LIKE
FLAMES
IN THE
NIGHT

Books by Connilyn Cossette

OUT FROM EGYPT

Counted With the Stars
Shadow of the Storm
Wings of the Wind

CITIES OF REFUGE

A Light on the Hill
Shelter of the Most High
Until the Mountains Fall
Like Flames in the Night

CITIES OF REFUGE • 4

LIKE
FLAMES
IN THE
NIGHT

CONNILYN COSSETTE

BETHANYHOUSE

a division of Baker Publishing Group
Minneapolis, Minnesota

Published by Bethany House Publishers
11400 Hampshire Avenue South
Bloomington, Minnesota 55438
www.bethanyhouse.com

Bethany House Publishers is a division of
Baker Publishing Group, Grand Rapids, Michigan

Printed in the United States of America

Library of Congress Cataloging-in-Publication Data
Names: Cossette, Connilyn, author.
Title: Like flames in the night / Connilyn Cossette.
Identifiers: LCCN 2019040932 | ISBN 9780764234330 (trade paperback) | ISBN
    9780764235542 (cloth) | ISBN 9781493422623 (ebook)
Subjects: LCSH: Murder—Fiction. | GSAFD: Christian fiction. | Love stories. |
    Mystery fiction.
Classification: LCC PS3603.O8655 L55 2020 | DDC 813/.6—dc23
LC record available at https://lccn.loc.gov/2019040932

Cover design by Jennifer Parker
Cover photography by Mike Habermann Photography, LLC
Map illustration by Samuel T. Campione

Author is represented by The Steve Laube Agency.

21 22 23 24 25 26   7 6 5 4 3 2

For the Wanderers who began
this journey with me
and the ones who've joined
along the way.

The Israelites did evil in the eyes of the LORD; they forgot the LORD their God and served the Baals and the Asherahs. The anger of the LORD burned against Israel so that he sold them into the hands of Cushan-Rishathaim king of Aram Naharaim, to whom the Israelites were subject for eight years. But when they cried out to the LORD, he raised up for them a deliverer, Othniel son of Kenaz, Caleb's younger brother, who saved them. The Spirit of the LORD came on him, so that he became Israel's judge and went to war.

Judges 3:7–10a

The Great Sea

Tyre

Mt. Hermon

Laish

Kedesh

ASHER

NAPHTALI

Hazor

EAST MANASSEH

ZEBULUN

Sea of Kinneret

Megiddo

ISSACHAR

Golan

WEST MANASSEH

Dotan

Shechem

Beit She'an

Edrei

Shiloh

Jordan River

EPHRAIM

Ramoth-Gilead

GAD

DAN

Ramah Gilgal

BENJAMIN

Jericho

PHILISTINES

Jerusalem

JUDAH
(Yehuda)

Hebron

Bezer

REUBEN

AMMON

SIMEON

Be'er Sheva

Arad

Salt Sea

MOAB

Kadesh-Barnea

☆ = Cities of Refuge

Part I

Tirzah

3 Tishri
1367 BC
Near Shiloh, Israel

Nothing would stop me from claiming this victory. Keeping my eyes on the rocky path ahead of me, I pushed harder as I came around a sharp bend in the road, ignoring the burn in my legs, the cramp in my side, and the squirming burden on my back that had somehow grown heavier with each stride.

My three-year-old nephew was breathless with laughter, his sweaty grip around my neck nearly choking me as we bounded along. This final portion of the road from Ramah to Shiloh was narrow, winding over and around many thick-forested hills. Since my brothers' children had begun to tire of the journey home, their complaints increasing throughout the day, I'd challenged them all to beat me to the top of the next rise. Much to my nephew's delight, I'd not held back when I bolted off, ignoring Malakhi's command to stop.

"Faster, *Doda* Tirzah!" Imri's little voice prodded, and although my calves screamed as I pushed up the steep incline, I submitted to his joyful demand, leaving the rest of our clan far behind and out of sight through the trees that lined either side of the road. Hitting a patch of loose gravel, my right sandal skidded to the side, but I caught my balance as Imri screeched in alarm.

"Have a little faith in your doda," I said, squeezing his ankles tight against my middle. "I've yet to lose a footrace."

"Not even against Abba?"

"Not since I was a girl," I said, stretching my stride even farther as we neared the pinnacle of the rise. The youngest of my brother Malakhi's children had me firmly wound about his smallest finger—twice, and I refused to disappoint him today. He cheered as I trotted to a halt, then twisted around to lift his fists in the air and jeer his siblings and cousins from his victorious perch on my back.

"There's no one there!" he said, clearly disappointed that his triumph had gone unwitnessed.

I turned back to take in the winding road we'd just ascended and indeed all that could be seen behind us was the shade-dappled path. Malakhi must have stopped the children from taking up my challenge soon after I'd run off. Now we'd have to wait for the rest of our caravan to catch up.

"See now," I said, poking a finger into his side to elicit a giggle. "Told you there was no cause to worry. They must have given up when they saw just how fast we were."

Bleary-eyed from sweat, I swung Imri to the ground, then bent over to catch my breath as we waited. "Doda Tirzah" may still be the fastest at footraces, but she was no fresh maiden anymore. Two years of marriage and two more of mourning had taken more out of me than I'd realized. I pressed a palm to the sharp pain in my side, determining that from now on I would run each morning with Malakhi's men as I used to—whether they wanted me to or not. I refused to be pinioned by weakness, physical or otherwise.

"And what do we have here?" came a voice from behind me, the clipped accent distinctly Aramean.

I jerked my body upright, slinging Imri behind me as I spun. Three soldiers blocked the path to Shiloh, all at least two handspans taller than me, their bronze-scaled armor flashing in the sunlight.

For once I wished I'd not run so far and fast. I prayed fervently that my brothers would see me standing on this rise. Willing the thrashing of my heart against my ribs to slow, I twisted my other arm back around Imri, not only to reassure him, but to hide the three fingers I'd lifted behind him, a signal that I hoped keen-eyed Malakhi would not miss.

"A young woman should not be out here alone," said the one who'd spoken before, his position at the head of the pack making his status clear. He was handsome, tall and lean, his fair skin and light brown hair speaking to a heritage far north of here. "Perhaps you have need of an escort?"

"Thank you, no. We are simply making our way back home from attending a wedding in Ramah." I thought it wise not to disclose where we lived, nor that in truth we'd also been celebrating Yom Teruah with my mother's family. Congregating in Shiloh for ingathering festivals had been banned by the Arameans, forcing us to find different methods of coming together to worship Yahweh. Wedding feasts were still allowed, for now.

The man narrowed his black eyes, a sneer forming on his lips. "You Hebrews certainly seem to have a lot of weddings."

His derisive tone provoked my ire, along with the reminder that it was because of men like these that I was a widow. I set my jaw and straightened my spine. "Our God commands us to be fruitful and multiply. We obey by marrying and filling the Land with our children so we can never be uprooted."

Two of the men laughed, entertained by the flare of pride in my people and my God. But the leader's top lip curled with disgust, and he advanced on me with slow, loose-limbed menace until I could see that his eyes were not black but a deep blue, like a spill of indigo ink. "Your people stole this land."

I held my breath, praying that the trembling of my hands was not visible to this awful man. The small flint knife tucked into my belt was useless against soldiers in full armor. What was taking my brothers so long?

"This land was given to us by Yahweh," I snapped, determined to show no fear and hoping to distract them for as long as possible. "The One who created these hills and valleys has every right to determine who should inherit them."

"Oh now, she's a feisty one, isn't she?" said the shortest of the three, a malevolent edge to his smile. "I bet she'd put on quite a show—"

The leader ignored him, those midnight eyes seeming to darken. "Your god is weak. We took this land with barely a fight eight years ago. It is *our* gods who have the power here. You stay on in these hills and valleys at the behest of our king, and only then to fill his coffers." Spittle formed at the corners of his lips as he spoke, and he moved so close that the bitterness of his breath filled my nostrils. "And when your people become too much of a problem, we will crush you into dust."

I'd had contact with Aramean soldiers many times before, both in Kedesh as they drove us from our inn a few months after our final defeat, and in Shiloh, where our clan had settled on my grandfather Ishai's vineyard. I'd been there when they'd hauled my husband off to forced labor with callous indifference, treating him and the other men as if they were nothing more than animals to be corralled, but this man's vitriol was shocking in its intensity. Something personal had shaped his fury toward my people. He regarded me with sheer malice, as if he did not see a young woman standing in front of him but an enemy on the battlefield.

"Come, Alek," said one of the men, shifting his weight as if unsettled by the force of his companion's rage. "We have messages to deliver."

Alek slid a contemptuous gaze to the man, a muscle twitching in his jaw, then locked his attention on me again. My heart faltered as the full force of his targeted glare hit me. "I will do what I please."

A flicker of movement behind the Arameans caught my eye, a shadow among the trees that lined this rough path. Then a swift flash of metal in sunlight flickered from the opposite side. The men of my family were moving into position, encircling us with silent skill. My knees threatened to waver, but I held steady, not allowing a hint of relief to show on my face.

"Please," I said with a feigned warble, hoping to give Malakhi and the others a few more moments to prepare their strike. "Please allow my nephew and me to turn back. We should not have run on ahead of our grandparents by ourselves." Let them think I was a brainless woman without effective escort, not the daughter of a master spy and in the company of some of Israel's most lethal warriors.

Alek peered over my shoulder at the road behind me. "Seems as though you ran a bit too far, little rabbit. There's no one anywhere in sight." He leaned down to rasp in my ear. "Or within shouting distance."

"Let my nephew go," I pleaded, everything inside me screaming for Malakhi and the others to hesitate no longer. "I'll do whatever you ask."

He ignored my plea, instead sliding the backside of his hand down my cheekbone, the touch causing a shudder deep in my bones. "Oh, that you will, little rabbit. And unfortunately for you, my father taught me well—"

I never would know what horrific thing he'd learned from his father, for in that moment his head slammed into my shoulder, a result of the stone that had smashed into the back of his skull and knocked him forward. I spun away, pulling Imri with me as the man toppled into the dirt at my feet.

My brothers, my father, and his enormous friend Baz barreled out of the trees, heads wrapped in their wives' scarves to obscure their faces. Eitan's sling whipped through the air again before letting another stone fly. The other two Arameans had already drawn their swords and turned to defend themselves, so the rock swished by without hitting its target. Unfortunately for our opponents, however, Eitan never missed twice in a row. The second soldier received a precision strike in the hollow of his throat. Choking and spitting, his hands wrapped protectively around his neck, he dropped to one knee. The third soldier engaged Malakhi, swords flashing, men grunting, and sandals scuffling as they slammed into each other.

Baz went after the man Eitan had hit in the throat and within moments had him on his stomach, hands bound behind his back with a belt. Coming to my senses, I realized that Alek, whom I'd thought had been knocked unconscious by Eitan's first stone, was moaning in the dirt two paces from my feet, but my father pounced on him before he had a chance to recover. Imri burrowed his face into my waist, his tears soaking my tunic as his small body vibrated with shock and horror.

I'd heard many tales of secret missions among the enemy from my father and Baz, and I'd seen Malakhi and Eitan spar and practice with weapons, but I'd never seen these four men actually engaged in a fight. They were as nimble as dancers and swift as wildcats as they subjugated the Arameans without even speaking a word to one another. It did not matter that my father and Baz were grandfathers now, their beards laced with silver; they were just as skillful as they'd been as young men fighting for the Land of Promise.

I was left stunned, in awe, and wholly frustrated by my own inability to defend myself. King Kushan's forces had swept into this land with unparalleled cruelty during his quest to build an empire to rival his Akkadian ancestors, horror after horror causing the tribes of Israel to bow far too easily to his yoke. They'd stolen our land and our wealth, violated our women, slaughtered our children, and aimed to break both our bodies and our spirits with forced labor. Yet the majority of us had been too cowardly, too complacent, or like I had been at fifteen years old, incapable of fighting back when they viciously drove us from our home.

But I was no longer a girl. In fact, I'd weathered so much loss and heartache since we'd left Kedesh that it seemed I'd aged far beyond my actual years. And I was part of a family who'd never given up the fight against the enemy, even if their efforts had gone from lauded among our people to clandestine. I could not lift a sword in battle, but there had to be *something* I could do, some way I could be useful in the struggle. I felt certain that I'd been made for more than the desolate and dependent existence of a childless widow.

My heart began to pound, but no longer with fear. Instead, a heady rush of anticipation flowed through my limbs as I vowed that I would never again be so helpless, so weak. I would arm myself with skill and knowledge and become integral in the fight for my people and our land. My husband may have died for nothing, but I refused to ever again surrender.

CHAPTER TWO

With the corner of my headscarf, I patted the sweat from my brow and neck. Not even the gentle breeze had any effect on my overheated skin as I knelt before the oven on this unseasonably hot day. I prodded a stick at the base of the pot in the center of the flames, shifting the coals so my root-and-barley stew would not burn and disappoint my mother.

She flitted about the kitchen courtyard like a butterfly, sampling dishes being prepared by my brothers' wives and the other women, and adding spices to her satisfaction. Our continually growing family, and those we'd absorbed into our clan along the way, necessitated a small army to prepare meals each day, but there was no one who cooked like Moriyah in all of Shiloh, so we yielded to her good judgment.

Using a thick scrap of wool, I lifted the lid to stir the fragrant mixture again. Satisfied that the stew was cooking evenly, I stood to stretch my back and cast my gaze over my grandfather's vineyard. Green spread in every direction, the towering vines replete with ripe fruit that was even now being harvested by the many hands of my family members, along with a number of other young men my uncle Yuval had employed to speed up the wine-making process over the next few days.

Since we'd been forced to leave the city of refuge, we could no longer rely on the Levites to provide food for our family, as we had when my mother was imprisoned there. Therefore we had adapted to the lifestyle of the rest of the tribes of Israel: plowing, planting, and praying for rain and a bountiful yield. The additional burden of tribute to the Arameans made the task more difficult, but this land, allotted to my grandfather by Yehoshua himself as a reward for his service during the conquest of Canaan, had continued to sustain us despite our being forced to give up half the yield to our enemies.

All day, as I'd been tending my duties, I'd been mulling over the problem of how to plead my case to Malakhi. When I was a girl he had indulged my affinity for carrying a sling about town and challenging the boys to shooting matches or footraces, even going so far as to allow me to take part in daily exercises with his trainees. But it was an altogether different matter to ask him to prepare me for battle.

For a few moments I considered how my older sisters, Abra and Chana, might react to the outrageous thoughts I'd been harboring. I suspected Abra might be supportive of me, as brash and outspoken as she was, but Chana would be full of concerns for my safety. With Abra living up near Merom with her husband's family since we'd been driven from Kedesh and Chana traveling with her husband's trading caravan, it had been far too long since I'd seen either of them, and I missed their sisterly counsel. They both had a number of children who I'd never even met. Even more reason to take part in this struggle, so those in our clan who'd not been able to travel to Shiloh for festivals would be reunited with us again soon.

"Where is your mind, Tirzah?" my mother asked as she lifted the lid off my stewpot and inhaled the fragrant steam.

Blinking at her sudden appearance, I stammered, "Nothing. That is . . . I was thinking of yesterday."

Surely she would not approve of the path my thoughts had taken. Although she'd had her own share of adventures as a young woman, now she longed for nothing more than to return to her beloved inn in Kedesh. Even after she'd been freed from her manslaughter sentence by the death of the High Priest of Israel, she'd chosen to stay in the city of refuge, in hopes of ministering to others in need of shelter. Being forced to leave the place she'd poured her heart into for over thirty years had been devastating for her.

Her lips pursed as she stirred the stew and hummed her contentment with my effort, which made pride surge in my chest. I may not enjoy cooking as much as she did, thinking of it more of an obligation than a joy, but she'd taught me well. She turned her piercing silver gaze on me. "I shudder to think what might have happened, had you been alone on that road. Or had Malakhi not had the foresight to stop the other children and follow after you and Imri."

As do I, I thought, restraining a shiver as I remembered the menace in Alek's gaze as he slid his knuckles down my cheek.

"I've apologized to Malakhi and Rivkah," I said, thinking of the desperate way my brother had held Imri to himself once he'd finished dealing with the Arameans. "I wish I hadn't put their son is such horrible danger."

"I know, my girl. The consequences of our foolish decisions are always made clearer when we look backward on the path we've traveled."

My mother always had a way of cutting down to the bone with such gentleness that I could not help but welcome the incision, no matter how much it stung. She spoke only the truth, as always. I had been foolish, and my nephew had almost paid the price for my recklessness.

"You are so much like her," my mother murmured, head tilted curiously as if she were inspecting something new on my face.

"Like who?"

"Alanah. If I did not know that you came from my own body, at times I would guess that you were born of my dear friend."

A gently reminiscent smile curved her lips as she spoke of the woman she'd not seen in over thirty years, but who I knew she considered as much a sister as those who shared her own blood. I also knew that she still mourned Alanah's absence, since she'd left Shiloh with her family to make a home far to the south before my parents even met.

For as long as I could remember, stories of the Canaanite woman who'd been captured on the battlefield in the year before our people entered the Land had enthralled me. As fierce as she was loyal, flame-haired Alanah had been changed by her time with those she once called enemies and had not only embraced worship of Yahweh but married Tobiah, the Hebrew warrior who'd discovered her on the battlefield. And she had saved my mother's life shortly after the brand that forever marred my mother's cheek had seared her flesh while she stood tied to a pole before the temple in Jericho.

"If only I had her courage," I said. "I emptied my stomach on the ground as soon as the men dragged off those Arameans."

"Oh, believe me, Alanah was just as terrified as I was when we were kidnapped together, and even as she stood up to the priestess who scarred me." She touched the blasphemous crescent moon and sun-wheel on her cheek. "Besides, although she is brave without question, and I am still in awe of how she sacrificed herself to set me free, I think it was her surrender to Yahweh that displayed the true depths of her courage."

Before I could ask her to explain her statement, my father arrived in the courtyard, head wet from washing in one of the rain-fed cisterns behind my grandparents' house.

"How goes the harvest?" my mother asked.

"We have plenty of hands, so we should be finished within the next couple of weeks," he said, pressing a kiss to her temple. "I wish the Arameans would allow us to celebrate the harvest the way we used to."

My parents exchanged a meaningful glance. The two of them had found each other during one such festival decades before, and I'd seen them many times sneaking off into the fields, hand in hand, to walk among the vines when the moon was bright. A pang of longing struck me hard as I watched their silent but affectionate interaction, so I averted my eyes, turning my attention back to my stew. Even living with my large family in this ever-expanding collection of tents gathered about my grandfather's home, two years of widowhood had been lonely. But I was determined to cling to the new purpose I'd set my mind to, not regret for what should have been. And besides, once I swayed Malakhi to go along with my plans, the hollow places would be plenty full again.

"I'd like to speak with you, Tirzah," said my father, drawing my attention upward again. A strange expression was on his face, something unreadable that caused a ripple of apprehension in my gut. "Come. Walk with me."

My mother took over my pot-stirring duties, giving me a smile that was no doubt meant to be reassuring, but that only made me more suspicious.

My father led me to one of the paths between vines, the sweet smell of ripened grapes enveloping us as we entered the field. "I've been meaning to talk with you about what happened on the road yesterday."

"I know," I said, brushing aside one of the long, unruly vines that had escaped its moorings. "I was foolish to run ahead with Imri. If I could do it all over again I would have—"

He lifted a palm to halt my explanations. "I have no doubt you learned a lesson. What I meant to say is that I am proud of you."

I blinked at him, stunned speechless.

"Your quick thinking and level head protected Imri, Tirzah. You did not panic. You did not fold under the pressure or give in to fear. And not only that, somehow you kept my little grandson fairly calm as well. There are a few men I know who might learn a thing or two from you." He grinned, pride in the brown eyes that matched mine, and I felt the compliment all the way to the tips of my fingers. That, coupled with my mother's comparison of me to a woman of strength and tenacity like Alanah, fanned my new yearnings into an even more fervent passion.

For as much as I adored my mother, it was my abba to whom I felt most connected over the years. Certainly he would understand my need to do something more than stir pots, bake bread, and tend to my siblings' children day after day, wouldn't he? He'd trained some of the most skilled spies in the Land, so his opinion was not a thing to be taken lightly. But just as I opened my mouth to beg his help in persuading Malakhi to let me be among those privileged few, his next words crushed my hopes.

"However . . ." He stopped and turned to face me, all levity washed away. "The incident yesterday also made me realize that a conversation between you and me is long overdue. It has been two years since Eliya's passing, and I think it time that we discuss your future."

I felt my blood drain into my feet. Although I'd been under my husband's authority during the two years I lived with his family just across the valley, they had wanted nothing to do with his childless widow. As Eliya had been the only son, there'd been no option of levirate marriage, so within days of his death, I'd returned to my father's house and willingly ceded to his authority and protection again. So far he'd not insisted I remarry, but it was certainly within his rights to do so.

"Your nieces and nephews are enthralled with you," he said, with a sweep of his arm back toward our tents. "And I know how much Rivkah, especially, appreciates your help when Malakhi has need of her pen."

Even as the mother of five and carrying the sixth, Rivkah still used her scribing skills to aid her husband's clandestine efforts, crafting missives to be sent to other circles of resistance among the tribes and translating those captured from foreigners. No matter how I tried to avoid it, I could not help but envy her, both for the precious voices that called her *Ima* and for her valuable contributions to the struggle against the Arameans.

"But perhaps," said my father, his mouth a determined line, "it is time that we entertain the idea of a husband for you."

A hundred excuses warred for supremacy on my tongue. How could I possibly make him understand my discontent, while at the same time avoiding the true reason I had no desire to ever remarry? My mother knew of the first two times I'd lost a baby, but the last one I'd kept even from Eliya, not wanting to see the disappointment on his face when I revealed that, yet again, I'd failed him.

Rightly determining that I was too stunned to speak, my father put his arm around my shoulder and pulled me close. "I have no desire to force this on you. After what happened with Rivkah and Malakhi, and even your mother and my brother, I would never push you to marry someone you do not approve of, nor someone you do not trust. But these are perilous times, daughter, as you witnessed firsthand yesterday. With the tribes of Yehudah and Simeon now making sure strides in the south, it is a matter of time before Shiloh becomes a center of conflict. The Arameans will only become more hostile in the coming months. It would do much to ease my mind if I knew you were cared for and protected in case anything were to happen to me or your brothers."

"Nothing will happen to any of you," I said, firm conviction in my voice. "There are no finer warriors among the tribes."

He laughed, the rich sound sparking memories of being tossed into the air and falling safely into his waiting arms. "That may be true of your brothers. But I'm an old man now."

I frowned playfully. "You are nothing of the sort, Abba. I saw you take down that Aramean on the road. That young fool didn't know what hit him."

He released me to massage his shoulder with a wince. "Maybe so, but your mother had to practically roll me out of bed this morning. These bones have seen more than their fair share of battle."

Although my father had ceded his command to Malakhi a couple of years after we'd settled in Shiloh, I'd avoided thinking of him as getting older. But now I took stock of the way his hair was more silver than brown and thinning a bit on the top, and the deep grooves that fanned out from his eyes. His body was covered with scars from his years of faithful service to the tribes of Israel, and I'd recently noticed that the limp he acquired during the war with the Arameans had become even more pronounced.

When he'd stepped down from leadership, I'd thought he might be restless here on the vineyard, but he truly seemed to be content tending my grandfather's vines alongside Yuval and entertaining his own grandchildren with tales of spying and warfare. As yesterday proved, he would not hesitate to take up a sword to protect his family when necessary, and he was always willing to give Malakhi counsel when asked, but otherwise he seemed more than happy—relieved, even—to leave the decisions in the hands of the younger generation.

He lifted his hands to cradle my face in his palms, his expression an earnest plea for understanding. "I know that it was difficult to lose Eliya, especially in such a senseless fashion, but it is time to move forward, daughter."

Although his words were meant to be encouraging, to make me accepting of the idea of another husband, they had the opposite effect. Instead they caused me to remember exactly *how* senseless Eliya's death had been. Instead of searching out the men who'd clumsily waylaid a caravan of provisions destined for Aramean soldiers, our enemies had rounded up fifty random Hebrews, Eliya included, and forced them into heavy labor with insufficient food or drink and plentiful lashings. Only ten survived, and my husband was not one of them. We'd not even been allowed to retrieve his body, buried as it was in a mass grave somewhere to the east.

I'd met Eliya soon after our arrival in Shiloh; he'd been kind to me and seemingly tolerant of my out-of-step ways, which is why I'd consented to the match when he approached my father for a betrothal. Even though my inability to provide him with a child gradually eroded much of the common ground between us, making our last year together one fraught with tension and disappointment, he did not deserve to die in such a way.

For as calm as my father had been as he'd asked me to consider marriage, the fear lurking in his eyes made it clear that yesterday's confrontation had shaken him. Darek was extremely protective of all of his children, but especially of me, his youngest daughter. Any notion I'd had of sharing my newfound convictions with him withered away.

"I'll think on it, Abba," I lied.

"Thank you," said my father, then kissed my forehead with a relieved sigh that made my gut twist with guilt. "That truly puts my mind at ease."

I could only pray that someday he might forgive my deceit. I'd already decided what my next step must be, and it had nothing to do with another marriage. Malakhi had to be persuaded, and soon, because I refused to molder away in useless, dependent monotony for the rest of my days.

◆◆◆

Once the children were shuffled off into the tents to begin their Shabbat rest, tucked into dreams with full bellies, the men gathered around the fire. Knowing that their nightly conversations usually included whatever information they'd recently gleaned about both our enemies and our allies, I fetched a full skin of wine—the perfect excuse to intrude upon their conversation unnoticed. Although Malakhi now led the group of spies my father had once commanded, he and Eitan never neglected to keep my father and Baz informed of their activities, continuing to lean on their wisdom and experience.

"Will he strike again?" Baz asked Malakhi as I filled his cup to the brim. The big man grunted something at me that resembled gratitude but otherwise ignored my presence. Although I was frustrated that I'd missed to whom he was referring, I said nothing, hoping they would all forget I was there and loosen their tongues. I stepped over his faithful canine companion, Toki, who panted at his side while staring into the flickering flames. Her graying muzzle matched her owner's perfectly, as did her enormous personality.

"The success that the men of Yehudah have had in the past few months is very encouraging," said Malakhi. "I've been in contact with one of their leaders. He assures me that Othniel is determined to clear the Arameans completely out of their territory. They've already recaptured Hebron and are rumored to have their sights on Be'er Sheva and Arad as well. It will not be too much longer before he turns his face northward."

A murmur of satisfaction went up among the group. Hebron was indeed a large prize. As the city in which our patriarch Avraham was buried, and one of the designated cities of refuge, Hebron back in Hebrew hands was not just a victory, it was the strike of flint against iron.

Othniel, the nephew of the great warrior Calev, was already famous among us for his exploits under Yehoshua's command when he was just a young man. I'd heard the stories from my own father, who'd fought beside Othniel in many a battle and said his valor was nearly unmatched.

Could it be that Yahweh was finally raising up someone who could fill the void left behind by Yehoshua? Had the pleas from those of us who remained faithful to him finally been heard? Perhaps, in the same way Mosheh had delivered us from Egypt, Othniel would deliver us from the Arameans. The thought made me even more determined to take part in whatever lie ahead.

"And Shechem? What word have you heard from your men there?" asked my father.

"None lately," said Malakhi with a sigh. "They simply cannot get close enough. They've embedded themselves among the laborers working on the high commander's home, but other than reporting shift changes and some of the movement of troops, they've gleaned little."

"The soldiers we encountered yesterday did give up some important information," said Eitan, then lifted a sardonic brow. "After a fair amount of persuasion, of course."

Once Imri and I had been secured, he and the others had dragged the Arameans off past the tree line to interrogate them. Our family waited only an hour before our men returned, faces finally uncovered and carrying the soldiers' clothes and weapons. Eitan was famous for extracting information from the most tight-lipped of enemies, so I was certain they'd been stripped of any knowledge they carried, along with their dignity. I felt not one shred of regret or compassion at the thought. Alek would have done far worse to me and my nephew had he gotten the chance, and he'd escaped with his life, a mercy we most assuredly would not have been afforded.

"They were carrying a written message that made it clear there is a new alliance of some sort in the works," said Malakhi. "But we aren't certain who the message was meant for, or with whom the Arameans might be plotting. It could be Egypt. Or Tyre or Sidon. Or perhaps even the Philistines. We need solid information about who is involved and what they plan to do."

"If the men you've already sent in to Shechem are ineffective," said my father, "perhaps you should send in someone new. You can only intercept so many messages, and even with Rivkah's skill in translating those messages, you have no way of knowing which are true and which are decoys. You need someone to burrow deep inside and keep ears on the commander himself."

A huff of air escaped my lips as hope flickered deep inside. *Me! Send me!* But having been so caught up in the conversation, I'd forgotten to slip into the shadows, and Malakhi looked up at me with a curious arch to his brow. "Did you need something, Tirzah?"

I dropped my eyes to the skin of wine in my hands, fumbling for a convincing excuse as to why I was lurking at the edge of their circle, listening to their war-talk. "I . . . I wanted to offer you more of those pistachio cakes Ima made. I think there are a few pieces left that the children did not devour."

In that moment, my conjured excuse somehow paired with my father's suggestion, and a clear idea of how I could prove my usefulness began to form—an idea that was as dangerous as it was brilliant, but one that I felt sure would yield the results they needed. However, I clamped my lips shut against the temptation to let it spill out of my mouth right then. The four of them together would quash my proposal without a second thought, and I would not waste my breath until I was armed for the fight.

Besides, as the commander of the unit, it was Malakhi alone who I needed to convince, both to train me for the mission and to keep it from my parents until the time was right.

The secret twitched on my lips even as they heartily agreed to my offer and I slipped away to retrieve the cakes, but I could already taste victory on my tongue. Because I was nothing if not skilled at convincing my doting older brother to capitulate to my whims.

CHAPTER

THREE

20 Tishri

I crept through the tent flap and emerged into the feeble predawn light. A shiver slipped down my back as chill morning air hit my skin. I was tempted to duck back inside and retrieve a warm woolen mantle but decided there was no need; I'd be warm soon enough. I gathered my hair into a tight braid and then roughly scrubbed my hands over my face to chase the remaining fatigue from my mind. I'd waited over two weeks, until the grape harvest was complete, but now I finally had the chance to prove myself, and I could not afford to be anything but arrow-sharp today.

Bending over, I reached for the bottom of my tunic and yanked it between my legs until it reached my waist. Then, with the expertise of a girl who'd spent her early years racing against the boys through the fields of Kedesh, I girded my loins by tucking the hem securely into my belt. It had been years since I'd done such a thing, so my first few steps were awkward, but by the time I'd slipped past the tree line into the woods at the back of the vineyard, I remembered how much flexibility such an arrangement gave me. Now I could stretch my legs farther, maneuver quicker, and jump obstacles with ease—actions that were imperative to my goals this day. Convincing Malakhi to allow me to be one of his spies would take more than just a race through the woods, but first I would remind him of my capabilities.

My breath huffed out before me in great white clouds as I moved through the trees, and my bare toes already ached from the cold, but I shoved those concerns from my mind. Although it had been years since I'd followed Malakhi and his men over the backside of the hill behind the vineyard and into the depths of the woods, I found the narrow path with ease, my eyes easily adjusting to the dim. A nightingale warbled farewell to the stars from the heights of a nearby cedar, the mournful sound dissolving into the icy breeze that lashed a few brown leaves across my path.

Holding my hand to my face, I breathed heat into the curve of my palm, hoping to thaw my nose as I listened for the sound of feet, the crack of a twig—anything that might hint at my quarry's presence.

When I'd nearly given up, thinking that Malakhi had chosen a different course for his men to run today, a flock of blackbirds suddenly startled into the sky about fifty paces southeast from my position, so I headed to the north of that spot, picking up speed with every footfall. As determined as I was to cut across their path, I ignored the whip of brush clawing at my bare legs and the press of sharp stones under my soles, fully accepting that I'd pay the price later but thankful that at least I was no longer shivering.

Malakhi's men were trained in stealth, their feet sure and their bodies honed for endurance, but nonetheless I found them, ghosting through the trees, dodging trunks and low branches, stretching their long legs over rocks and logs, and breathing with such precision that only tiny white streams of frozen air slipped from their lips.

Heart pattering with nerves as much as exertion, I plunged in among them, weaving into their group without a word and keeping my eyes trained on my brother, who led the silent chase through the woods. Malakhi was now past his thirtieth year, but he ran with the agility of a youth and all the skill and tenacity of the warrior he was. He was a born leader. The men he commanded obeyed him without question, their respect earned in battle and their love by his uncompromising devotion to our people and our God. And I would not give up until I was one of them.

From the corner of my eye I noticed Eitan's head whip around as I passed him. Although pleased that I'd outpaced my long-legged oldest brother, I refused to look his way or acknowledge the silent questions undoubtedly being hurled at my back. I dodged a few more trees, then hurdled over a fallen one and sucked in a breath as I landed on a pine-cone; but I did not break stride as I passed up three more men, including Eitan's two oldest boys, Yoni and Zekai. Although only sixteen and seventeen, they had recently begun training with their father in anticipation of their twentieth year, when they'd be allowed to join the fight.

My shins ached and my thighs quivered, but I pressed on, calling up the helplessness I'd felt before the Arameans two weeks ago and using it to drive myself onward as the dawn began to push above the farthest ridge. I embraced the pain and named it victory.

When Malakhi slackened his pace, slowing to a jog before he trotted to a halt, I was disappointed, wishing for just a few more moments of the freedom I'd reveled in as I ran unfettered for the first time in years.

I was not the first of the runners to catch up to Malakhi; six other men stood at my brother's side as I skidded to a stop, but I was by no means the last. Although I felt like tipping my head back and crowing, I held my expression as I approached, valiantly pushing aside the shaking in my muscles and the urge to gulp for air. Seven pairs of eyes tracked my movement until I stood before the group, chin high and gaze steady.

"Tirzah," said Malakhi, frustratingly unruffled by my appearance. "What are you doing?"

Forcing my harried breaths into a slow rhythm, I shrugged a shoulder. "Running with you. Like I used to. Before Eliya."

A deep wrinkle formed between his black brows, one I'd not noticed before now on his handsome face. It was not only my father who was showing signs of age lately; perhaps the burden of Malakhi's responsibility was weighing on him. "Why?"

Feeling the tension emanating from the twelve men who now encircled me, I braced my body for the fight that was sure to come. "I want to go to Shechem."

Malakhi's head reared back and his silver eyes flared wide. "You what?"

I fixed my jaw like iron and refused to soften my stance. "You need a spy in the commander's house. Send me."

Exclamations came from all around the circle, a mixture of scoffing, breathy laughter, and from Eitan a sharp "no"—all of it in defiance of the strict orders they had to keep to a hush during this predawn training. But I did not move, I did not turn my head to defend myself, and I did not waver as I stared at Malakhi with intense determination.

"Go on back," Malakhi said, his voice ringing with the same authority my father's had when he'd been the commander of this unit.

At first I thought he was addressing me, but then his eyes lifted over my shoulder and swept around the group. "Training is over for the day. I need to speak with my sister. And keep this to yourselves."

As the men silently filtered back into the forest, most likely mocking me as they headed back to their tents, Eitan strode to my side and yanked my arm to force me to look at him. "What are you thinking, Tirzah? You may have had some fun running with us when you were a girl, or slinging stones and climbing trees, but you are not a man—"

Malakhi lifted a palm, halting Eitan's tirade. "Let me."

Steam billowed from Eitan's lips into the chill, his hazel eyes burning like coals. My oldest brother was extremely protective of me and had been for as long as I could remember, so I understood his irritation with my outrageous request. But I would not capitulate.

"I'll handle this," said Malakhi. "Go on back."

Eitan pursed his lips and shook his head at me.

"Go," said Malakhi, abandoning his previously commanding tone as he addressed our elder brother. A mischievous grin curved his lips. "Crawl back under the blankets with your wife for awhile while I sort this out."

Eitan huffed, still glaring at me, but soon his annoyance melted into a soft laugh. "I think I'll do just that. While you two freeze your noses off talking nonsense, Sofea will warm me up."

He wiggled his brows suggestively, so I screwed my face in disgust and shoved his shoulder. Amusement twinkled in his eyes as he poked a finger between my ribs and then sauntered off, assured that Malakhi would talk me out of my notions of spying.

"You have enough children for now," Malakhi called out, his voice taunting. "Let Rivkah and me catch up." Eitan's laughter trailed behind him as he disappeared into the trees.

"You're both terrible," I said, but I could not keep the affection from my tone. I adored the way both of my brothers cherished their wives and doted on their children. Neither of them were perfect by any means, but they were men of honor and devoted to their families.

"All right," sighed Malakhi. "Now what is this absurdity about Shechem? I thought you were spying on us that night around the fire, and now I know why."

Feeling gooseflesh prickle on my now-wobbly legs, I unwound my tunic hem from my belt and brushed the fabric back down over my knees. "You said you need someone who can get close. Much closer than the men you've already sent in. I have a plan."

He shook his head. "I am not sending my sister into a hornet's nest. Forget this."

"I won't." I gritted my teeth. "I spent all of my younger years practically training alongside you. Running. Shooting. Wrestling. Sword-fighting. I may not be a man, but for a woman I am more than capable. I've wasted a few years, of course, but it won't take long for me to get back into the form I was in before I married."

He opened his mouth to protest, but I was quicker.

"I have much to learn, I know. But I am the daughter of one of the most talented spies our people have ever had. You may have noticed me listening the other night because I was not trying to be that careful, but next time you won't know I am there, I guarantee it. I will train hard. I will do anything you ask of me—anything, without argument. But I can do this, Malakhi."

With his chin tilted to the side, he kept his one good eye pinned on me, searching my face intently—for what I could not guess—but I could tell that he was wavering by the softening of his mouth and the contemplative expression on his face.

"You have plenty of men in your company who can get into Shechem," I continued. "But for this task you need something different. You need a cook who can go into the high commander's home every single day without suspicion, who can serve at the Aramean's table and keep her ears and eyes wide open as she does so. You need a woman who understands the importance of this mission and yet is unmarried and without children. You need *me*."

Since the day I'd spoken to my father about remarriage, I'd only become more convinced that since Yahweh had not seen fit to give me children, *this* was the path he'd determined for me. I may never be a mother, but I could fight to ensure that Imri and the rest of my nieces and nephews lived without fear and that future generations would enjoy the Land of Promise in freedom and peace.

"Let me be of service to Israel, Malakhi. Let me fight against the monsters who slaughtered Eliya and tossed his body into a ditch with the refuse." My voice quavered, but I swallowed the emotion and forged ahead. "Like you said, the time is *now* to take a stand against Kushan. Now, when Othniel has been making so much progress. If our generation does not throw off these chains soon, there will be nothing left of us. I may be a woman, but I am ready and willing to stand for Yahweh."

The speech had poured out of me in a torrent, each word growing stronger as I spoke, and my body had warmed with the heat of my passion—passion I didn't even know I'd been harboring. By the time I finished, Malakhi stood blinking at me, his jaw slack, looking nearly as shocked by my outburst as I was.

He lifted a hand and scrubbed at his forehead, as if it pained him. "You . . . you want to go in and cook?"

"Yes. Ima has taught me more than enough to secure a position in the commander's kitchen. And I've been around you and your men enough to know that lips loosen when the wine and beer flow."

He narrowed his eyes, that new wrinkle making another appearance. "No. No, it's not safe."

"You already have men in the city, don't you? They can watch over me. And I'll be with the other cooks, so I won't be alone. Ima has trained me well; I'll have no problem making myself invaluable in the kitchen. And you'll teach me to protect myself, should anything go awry."

He growled under his breath. "This is foolish."

Whether he meant my idea or the fact that he was considering my idea, I wasn't sure, but I plowed ahead. "Please, Malakhi. Train me. If you don't feel comfortable with my skills, then you don't have to use me. But give me a chance to prove myself. This is the only way I can fight for my people's freedom. I need to do this."

He stared off into the distance, his jaw twitching as he considered my argument, letting silence fall between us. As the sun lifted higher in the sky, the birds and insects began to fill the space with song, and the longer Malakhi went without saying no, the larger my hopes swelled.

"Eitan will kill me," he said, his silver eyes glittering in the soft morning light. "And then Baz and Abba will flog my dead body."

Glee rippled through me, and I grabbed his arm. "You'll do it? You'll let me go?"

He pressed his lips so tight they went white, as if he were fighting against the words. "I'll train you—"

I threw my arms around him and squeezed, cutting him off. "Oh, thank you, Malakhi. I won't let you down. I'll work so hard, I promise. I won't give you any cause to doubt that I am ready for this."

He pressed me back to look into my eyes. "I said I will train you, Tirzah, but it's not just me you'll have to convince if this is to work. You'll have to prove your worth to the entire team. You'll have to convince all of us that you are deserving of our trust and that you are fully capable of protecting yourself without hesitation before I will let you step one tiny toe in that city."

"I vow to you that I will do all of that and more."

"And you'll obey my every command? Keep your smart remarks

to yourself? Forget that I am your brother and respect me as your absolute superior?"

If Eitan, who was eleven years Malakhi's senior, could submit himself to his younger brother's command, then I certainly could. Besides, Malakhi and I had always had an easy relationship. He understood me better than anyone, and I trusted him implicitly. I dipped my chin with a firm nod. "I will."

"If we do this, you cannot breathe a word to anyone else beyond Eitan," he said, a weighty note of authority in his tone. "Until I determine whether you are fit for such a mission, none of the other men are to know you are even training. Understand?"

"Without question," I responded.

He heaved another long-suffering sigh, his gaze flying upward. "Once Baz and Abba are finished with me," he mumbled under his breath, "Ima will put me in a stew."

Overjoyed by his capitulation, I tugged at his arm with a laugh. "Come on, I'll race you back. Perhaps Rivkah is waiting to warm you up too." I winked and broke into a run, enjoying the sound of my brother's laughter at my back.

For as light as my heart felt while my feet swished through the underbrush headed for home, the gravity of this moment was not lost to me. No woman among our people had ever done anything like this, and I was determined that Malakhi would never regret giving me the chance.

CHAPTER
FOUR

Liyam

25 Tishri
Near Arad, Israel

A song of victory vibrated in my bones as the three hills that encircled our valley appeared ahead on the horizon. The walk from Hebron had been a miserable one—grit coating my tongue and stinging my eyes, the armor on my body still encrusted with the blood of my enemies—but I lengthened my stride toward home as I imagined its terraced hillsides painted with gold and green trees that would soon scatter their leaves, and the wheat fields waiting to be plowed and sown. The nearby wadi beckoned as we passed by, calling me to wash in its stream-fed pool and allow its hidden waterfall to rinse weeks of war from my skin. Yet no amount of fresh, cool water could ever flush the smell of death from my nostrils, the sound of battle-anguish from my ears, nor the feel of my blade dispatching the wounded into the embrace of their powerless gods.

At least the remaining Arameans had finally skittered away like the diseased rats they were, tossing aside their arms and fleeing before the forces of Yehudah after we'd laid waste to the once-feared army. Hebron, the final resting place of our forefathers, and a city of refuge, was ours once again. I could not wait to see the look on my father's face when we told him of the triumph we'd finally secured over our oppressors.

Tobiah had battled the fearsome forces of King Og at Edrei under Mosheh, had been there when the walls of Jericho fell, and rescued my mother, Alanah, from the rubble. He'd fought many battles under the mighty commander Yehoshua as they'd struggled to claim Canaan for Israel. But now as a man of nearly sixty years with a body wearied by war and heavy labor, he'd made the decision to step aside and allow my generation to reclaim what his own had so recklessly lost.

I'd never forget the mixture of pride and envy in his eyes when my five older brothers and I had marched from the valley with the goal of pushing the Arameans from our tribal territory two months ago. The fact that we'd already accomplished a major victory, even though we'd had one sword for every four men, was nothing less than a miracle of Yahweh, one that I hoped would inspire the rest of Israel to rise up and throw off the yoke Kushan had slipped about our necks with far too much ease. With Othniel as our leader, and this first decisive triumph in hand, it finally seemed a real possibility. We'd secured Hebron, Be'er Sheva and Arad were next, and then we would push north until every last Aramean was driven from the Land of Promise.

My cousin Yavan appeared at my side, jamming a sharp elbow in my ribs with a grin. "I don't know which I am most anticipating: scrubbing this stink from my bones or my wife's cooking."

The familiar pang of jealousy struck particularly hard in that moment. Eight years ago when we'd returned from battle, stunned and demoralized by our defeat, the soft embrace I'd been able to fall into had done much to ease the sting. The gentle hands of my wife, Havah, the ones that had aided me in removing my armor upon my return and had wiped the filth from my face as I mourned those who'd fallen, would not be there to soothe my bruised body today. The pang swelled into an ache, one that even seven years after her loss seemed nearly as sharp as it had the day I'd buried her.

Yavan flinched at my expression. "Forgive me," he murmured, scratching at his wiry black beard. "I didn't think—"

I slapped his back and forced a smile. "For as much as Nena's cooking is worth the anticipation, you smell like the corpse of a plague-ridden mule left to rot in the sun for a month. Head for the stream first."

My cousin and closest friend snatched up the bait. "Me? At least I don't stink like the hind end of a camel after it's been grazing on moldy barley."

Grateful to veer my thoughts away from the past, I returned his insults with a few of my own, each volley becoming more and more descriptive until not only were he and I howling with laughter but my five brothers, along with Yavan's three brothers, had joined in with a few creative jabs of their own. The fact that every one of us who'd set out from this valley were returning relatively unscathed was yet another miracle. Last time that had not been the case. Two of my uncles, including the one I'd been named for, had been among the thousands of Hebrews to fall the day we'd lost the last of our ground to Kushan's forces.

Coming around the last bend, we entered the valley, my chest aching at the familiar sight. Olive groves lined the hills all around us, along with numerous vineyards and orchards. Many of the trees bowed deep from the weight of their fruit, the product of my father's tireless efforts over the years. We'd returned just in time to aid the rest of the family in bringing in the last of the harvest—a provision granted by Othniel, with the expectation that we would return in a month, refreshed and prepared to march on Arad before Aram could muster enough reinforcements to halt our momentum. Perhaps the entirety of Yehudah's territory would be in our hands before the early rains poured out Yahweh's blessing upon our thirsty soil.

My greedy eyes traveled past the fertile bounty and toward the grouping of homes that had grown from three to twelve in the years since my father and mother had returned to the valley once inhabited by her Canaanite kin. Although my wife was no longer among the women who awaited us within those dwellings, a pair of brown eyes that matched hers perfectly would no doubt be among the first to spot us. Yavan may be anticipating good food and a washing, but nothing would ever be as satisfying as holding my daughter in my arms. My ears already anticipated her little voice calling out "Abba!" and her tiny hands patting my bearded cheeks as she regaled me with tales of explorations over the weeks I'd been gone.

However, as we came closer to the cluster of mud-brick homes that our family had built over the years to cope with our ever-expanding clan, I noticed an oddity. Not only did Nadina not fly to greet me, but the ever-present sounds of children playing in the orchards were missing, along with the bustle of family members tending the fields or weeding the enormous vegetable garden at the foot of the southern slope. With the exception of two of my brother Lev's boys herding a few brown-and-white goats atop one of the stone-lined terraces off in the distance, not a soul could be seen. The entire valley seemed blanketed in a hush.

"Where is everyone?" asked Yavan, echoing my thoughts, his tone causing wariness to buzz through my bones. Around us my brothers and cousins had also gone on alert, sensing something was awry. Had there been an attack? Had the Arameans come here after retreating from our forces? My heart took up a stuttering beat as I swept my gaze around the farm. Yet the plows sat untouched, donkeys and sheep ambled about blissfully unaware within the stone corral, and the garden overflowed with bounty that would help sustain our clan through the cold months ahead. Nothing seemed amiss.

The door of the largest house swung open, my mother stepping over the threshold, followed by my father, who slipped his muscular forearm about her waist as they awaited our approach. A rush of relief hit my chest.

My mother's curls fluttered in the breeze, the red tendrils now faded and interspersed with white, but no less lovely than they had been when I'd long ago made a game of winding the coils about my fingers as she hiked through the wadis, bow in hand, with me strapped to her back. The smile that had sparked from the unbidden memory melted from my face as I realized my parents did not return the gesture and that, although I was walking in the very center of ten men, their eyes were focused on me alone.

My mother stepped forward, her bleak expression making my uneasiness thicken into black, oozing dread. I'd seen that look on her face before—the moment she'd emerged from my bedchamber with my wife's lifeblood on her tunic and futile apology in her blue-green eyes.

My feet halted, refusing to take another step toward her and whatever horrors were locked behind her flat-pressed lips.

My father pulled her to a stop with a gentle tug on her elbow. "Alanah," I heard him mutter. "Let me."

"No, Tobiah." She pried his hand from her arm with a grimace, her stubborn chin lifting. "I will tell him."

I'd just spent weeks engaged with the most brutal of enemies, lodging my battle-ax and dagger into the flesh of myriad faceless men without remorse. When the slaughter had been complete and the victory claimed, I'd spent days hauling corpses to burn piles after searching them for any useable weapon on the bloodstained battlefield. But the sight of my mother coming toward me with desolation on her lovely face was enough to make me retreat. My feet took three stumbling steps backward. My eyes jerked away from the pity between her fiery brows to the doorway, where my two oldest sisters stood on the threshold with tears on their cheeks. My throat burned as I searched behind them, desperate for a glimpse of brown eyes, pink-petal lips, and hair the color of roasted barley.

"Liyam." My mother reached for me, but I tripped another two steps back, refusing to let her touch my skin, rejecting whatever she was going to say before her mouth even opened. "There was an accident three days ago. We sent Beriah to fetch you, but he could not find you in the chaos."

I squeezed my eyes shut, my head spinning as my mind sped ahead of her words. Not after Havah, surely Yahweh would not be so cruel . . .

"Son. Our precious little Nadina—" Her voice shattered, hitting me with the impact of a thousand arrows slung from her expert bow, driving me to my knees in the dirt. "Your daughter is gone."

CHAPTER FIVE

I squinted, attempting to merge the two bleary outlines before me into one man and failing miserably. I tried again, my fingers gripping my quarry's tunic tighter as I shook him and screamed into both his blurred faces, uncaring that the entire marketplace of Arad was standing witness to my inebriation. "Stand. Still. And tell me who he is."

The grizzled peddler tried to fold himself down, no doubt retreating from my shouts and my breath, both of which were likely terrifying after two days of drink and grief-induced fury. I did not care. He would give me a name or I'd kill him too. He was hiding a murderer. Everyone is this godforsaken town was. They refused to give me any information that would lead me to the trader who had plowed over my seven-year-old daughter with his horse-drawn wagon nearly a week ago.

"I told you, all I know is that he is Moabite," whimpered the peddler, cowering. "And he has one eye."

"Where did he go?" I shouted, shaking him again. "What is his name?"

"I don't know!" His voice warbled a plea, his palms lifted in supplication. "He was only here three days, selling spices and cloth from Egypt. Then he was gone. Please, I don't know anything more than that."

"He killed my daughter! I want his name. I *will* have his blood," I snarled, my sight going bleary again and my head swimming. "I will have justice."

Two sets of enormous hands suddenly gripped my arms, tearing me away from the trembling peddler, yanking me backward until my heels skidded over stony ground.

"Liyam!" said the voice of my brother Shimon. "Stop this. He doesn't know anything."

Shimon and Yosef, my brothers closest above me in age, had a tight grip on me. Yavan stood nearby, his brows furrowed. Obviously the three of them had followed me to Arad, likely determined to keep me from doing what I must. But I refused to back down, struggling against their hold.

"He knows," I bellowed, then swung a finger around at the blur of gawking merchants and customers who filled the town plaza. "They all know who murdered her. And I will have a name or I will burn this market to the ground."

"That's enough. Look," ordered Yosef, jerking me to the right. "There are soldiers right over there, watching you act the drunken fool."

My head lolled to the side, eyes trying to focus in the direction he'd turned me, but in the past minutes the sunlight had somehow become far too harsh and I saw nothing but glare.

"Bring them on!" I spat, trying to blink the swirling lights away. "They know too. I'll have their coward blood as well!" I let out a few curses toward the Arameans who still held this town, reminding them that Othniel would be here soon to take it back.

"Cease this foolishness," Shimon hissed, his face close to mine. "The three of us are not prepared to take on a garrison of Arameans whom we've just humiliated in battle. And you are far too gone to even lift a sword in the right direction. This is not the way to bring about justice, Liyam. Assaulting innocent men will not bring her back."

"Innocent? My *Nadina* was *innocent*." Her name plunged the poison-tipped spear even deeper in my gut while her precious face floated just out of my mind's reach, as if already fading from memory. "But that didn't keep her from being left in pieces in the middle of the road."

A small group of my older nieces and nephews had been with Nadina that day, oblivious to the encroaching danger as they walked home from the market late in the afternoon. The trader's wagon and team had come from the direction of Arad, barreling around a curve at a breakneck speed. Distracted by a lizard, Nadina had darted after it like the quick and venturesome little thing she'd been, so she'd been unable to hear her cousins' agonized warnings over the thunder of horsehoofs. All five of them blamed themselves for not keeping a closer eye on her and allowing her to run ahead of them, and they'd each come to me separately with brokenhearted apologies on their lips. But none of them had held the reins that day. Only *he* was guilty of murdering my only child.

A choking sound from a few paces away made me swing my head around, my vision blurring again from the sudden movement. A stranger, a woman a little older than my mother, sat on a stool next to her table of wares, a palm over her mouth and pity in her eyes. I didn't need some stranger's tears. I needed my little girl.

But she'd already been in the ground when I arrived home to crow over my worthless victory. Her precious bones rotted in the dirt. Her lilting voice and laughter silenced. Those tiny hands that fluttered like butterflies as she described all the wonders of the valley stilled forever.

Yavan's voice was gentle as he moved in front of me. "He's long gone, my friend. He could have taken any of the trade roads once he left the area. He could have gone east over the Jordan into Moab or Ammon. He could have gone back south to Egypt. Or he could have moved deeper into Hebrew territory. There is no way to know. Besides, he has five days' lead on us, even if we did know which direction he traveled."

I growled like the rabid dog I'd become. "Someone had to have seen him. Someone here has to know his route."

My cousin shook his head. "It's useless to thrash about screaming at these people, Liyam. It won't help you know anything more than you already do."

"I know now that he has only one eye," I said, conjuring an image of a slavering beast with his sole hooded pupil trained on the last of my earthly treasures before he trampled her into the dirt. "And I know that I am going to dig out his other one with my dagger before I tear him limb from limb."

My stomach lurched and acid burned a path up my throat before I jerked from Shimon's hold to vomit on the cobblestones. Doubled over, my chest aching from the force of heaving up two day's worth of beer, I wiped my mouth with the back of my hand.

Until my own heart stopped beating and I was laid alongside my girl and her mother, I would not stop searching for him. I'd vowed it again and again as I lay on my back, searching the black sky for answers the past two nights. I'd refused to pass over the threshold of my home and take any rest in the place where Nadina had laughed, sung songs, and laid her sweet head down to dream.

"You are no good to anyone in this state, Liyam, least of all Nadina," said Shimon, his older-brother tone as stern as I'd ever heard it. "How can you expect to honor her memory with your head stuck inside a beer jug? I, as much as anyone, want my niece to be avenged." He slapped a palm to his chest, making me flinch at the sudden movement. "I know what it's like to lose a child. But if you don't pull yourself together and stop harassing these merchants and poking at the Arameans, you'll find yourself in chains, or worse. You won't ever have justice for her if you are dead too."

Regardless of my swirling senses and the rising urge to again empty my belly on the ground, the truth of Shimon's point somehow collided with the small part of my mind that still functioned properly. He was right. I'd wasted two days guzzling down any drink I could find in the valley, welcoming the sensation of grief being swallowed up in numbness. Then, when the effects had worn thin and none of my family members were willing to replenish my dwindling supply of beer, I'd stumbled the two-hour walk to Arad in search of stronger drink and information about the monster who'd crushed my child.

If the merchants here refused to give me answers, then I would find them elsewhere. And to do that I had to be clear-minded and focused on my mission alone. I was no longer a husband or a father, I was simply a *go'el haadam*, the next-of-kin who had every right to avenge my daughter's blood. The one-eyed Moabite would pay, even if I had to search the face of the entire earth to find him.

"This is a fool's errand, son," said my father, swatting away the smoke that had shifted on the breeze. He tossed another handful of twigs onto the burn pile we'd built in an open patch near the olive grove. "You will never find him. You are needed here for planting and then in the battles for Arad and Be'er Sheva, alongside your brothers."

I glared into the flames, arms crossed over my chest, refusing to acknowledge his admonishment. My head still throbbed from my two-day marriage to the lip of a beer jug, and even now the hole in my chest cried for more, but after my brothers and Yavan had dragged me home and forced me to sleep off my inebriation, I'd remained sober, using the full force of my crushing grief as fuel for my single-minded purpose instead of seeking to quench it.

"You have plenty of help, Abba. And one man will make little difference in battle," I said. "Besides, I have every confidence that our tribe will be victorious with Othniel in command."

Our scouts had brought back word of rumors among the Arameans that we'd had the Ark of the Covenant on the battlefield in Hebron and therefore their swords had dissolved to ash as we advanced. Of course the Ark was still safe within the Mishkan at Shiloh, but their terror was a gift to Othniel for sure. And knowing how shrewd our commander could be, he'd likely use such fears to his advantage, sending in spies to embellish the stories, layering myths atop truths until the rumors became legends. Soon Othniel himself would be the very embodiment of Mosheh, the great commander who'd brought Pharaoh to his knees and split the sea in two, face shining with the glory of Adonai and his staff spewing a cloud of fire. Israel had little need of my sword, and I had my own sacred duty to fulfill, no matter what my father said.

"And so you will go off on your own? Spend weeks, months, perhaps years searching for this man?"

"Yavan has offered to come, and Shimon too."

"They have families, Liyam." My father's voice had gone hard.

"Which is why they understand the importance of bringing the swine to justice."

"You don't want justice, son. You want blood."

"Blood *is* justice. It has been written so from the beginning, and I have every right to act as Blood Avenger for my daughter."

After a few moments of intense scrutiny, he nodded begrudgingly, his brown eyes softening. "This is true. However, Hebron is now ours again, so I take little issue with you searching out this trader for the purpose of bringing him back to the city of refuge for trial."

"There has not been a fair trial in this territory since the Arameans seized control. I will not take the chance."

"Things are changing. Elders of the tribe of Yehudah will soon stand judge at our city gates to uphold the Torah. By all accounts this was an accident—" At my snarl of disagreement he lifted a staying palm, his expression sympathetic. "A horrific one without a doubt. But we don't know what happened that day. He has the right to stand before a council of elders and give his own account, even as a foreigner. Your nieces and nephews will stand as witnesses to what they saw."

"I cannot wait for however long it takes to reconstruct our justice system, Abba. I won't. The man tore through the countryside as if pursued by a demon—" I cleared my throat, using my anger to barrel over the break in my voice. "They said he did not even slow down as his horses trampled over her, nor did he look back after his wagon wheels crushed her tiny body."

My father opened his mouth, but I spoke over him, doing my best to sound respectful in spite of the venom coating my insides. "I am not asking your permission. I am simply telling you that I am leaving at first light tomorrow. And if Yavan and Shimon want to come with me, I'll not stop them but will only be grateful for their assistance. If it takes longer than a few weeks to find Nadina's killer, I'll send them home to their families. But I will not return until it is finished."

My father regarded me with tight-lipped severity, his brown eyes full of equal measures of frustration and compassion. He may be a grizzled warrior, with scars marking his bearded jawline, his forearms, and one particularly deep one traveling the length of his thigh, but he was still my abba, and though I was nearing my twenty-eighth year, I was still his youngest child. Even now I could remember the sensation of perching atop his broad shoulders to pick fruit from high branches and chattering away as I rode astride the donkey while he plowed the barley fields, replete with pleasure at having my father's attention all to myself as my older brothers labored elsewhere.

And I would never forget the moment I laid my newborn daughter in his arms, hours after my wife had perished in childbirth, and he'd pulled me into his strong embrace as I wept over the woman I'd married by arrangement but had come to cherish nonetheless.

The release of tension in his shoulders, paired with the pinch of sorrow between his brows, told me everything I needed to know: He understood. If it had been one of his children—if it had been *my* body crushed in the road—he would have chosen the same path I set my foot to now.

My mother appeared beside me, her arm sliding around my waist as she too gazed into the growing flames of the fire before us. "Of course we will not stop you, Liyam. We feel your pain and will aid you in whatever way we can. You know that we lost two unborn babes after Lev and one more to illness before you were born. Tobiah and I are not strangers to grief, nor the wish to undo what has been done." She turned to face me, then lifted both of her callused hands to my bearded cheeks, her blue-green eyes flickering with ferocity as she held my gaze.

"But do you remember, my precious son, that I once left this same valley with a heart full of vengeance? I strapped on armor and set out to kill Hebrews in retribution for my father's and brothers' deaths. I plowed onto a battlefield alongside thousands of my fellow Canaanites, a lone woman with only a bow and a few arrows, so blinded by hate that I rejoiced when I shot your uncle Shimon in the chest. I stole your Doda Tzipi's husband and the father of her four boys because of my bitterness. It was only by the grace of Yahweh that Tobiah found me half-dead in the aftermath and saved my life. You may have every right to take the trader's life, Liyam. But at what cost?"

Tirzah

15 Shevat
1366 BC
Shechem, Israel

"Are you sure they will come?" I asked Malakhi, huddling closer to him for warmth. My breath came out in a frosty puff, and I pulled my woolen mantle tighter around my neck, fighting a shiver.

Cradled between two tall mountains, Shechem slumbered through these last hours before dawn, only a few distant flickering lights from its walls visible in the darkness. My brother and I had camped within this stand of trees on the southeast slope of Har Ebal last night to await the men who would escort me down into the Hebrew camp, where I would begin the mission I'd spent the last four months preparing for.

My brother wrapped his arm around my shoulders. "They'll come. I designated this meeting at the full moon the last time my men exchanged information, and I have every confidence in Hanael and Sheth. You can trust them to watch over you."

I lifted a tight smile, hoping to mask the trepidation that had surged higher with every step away from my home. "If they endured the same training regimen I did, then I have no choice but to believe you."

Under Malakhi's guidance, I'd pushed my body to unimaginable limits, practiced evasion techniques until I could do them in my sleep, and learned how to defend myself against a man twice my size using little more than the weight of my own body. I'd learned how to use swords, daggers, and slings with a proficiency few women could boast. I'd thrown knives again and again and again until the movement was ingrained in my aching muscles and even meticulous Eitan was satisfied with my aim. And as I'd promised Malakhi, I'd not spoken one word of complaint. I'd obeyed his every command with the same unquestioning respect as did the rest of his men.

By far the biggest challenge had been hiding my training from the rest of the family. But I'd learned to evade questions about my whereabouts, to slip out of our tent silently and find my way back in without detection, to concoct convincing falsehoods, and to play the role of compliant, devoted daughter and favorite doda to the children—all while listening in on conversations with the efficiency of a seasoned spy.

My older brothers had taught me to lie, to steal, and to kill, and how to determine when each was necessary. But as intensive as my training had been, and as encouraging as Malakhi was about my progress, nothing could quell the flutters in my stomach when I woke this morning with the realization that today I would walk into Shechem without him.

He pulled me close to his side and placed a kiss on my temple. "You can do this, sister. I had my doubts that first morning when you crashed into our run like a boar, but you have proved yourself over and over to me. And you were right."

I scrubbed at the gooseflesh on my arms, wishing we'd been able to build a fire in our hiding place. "What do you mean?"

"You were right when you said that we needed a woman on this team. There are so many things a woman can do—and places you can go—that a man cannot without raising suspicion. And you've shown a remarkable knack for understanding people, finding their weaknesses, and exploiting them for your purposes." He barked a laugh. "Who knows, if Mosheh would have sent in ten women to spy in Canaan, we might have spent forty years less in the wilderness."

His confidence in me calmed some of the roiling in my gut, but my hands still trembled. "If something should happen, tell Abba that I am sorry—"

He cut me off. "Nothing will happen. My men will be watching over you. They've already secured you a place among the cooks. And if they have even the slightest concern that you are under suspicion, they will get you out before the sun sets. I would not send you in if I did not have every confidence in your ability to uncover exactly who the Arameans are allying themselves with and what their plans are. The only thing I will tell our parents is that I have delivered you to our cousins in Ramah safely and that you will return as soon as they have no more need for your assistance."

The story my family had been given was that my mother's sister, Meital, had requested my help for her own daughter, who, pregnant with twins, required extra hands over the next few months. Thankfully, the falsehood had been accepted easily. Once I'd informed my father that I was still not ready to remarry after such a horrific loss, it was clear that they attributed my elusive behavior and frequent disappearances for belated grief over Eliya. Therefore they'd seemed all too glad to send me off for a while, hoping the time away would help me heal, and perhaps that I might even return with a different perspective about another husband.

"As for your apologies to Abba, they will hold until you return. You and I will both have much to answer for with regards to this scheme. But once he finishes yelling and threatening to tear me limb from limb, he'll be proud of you, sister. I know I am." He wrapped his arm about my shoulders and pulled me into an embrace. "What you are doing for the sake of our people is beyond admirable, Tirzah. I pray that Yahweh, the One Who Sees, the One who led Yocheved to place Mosheh in a basket among the reeds, will bless you with wisdom. With courage. And with divine protection as you go now into battle."

Malakhi's blessing over me caused a multitude of overlapping emotions to rise to the surface. Fear, doubt, apprehension, panic, hope, and excitement all rushed through my body in a swirling torrent that nearly had me begging my brother to take me home.

But the comparison he'd made between myself and the brave woman whose small, yet faithful actions had saved the baby who would one day deliver my ancestors from slavery in Egypt settled my conflicted heart, reminding me why I was here and what I needed to do to accomplish our goal.

Two men stepped out of the deepest shadows to approach us, dressed in threadbare tunics stained with grime from their long months of labor while they hid in plain sight, and the rest of my nerves dissolved into nothing. Our people, our land, and our entire way of life was at stake, and if I had to give my own life for this mission, I would.

"When Malakhi told us he was bringing a woman, we were surprised," said Sheth after we'd parted ways with my brother, his low voice seeming too loud against the hushed morning. "But his sister?" He blew out an incredulous breath that feathered the disheveled brown waves over his forehead. "That I could not believe."

"I know what I am doing," I snapped.

"Oh, I don't doubt that for a moment," he said, his dark eyes going wide. "Malakhi wouldn't send you in if he hadn't prepared you well. You probably could gut me like a deer and I wouldn't know what had hit me."

I stared him down for a moment, thinking he was mocking me, and although his eyes gleamed with a hint of mirth, I sensed there was sincerity behind the statement.

"That I could," I said, lifting one brow. "And then I'd season the stew so well no one would ever know." After a few tense breaths, Sheth burst into quiet laughter, and I smiled in spite of myself. There was something about him that reminded me of Malakhi in his younger years, before war and loss had filed away some of his carefree mischief. And just like my brother, he was far too handsome for his own good.

"Ah yes," said Sheth, with an amused glance back at Hanael, who'd been silently walking behind us on the narrow trail toward Shechem. "There is no doubt you are Malakhi's sister."

"That I am," I replied, feeling a rush of pride at being compared to my well-respected brother.

"And therefore," said Hanael, his solemn tone a stark contrast to Sheth's teasing one, "we will protect you with our lives, Tirzah. We vow it."

I paused on the trail to look back at the other man Malakhi had entrusted me to. With his serious brown eyes and his closely cropped hair, he looked to be a few years older than Sheth, whose easy manner gave him the air of a carefree youth—something I knew to be nothing more than a carefully cultivated illusion since both men were masters of their trade. Where Sheth reminded me of Malakhi, Hanael brought to mind my second oldest brother, Gidal, who'd died when I was only nine. Stoic, yet kind, Gidal had doted on me when I was a girl, and I'd loved to spend time with him out among the fruit trees he'd tended in Kedesh, simply soaking up his warm and steadying presence.

"My brother has told me much about the two of you," I said. "The fact that you've been here for months, enslaved to our enemies and enduring so much hardship for the purposes of gathering information is heroic. I only hope that I can be of help to you in such a worthy goal."

Hanael dipped his chin in response, his lips pressed into a tight smile. "We have found a place for you among the women. Sheth befriended the head cook weeks ago, when Malakhi first sent word of this plan, and asked if she had space for you among her cooks. You are the recent widow of Sheth's cousin and desperate for work."

"And she agreed?"

"I can be most persuasive," said Sheth, flashing a lascivious grin, making plain exactly which tactics he'd employed against the woman.

I stifled a laugh when he dropped a wink to drive his point home, then clucked my tongue. "Poor girl. You'll break her heart in two."

"She'll survive," he said with a casual shrug. "She's married anyhow, and at least seven years my senior."

His statement took me by surprise. I'd not considered that I may have to employ such strategies myself at some point. Would there be a time when I'd need to utilize feminine weapons to obtain the information I sought? Perhaps feign interest in some Aramean soldier? Malakhi had not mentioned such things, and in fact made much of teaching me how to avoid or fend off advances, but perhaps I should consider every possibility. Our people's very existence was at stake.

"Roma knows you are coming and has consented to having you work with her girls in the laborers' camp for now. You will have to prove yourself worthy in order to be promoted to the commander's kitchen. The man is notoriously finicky," said Hanael. "He is the head of the entire Aramean army within our territories, but he thinks of himself as more of a king than a simple general, and therefore eats like one."

I patted the leather pack slung over my shoulder, which carried my secret weapon against the commander's palate. "My brother may have trained me to be a spy, but no one cooks like my mother. I learned from the best."

As we descended the trail into the valley, the rising sun crested between Har Ebal and Har Gerizim, bathing the walls of Shechem in a golden glow. In the shadow of these same two mountain peaks, Yahweh had cut the eternal covenant with Avraham, Yehoshua had erected a white memorial stone to confirm that covenant hundreds of years later, and Yosef's mummified bones were laid to rest. And now this city of refuge awaited liberation from the grip of our enemies. I thrilled at the idea that I might have a small part in recapturing such a strategically and historically significant prize.

"Where are the two of you from?" I asked, hoping to make the last stretch pass quickly and take my mind off the destination.

"Not far from here," said Hanael. "To the southwest, near Afek. We are of the tribe of Ephraim."

"How did you cross paths with my brother, then?"

"He and a few of his men were traveling through on a mission to scout on the coast, quietly recruiting along the way," said Sheth. He waved a dismissive palm in the air. "At first we laughed at him, with his talk of underground revolt and his fervent insistence that if a few of us would stand against the Arameans more would follow. But the longer he talked and the more he reminded us of the legacy our forefathers left behind and the responsibility our generation has to reclaim what had been stolen, the more convinced I was." Passion glowed on his face, overshadowing any trace of his earlier playfulness.

"Did you follow him back to Shiloh for training?"

"No," he said. "It was a few more months before I could talk Hanael into going." He grinned at his friend, easily slipping back into his charming persona. "But I wore him down in the end. Told you I could be persuasive." He winked again, and I barely resisted the urge to shove his shoulder like I would my own brothers.

"Do you both have families back in Afek?" I asked.

"I'm unmarried," said Sheth with a shrug. "It was simple for me to go wherever Malakhi needed me."

"And you?" I asked Hanael.

"I have a wife and three boys," he said, his gaze lifting to meet mine with sudden intensity. "And it was they, and not Sheth, who convinced me that I could no longer close my eyes. When I looked at my beautiful wife and my precious sons and considered how I would explain away my inaction in the face of all the atrocities the Arameans have committed against our women and our children, something lit inside me that burned away all my excuses."

I mulled over his response as we entered the camp that lay near the foot of Har Ebal, southeast of the city walls. Threadbare tents were packed together here like sheep in a pen, the squalid and overcrowded encampment housing the many families who'd either been pushed out of Shechem when the Arameans stormed in or had abandoned their farms in the Jezreel Valley, unable to bear the heavy burden of tribute our overlords demanded.

Now that the sun was rising, the camp was halfheartedly stirring to life, a line of men already making their way toward the city, where a long day of enforced labor awaited them, the price the Arameans demanded for those who could not afford the taxes they'd inflicted on us. Eyes on the ground as they trudged toward Shechem, none returned my curious gaze.

"Has word of Othniel's victory not made it here?" I asked as I watched another group of unsmiling workers shuffle by. A pall of defeat hung over the entire camp; even the few goats that stood tied to tent pegs hung their heads in shame.

"There have been rumors of course," said Sheth. "And we've done our best to spread word about the strides the tribe of Yehudah has made toward freedom. But Shechem was among the first cities to fall on this side of the Jordan eight years ago. The people here were so cowed by the horrific stories out of Edrei, Golan, and the other eastern territories they practically stretched out their necks in the dirt, waiting for Kushan's iron sandal to crush them."

"After that," said Hanael, frustration in the taut set of his jaw, "it was simple for the army to sweep in and to confiscate every weapon and metal tool for their own use. And now, no matter the vastly superior numbers of those in this camp, they have little interest in joining our cause, regardless of the reports of Othniel's faraway victories."

In Shiloh, the Arameans kept a tight rein on our leadership, but a semblance of worship of Yahweh was still adhered to and our priesthood remained fairly intact. The stories of Mosheh and Yehoshua were still told by firelight on Shabbat, and the Mishkan, with the stone tablets of the Covenant at its heart, was within plain sight. The people there were oppressed to be sure, but a swell of hope had been growing, instigating a hushed but ardent call for Yahweh to deliver us from the Arameans. The number of men approaching Malakhi and Eitan under cover of night with uprising on their minds had multiplied tenfold since Othniel had lifted his banner.

And yet here, only two hours' walk from my home, these people—my people—were as much enslaved as they had been under Pharaoh.

After Hanael parted with us, saying it was best that he report for his daily duties on time to avoid suspicion, Sheth brought me to the very center of camp, where a group of women bustled about preparing daily bread. In a fascinating swirl of motion, the army of cooks stoked fires, ground flour with rhythmic efficiency in front of saddle querns, and slapped flat rounds of dough on the insides of open-faced ovens. The scent of fresh-baked bread filled the air, making my mouth water and causing a sharp spike of longing for home that I pointedly brushed from my mind.

"Roma," said Sheth, snagging the elbow of a tall woman who'd been directing a group of four girls with the distinctive tone of someone who savored her authority. Roma turned, revealing that not only was she quite lovely, but, by the shy smile and the wash of pink on her cheekbones, she was smitten with Sheth.

He responded to her wordless admiration with another of his cajoling grins. "This is my cousin's widow, Tirzah, whom I told you about. She is eager to begin."

"Begin?" Roma's brows furrowed. "What do you mean?"

"You said she could come work for you, don't you remember?"

Roma slid her gaze over to me, her mouth slightly ajar. "I don't . . . I have plenty of help."

Sheth's face crumpled into the most sincere illusion of disappointment I'd ever seen. "Oh, but Roma. You must help her. My cousin was murdered by brigands only a few weeks ago, and Tirzah's entire family was slaughtered in the melee. She has nowhere to go and is destitute. My family is too impoverished to offer her respite."

Resisting the very real instinct to roll my eyes at his overwrought narrative, I digested the details he'd thrown out, making sure to lock them into my mind in order to avoid contradicting them later.

Sheth reached out to grip the woman's wrist. "Please. I cannot bear to see her tossed into the streets." He slid his palm up her arm, making the most of her sleeveless tunic, and then leaned forward to whisper something low in her ear.

The pink on Roma's cheeks blossomed into roses, and she blinked rapidly, completely entangled in Sheth's snare. But when someone nearby dropped a pot atop a cook-stone, the sound shattered her stupor.

"Well, yes . . ." she said, clearing her throat and glancing about, likely wondering whether the other women had seen her melt in the face of Sheth's talented persuasions. "I suppose we can always use another pair of hands."

She pursed her lips as she glared at me in a show of reasserting her authority. "You'll start by fetching water." She jerked her head toward the group of four young woman she'd been speaking with before. "Grab an empty waterskin and follow them."

I nodded in silent submission, wondering how I would possibly prove that my skills were sufficient for the commander's kitchen if I was stuck hauling water.

Sheth smiled broadly, ignoring the terse manner in which Roma had addressed me. "You are sent from the heavens, my dear. You cannot know how much it means to me that you are helping my poor cousin's widow." He leaned forward again, his lips brushing the line of her jaw as he murmured, "And I meant what I said," in a tone so seductive I felt my own cheeks warm. The man was *truly* a master of his trade.

With her jaw slack, Roma's face burst into deep red again as a grinning Sheth spun away with a flippant farewell. We'd already agreed on the time and place of our next meeting, so I knew he and Hanael would steer clear of me until then. They'd secured me a place in the camp as they promised, but now the rest was up to me.

CHAPTER

SEVEN

I shifted on my pallet, wishing I had more than just my leather pack to lay beneath my head. But no soft, goose-down pillow could be more important than what was inside the bag—the wool-wrapped jar of honey I'd brought from Shiloh. However, if Roma continued to thwart my every attempt at proving my cooking skills, I'd never have the chance to use it.

It had been a week. Seven long days of tramping all over the valley tending to Roma's endless and mundane tasks, and I'd still not been allowed to so much as handle a mortar and pestle. But this morning, when no one was looking, I'd wrapped a small measure of flour inside a piece of linen and tucked it inside my bag, a plan forming in my mind as I did so.

"How can you still be awake?" came a whisper from my right, where Odeleya, one of my fellow errand-runners, was pressed tightly against my side. In a small goat-hair tent filled with ten women, there was little choice but to sleep shoulder to shoulder, but at least the tight quarters kept the chill of icy nights like this one at bay. And with such a thin body, the girl was nearly always shivering when she was not hard at work.

"Why are you?" I asked, surprised that after a long day of hiking all over the slopes of Ebal, searching for downed branches, twigs, and dried animal dung to fuel cook-fires, Odeleya had any energy left to even whisper. I'd realized three days ago just how grateful I was that Malakhi had pushed me so hard during training. I was exhausted at the end of each day, to be sure, but nowhere near what I would have been a few months ago.

Her response was so quiet I barely understood the words. "Missing home."

Although I'd spoken to the girl over the past few days, our conversations had been limited to the tasks at hand. None of the women had been unkind; in fact, they'd been more than generous in inviting me to share their tent, but I'd decided it was best to keep my focus on my mission and not distract myself with forming attachments. Therefore, I kept to myself and instead spent every possible moment listening and observing as I went about my duties, knowing that at any moment I could stumble across information that might be valuable to Malakhi and his men.

But Odeleya could not be any more than twelve years old at most, with a wide-eyed innocence and a soft, sweet voice—and she was obviously hurting. No matter that it was best for me to avoid distractions, my mother would be ashamed of me if I turned away from this girl who seemed to be alone here in this labor camp.

"Where is your family?" I asked.

I felt the twitch of her shoulder against mine. "They sent me here a few months ago. They could not afford to feed me after the drought withered what was left of their crops. Nor could they afford their tribute atop my father's debts. It was this place or . . . well, you can guess what else they considered. I am fortunate Roma allowed me to stay."

Nausea swelled in my gut at the thought of Hebrew parents sending their daughter into a labor camp to satisfy their debts or selling her to be used by degenerate men. And yet, since our territories had been overrun eight years ago, our every stalk of barley and cluster of grapes taxed, and a cycle of droughts and damaging storms finishing off what was left, many was the story I'd heard of the people of Yahweh taking desperate, horrific measures to ensure their survival.

"And will they return for you?" I asked. "When the debt is satisfied?"

She went rigid. "No. They made it clear that they have washed their hands of me, that I am a drain on their meager resources and without dowry. This place is my only choice."

As I was still reeling from the revelation that she'd been purposely orphaned, she asked, "Where is your family?"

"Gone," I responded, having repeated the falsehood many times since I'd come into the camp. "My family was killed, and I too had no choice but to come here."

"What happened?" she asked. "How did you survive?"

Surprisingly, this was the first time I'd been forced to come up with a story about the attack, since the others simply wished shalom for my poor family's lost souls but did not push for details. However, Odeleya had no such reticence. She pressed closer, and I felt her eyes on me even in the dark.

"I was not at the house when they came," I said, hoping my vagueness would satisfy her.

Instead it seemed only to whet her thirst for more details. "Where were you?"

I pulled an answer from the air around me. "I'd gone to deliver milk to an elderly woman who lived nearby."

"But how did they not find you there?"

The girl was determined to test my story, no matter how innocent her intentions. "We heard the commotion and we . . . we hid in a cistern. When we emerged a few hours later, everyone was gone."

A small gasp came from her lips. "Oh, that must have been so frightening. I cannot imagine, hearing such horrors . . ." Her voice trailed off and I let the silence hold, hoping she would take the pause for an attempt to control my emotions.

I forced my voice to warble. "It's not something I enjoy speaking of."

"Of course not," she said, gripping my hand in sympathy. However, she must have determined that my reticence did not apply to her, since she continued probing.

"Please," she said, her voice small and apologetic, "tell me that you did not lose children in such a terrible way."

This time a very real bolt of emotion hit me in the center of my chest, and I could not control the flinch. "No." I pulled in a breath through my nose. "No, I do not . . . I did not have any children."

"But you were married?"

"Yes," I said, allowing a shadow of the truth to bleed through my lies. "Eliya and I had not been blessed in such a way."

"Oh, how sad." But then after a few moments wherein I hoped she'd fallen asleep, she squeezed my hand again, her tone drowsy. "But you are still young. My ima was nearly thirty years when she gave birth to me, and I am the youngest of eight. You'll marry again and have babies."

My heart thumped unevenly, and I pressed my lips together to keep the scalding hot truth from pouring forth. *No, it does not matter how young I am, or even if I did submit to another marriage, my body refuses every attempt at pregnancy. All I have now, all I will ever have, is this mission.*

"Of course," I lied, and then pushed the knife deeper into my own wound. "If Yahweh wills it so, I shall."

After a few long moments in which I prayed she would not pursue any more details of my past, real or imagined, Odeleya began to breathe evenly, thereby ending her interrogation. Grateful for the reprieve, I settled into my makeshift pillow and stared at the black ceiling, doing my best not to dwell on the pain her innocent questions had churned up. Instead I told myself the story I'd fed Odeleya, making sure to plant the false details in my mind so neither she nor anyone else in the tent who might have overheard our whispered conversation would ever have cause for suspicion.

I let my eyelids drop closed, embellishing the story in my head, conjuring an image of the village I supposedly lived in, the house, the jug of milk I'd carried to the old woman across town. I even thought of how bone-chilling it would have been crouching inside a half-full cistern, listening to the sounds of slaughter all around and imagining what horrors I would have emerged to find. After a time,

I'd half-convinced *myself* that such an atrocity had actually happened. When I repeated the story again, I'd be more prepared. Perhaps I'd even be able to dredge up a tear or two during the telling.

Odeleya curled in closer to my side, a reminder of my nieces and nephews who argued each night over who had the privilege of laying next to their favorite doda. I missed their squirmy little bodies and their sweet sleep noises. I missed the sound of my father and brothers murmuring quietly around the fire late into the night. I missed my mother's gentle voice, her warm palms on my cheeks, and the way her very presence seemed to infuse me with strength. I hoped my parents would not be disappointed by my choice to come here once they discovered my duplicity, that they would understand my reasons and be proud.

I could not fail my people, for although my own story of violence was nothing but a lie, many horrors had been perpetuated on the tribes of Israel under the king of Aram-Naharim. I needed to uncover the Aramean commander's plans and discover who he was plotting with *before* Othniel came north. I could no longer wait around for Roma to give me a chance to show what I'd learned at my mother's knee. I had to find a way into that commander's kitchen.

Too anxious to lay still and beginning to feel overheated by Odeleya's small body so close to mine, I shifted away from her one tiny increment at a time, all the while keeping my ears attuned to the sounds of the other women breathing steadily inside the tent. Although it took me much longer than it did when I slipped away from my nieces and nephews, I managed to free myself from Odeleya's entanglement, tucked the blanket tightly around her, and carefully slid out of the tent—the pack holding the all-important portion of flour and my precious golden treasure tucked carefully under my arm.

Once I finally stood outside the tent flap, I waited for a few long moments to ensure that no sounds of stirring came from within. It would not do for any of the women to notice my sneaking about and report it to Roma. Barefoot in the black night, I headed for the cook-fire, praying that some of the embers there still glowed. I had bread to bake.

I scrubbed at my bleary eyes with my fingertips as the women stirred around me in the tent, murmuring together sleepily, combing tangles from their hair, and wrapping their heads in scarves before leaving to begin their daily tasks. After a long night of blindly finding my way around the campsite to bake bread in secret, dawn had come far too soon.

But tucked in my pack, wrapped in the linen cloth that had once held the pilfered flour, were six pillowy rounds of bread, made with honey saved from Gidal's hives before we were driven from Kedesh—the best honey I'd ever tasted—and the dregs of the sour goat-milk yogurt I'd squeezed from the skin-bag I'd found hanging from a tripod near the fire.

The lessons I'd learned from Malakhi—keeping attuned to the sounds around me, measuring my breaths, and rolling my feet to keep my steps silent—had all served me well. Only once had I been in danger of being found out, when a man stumbled from his tent in the middle of the night to relieve himself. But I'd skittered into the deep shadows away from the glow of the fire, and somehow he'd not seen me.

I emerged from the tent with Odeleya close on my heels. Like a lark she chirruped morning greetings to the others with astounding brightness for a girl who'd been abandoned by those who should love her most.

"You," said Roma, pointing at me from across the campsite. She had yet to address me by name, and I wondered if she even remembered it. "Go fetch water right away. Someone managed to spill one of the jugs last night. We have only just enough for bread, but we'll need more for porridge."

I swallowed my annoyance with her condescending manner, knowing that this antagonism was likely because I'd witnessed her fawning over Sheth. She seemed determined to show me my place and probably thought that if I was desperate to keep my position in the camp I would keep my lips sealed. And I would, but not for the reasons she imagined. Besides, it *was* me who'd tipped the jug over during my late-night mission.

"I will go with her," said Odeleya, already slinging two empty water-skins over her shoulder. I hesitated, willing Roma to contradict the girl and order her to stay with the other women. But I was disappointed when Roma nodded and reminded us both that we must hurry since the well was all the way on the opposite side of Shechem, as if we'd both not made the trek around the city walls many times.

As Odeleya had done, I collected two empty waterskins, along with a sturdy pole that I could lay across my shoulders and balance the full bags on the return journey. By habit, my fingers found the small knife secreted within my leather belt, one that matched the other on the opposite side of my waist. Master craftsman that he was, Eitan had created the weapons specially for me by melting down a broken dagger one of Malakhi's men had scavenged from a burnt-out village. Eitan had made the arrow-shaped knives small, only the length of my hand, but wickedly sharp and able to be slipped easily into near-invisible sheaths between the double-thick sheets of padded leather tied about my waist.

The other women looked at me oddly when I did not remove my wide belt before crawling into bed each night, but I could not chance one of them discovering my only means of protection. Whether I would have the courage to use those knives to their fullest purpose was still to be seen, but I certainly wished I'd had them when Imri and I had encountered the three Arameans on the road. The very presence of the knives within my belt lent me a new measure of boldness.

With the empty waterskins slung over my arm, next to my own pack, I ushered Odeleya from the campsite, halfheartedly listening to her chatter as we made our way through the maze of tents toward the path that led down into Shechem. Near the entrance to the camp was a group of Aramean soldiers standing guard, tasked with ensuring that we Hebrews minded our masters peaceably.

Until now I'd always slipped past the soldiers with my head down and my ears open, doing my best to remain unnoticed, but today I'd have to throw off that invisibility and pray that the outcome would be worth the cost.

Odeleya stared in wide-eyed shock when I halted in the path, handed her the stick I'd been carrying, and told her to wait for me to return. Then, with breathless words of supplication to the God who was able to make the sun stand still for Yehoshua, I made my way to the Aramean I'd concluded was in charge of this group of guards, knees trembling.

As I approached, I slipped my hand inside my pack, willing it not to shake as I removed the bread I'd made, and hoping that the honey and the yogurt had done their job.

The head guard looked down at me with curious confusion, a predator surveying a mouse that had foolishly crossed his path. A flash of fear that he could somehow see the outline of knives inside my belt nearly halted my steps, but I pushed forward and lifted my linen-wrapped offering to him, hoping that a man tasked with overseeing Hebrews understood our language. I had no intention of giving away my comprehension of theirs.

"Roma, the head cook, asked that I deliver this bread I made to you and your men," I said, pausing to clear the warble from my voice. "If it pleases you, I hope you will accept her gratitude—and mine—for your protection of her charges in the camp."

His brows lifted, and to my relief, he responded in my tongue. "Is that so?"

I bobbed my head, keeping my eyes lowered and my posture sub-servient. "We are all so very grateful for the chance to work here in peace." The lie slithered from my mouth, leaving an oily residue behind.

The head guard lifted the bread to his nose and inhaled, his eyes flaring in surprise at the sweet scent. It would have been better for the loaf to be hot, but I had every confidence that even cold it would taste far better than the standard, tasteless flatbread I knew to be their daily ration.

"Perhaps the girl has brought us poisoned food," said another of the guards with a gruff laugh. "Make her eat some first."

I forced myself to not react to the goad in a language I supposedly could not understand and kept a placid smile on my face.

"No," said the head guard as he passed the other loaves to his companions. "No Hebrew would be so foolish. The commander would have the heads of twenty or thirty of them if they so much as lifted a pitchfork in threat."

After a menacing grin toward me, he took the loaf between his teeth and ripped off a large chunk. To my satisfaction, not only did he hum in appreciation of the taste, he finished off the bread and then licked his fingers. "You made this?" he asked.

I dropped my eyes in feigned humility. "I did, my lord."

"Well, if it *was* poisoned, it was certainly a delicious way to perish." The humor in his voice surprised me, and I braved a glance upward.

"I am pleased that you enjoyed it," I said, then nodded and turned away, praying that my efforts would yield fruit. A few paces away Odeleya stood like a cornered gazelle: pale, eyes as large as pomegranates, small mouth hanging slack. Not only must I find a way to explain my behavior today, but now I also had to plan how I might avoid her company as I maneuvered myself into the commander's kitchen—for the sake of my mission, and for her protection. She was a sweet girl, but I could not allow her to thwart my efforts, no matter how innocent her intentions.

"What is your name?" came the voice of the guard behind me, before I could take more than five steps toward my astonished young companion.

I halted and looked over my shoulder. "Tirzah, my lord."

He nodded and brushed a hand through the air, dismissing me without a word of thanks, but the satisfied expression on his face made triumph pound in my veins. I was one step closer to my goal, perhaps even two.

Without a word to satisfy Odeleya's curiosity, I led her away from the labor camp and down onto the valley floor, taking my usual northern route around the city walls. The girl did not question my unconventional course toward the well of Yaakov, regardless that it was almost twice as long, but her confusion was nearly palpable at my back.

What Roma had not accounted for in her campaign to keep me busy with countless trips back and forth to the well was that such mundane errands afforded me the perfect opportunity to scout the area around Shechem. I'd not yet been inside the city, but in addition to the labor camp, there was also a military encampment at the foot of Har Gerizim. To my delight, soldiers' voices echoed across the narrow valley, sometimes with perfect clarity.

Although my instinct was to steer clear of the soldiers as I'd been accustomed to doing in Shiloh, I'd made a habit of taking the longer route to the well, allowing for the possibility that I'd chance over-hearing something along that way. So far, I'd heard nothing more than useless information about training maneuvers and a litany of crude jests.

But at least listening in on the conversations of the soldiers who traversed the same path gave me the opportunity to acclimate myself to the strange cadence of their speech. It was stilted on my own lips, but I understood far more than I could speak. Hopefully I could control my reactions well enough that the commander and his men would have no suspicion that I was listening in on their every conversation.

After we'd passed another tight-lipped group of soldiers heading back toward the gates of Shechem, Odeleya's exasperation with my silence boiled over. "Are you ever going to tell me what just happened?" she asked, coming alongside me. "Why did you give those men bread and say it was from Roma?"

Thankfully our silent walk had given me enough time to prepare a smooth response. "I am a cook—a good one. I want to use my skills instead of packing water back and forth like a mule and scavenging the woods for tree branches."

Frowning, Odeleya jerked her shoulder to keep the empty skin-bags from sliding down her arm. "But why did you not just give Roma the bread? Show her what you can do?"

I was impressed by her quick mind but hid my reaction with a care-less shrug, one that would also disguise my fear that my plan, however well thought out, might still go awry if Roma did not react the way I guessed she would. Nevertheless, I spoke with certainty.

"Giving her credit for such generosity to our masters will make her look good in the eyes of the guards. And once she is beholden to me, she won't forget my name again."

EIGHT

1 Adar

From my hiding place crouched between two brushy pines, long before the gray light of dawn, I caught sight of the barest sliver of the new moon. The herald of the beginning of the month had been the signal that Sheth and Hanael would meet me on the slope of Ebal in the very same place my brother had left me in their care.

And thankfully, I would have progress to report. My scheme with the bread for the Aramean soldiers had worked even better than I'd hoped.

Not a sound accompanied the arrival of the two men, but I sensed their presence even before they slipped into the small clearing. Hands hovering at my waist where my knives were hidden, I waited until Sheth whispered a low greeting before I unfolded myself to standing and stepped out of the cover of the pines and into the starlight.

"Malakhi trained you well," he said, a smile in his voice. "I could barely see you there."

I restrained a grin at the praise. "It's fortunate that my chattering teeth didn't give me away. I've been waiting for hours."

"Apologies," said Hanael. "There was a disturbance in the camp near us. Guards were called in to search a tent nearby. We were forced to wait until they cleared out before leaving."

"What happened?" I asked.

"We don't know. A theft or something of the sort, most likely," said Sheth. "But the Arameans are on edge. Something has them unsettled."

"Othniel?" I asked.

"I would guess so. We've heard they have taken Arad now, which means nearly the entirety of Yehudah's territory is back in the hands of their tribe."

"And Be'er Sheva has been returned to the tribe of Simeon," said Sheth. "Othniel's victories have already become the stuff of legends. They say he cannot be stopped."

A frisson of excitement coursed up my spine. "And what is next?" I asked. "Are they coming north as we hoped?"

Hanael let out a small sigh. "Yes. There's been word that the army is growing, day by day. Men from all the tribes are finally throwing off their cowardice and making their way into the ranks of Othniel's company."

"No wonder the Arameans are nervous," I said.

"They have cause to be," said Sheth. "But we suspect Kushan is looking to make alliances with some of our enemies. And if he succeeds, Othniel may find himself fighting a war on two fronts, or worse."

"Malakhi believes this as well," I said. "Have you found proof?"

"We've been told that the addition to the garrison we are building must be finished within the month, and the men working on the commander's villa have been informed the same. They are expecting guests. Important ones."

"And you?" Hanael asked. "Have you had any success?"

Now I did give myself leave to smile. "I have. I am to report to the commander's kitchen in the morning."

"You talked Roma into sending you?" asked Sheth, his tone appreciative.

"It took some doing. She spent the first week making me haul water and wood. But I outwitted her." I told them of how I'd made special bread for the guards and attributed the gift to her.

"Was she not suspicious?" asked Hanael. "We cannot afford for anyone to question your reasons for being inside Shechem."

"When she came to me the next day, asking why I'd done such a thing, I told her it was purely from gratitude for allowing me to stay and that I only hoped to serve in whatever capacity she needed me," I said. "At first she did not believe me, but then I told her about how my poor murdered ima had taught me to cook and how even baking bread made me feel close to her memory."

The false grief had poured from my lips like date honey. I'd managed to draw mist into my eyes by conjuring the very real memories of sitting at my ima's knee as we patted rounds of bread between our palms. By the time I'd finished my story, Roma had practically begged me to cook.

"And when I told her how much you would appreciate her kindness to me," I told Sheth, "she blushed and stammered and fluttered her hands as she directed me in my new duties. I don't know what you've done to that woman, but you've done it well."

Sheth laughed a bit too loudly, so I shoved his shoulder and hissed for him to be quiet.

"No one is up here," he said. "Who other than the three of us would climb a mountainside hours before dawn? So tell us, how did you come to be appointed to the commander's kitchen?"

"I give the credit to my honey-yogurt bread," I said with a casual shrug. "One of the guards must have said something to his superiors, because two days ago one of the cooks was caught stealing. Whoever came to Roma with the request for a replacement asked for me by name."

"I'm impressed," said Sheth. "You got inside faster than I expected. Your brother will be proud." His words filled me with satisfaction, as if Malakai himself were speaking them.

The sound of voices nearby caused the three of us to drop to the ground as Hanael blew out the oil lamp.

"Arameans?" I breathed.

"I don't think so," whispered Hanael, then gestured for Sheth to follow him. "You stay here," he told me.

"No chance of that," I said, drawing out one of my knives.

He huffed a laugh and slipped through the trees toward the voices that, as we moved closer, could clearly be distinguished as Hebrew.

In a clearing not fifty paces from where I'd met Hanael and Sheth, and very near the summit of the mountain, five Hebrew men were gathered. With two oil lamps on the ground in the center of their circle, they stood with hands uplifted, a quiet *Shema* on their lips. We waited as they spoke words written by Mosheh, reverence for the sacred call to the people of Israel to hear and obey the law of our One God drilled into us from birth. As soon as the last word was spoken, Hanael stepped forward.

The men startled, three of them skittering off into the trees like hares. Only two of them stood their ground as Sheth and I moved into the dim circle of lamplight. One of them held a chip-edged bronze dagger, a shoddy weapon that would likely do little if they were actually under attack.

"We mean no harm," said Hanael, palms upward to display his own empty-handedness. "We are simply curious as to why you men are meeting here in the dead of night."

The man with the dagger did not relax his stance, his eyes narrowing. "I will ask you the same. Who are you and what is your purpose here?"

Hanael and Sheth shared a glance as I wondered what sort of story they'd concoct to explain our presence.

"This is my cousin's widow." Sheth gestured over his shoulder at me. "She works among the cooks and sent word that one of the guards made advances toward her. I asked her to come here to ensure she was not harmed and to discuss whether we should send her back to our village."

The man divided a suspicious look between the three of us, so I did my best to look cowed, as if truly fearful for my virtue and dependent on my "cousins" to protect me.

A softening of the man's shoulders made it clear Sheth's excuse had been accepted as truth. He let out a sigh. "We are Levites. And it is Rosh Chodesh." He gestured in the direction of the moon. "We meet here in secrecy at the head of every month to worship and plead with Yahweh for deliverance."

"You are priests?" asked Hanael, his gaze moving to the three cowards now emerging from their hiding places among the trees.

The first man shook his head. "We are of the line of Gershon, not Aharon. But we have all served at the Mishkan in Shiloh over the years in various capacities. The Arameans won't allow us to gather, of course, but we five refuse to submit to such an edict, so we come here." His jaw firmed, as if it were the three of us standing in the way of their worship instead of our common enemy.

"Have you found others still holding fast to the Torah in the camp?" asked Hanael.

The Levite pursed his lips and folded his arms over his chest. "We gather here in secret, as we've done since we were chased out of our homes seven years ago. How would we know?"

"But you are Levites," said Hanael. "Is it not your job to call our people to worship and repentance?"

"The Arameans may allow some semblance of worship to continue in Shiloh, but here they tolerate none of it," the man said. "They would consider a public call to return to Yahweh an act of war against their gods. We could very well lose our lives."

As I listened to the Levite and Hanael, my eyes were drawn to a circle of stones nearby. Realization struck about where exactly we were.

"This is the altar Yehoshua made, isn't it?" I said, pointing to the stones. The five men turned to me, confusion blinking in their eyes.

"It is," said the Levite. "The Arameans destroyed it years ago, but we rebuilt it. Of course we cannot conduct sacrifices here since it is too much of a risk, even under the cover of darkness, but it is why we chose this place to gather nonetheless."

It was on this very mountain that Yehoshua offered sacrifices to reconfirm the Covenant between Yahweh and his chosen people. From this place he reminded those born from the wilderness generation how the One True God chose us from the nations, brought us out of slavery, and led us to many miraculous victories against the Canaanites.

My father had recounted the awe-inspiring rumble of thousands of Hebrew voices committing as one to live in Covenant, their obedience a testimony to the power and righteousness of the Almighty. And here were the men charged with teaching our people how to uphold that sacred duty to Yahweh trembling in fear and hiding among the trees in the night.

A sudden rush of righteous anger surged upward, spilling out of my mouth. "You have enough courage to reconstruct this altar but not enough to call for repentance? No wonder the people in the camp down there are so fearful. They have no hope, no leadership. How can you even call yourselves servants of Yahweh if you stay silent?"

The Levite sputtered a half-constructed excuse that I ignored completely as I talked over him, gesturing to the two oil lamps still flickering between us. "You can keep the truth within the circle of these shadows, recite the Shema to each other, and be safe. Or you can take your heritage seriously and spark a fire among the people. Don't you remember the reason Yahweh finally sent Mosheh to lead us from Egypt? It was because we started crying out for deliverance." I flung my hand toward the altar. "Has Yahweh disappeared? Has the power that split the sea diminished since the Arameans seized control? Or have we simply forgotten who we are?"

Seven pairs of incredulous eyes were fixed on me and all mouths gaped. My own lips snapped shut, and my heart began to pound. Where had those words come from? I'd not consciously decided even to speak such admonishments to these men, but somehow they'd poured out in a torrent. Heat rose on my cheeks, and I was glad the evidence of my embarrassment would not be highlighted by the feeble glow of the lamps.

"She is right," said Hanael. "You have heard of Othniel's victories, have you not?"

The Levite nodded. "We have. Although some say that he will be satisfied with the retaking of Yehudah and Simeon's lands and will leave us to the Arameans."

"No." Sheth glanced at Hanael, a plea for permission in his eyes. After a few moments, Hanael nodded. "Othniel *is* moving northward— and soon. We can give no more detail than that, but like my cousin said, we must be ready when he arrives."

"We should go," said Hanael. "Dawn is coming. We did not see you, and you did not see us. Yes?" He lifted his brows, a silent command in the gesture, one that reminded me of the looks my father had given Malakhi and Gidal whenever they'd been up to mischief.

The Levite looked back at the rest of his companions, who nodded their agreement. Then he set his gaze on me, something pensive in his expression that made me flush all over again. "Agreed."

Still reeling over the unbidden words that had flowed from my mouth, I followed Sheth and Hanael from the clearing and down the mountain path. When the time came to part ways, Hanael turned and placed his hand on my shoulder. "One of Malakhi's men will come when the moon is full to relay any intelligence we gather, so if you discover anything of importance between now and then, send us word. Do you remember my instructions for leaving us a sign?"

"Yes, the fifteenth brick on the fifth row down on the south fence of the courtyard," I recited, hoping that I would find the tiny gap there with ease.

"Excellent," said Hanael. "I would remind you to be safe and not take too many risks, but after tonight I think you might be the bravest woman I've ever met, so I have little doubt you will be fine."

Sheth snorted a laugh. "I thought those Levites would drop to their knees and kiss your feet by the time you finished flogging them like mules."

I let out a groan. "I don't know what came over me. My mother is the one to speak such bold things. I am only here to gather information and do my best not to get killed in the process."

"Perhaps some of your mother's boldness has been passed on to you. Those Levites will be mulling over your words in the days to come, I am certain of it." Hanael smiled at me and squeezed my shoulder. "I have a feeling we were meant to come across those men tonight, as if Yahweh himself placed them in our path."

I considered his statement all the way back into camp, but as I slid through the tent flap and beneath my blanket next to Odeleya, I shook off the idea. I did not know what had taken hold of my mouth tonight;

perhaps a lack of sleep had melted away my good sense. I would keep my hasty words to myself from now on.

"Where have you been?" came Odeleya's whisper in the dark.

A spark of fear shot through me. Had she noticed that I'd been gone most of the night? I prayed she would say nothing to Roma.

"Only to relieve myself outside the camp," I whispered. "I prefer not to use a pot in a tent with nine other women watching or listening."

She murmured agreement with my falsely modest sentiments. "I don't like it either, but it's too cold out there for my taste." She shivered at the thought and snuggled closer to me. "Are you not frozen through?"

"I'm fine. Rest now," I said and settled my side against hers, as had become our habit in the past couple of weeks, hoping she would drift back into sleep with no further questions.

"It's nearly dawn. There is not much time before we must report to the commander's kitchen," she said with a yawn. "We'd best not sleep anymore."

My body went rigid. "What do you mean 'we'?"

"Did Roma not tell you? I begged her to let me assist you in Shechem and she agreed."

"Why would she do that? You belong here." My jaw tightened as I sifted through excuses to feed Roma so she would reverse the foolish decision. I could not have Odeleya there with me. Watching over her would be a distraction from my mission and endanger us both.

"I've already learned so much from you since you arrived, and I want to know more." The girl had been closer than my own shadow, her happy chatter a pleasant diversion as we cooked and baked and cleaned, sunrise to sunset, in order to fill the bellies of the Hebrew laborers. The thought of such an innocent girl inside the home of the high commander of the vicious Aramean army made my skin prickle.

"No," I said. "It's not safe. There are plenty of other women to learn from here in camp. I cannot have you under my feet while I work."

A little gasp burst from her lips, and guilt immediately coated my insides. I'd not meant to wound the girl, only to protect her from dangers she could not comprehend.

"Please," she said, her whisper a mournful plea. "I promise to be of help to you. I will do whatever you ask. I just want to . . ." She paused. "I just want to stay with you."

The desperation in her voice reminded me that Odeleya's family had sent her off to fend for herself in a place where a multitude of enemy soldiers were garrisoned—soldiers who were notorious for their unscrupulous behavior. This tenderhearted girl, undoubtedly starved for any amount of kindness, had for some reason chosen me to cling to, and if I was honest with myself, she'd already slipped past my defenses. And Roma *had* insisted that the women in the commander's kitchen were guarded well in exchange for satisfying his demand for well-crafted delicacies that could grace the table of Pharaoh himself.

"All right," I said, already regretting my softheartedness. "But if I feel you are in any danger, you will be sent back directly. Do I make myself clear?"

"Oh! Thank you, Tirzah. I will not let you down." She hugged my arm and kissed my cheek with a giggle that earned her a hissing command for quiet from an annoyed tentmate.

But satisfied with her victory, Odeleya lay silent beside me until dawn, allowing me to think back through everything Malakhi had taught me over the past months. No matter how brave Hanael and Sheth might think me, walking into the enemy's house with the purpose of stealing military secrets was a terrifying prospect, even without a twelve-year-old girl relying on my protection. I only hoped I did not disappoint her, or my people, as I plunged into the many unknowns in the days ahead.

NINE

Although the recipe I'd prepared was one my mother had perfected years ago using deer or gazelle meat, the commander preferred pork be served to him at least three or four times per week. Even touching the meat Yahweh had declared to be inedible caused my gorge to rise, but for the sake of Israel I swallowed my disgust and prepared the unclean food without complaint. Unable to taste the dish and ensure the spices were balanced with the roasted meat and date sauce, I was forced to rely on my nose instead.

As Zimora, the head cook, carried the still-steaming pot into the house, I prayed that today of all days my keen sense of smell had not betrayed me. For if I'd learned anything in the past ten days about Barsoum, the high commander of Kushan's forces in the Hebrew territories, it was that there was no such thing as a second chance within his household.

Contrary to what Roma had said, I'd discovered that the woman whose place I'd taken in the kitchen had not stolen anything at all, but simply neglected to return one of the silver plates to the treasury room following a banquet. The plate had later been found beneath a basket, fully intact, but the unfortunate woman had already been taken outside the city and executed. Whether Roma knew the entire story and had hidden it from me for her own purposes I could not guess, but it had only taken one day within the walls of Shechem for me to regret allowing Odeleya to come.

I brushed my hands clean on my tunic and glanced around the kitchen courtyard, searching for my young friend, feeling the impulse to check on her before I moved on to my next task. As usual, however, she was off running errands for the cooks. Thankfully the girl was hardworking and compliant and had already made herself indispensable in the commander's home, so she was relatively safe for now. And as Roma had assured me, there was a rotation of guards on duty at all hours for the purpose of protecting the fifteen women who worked in the commander's kitchen. Although, as my gaze landed on the two men now standing a few feet from our preparation area, their eyes ever trained on us, I wondered if they were there more for the purpose of preventing assassination attempts. For truly, it would take only one determined cook and a few oleander leaves to bring down Barsoum.

However, as I was informed upon my arrival, if anything were to happen to the commander via foreign ingredients in his food, a hundred Hebrews would be burned alive and our own families summarily slaughtered in front of our eyes. There was little likelihood that any of the women who spent their days cooking for the commander and his guests would take such a foolish risk.

Wishing I could keep my eyes on Odeleya at all times and yet knowing my mission in Shechem was of utmost urgency, I lifted a silent prayer for her safety and set about making bread for the commander's next meal.

Lost in the repetitive activity of kneading dough and busy repeating a few new Aramean phrases I'd picked up over the past few days in my head, I barely heard my name over my thoughts. I looked up from where I knelt before the trough to find Zimora standing above me, her expression grave. "You have been summoned before the commander."

The list of spices I'd used in the roasted pork barreled through my mind as my pulse overtook the familiar sounds within the kitchen courtyard. Had I mistaken one for something bitter? Or perhaps the meat had been dry? Would my life and my mission end today because I'd refused to compromise my commitment to the Torah and taste the pork?

Gathering together every moment of training I'd been gifted by my brother, I pushed any fearful thoughts to the side, lifted my hands from the trough of dough, and wiped them clean with a nearby cloth. Then I asked her to lead the way, as I'd gone no farther than the kitchen courtyard and the servants' quarters since we'd arrived.

The laborers were nearly finished rebuilding the eastern wing of the villa, which had been partially destroyed during the initial Aramean invasion into Shechem. Although I'd kept an eye out for Sheth and Hanael among the many Hebrews tasked with the construction, I'd only seen Hanael once. Of course we'd both averted our eyes immediately, lest someone notice even a hint of connection between us, but knowing that he and Sheth were nearby gave me a constant infusion of courage as days went on. Hopefully, if my own fate now matched the woman whose position I'd filled, Roma would keep what she knew of my relationship to Sheth to herself for his sake. I could not bear for such brave men to suffer on my account, let alone Odeleya.

Eyes on the ground, I followed Zimora past the completed renovations, and into a large chamber. Centered in the room was a long cedar table surrounded by twelve ornately carved chairs, five of them occupied. Knowing that to meet the eyes of my master unbidden was equal to summoning death, I kept my gaze on the tiles under my feet as the servant girl came to a halt near the head of the table.

"Tirzah, my lord," she said, gesturing toward me without raising her own eyes to the man who held our lives in his palms. "Her hands alone prepared the dish you enjoyed so much."

A rush of relief traveled from the base of my skull to my feet as I realized that my food had not been rejected by Barsoum. But thanks to my training, I did not allow myself to so much as twitch a finger at the realization, especially since the head cook had addressed the commander in his own language.

"Ah, thank you, Zimora," said a cool voice from the head of the table. Although I was unable to see the commander's face, his devotion to food was obvious. His lower body spilled over the edges of the seat of his chair, his bare shins as big around as a normal man's thigh. "I am glad to have the chance to relay my gratitude to the cook herself. From where do you hail, young woman?"

I did not respond, but kept my breathing steady as I waited for the inevitable translation.

"She does not speak my language?" Barsoum asked Zimora.

"You do not speak the language of the Arameans?" Zimora relayed to me in Hebrew.

Now I shook my head, shoulders tight, hands purposefully fidgeting with the seams of my tunic, as if I were terrified to be in the man's presence. And although I should in fact be fearful, for some reason my heart beat steadily and I felt nothing but a buzz of energy that heightened my awareness of everything around me: the smell of the food on the table, the pop of a coal inside a nearby brazier, the creak of wood as the commander shifted his bulk on his chair. My own curiosity about the rest of his appearance would go unsatisfied, for I would play the part of dutiful, timorous servant well today.

"You will tell her that I have not been served such a delectable dish in my entire time in Shechem," he said. "The pork was tender and flavorful and the heat of the spices perfectly balanced with the sweetness of the date sauce."

Zimora unnecessarily repeated the words, and only then did I allow a small smile to curve my lips, my posture subservient as I timidly nodded acceptance of the praise.

"It is my pleasure to serve in this household, my lord," I replied in Hebrew, then waited as she translated my response.

The commander asked how long I'd been in Shechem and where I'd come from, then awaited the translation of my answer with surprising patience. Unlike with Odeleya, I kept details of my concocted past to a minimum in a soft voice that I knew even Zimora would strain to hear.

"Must be one of the villages I had destroyed a few months back. The elders of Manasseh did not heed my warnings about their incomplete tribute. It's a wonder this one survived," Barsoum said, addressing his tablemates with an air of disinterest.

"Likely not unscathed," said one of the other men. "If I remember clearly, your orders were to kill the men, burn the villages, and let your soldiers do whatever they wished with the women and children."

"Yes . . ." said the commander, drawing out the word as if truly considering what might have happened to me. The inquisitive gaze I felt focused on me made my skin prickle, and I hoped that my vague explanation would not be challenged. "She does seem a bit . . . subdued, doesn't she? They likely passed her around before bringing her here." He chortled, as if the thought of my violation amused him. I willed the nausea back down my gullet as he slapped a palm on his meaty thigh. "Well, regardless of whether my men sampled her or not, that pork was nothing less than paradise. I want more."

All five men burst into laughter, and I forced a flinch at the sound, eyebrows drawn together as if confused by their supposedly unintelligible conversation. Their amusement over the suffering of my people, over the many women and children who actually endured such horrors since they'd invaded our territories, seared through my limbs like molten iron. Here I stood, not three paces from the depraved beast who, at the behest of his equally wicked king, had been the source of so much torment, and I could do nothing but bow my head and feign bewilderment. My palms itched for the weight of the knives inside my belt.

"Tell her that she is now in charge of preparing my personal meals and delivering them," said Barsoum. "I want more of what she made here. And make sure that cook I bought from Egyptian traders last month teaches her everything she knows about food from her land. I have a feeling that in this woman's talented hands such knowledge will ensure that I will be dining just as well as Pharaoh."

"Of course, my lord," replied Zimora. Then with a deep bow, one that I copied, she left the room with me two steps behind, still the very picture of submission with my eyes on the floor. But inside, I was shouting for joy. Not only had my skills won me the access I'd hoped for, but from the conversation I'd overheard, neither the commander nor his companions had suspected that I understood every word. If I could keep up the ruse and stay in the good graces of the murderous tyrant who lorded over Shechem by keeping his ample belly satisfied, it would not be long at all before I could leave a note for Hanael and Sheth in the courtyard wall with information about this secretive coalition. My contribution may be small, but it would be one more step toward freeing my people.

◆ ◆ ◆

Never once in my imaginings of what it would be like to spy within the household of the Aramean commander had I guessed that I would spend a fair amount of time scrubbing vomit from the floor.

Barsoum, as I'd come to discover over this past month, was famous for raucous, drunken banquets. He regularly invited soldiers he deemed worthy of reward to partake of their fill of his drink, his meat, and his women. And my duties were to keep the guests' bellies satisfied and then to scour the room after the festivities had concluded.

This night was my third such experience, and I'd already become fairly desensitized to the sights, smells, and sounds of such debauchery. But scrubbing the stone floor free of the contents of more than one stomach was an exercise in controlling my own instinct to retch. However, determined to not bring the slightest amount of attention to myself—a challenge that I'd actually come to relish—I breathed through my mouth as much as possible and latched my mind onto other things as I worked.

In the last few weeks, I'd uncovered a number of potentially helpful pieces of information: a burgeoning connection between the king of Tyre and Barsoum that involved large shipments of cedar being traded for copper ore from the southern mines, though no talk of a military coalition; an expected caravan disguised as Aramean traders carrying weapons down from the north; and a call for foreign mercenaries willing to fight, without scruples and for an impressive wage, against Othniel's ever-expanding army in the south. I'd scribbled each bit of intelligence in code on bits of papyrus and tucked them behind the brick in the courtyard, imagining each note flying directly to my brothers' hands. Eitan in particular would be very interested in the caravan of weapons and the estimation of its arrival.

The longer I served at Barsoum's table, the less the men noticed me. I became nothing more than an invisible pair of hands filling their plates and topping off their cups of beer and wine. If their lips continued to be as loose as they had been in my presence thus far, it would not be long before my mission here was complete.

I'd also counted the number of steps between each room, memorized where every chamber lay within the villa, and noted which contained windows or other points of entry, and I'd become well acquainted with Barsoum's daily patterns, from sunrise to sunset and beyond. He may have once been a ruthless warrior during the war with our tribes, but apart from his lavish banquets, he did little more than meet with his men, eat, and indulge himself in various other pleasures. When we took this city back—and I had every confidence we would at some point—I would have passed on all the necessary information to take him down easily. And after listening to the filth and horror that spilled from the man's lips and witnessing his depravity firsthand, I would not shed a tear.

So far this mission had been almost too easy. I'd had no problem leaving notes for Sheth and Hanael in the gap between bricks in the courtyard wall, no matter that my heart pounded and my fingers shook each time I skittered out in the blackest part of the night to do so. And none of the cooks even looked at me askance, seeing me only as one of them as I chopped vegetables, skinned animals, kneaded bread, and concocted new dishes to satisfy Barsoum's decadent and ever-evolving tastes.

A snore from one of the soldiers still seated at the table startled me. The man was cheek-down on his plate, his arms dangling nearly to the floor. Two more of Barsoum's men were sleeping off their drink on a couch across the room, alongside one of the scantily clad women who'd been brought in to entertain the group. I noticed during the height of the revelries that she'd imbibed nearly twice as much as the men and wondered if she'd done it on purpose to escape whomever of his favorites Barsoum had planned to offer her up to as a prize.

Remembering the fate of the woman who came before me, I crawled on my hands and knees, making my way beneath the table to retrieve a fallen plate and sweep up the half-eaten delicacies that had been crushed into the floor by a heavy-footed sandal.

From the corner of my eye, a glint of metal caught my attention. Near one of the rough-hewn table legs lay a bronze knife one of Barsoum's men must have left behind in his drunken state.

My heartbeat tripped and then sped as my gaze moved around the room from my vantage point beneath the table. Other than the four people sleeping off their excess, I was alone in this room, left behind with orders not to leave until it was spotless.

The one thought that kept cycling through my mind as I brought my attention back to the abandoned knife was how hard Malakhi and Eitan had worked to stockpile weapons and how thrilled they would be to receive such a finely crafted blade. I could almost see Eitan's eyes flaring wide as he brushed a long, callused finger along its well-honed edge. Even I could see that it had been made by a master of the same skill level as my oldest brother.

Swallowing hard, I scuttled closer to the blade, seeing my own reflection on its flat, alongside the flicker of light from the lampstand in the corner. I held my breath for the count of ten, listening for any movement among the sleepers. Then I reached out, snatched it up by the handle and slipped it inside the neck of my tunic. It slid all the way to my waist, held securely there by my belt. Pulling up to my knees, I adjusted the folds of my garment, loosening it enough to ensure that no one might see the outline of the weapon within. Then I shuffled out from under the table, stacked the last silver plate atop the neat pile to be scrubbed and delivered to the treasury, and finished my duties in the room with all haste. The blood pulsing through my limbs drove me to move even faster than I normally did, and I managed to flee the room before any of the drunken guests opened their eyes. Thankfully, it was well past nightfall, because I already knew the exact tree under which I could bury this prize. I would leave instructions for where to find it in the wall, and hopefully it would be in Eitan's hands within a matter of weeks. What I wouldn't give to see his face when he was told who had managed to get it out of the commander's house in the first place. If anything, it would do much to reassure both my brothers that they'd made the right choice in sending me to Shechem.

CHAPTER
TEN

Liyam

29 Adar
Shiloh, Israel

"What business do you have in Shiloh?" demanded the soldier, as three of his companions spread themselves across the road to prevent Yavan and me from passing. Over the Aramean's shoulder stood the Mishkan on its sacred mound, the once-vibrantly woven gates to the Tent of Meeting looking shockingly worn after eight years of Aramean control.

Even after all the months we'd searched for the Moabite trader, somehow my cousin and I had avoided direct run-ins with enemy soldiers. But it seemed no such blessing was upon us today.

"We've come up from Ramah to visit family," I said, wrapping the truth within a lie.

The man's eyes traveled over me, likely checking for weapons. Hopefully he'd not physically search me, or the knives strapped to my thighs would be discovered and confiscated.

"You don't look Hebrew," he said, his gaze snagging on the *tzitzit* at the hem of my knee-length tunic. Where many Hebrews had discarded the practice of wearing knotted fringes in obedience to Torah law, I wore mine with pride, thankful they displayed my true allegiance, especially since my father's heritage had failed to overcome the red hair and green-blue eyes I'd inherited from my mother. Therefore, I'd been glad to stash my Moabite-style clothing away in my pack as soon as we'd reentered the Land.

"My mother is Canaanite. Her mother's people came from the far north, and her father's people from Edom long ago," I said, the explanation I'd used all throughout our travels in foreign territory springing to my tongue.

The Aramean directed an accusing glare at Yavan, who remained stoic, before returning his attention to me.

"This is my cousin by marriage." I supplied the easy truth, since Yavan's features were plainly Hebrew.

Regardless of my explanation, the suspicion in the Aramean's eyes did not wane. "And who are your relations here?"

"Ishai the Egyptian. We are kin by marriage as well." I gestured toward the familiar path we'd been heading for when intercepted by the company of soldiers on the road just outside of Shiloh. "His vineyard is just there, on that hillside above the Mishkan."

I'd not seen the elderly vintner for nine years, not since the last ingathering celebration before our territories were overrun and large-scale pilgrimage festivals forbidden by our oppressors. I hoped Ishai still lived—although, if he did, he would be well into his eighth decade on the earth. I could only pray that the long-held bond between our clans, and his extensive connections, might yield more clues to the trader's whereabouts, since the trail we'd followed from Jericho had grown colder the farther north we traveled.

"What would bring the two of you, alone, to visit family here?" the soldier asked, skepticism in his tone and his palm moving to the hilt of his sword. Whatever lie I spun must be convincing, or our hunt for the Moabite might well end today, and with the two of us in chains.

Even though Shimon had begged us to return to the valley with him when he'd parted ways with us months ago, I would not give up. I would search beneath every rock for the snake who took my precious child from me. If Ishai had no information to offer, or if he'd died and no one in Shiloh remembered us, I'd simply move on to the next city, and the next.

"A woman." I seized the first answer that came to me, along with a lascivious grin. "What else?"

The Arameans brows went high.

"I need a wife. Mine died," I said, with a casual shrug. "So my father sent me here." Yavan's body was so still next to mine that I wondered whether he was even breathing.

"A woman," stated the soldier, the word curling strangely on his foreign tongue.

"My bed has been cold for far too long," I continued, leaning forward as if I were sharing a great secret. "There are none whose . . . company I prefer in our village. I've been promised a fresh selection here. He"—I jerked my chin toward Yavan—"needs one too. He's tiring of the one he has, but I get first pick." I forced out a bark of laughter.

The Aramean scrutinized my face, but I kept my features friendly and open. After a few more long moments, the soldier sighed. "Carry on, then. But I'll be keeping my eyes on you. You don't belong here. Get your women and then go home."

We stood unmoving, like two stones in a stream, as the group passed around us. There were a few Canaanites among the crowd, three who looked distinctly Amorite, and one particularly dark-skinned man whose heritage eluded me.

Kushan had gathered soldiers from among the enemies Yehoshua's forces had pushed north out of the Land nearly forty years before, fomenting their anger against us and arming the many wandering Amorite tribes over the years. When he swooped in with his surprisingly well-organized army, it took little to convince the remaining Canaanites to join him by promising to return their territories in exchange for their loyalty. It had been one of the reasons our people had fallen as easily as they had, infiltrated as we were by the enemy we should have vanquished under Yehoshua. However, Kushan's promises to the

Canaanites had gone largely unfulfilled, since thus far he was satisfied with the yearly tribute the Hebrew tribes offered. Even so, nearly a third of the Aramean army here was of Canaanite or Amorite origin.

"You are fortunate Nena was not here to hear you say I've lost interest in her. Or that I'm searching for a replacement," said Yavan with a grin as we turned to head up the path toward the vineyard. "You think those Arameans are dangerous . . ."

"It was the best I could come up with in the moment," I snapped. "Did you have a better excuse for why we are here?"

Yavan's smile faded, and I immediately regretted that leftover anxiety from our run-in had ruled my mouth. My cousin had been nothing but loyal and far too patient with me over these past months. But the man I'd been had died alongside Nadina and nothing, not even my closest friend since birth, could resurrect him.

Instead of responding to my swipe, Yavan slackened his pace until he was walking behind me on the well-worn path up the hillside, making me feel even worse for how much I'd pulled away from our friendship during this journey, one he'd volunteered to join for my sake. He deserved more.

To my surprise, the vineyard had changed little, even after years of enemy occupation. A multitude of vines still danced along the hills in long strings, held aloft by makeshift fences. This early in the season they remained devoid of leaves, but it would not be too much longer before the first green shoots burst to life, ready to produce grapes that would eventually be pressed and fermented. Ishai's vineyard was widely known to produce the best wine in the northern territories, and I had memories of my father and Ishai talking by the campfire during festivals, comparing growing techniques late into the night. I wondered if the oppression we'd suffered under the Arameans had affected the yield of this once-thriving farm, or if the heavy tribute demanded of every Hebrew had worn Ishai's former prosperity thin.

Halfway up the side of the mountain, the path led us to a small one-level home, surrounded on three sides by enormous poplars. Encircling that lone dwelling was a gathering of twelve tents, ranging in sizes from eight-paces-square to one that looked large enough to house a three-generation family. By all appearances, the tents had been anchored to the spot for a long while and the large group that lived within them well entrenched. At least thirty-five people were gathered in groups on the ground around the central open area, partaking of a meal together, voices young and old overlapping. But all too soon every man, woman, and child in the vicinity had ceased their conversations and activities to watch Yavan and me approach. Unnerved by the focused attention of so many eyes, I lifted a palm in greeting when we were still twenty paces away, offering a hearty "Shalom" as we neared. Scanning the gawking crowd of strangers, I did not see Ishai anywhere, and my hopes began to dwindle. Perhaps this had been a wasted trip after all.

A man and a woman stepped forward to meet us, returning my greeting with wary smiles. Any brown left in the man's hair had been almost completely taken over by silver, and the woman's long, straight tresses were black with a multitude of threaded white glimmering in the waning sunlight, but the two of them together exuded an unusual vitality for people of their age.

Two younger men stood a few paces behind them, suspicious gazes latched on us. A sling leisurely dangled from the fist of the tallest one, even though his long and lean body was at ready attention, but it was the menacing stare of the second that truly unnerved me. Even with his chin tilted slightly to the right, the man's gray eyes were trained on my face, as if they could see past any artifice I could erect and dared me to make a move. In that moment I was grateful I would never have to stand on the opposite side of a battlefield from either of them. Everything about these men screamed their status as formidable defenders of Israel.

"Welcome," said the older man, wrapping his arm about the woman and pulling her protectively to his side. In contrast to the intimidating expressions of the younger men behind him, his tone was almost inviting. "I am Darek." He gestured to the two warriors behind him. "These are my sons Eitan and Malakhi. How can we be of service to you?"

I loosened my stance, aiming to display our peaceable intentions. "I am Liyam, and this is my cousin, Yavan. We are seeking a vintner named Ishai. Does he still live here?"

"What business do you have with Ishai?" asked Darek, brows lifted. "Trade?"

"No," I replied. "We seek information about someone he may have come across recently. A trader from Moab."

"You don't seem familiar," said Darek, ignoring my explanation as he looked between Yavan and me. "You are not from Shiloh."

"We are not, although we visited this vineyard almost a decade ago with our family."

Surprise lit the man's eyes. "Then you are personally acquainted with Ishai?"

"My parents certainly are. My mother was good friends with his daughter many years ago, before our people came into the Land."

The woman gasped and took two quick steps toward me before her husband jerked her to a sudden standstill. "Who is your mother?" she demanded.

Shocked by the urgency in her tone, I responded without pause. "Alanah, wife of Tobiah, from the tribe of Yehudah."

"Oh! Darek! It's Alanah's son!" Shaking off her husband with determination, she crossed the distance between us. Once she stood in front of me, I saw tears glimmering in her silver eyes and a large scar covering one of her cheeks, one in the shape of a crescent moon curved around a sun-wheel. The familiar story of my mother's time in Jericho and the hateful priestess who'd had her young friend branded with the mark of Canaanite gods flooded back to me from earliest childhood.

"Moriyah?" I asked, astounded that the woman I'd heard about my entire life now stood before me, especially since I'd been told she'd moved north decades ago.

"Oh, I am so glad to meet you, Liyam. I should have recognized you immediately by the color of your hair, you look so much like her. You even have her eyes, that unparalleled mix of blue and green. I have not seen her in, oh heavens . . ." She let out a quick huff, a palm to her heart. "It must be nearly forty years! She, like me, must be a grandmother many times over by now."

"That she is. I have five brothers and three sisters, so there are thirty-nine grandchildren." I paused to clear a sharp spike of pain from my throat. "I mean . . . thirty-eight."

A flicker of curiosity came across Moriyah's face at my blunder, so I offered a distraction. "She also has six great-grandchildren now, and two more on the way."

"It cannot be possible," said Moriyah, shaking her head in bewilderment. "It seems only yesterday the two of us were running through the countryside disguised as boys, stealing fruit from Canaanite farmers." With her fingers pressed to her lips to suppress a giggle and humor dancing in her eyes, she seemed nearly as young as she was in her memories in that moment.

As their mother gushed over me, insisting that we would sit down to a meal and then tell her everything about my family, Eitan and Malakhi softened their defensive posture and approached us. After patting my cheek with a satisfied grin, just as my own mother might do, Moriyah spun away, a whirlwind of colorful skirts and fluttering headscarf, asking some of the women who stood nearby to assist her with the meal. My stomach snarled at the welcome thought. Yavan and I had traded away the last of our silver for information back in Ramah and had been scavenging provisions for the past two days.

"Now that my mother is occupied with feeding you," said Malakhi, with an open grin that stood in stark opposition to his earlier hostility, "let's discuss why you are here. What information do you need from my grandfather?"

"Is he still living?" I asked.

"He is. My grandmother insisted he go into the house earlier to rest."

"I am glad," I said with all sincerity. "My father admires him greatly. Both for his vineyard and his record as a warrior under Yehoshua's command."

Malakhi's grin grew even wider. "He is a great man. We pray that we will have many more years to glean from his wisdom."

"As do I. As for your question, I am searching for a traveling merchant, a Moabite who goes by the name Zarosh. He trades in spices and cloth and is distinctive in that he has only one eye and drives a wagon led by two enormous black-and-white horses."

It had taken months of traveling between Moabite cities, seeking out every merchant we came across, to discover the name of the trader and that he hailed from a village that had been destroyed by Amalekites six years earlier. Shortly after Shimon had decided to return to our valley, we'd crossed paths with a group of Egyptians who'd pointed us north, having seen our quarry on the road outside Jericho.

"I have not come across anyone with such a description here in Shiloh." He turned to his brother and father. "Have either of you?"

"Not that I can recall," said Darek.

"Are you certain he came this way?" asked Eitan, his manner now just as relaxed as his brother's as he scratched his bearded chin in thought. Apparently my reunion of sorts with their mother had convinced these two that we meant no harm to their loved ones.

"We've followed his trail from Moab, up through Jericho, and were directed this way in Ramah," I said.

Malakhi blinked in astonishment. "Why would you chase one lone trader so far? And through enemy territory at that?"

My jaw clenched as I considered whether to reveal the truth to these strangers, but something urged me to lay it before them. "He killed my daughter. And now I will have justice."

Three set of eyes stared at me for a few silent moments, the friendliness in them suddenly swallowed up by wariness. Although unsettled by their strange reaction to my declaration, I held my head high.

"You are . . ." Darek paused, a pinch of something that looked like pain between his brows. "You are a Blood Avenger?"

"I am," I stated, unapologetic. "I have vowed to search him out, no matter how long it takes or how far I have to travel."

The men traded glances back and forth, an entire conversation held without a spoken word.

"Do you mean to capture this Moabite and take him to trial?" asked Malakhi.

"I mean to take his life in payment for the shedding of my daughter's blood," I said. "As is my right as her father and next-of-kin."

Eitan sucked a sharp breath through his nose, and Darek flinched. I'd told many Hebrews along our journey about what sort of prey I hunted and why and had not received any responses other than understanding, and even blessings that I might find my daughter's killer with all swiftness. Why were these men seemingly so dismayed? Surely warriors such as these would have no reason to begrudge my right to justice.

Malakhi broke the tension first. "You both are welcome to stay here for as long as you like. Enjoy my mother's hospitality. Her cooking is unparalleled, as you will soon see. But we can do nothing to aid your search for this Moabite you seek."

Dumbfounded, I flung my arms out in frustration. "Why ever not? The demon plowed over my seven-year-old child with his horses and then fled from his crime without remorse."

All three men regarded me with identical expressions of horror and pity.

Brushing a hand through his graying hair, Darek released a mournful sigh. "We truly empathize with your loss, Liyam. Please, believe me. We all have daughters whom we would fight to the death for. But you have stumbled across the wrong family to help you perpetuate a blood feud."

"You would see my little girl's death go unsatisfied? Her blood wasted?" The boiling anger I'd kept cinched so tightly threatened to burst free. I turned to Yavan, who watched our exchange in uncharacteristic silence. "Come," I said. "There is nothing for us here. Let's move on."

"Please," said Darek, his hands outstretched in supplication. "Do not leave. Stay. Take a meal with us, and give us some time to share our story, for there is nothing simple about this conversation. Besides, my wife will be devastated if you go without indulging her in news of Alanah and your family."

Yavan's palm came down on my shoulder. "We should accept their offer, Liyam. Even one night of good food and rest will benefit us greatly."

Turning my head, I met my cousin's earnest gaze. Deep shadows underscored his pleading eyes, and he looked gaunt after these last couple of weeks with spotty nourishment. Another wave of guilt crashed over me, causing my resolve to waver. I'd done nothing but push us forward day after day, week after week, driven by my single-minded compulsion to find the one-eyed Moabite. I'd not even noticed that the man I considered closer than my own brothers was beyond weary, as if one more step forward might cause him to cave in on himself like a gutted oak.

My eyelids dropped closed as I inhaled a few slow breaths, relenting solely for Yavan's sake, although exhaustion seemed to be catching up to me as well. "All right. We'll stay for a day or two. Refresh and replenish before moving on."

"I am glad to hear it," said Darek with a relieved smile. He moved between us and slung an arm around both our shoulders. "Come, let my wife fill your bellies, and we will trade stories around the fire. Perhaps what we have to say might cause you to look at this situation in a different light."

Too drained to argue, I allowed the man to usher me forward through the crowd of family members who had watched our entire conversation with eager curiosity. He led us toward the courtyard, where his wife and the other women kindly washed our feet before offering us bowls of warm stew and cups of Ishai's exquisite wine. Once we were sated, I submitted to answering question after question about my mother and the ever-expanding clan that had sprung from the unlikely union between my mother and father—a Canaanite captive and a Hebrew warrior. For the first time in weeks Yavan seemed to relax, the antics of a few of Darek and Moriyah's young grandchildren even causing him to chuckle. The familiar sound made me realize that it had been nearly two months since he'd last made an attempt to raise a laugh from me—a battle he'd finally forfeited after I'd snarled that I found nothing humorous while the spilled blood of my girl went unavenged.

It was past time to send him back to the valley. I'd been selfish to keep my cousin away from his wife and children as long as I had. I did not look forward to continuing on alone, but no matter what story these people had to tell, nothing and no one would alter my course.

ELEVEN

"Do you mean to tell me that you kept a foundry secret from the Arameans for *eight* years? How is that possible?" I asked Eitan, as I swept a finger along the flat of the perfectly balanced blade he'd just handed me. Flickering light from the cook-fire danced on the metal, transforming the weapon in my hand into a thing of terrible beauty.

An icy rain had taken up residence over Shiloh shortly after our arrival, so we'd sheltered beneath the largest tent with Malakhi, Eitan, and their families, trading stories back and forth in the smoky air for the past two days. As the hours built one upon the other, a sense of honor had grown inside me as I considered how much sensitive information these men had entrusted to Yavan and me after such a short acquaintance. But even more surprising than their trust in us was the depth of kinship I already felt with Malakhi and Eitan, a connection I'd only ever had with my brothers and cousins. It was as if the bond formed between my mother and Moriyah during their flight to Jericho so long ago had somehow transferred to their sons.

Eitan, whom I'd discovered was a master of metalwork and weaponry, grinned widely, pride glinting in his hazel eyes. "The foundry is well hidden out in the woods. We keep it guarded at all times by a rotation of men, since it's far too important to take any chances. We only stoke the fires when there is enough of a breeze to dissipate any smoke. Besides, the soldiers here have gotten complacent over the years. Although since you and your tribesmen have been taking back your territory, things are beginning to change in that regard."

"And how do you come across the materials to make weapons such as these?" I handed the dagger back to its creator, still awed by the craftsmanship. "Complacent or not, the Arameans still have a choke hold on the metal trade here as well, don't they?"

"They do. Ore is scarce anywhere in Hebrew lands. Most copper mined in the south gets sent either to Aram-Naharim or to Egypt, and imported tin is a rarity," replied Malakhi. "Unfortunately, far too many of our brethren complied with the edict to surrender their weapons to the enemy, but we established a network years ago so that any broken metal implements and any found or stolen weapons are smuggled here, to be mended or melted down and repurposed, then distributed among those we have been training to rise up against Kushan. There have even been a few northern-bound shipments of ore that have"—he cleared his throat—"managed to make their way here."

I laughed. "You've been stealing ore from the Arameans?"

He splayed his palms wide with an expression of false innocence. "Not stealing so much as . . . misdirecting toward a worthy purpose."

As I'd learned over the past two days, Ishai's family and the thriving vineyard they ran was far more than it appeared. The way Malakhi and Eitan had transformed a small group of spies led by their father many years ago into an organized, well-connected, and rapidly expanding covert resistance against the enemy was astounding.

"How have you managed to train hundreds of young men in Shiloh without bringing attention to your efforts?" Yavan asked. "We were stopped by soldiers before we even reached the gates of the city."

"The vineyard has been an excellent cover," said Malakhi. "Years ago we secured permission from the city elders, along with the Aramean commander who heads the garrison here, to employ rotating groups of young men from neighboring cities to help with the planting, maintenance, and harvesting of the grapes. If two or three of those young men just happen to disappear every day, well . . ." He shrugged. "So far we've had only a few near misses, mostly with other Hebrews who've figured out what we were doing and begged to take part. Only once were we forced to deal with a soldier who stumbled across Eitan teaching the sling to a group of Benjamites out in the woods."

"But he really should have been paying attention where he was walking," said Eitan, his expression blank. "A man can trip and fall over the edge of a ravine far too easily at twilight." The ruthless edge to his statement was not surprising; these men were committed to freeing our lands by whatever means necessary. Our people, and our way of life under the Torah, must survive.

"The abundant productivity of this vineyard has been nothing less than a gift from Yahweh," said Eitan. "The Arameans tend to avoid questioning the supplier of the best wine in the region, especially when Malakhi ensures that the soldiers stationed in Shiloh receive more than their fair share of the choicest vintages."

"My sons have accomplished far more than I could have ever imagined," said Darek, pride evident in every word. "Once Othniel began making strides in the south, the number of young men begging for training grew so quickly that they've now established trusted leaders in each region to replicate the successes here."

"It is only by the will of Yahweh that we have done so," said Malakhi. "I vowed long ago to inspire the younger generation to rise up against our oppressors beneath his banner in whatever way I could. We can only pray that those we train will return home to pass on the knowledge they gained here and spread word that the sons of Israel will no longer stretch out our necks for Kushan's sandals."

Having been at the battle for Hebron to experience the shared thrill of that very first victory with my tribal brethren—most of whom were the younger generation he spoke of—I had little doubt that the influence of these men, merged with Othniel's determination and fame, would grow to be an unstoppable force. The temptation to take part in this underground resistance was almost overwhelming. But as soon as

I considered the prospect, the image of Nadina, arms outstretched as she ran to me across a field, arose in my mind. *No.* I could not, would not, be swayed from my purpose.

"Have you decided your next steps?" asked Darek as if he'd heard the silent struggle within me. Seated next to his wife—whom he'd ordered to rest after she'd prepared yet another delicious meal—Darek kept a possessive arm about her shoulders. The sight of their casual and unapologetic affection caused a small ache under my ribs. I'd once envisioned such a long future with Havah, with grandchildren at our feet. Now my line would end with me. If I had nothing to hold in my hands, there would be nothing for Yahweh to strip away.

"It's past time for us to move on," I said. "Yavan and I went down to the market this afternoon and asked about the Moabite, but no one has seen him here in recent months. Perhaps we will head west. He may have gone toward the coast to replenish his wares at one of the ports."

Disappointment was plain on Darek's face. I knew he'd hoped that the tale he'd shared with us about Moriyah's past, and the long years of estrangement between himself and his brother who'd vowed revenge on her, might change my mind. But although I now comprehended their reasons for refusing to aid my own vengeance, it changed nothing. Moriyah's situation had been the most innocent of accidents, and she'd been more than willing to take responsibility for mistakenly killing Darek's nephews. The Moabite was at best a spineless coward and at worst a monster who took sick pleasure in trampling little girls.

I glanced over at my cousin, who looked well rested after two days of pampering by Moriyah and the other wives of Darek's clan, but his gaze was trained on the flames, brows furrowed with what I assumed was the weight of his double-mindedness. Yavan was loyal beyond all things and would without a doubt lay down his life for me, but I must not allow him to do so any longer.

"Actually," I said to Malakhi, "I have a favor to ask of you. Do you plan to send anyone south to Othniel anytime soon?"

Malakhi's brows lifted. "We do."

"I'd like Yavan to go with them," I said. "He needs to return to his family."

"No, Liyam," argued my cousin. "I will stay with you for a few more weeks—"

"You will not. I've kept you from Nena long enough." I glared at him. "It is time. Go home. Help get the early planting in before Othniel calls up the army to push north."

He opened his mouth to disagree but was interrupted by a commotion outside the tent.

Led by the bear of a man named Baz who had been connected to this family for many years, two young men entered the tent, dripping wet and chests heaving. Malakhi stood to greet the newcomers, who'd obviously come some distance with great urgency. Moriyah jumped up, already in motion to find dry clothing for the men and bring them food and drink.

"They have news, Malakhi," Baz said, brushing an enormous paw over his own wet beard. "But they refuse to speak to anyone but you."

"Word from Sheth and Hanael?" Malakhi asked. "We've been wondering what took you so long. We expected you back two days ago."

"We came directly here from Shechem. We bring tidings," said one of the young men, his face drawn and eyes weary. "But none that we rejoice to carry."

"Tell me," said Malakhi, with sharp-edged authority.

"We waited at the appointed meeting place on Ebal at the new moon, as you ordered," said the young man, scrubbing his fingers through dark shoulder-length locks now plastered to his head by the rain. "But neither man appeared."

"Perhaps they were prevented by their overseer? They've missed appointed meetings before."

The young man shook his head. "We thought so too, so we took a chance and made our way into the camp, hoping to blend in and perhaps discover where they might be." He paused, his gaze dropping.

"And? Did you find them?" Malakhi prodded, his posture rigid.

"They'd been taken."

Malakhi took a step forward, his hands fisted. "Taken? What do you mean?"

"The rumor is that two Hebrews were arrested for spying—men who were on the labor crew for the commander's house."

Malakhi's silver eyes darkened. "No. That can't be. Sheth and Hanael are my best; they would not be so careless."

"It is worse." The messenger's sigh was weighted with sorrow. "One of them, we don't know which, was killed in the main plaza. Beheaded as a warning. No one knows whether the other is alive or dead. There was nothing we could do but turn back."

Malakhi, the leader of men who I'd come to think might be practically fearless in the struggle against the Arameans, jammed both hands into his black hair, his face now almost completely devoid of color. "No," he whispered. "No."

Eitan also appeared stricken by the news, his breath coming in great pants before he sank to the ground to lay his head in his hands, his lips moving silently as if he were pleading with Yahweh.

"These men were well aware of the risks when they entered Shechem," said Darek, dividing a confused look between his two distraught sons. "We've lost men before, and we will again."

"You don't understand, Abba," said Malakhi, his voice teetering on the edge of panic. "Sheth and Hanael have been in Shechem for over a year gathering intelligence, but two months ago they were given a special mission. They were told to protect something of utmost value, and if they've been compromised, then that means she—" He stopped and released a tortured groan. "What have I done?"

Darek's eyes were wild as he moved to grip his son's shoulders. "*What* were they supposed to protect? Tell me!"

Malakhi's eyes dropped closed, as if he could not bear to answer his father's near-hysterical question while meeting his gaze. "Tirzah. They were supposed to protect Tirzah. And now she is there, in the commander's house. Alone."

TWELVE

All discussion of my quest and Yavan's journey south was quickly forgotten after the revelation that Malakhi had secretly sent his youngest sister into Shechem as a spy. The explosion of fury from Darek's lips was painful to witness, but nothing if not understandable. I, above all others, knew the pain of losing a daughter, and for his sake I hoped that the young woman would be safely returned to his arms.

For the second night Yuval, the one-time steward of Ishai's vineyard and the man he'd adopted as a son, allowed Yavan and me to take refuge from the incessant rain inside the two-room home he shared with his wife and four children. Although the Canaanite-born man bore lion-inflicted scars on his face and body, he and his wife, Tzipporah, were generosity personified as they welcomed us to their home—a defining characteristic of this entire clan, it seemed.

Lying on the floor near the glowing embers of the small fire at the center of their home, Yavan and I whispered our speculations about the situation with Malakhi's sister.

"What sort of woman would take on such a precarious mission?" Yavan had asked.

"A foolish one, no doubt. I cannot understand how she talked Malakhi and Eitan into it. Especially without their father's knowledge."

"She must be unmarried. I heard no talk of a husband."

I hummed in agreement. "No sane man would allow his wife to put herself in such a position."

"From what Malakhi indicated, she was very well trained and plenty capable of doing the job she set out to do."

"Regardless. Sending her into the Aramean commander's home was nothing but foolish. I truly thought Malakhi was wiser than that." But even as I declared it, I had to acknowledge that no matter how successful he'd been over these past years, no one was perfect, and even the most acute military minds were bound to make a mistake or two. And by the devastation on Malakhi's face, I knew he'd be thrashing himself over this decision for a long while.

"I wonder how they will extricate her without raising suspicion," mused Yavan. "The Arameans will now be twice as vigilant after discovering spies in their midst."

"Maybe she's already dead," I said. "And there will be no need."

My cousin flinched at my callous response. "For Malakhi's sake, as well as the rest of this clan, I certainly hope not."

I hefted a deep sigh, sorrow building as I thought of my own losses and the hollow place in my chest that would likely not heal for the rest of my days, whether I found the one-eyed Moabite or not. "As do I, cousin. As do I."

Just after we awoke the next morning, a knock sounded on the door to Yuval's home. Tzipporah opened the door to admit a stoic Eitan, who asked that we join Malakhi on the rooftop of Ishai's home, more than likely to discuss Yavan's travels with the group going south.

After thanking our hosts for their hospitality and pulling our woolen mantles tight about our bodies, we followed Eitan into the drizzle, through the barren-limbed vineyard, and up the stairs to the rooftop where Malakhi stood beneath a black wool canopy, his back to us and defeat evident in the slope of his shoulders.

"Shalom," I said, truly wishing that the man who'd been so open and gracious to us might find some semblance of peace, even in the midst of this trial.

He turned, and though I'd expected defeat also to be mirrored in his silver eyes, instead I was greeted with an expression of firm determination.

"Good morning," he replied. "I trust you both slept well?"

"We did, thank you. I understand that you have much more important matters to attend to, but I must be on my way today, and I want to make sure that Yavan will be allowed to travel with your men."

Malakhi stared at me for a few long moments, something about his pointed scrutiny making me uneasy. Then, as if suddenly realizing that my cousin stood at my side, his gaze flitted over to Yavan. "Yes, of course. You are welcome to stay here until they depart in a few days." Then his attention moved back to me. "But I have a proposition for you, Liyam."

I lifted my brows. "Me?"

"Eitan and I spent the entirety of the night up here discussing what to do about Tirzah. We cannot allow our sister to stay in Shechem. Not after one of my men, or perhaps both, was executed."

I opened my mouth to ask what their dilemma might have to do with me, but Malakhi lifted a palm to halt my words. From the corner of my eye, I noticed that Darek had joined us. He stood at my right, the rigid lines of his war-marked body and the firm set of his mouth communicating that in no way had he forgiven his sons for their decision to send his daughter into such danger.

"From what the messengers said," Malakhi continued, seemingly unaffected by the fury radiating off his father, "the commander's house is now locked down. Even the remainder of the building project has ceased until they determine whether anyone else is a spy. It is only a matter of time before someone makes the connection between Sheth and Hanael and my sister. We need someone to go in, get her, and bring her home." His silver eyes were piercing. "I need you to do it."

I reared back. "I don't even know your sister."

"What does that matter? She is a woman in distress. I've only known you for two days, but I have deduced that you are an honorable man. A man with what might be the most single-minded determination I've ever witnessed. Even if I feel that your dedication to a blood feud is misguided."

I brushed aside the subtle dig. "What makes you think I could accomplish that, even if I were willing?"

"You don't look Hebrew," he said, gesturing to my red hair. "You told me yesterday that you were able to pass as Moabite west of the Jordan River, due to your mother's foreign heritage."

The clothing I'd procured there and the dialect I'd learned from my mother had been a great help in that regard. "I did. But what would that mean in Shechem?"

"Although Tirzah has only been in the commander's house for a few weeks, she already sent us numerous helpful pieces of information. One of which is a call for mercenary soldiers. Barsoum, the high commander, is offering an impressive wage to anyone willing to fight alongside his men, regardless of their heritage."

"And you mean for me to answer this call?"

"We do. Your appearance makes you uniquely qualified to pass as a foreign soldier. From the stories you and Yavan told us of your time under Othniel's command, I have no doubt that you possess the necessary skills to prove competent. And because Tirzah does not know you, there would be no chance she might accidentally divulge your connection before you can reveal the truth to her."

"You have plenty of other men. You told me you have spies all over the territories and beyond. I am certain you know someone else who can pass for Moabite. Someone she does not know."

"None who can be fetched in time. You are the only one. We need your help, Liyam."

I glared at him, feeling cornered. I truly felt for his plight and could see that he considered me to be his only hope in this circumstance, but as much as I'd already come to respect Malakhi, I'd made a vow on Nadina's memory. I would not let her down.

"No." I shook my head. "I need to move on or the man who killed my daughter will get farther away. I'm sorry."

"Please," said Darek, moving into my line of sight, breaking his silence for the first time since he'd joined us. "This is *my* daughter's life we are speaking of. *My* little girl who is unprotected in the house of one of the most ruthless men to ever lead an army. Although I cannot condone your mission to destroy the man who killed your daughter, I can certainly understand the urge. I would do anything to bring Tirzah home. If I could go into Shechem without further endangering her, I would already be there."

Darek slanted a wrathful glance at his sons, making me certain that this idea had already been argued and discarded. Then he turned his dark brown eyes on me, and the pain there was a reflection of the hollow place in my chest. Before I'd lost Nadina, I'd not understood the lengths I would have gone for one more glimpse of her precious face, one more embrace, one more word from her lips. That same desperation was in Darek's eyes now.

"I will help you find the one-eyed trader," Malakhi declared, his tone full of confidence. Surprised at his change of heart after the vehement argument he'd made against my quest, and affected by Darek's impassioned plea, I wordlessly gestured for him to continue.

"You are right that I have men all over the territories, and in other places as well, among both friends and foes. I will use them to search out the man who killed your daughter. Then you can do with him whatever you please."

If Malakhi utilized his connections, I would not have to spend years searching for the killer myself. His network could root out the murderer much faster than I could ever hope to do alone.

My resolve wavered further. "It may not work. Your sister could already be compromised. Will you still hold up your end of the bargain, even if I fail?"

"You won't fail. I've heard the stories of your mother and father since I was a boy. I have complete faith that a man raised by two brave and resourceful warriors is plenty capable of bringing Tirzah home."

Dragging my fingers through my hair, I glanced back at Yavan. My cousin returned my searching gaze with a helpless shrug. He, above all others, understood what I'd endured over the past few months of searching but had never attempted to dissuade me from my course. He would not challenge my decision either way.

I turned my back on the four men to face north, toward the Mishkan down in the valley. Even setting aside the profound way Darek's grief had impacted me, what Malakhi offered was a far better solution than wandering all over the Hebrew territories on my own, regardless that his proposal was one that might end with my head separated from my neck. However, if this detour ended with Nadina's lifeblood avenged, then it was worth whatever risk I might have to take.

"All right," I said, not taking my eyes from the place where smoke curled into the air from the morning sacrifice. "Tell me what I need to know."

Tirzah

6 Nisan

Any burns I received from the scorching heat of the pot I'd just plucked directly from the flames were well deserved. My friends were dead, and I was to blame.

I strode toward the commander's chambers, my hands barely protected by a double-layer of wool cloth, guilt and fear roiling in my gut. I'd learned the hard way that the Aramean commander did not eat what *he* considered cold meat, which meant it must still be visibly steaming. It had taken only one incident of him bellowing about what inedible rot I'd served him to ensure that my feet never paused between the kitchen courtyard and his table.

However, since Hanael and Sheth had been arrested two weeks ago due to my failure, a few filthy epithets were the least of my worries. With both men who'd been entrusted with my safety gone and no way of sending word to Malakhi, I was completely on my own and more than likely the next to suffer a traitor's execution.

I'd not been foolish enough to ask around for a description of which of the two had been slaughtered in the main plaza, but I hoped that the second man had already died wherever he'd been imprisoned. I was only too aware of how savage these Arameans could be and knew the horrific measures they took to pry information from their enemies. The gory tales the commander and his men laughed about over their meals turned my stomach inside out.

Pausing for only a brief moment at the threshold of the dining chamber, listening to the sounds of yet another of Barsoum's debauched banquets, I swallowed against the nausea that rose along with the images of kind, gentle Hanael or spirited, brash Sheth being tortured for my rash decision to steal that knife. Regret had been my constant companion since the moment I'd overheard that one of the men had been seen digging it up and unwittingly led an informant to the other. If only I'd held to my mission of retrieving information and not pushed for more glory . . .

An unfamiliar laugh from within the dining chamber jolted me from the cycle of torturous thoughts, reminding me to keep my focus where it belonged. My connection to Hanael and Sheth would undoubtedly be uncovered since I did not trust that Roma would keep our relationship a secret, but until then I must continue collecting information about every guest at Barsoum's table. Sick with dread or not, I had a job to do, and I vowed to continue until my dying breath. Otherwise my friends' sacrifices would be in vain.

Head down, I padded across the room to offer the dish to the commander's head manservant—the unfortunate man newly charged with tasting his master's food for poison, following the revelation that enemies had infiltrated this house. Grateful that all attention was on the flock of dancers entertaining Barsoum's guests with little more than feathers, beads, and henna to hide their modesty, I placed the pot on the wooden table, ladled a large portion into a bowl, then stepped back to await the commander's assessment of the stewed goose with root vegetables and leeks that I'd prepared.

The sound of lips smacking against fingers and the hum of appreciation as he chewed made my pulse slow a small measure, but I did not even dare shift my feet as I awaited the verdict. Once he signaled me to serve the rest of his guests, I breathed easier, knowing that at least today my cooking had met his exacting standards.

Retrieving the pot, I began to serve the other men who'd joined the Aramean leader at his table, although I kept my head dutifully bowed as I scooped a steaming portion into each bowl.

The two soldiers seated to Barsoum's right were well known to me and frequent guests of the commander. The black-haired one was named Ishmid, and the one whose head was shaven clean, Khaled. Ishmid ignored me, as he always did when I served him, his eyes instead trained on the half-naked women twirling about the room. However, Khaled peered up at me as I dipped my wooden ladle into the pot, his knowing smirk raising the hair on the back of my neck. Once, when the commander had not been looking, Khaled had covertly slid a finger up the outside of my thigh, so I now held my breath whenever I was near him, doing my best to remain invisible and serve him swiftly, and at arm's length.

Most of the remaining guests were familiar. I'd seen the other soldiers at this table various times before, but the man seated at the end was a stranger, his dress indicating he was something other than Aramean. His dark red hair and full beard were distinctly ragged in comparison to that of the well-groomed and oiled commander and even the rest of the soldiers, making me wonder why such a rough-edged visitor would be allowed at the table of the man who answered only to King Kushan. But perhaps this man had something to do with the alliance Malakhi had been so certain was in the making. I determined not to miss a word of what was being said, even if my chances of getting a message to Shiloh now were painfully slim.

Sprawled in his chair with the air of a satisfied lion, the stranger tipped his head back and laughed at something the man next to him said, making me realize that it was indeed his voice I'd heard outside the threshold. The sound was deep and rich, but with a dangerous edge that made my skin prickle. I'd do well to avoid this man at all costs.

Thankfully he seemed to be of the same mind as Ishmid and ignored me as I continued moving around the table, distributing fresh rounds of bread and refilling wine cups.

Once my task was finished and every man engaged in eating, I placed my back to the far wall and dropped my eyes to the floor, melding with the shadows and harnessing the complete stillness I'd learned from Eitan. The thought made a sudden pang of longing and grief slam into me since it was more than likely I'd never see my oldest brother or the rest of my family again. All because I'd touched that cursed knife.

When the dance was complete, the commander lifted his cup of wine, a signal that he desired more. I complied with all haste and then continued around the table, filling each man's cup to the rim.

"I lift my cup to our new friend," said Barsoum, "who succeeded where my men did not. And in less than a day."

Trapped into acknowledging the double-edged words, the commander's underlings raised their cups toward the stranger, yet the expressions on Khaled and Ishmid's faces were anything but complimentary.

The red-haired man dipped his chin to accept Barsoum's appreciation, but his smile was short on humility. "It was a pleasure to assist you, my lord."

His words were oddly accented and a bit stilted as he spoke Barsoum's language, furthering my guess that he was a foreigner.

"Tell us," said the commander, his cool, dark-eyed gaze moving between Ishmid and Khaled, "what did it take to finally break the Hebrew spy?"

A slow, malevolent smile curled across the stranger's lips, one that made the sharp planes of his face seem feral. He reached out to stroke the serrated dagger that lay beside his bowl on the table. "My father is a butcher. I come by such skills naturally."

It took every lesson that Eitan had drilled into my head and every admonition Malakhi had delivered to keep my body still and my chest from heaving in horror. But even so, I had to swallow hard against the instinct to cry out. It was *my fault* that my friend had suffered. *My fault* that he'd endured excruciating pain at this beast's hands. It should have been me at the end of that knife.

Khaled's eyes were no more than slits as he spoke. "And what, may I ask, did you discover that we did not?"

The stranger turned his head to Barsoum's second-in-command, danger radiating from him like ripples on a pond. "You say that as if you actually learned something. From what I understand the only thing you accomplished was taking the head off one of them."

"The older one was more than half dead by that time anyhow," said Khaled with a dismissive sniff. "And we needed to send a message to any others who might have the gall to risk such folly."

My stomach lurched, pressing acid into my throat as Hanael's kind face floated across my vision. My soul silently wept for his wife, his children.

"Yes, I noticed the body hanging from the wall as I entered Shechem. I have no doubt it will have the desired effect. None of the *Hebrews*"—the stranger spat out the word as if it had been fashioned from poison—"will dare lift a finger against you again."

"That is the hope," said Barsoum with a sigh, then took another deep draft from his cup. "But they are a sneaky lot, and I have taken measures to prevent any more breaches in security." He waved a hand toward his manservant, whose life was in the balance every time he sampled his master's food and drink.

"I must say," he continued, "when you arrived here, looking for work as a mercenary, I was not sure you'd be of any use to me. My men are quite skilled at encouraging tongues to loosen. I taught them myself, of course." He grinned, gesturing to Ishmid and Khaled, who remained still as statues in their chairs but whose resentment filled the room like smoke. "But they failed to get more than the usual claims of innocence and vows that he and his friend were working alone. However, when you emerged from the spy's cell with detailed information about their network, I knew I'd been right to send you in." He tilted his cup at the stranger again with a chuckle.

To uncover knowledge of Malakhi's operation, this man must have truly put Sheth through a terrible ordeal. I knew for certain he would have rather died than reveal such damaging information. The torture must have been beyond agonizing.

"And where does this supposed training of Hebrew spies take place?" spat out Khaled.

The stranger's brilliantly colored brows rose at Khaled's barely constrained aggression, and an arrogant, vicious smile lifted the corner of his mouth.

Panic banged hard against my ribs. I had to get back to Shiloh and warn my brothers before the Arameans descended on them. My mind whirled with possibilities and plans, all of them useless. With the suspicion that more spies were in the household, I could not chance bribing someone to take a message out of the city, nor even make it known to anyone that I was of a mind to do so. It had been rumored that the man who betrayed Sheth and Hanael was himself a Hebrew. Other than Odeleya, whom I would never put in such danger, there was no one else I could trust inside these walls.

"South of here," replied the stranger. "Not too far from Yaffa, outside a town named Azor."

Confusion buzzed in my head. Had I misheard?

"Azor?" said Ishmid. "That's on the very edge of Philistine territory."

"Apparently there are a series of caves nearby that they utilize for their endeavors," said the Moabite. "Although he was weeping fairly loudly at the time, he made it clear that your men veer away from the area, out of respect for your treaties with Yaffa. They've been getting away with building a rebellion right between your eyes."

Khaled sneered. "And how do we know this information is correct? The Hebrew is dead, so we cannot confirm these details. And what loyalty does a Moabite have to Aram anyhow?"

"I have no reason to lie," said the mercenary, leaning back in his chair, far enough that the joints creaked. "It won't take much for your men to confirm such things anyhow. And my loyalty is to whomever pays me a healthy wage. Besides"—that malicious grin curved his lips upward again—"that Hebrew was far too eager to spill his guts as I peeled the skin from the soles of his feet."

You are stone, I told myself, desperate to control both the bile and anguish that threatened to spew from my lips. *Do not twitch a brow. Do not grind your teeth. Do not quirk a cheek.* Obviously Sheth had used his final breaths to give misinformation to his torturer, and I would not let his valor be erased by my foolhardy reactions. *Give him peace, Yahweh,* my mind pleaded. *Usher him into the olam ha'ba with honor, O Merciful Creator.*

A bark of laughter burst from Barsoum's fleshy lips. "A butcher, you said? Sounds as if your father taught you well."

The Moabite shrugged, as if the effort to torture a man were nothing.

How could men revel in such things? How could anyone with a soul find pleasure in another's suffering? I'd known there was evil in these Arameans; I'd heard the stories of the atrocities they'd committed against women and children in the war eight years ago. But as I listened to the commander chortle over Sheth's torment, I became witness to fathomless darkness. We *had* to win this battle, or men like this would eventually swallow our people whole.

I will not let your sacrifice be in vain, my friend, I silently vowed to Sheth.

"As I said, I was not certain of you," Barsoum continued. "And my men advised me to send you from my gates. They did not think my idea to test your loyalties by working on the Hebrew was a wise one." The commander's gaze traveled around the room, landing on Ishmid and Khaled. "But they were wrong. And should *not* have questioned my instincts." Both men paled at the chastisement and dropped their eyes to their empty bowls.

After a long pause, in which I half expected his lackeys to melt into puddles of humiliation beneath the table, Barsoum pointed a thick finger at the Moabite. "So now I find myself in your debt."

"It was my pleasure to aid you, my lord," replied the Moabite. "I am happy to serve as a mercenary within your army. That is plenty of thanks."

The commander waved his argument aside. "No, no. I pay my debts. What will you have? A measure of silver? I have an Egyptian *kopesh*, crafted in Avaris, that might be of interest."

The Moabite leaned back in his chair, arms folded, contemplating the offer for a few long moments. "I'll take her," he said.

"Who?" asked the commander, seemingly as bewildered as I by the strange request. "One of the dancers?"

All of the guests directed their gazes toward the women who'd continued to sway blithely about the room all throughout this horrific conversation. None of them reacted to the Moabite's demand, likely used to being offered up as prizes at Barsoum's whims.

"No. The girl who served us today. I'll take her."

Blood rushed to my face, pounding in my temples, burning up my neck, and echoing in my ears. The Moabite wanted *me*? I could only pray that the commander did not see a flush in my sun-bronzed skin or he would know that I'd understood every word that had passed between them.

"You want my *cook*?" Confusion reigned in the commander's tone. "But she is the best I've had in a long while."

"I care nothing about her skills in the kitchen," said the Moabite with a lurid chuckle.

I could feel the eyes of every man in the room on me but kept my own locked on the stone floor beneath my feet. Why would he want me when he could have one of the curvaceous dancers instead? It made no sense.

"Tirzah," said the commander, speaking my name for the first time in all the weeks I'd been in the household. He clapped at me, giving me leave to look at him. I affected a confused expression as he gestured for me to step forward and stand next to the Moabite's chair.

"She continues to cook for me. I won't have my kitchen in any way affected," he warned. "But as long as you return her at dawn, she's yours at night for as long as you are in Shechem."

Horror curled around my bones, and my body began to tremble. What had I done to myself? Why had I badgered Malakhi into sending me here? I'd known the dangers, of course, but after weeks of living in the commander's house with nothing more than a few lewd suggestions by men who did not know I understood their words, I'd slipped into complacency, thinking the commander would not risk his precious stomach by allowing anyone to manhandle me.

Before I could prepare myself, I was jerked from my feet by a long arm and swept into the lap of the Moabite. A cry burst from my lips as the red-haired stranger grinned down at me, his odd green-blue eyes seeming to pierce directly through me.

"My thanks," he said, his long fingers curving around my waist. "I shall enjoy my reward."

My body went rigid as I suddenly realized that the hand of the man who'd killed Sheth was directly atop one of the knives hidden within my belt. The pressure of his palm increased against the leather, making the tip of the blade press through the padding and into my abdomen. A shudder traveled from my shoulders down to my toes.

Of one thing I was certain: this man had just found my knives. I'd been discovered.

But to my shock, instead of revealing my duplicity to the Arameans, the Moabite slipped his huge, callused palm around the back of my neck and forced my lips to his. I struggled against his hold, but he held me fast, his strong fingers digging into my waist as he pulled me closer. Briefly I considered using my teeth against the assault on my mouth, but just as quickly tossed the idea aside, knowing it would only win me a beating.

Then, just as suddenly as he'd kissed me, the mercenary pushed me from his lap, making me tumble to the ground, shaking and dazed.

"I'll wait until she's finished with her duties," he said to the commander, with calm that belied the violence he'd just inflicted on me. "And have her back in the kitchen by dawn."

"You have a deal," said the commander, as if the two were bartering over a goat and not my body and dignity. "I'll have my men lead you to your quarters. Tirzah should be finished here soon, and then you can do with her what you like."

❖ ❖ ❖

For the first time I wished I did not know these halls so well, did not know exactly how many steps stretched between the kitchen courtyard and the mercenary's chamber. Barsoum always put his current favorite soldier or visitor in the last room at the very back of the house, so I'd delivered many a meal there. Now I was the one being delivered to that door by two of Barsoum's stone-faced guards.

Only thirty steps now lay between the brutal stranger and me, and each one was more excruciating than the last. I was under no illusions about what would happen after I crossed the threshold. The man was at least a head taller than me, with a body honed by war. No matter the defense tactics Malakhi had taught me, I would be no more than a kitten fending off a bear. And since the man had felt the knives at my belt, I had lost the element of surprise. The question still remained as to why he'd not said anything to Barsoum when he'd discovered them, but perhaps he assumed I knew nothing of how to use them. He would be wrong.

I'd spent the first fifteen years of my life shooting a sling and tossing knives at tree trunks with the boys of Kedesh, and my last four months in Shiloh honing those skills with Malakhi. I knew how to slip the blades free in one swift move, how to fling them in tandem at a target thirty paces away, and just where to plunge the razor-sharp tips into a man's body to do the most damage. But I also knew that if I attempted any of those things tonight, while trapped within the Moabite's room, I would not live to see the dawn.

Fifteen steps now remained between me and the door to my undoing. The entirety of my body trembled, including my jaw, and my bones were frozen solid. I stumbled on a cracked tile, coming to an abrupt halt so I did not tumble to the ground, but one of the guards jabbed me in the shoulder blade with an order to step up my pace. The two brutes had waited for me in the kitchen courtyard as I'd finished the last of my tasks, their knowing eyes trained on me as I scrubbed and rinsed and swept until I had nothing else to postpone my humiliation at the hands of a savage.

By the time I stood in front of the doorway, blinking away hot tears, I could barely contain the bile that stung my throat. It was possible that I might lose my stomach before the man even laid a hand on me. But even so, I drew in a long, deep breath, determined to hold myself with dignity for as long as I could. No matter what the Moabite did to my body, I refused to let him steal pieces of my soul.

One of the guards knocked on the door, and after only a brief pause, it swung open. The Moabite's head nearly touched the lintel. I'd known he was tall from when I'd seen him stride out of Barsoum's chamber earlier, but up close I realized that although he was just as tall as Eitan, his build was closer to Baz's. My earlier thought of crossing claws with a bear was an apt comparison.

His brilliant blue-green eyes met mine for a brief but intense moment, making my skin flash with a wave of heat. Then, after they flickered once over my shoulder to my escorts, they perused the length of my body. A hum of appreciation came from his throat before he stepped back to give me space to enter.

You will not crumble, I lectured myself. *You knew the dangers when you begged for this assignment. Hold your head high. For the sake of your people you must endure, no matter the cost.*

I took the final steps over the threshold as the Moabite thanked the guards for bringing me to him. Then I crossed the room, knees trembling and gut churning like the sea, breathing prayers to the One Who Sees and pleading for the strength to pass through this dark valley.

As if my desperate call had been heard, I was immediately infused with a surge of courage, and something in the depths of my soul whispered, *"All will be well."*

By the time I turned to face the man who'd murdered Sheth and now meant to destroy me, my arms were locked over my chest, my jaw was set, and I'd determined to focus solely on the mission I'd been given and press anything else deep down into the same abyss where my other hurts lie. He would not win this battle.

CHAPTER

FOURTEEN

Liyam

I'd expected Malakhi's sister to break down as she entered my quarters, to weep or to plead for me to spare her virtue. I'd seen the flash of horror on her face when I'd told Barsoum I wanted her before she locked it away and felt her body shake as I slung her onto my lap and assaulted her with my mouth. But even though Tirzah was terrified, her spine was straight and her expression a blank wall as she strode across my room and then turned to face me.

What an extraordinary woman.

Keeping my eyes on her, I leaned back against the door, hoping the guards would leave, but their low murmurs and crass whispers made it clear that they'd reveled in delivering a lamb to this lion's den.

I'd had only a few brief moments to study Tirzah during the meal earlier, not wanting to draw attention to her, but there was no doubt she was Darek's daughter. Her hair was perhaps a shade darker than his had once been, but the eyes that now met my own with shockingly brazen challenge were the same deep brown. Moriyah was there in her features as well, the exotic cut of cheekbone, the shape of her lips and brows reminiscent of Egypt. Hers was not a bold or extravagant beauty but one I found myself appreciating nonetheless. However, it was not the curve of her long, graceful neck, the depth of her dark eyes, or the smooth bronze skin that I found myself admiring most.

It was the courage written on every line of her intriguing face.

Since the glow of torchlight still shone beneath the door, I decided that the guards had no intention of leaving for now, so I held Tirzah's gaze and lifted one finger to my lips.

She flinched at the unexpected move, her brows furrowed and her palms moving to her hips, directly atop the secret weapons I'd felt earlier while she'd been in my lap.

Lifting my other hand in a gesture to remain still, I took a few steps closer, then paused, hoping she would see that I did not mean to overpower her. If she was as skilled as Malakhi boasted, it would not take much for her to whip out those knives and skewer me.

Her face was a mask of confusion as I crept closer with caution, slowly collapsing the distance between us. Her breathing quickened, her eyes stretched wide, and the full lips I'd recently tasted pressed into a tight but shaky line. The trembling of her body made her dark curls quiver as I leaned down to bring my mouth as close as possible without actually touching her. Her breath hitched audibly, but she held fast.

"You must trust me," I breathed into the shell of her ear, in our shared language. "I need you to cry out. Tell me 'no'—loudly, and with force." The guards would not walk away to report to their master until they were satisfied that I was pleased with my prize.

She jolted, jerking back to look me in the eye, but admirably kept her feet locked in place. *Such bold courage.* I could almost see my mother grinning her approval.

"Go on," I whispered, tipping my head back toward the door. "Make it sound real."

She blinked a few times, her lips opening and closing as if searching for words, and a thousand questions brewed in her brown eyes. Then, as if somehow she'd accepted I truly meant what I said, she squared her shoulders and exclaimed, "No! Leave me alone."

I nodded to her, voice low. "Yes, good. Convince them."

"Please, you can't do this!" she called out, her voice growing louder and more strained. "No! Stop!" and then she let out a tortured, mortified wail that sounded as if I was stripping the clothes from her body.

For the benefit of the guards, I loudly ordered her to stop her useless squalling as I slipped my arm around her waist and slapped my palm over her mouth. Although she went rigid, to my surprise she did not fight as I pulled her closer in case one of the guards peered through the crack of the door, expecting to witness a struggle.

"Keep going," I urged in a whisper. "I don't think they've left yet."

She complied as my hand loosely muffled her cries for mercy and the surprisingly authentic weeping that emanated from her lips. If I did not have the woman pressed against me, feeling the rigidity of her muscles, I might have guessed she was enjoying making fools of the men who'd thought they had delivered her up for violation.

Mumbling a few foul words and snarling at my "victim" to hold still, I played my own part in the game, hoping it might convince the guards of my satisfaction with their commander's offering. After a quick glance over my shoulder, I breathed easier when I saw that the glow beneath the door had already melted into blackness.

Tirzah and I stared at each other, both of us breathing hard as I strained my ears, listening for any sign of rustling outside the door, but all was silent.

Then, realizing I was still clutching Malakhi's little sister against my body, I dropped my arm from her waist and slowly lifted my palm from her mouth.

"Malakhi sent me," I said in a rush. "I'm here to get you out of Shechem."

She sucked in a breath, her jaw going slack as she worked through what I'd said. Then with a huff, she tripped backward, out of reach.

I expected relief, perhaps even a tear or two of joy that someone had come to rescue her after what had happened to Malakhi's men. But instead of lifting into an expression of gratitude, the face I'd been admiring went hard.

"I don't know anyone by that name," she stated, her tone as flat as the plains of Moab.

I stood blinking at her, my jaw agape. "What do you mean? Your brother Malakhi has been sick with worry over you. Eitan as well."

"You must have me confused with someone else." There was no movement of her features, nothing to indicate that the names of her brothers meant anything to her.

I was struck dumb by her swift and unapologetically false response, but at the same time was impressed by her quick thinking. She was right to be suspicious. She knew nothing of me other than the front I'd constructed for Barsoum. She'd heard me discuss torturing her friend for information and had no way of knowing whether I'd pried the names of her brothers from the spy's lips. Obviously, Tirzah was no fool. If the commander had any reason to believe she'd been involved with the two Hebrews he'd arrested, it would make sense that he would use me to force a confession.

I sighed, running my hands through my hair. It had gotten so long during the months I'd been away from our valley that it hung around my shoulders in tangled rust-colored waves. Between the wild mane and the unkempt beard that had overtaken my face, I likely looked more like a beast than a man. Somehow until now I'd neither noticed nor cared. All I'd thought about was vengeance for Nadina since the moment my mother had revealed the tragedy.

"All right," I said, taking a couple of steps backward, hoping to ease the tension between us. "You are right not to trust me. If it was me, I would be wary too." I gestured to the bed. "You have no doubt been on your feet all day. Sit. I will tell you how I came to be here."

Her brows bunched together as she weighed my words, her eyes flitting between me and the bed bedecked with soft linens, a plush cushion, and goose-feather pillows.

I pointed at the tile beneath my feet. "I will not move from this spot, I assure you. Besides"—I affected a tight smile, lowering my voice—"I know what's in your belt."

Her eyes narrowed, but she moved to the bed and sank onto its softness, keeping me in her sights as she did so.

"I understand that you have no cause to trust me," I said. "I am a stranger to you, but not to your family. I came through Shiloh last week, searching for someone, and went to Ishai's vineyard to see if he might have knowledge of the man I seek."

As I spoke the name of her grandfather, there was an infinitesimal softening of Tirzah's expression. Encouraged, I continued.

"My family used to stay on his vineyard during ingathering festivals many years ago, before the Arameans took control. I remembered his and your grandmother Ora's hospitality well from the time I was a boy. I assure you, I am not here to hurt you or to turn you over to Barsoum. When messengers arrived with news of your friends, my cousin and I were there, and your brother decided I would be the best man to extract you, since I am half-Canaanite and just returned from a sojourn in Moab."

Her mouth pressed into that rigid line again for a few moments, but then a hint of reluctant acceptance crept into her expression. "Why would he trust you with such a mission?"

Not wanting to reveal anything of my bargain with Malakhi, I gave her a different piece of the truth. "Our mothers are friends," I said, then pointed to my cheekbone, the same place Moriyah was marked with the symbols of Canaanite gods. "My own was there in Jericho when the priestess branded her with the sun and moon."

She sucked in a breath, eyes growing wide. "You are *Alanah's* son?"

"I am," I replied, more than proud to claim her. "My name is Liyam ben Tobiah. I am her youngest."

"I have heard stories of her for as far back as I can remember." Her voice was incredulous, but somehow I knew she finally believed me.

Relief poured into my limbs, and behind it came a wave of exhaustion. I'd been on edge from the moment I'd set foot inside Shechem, hadn't slept more than a couple of hours since Shiloh, and now that I'd found the object of my mission, my body screamed for rest.

Suddenly Tirzah flinched as if she'd been pricked with a dagger and jolted back to her feet, face pale. She jabbed an accusing finger at me. "You! You told Barsoum—"

My gut wrenched because I knew the connection she'd just made. I'd hoped we might put off this conversation until tomorrow, or at least until she trusted me more.

"You convinced Barsoum that you were a mercenary by *torturing* Sheth." Her fists clenched at her sides, her voice dropped into a menacing tone that pierced me straight through. "Did you . . . ? Did you *kill* my friend?"

Letting out a slow breath, I dropped my head, hands on my hips.

"You animal!" she spat out before I'd found the right words to respond. "How *could* you do such a thing? To a fellow Hebrew no less!"

If only I could go back and erase the details I'd been forced to reveal at Barsoum's table, to wipe them from her mind. It had been terrible enough to be in that dank, rat-infested cell with the young man, so bloodied and battered that he barely looked human, and to hear the death rattle in his chest as he pleaded for me to end his suffering, I did not know how I could possibly make Tirzah understand the impossible choice I'd had to make. But if I'd learned anything about this woman in these past hours, it was that she was nearly as brave as Sheth had been in his final moments.

"It was painless," I said, keeping my tone low and even, hoping to assuage her wrath before the guards heard her tearing into me. "I only made it seem as though I tortured him. I promise you."

All night I'd snatched glances at Tirzah across the room as she hovered in the shadows, head down and posture subservient as she played her role, moving around the table with such silent steps that none of the others seemed to even notice she was there until I'd pointed her out. But the woman standing before me now, practically vibrating with fury and looking as if she might even yet pull out those knives and slit my throat, was no cowering shadow. She was magnificent.

"If I did not give him relief, they would only have stretched the torture out longer. You can't imagine all they did, Tirzah . . . *they* are the animals." I dragged my hands down my face, wishing I could wash the images from my own mind. "I could not leave him in agony, knowing that I could offer him a peaceful end instead."

My little Nadina flashed through my mind as I spoke, reminding me of my own torment and how many times I'd wished for just such an end when the image of her tiny body being crushed into the ground tortured me.

"I thought through every possible choice. Every possible outcome. If there would have been *any* way to save him, to get both him and you out of Shechem safely, I would have done it." I shook my head, wishing I'd never been placed in such an unthinkable situation. I'd killed men on the battlefield, but never one of my brethren.

"But I can tell you," I said, "your friend died with honor, in service to our people. He was the one to offer up the misinformation about the training grounds near Yaffa. The Arameans will find a camp there that was abandoned a few months ago, but it will solidify my story in their eyes. He held his secrets to the very end. Even at a terrible cost . . ."

Tirzah's eyes glistened, but even though her grief was palpable, her features remained unyielding, and her tears did not fall. The urge to erase the distance between us and comfort her was surprisingly strong, but I forcefully pushed it aside, knowing she would not accept consolation from the man who'd killed her friend, regardless of my merciful intent.

Besides, she and I could not waste any more time tonight. We needed to plan our escape so I could get on with the task of finding the one-eyed trader. When I was through with him, he'd wish for a swift passing as well.

"You'll stay here tonight, to keep up the ruse," I said, hoping the brusqueness in my tone would draw her focus back to escape instead of dwelling on her friend's horrific last days. "And tomorrow night we'll get out of the city. I assume you know the best way to slip out of this house?"

Tirzah folded her arms over her chest, her backbone snapping straight and all traces of grief wiped away. "No. I am not finished."

"Finished with what?"

"My mission is not complete," she replied, her chin lifting in defiance. "And until I have what I came here for, I'm not leaving this city."

FIFTEEN

Tirzah

I awoke with a start, my body attuned to arise the hour before dawn, and immediately came to the realization that I was not in the women's quarters beside Odeleya, but instead in the exceedingly soft bed of a stranger. Liyam's heavy breaths from across the room, where he slept atop a makeshift pallet, brought back the events of the night before and his gut-wrenching confession about Sheth.

It was still difficult to believe that the ruthless Moabite mercenary was actually an ally Malakhi had sent to rescue me. But as soon as he'd mentioned my grandparents' names I'd known he was telling the truth. Then when Liyam explained his connection to Alanah, a woman whom I'd looked up to since I was old enough to understand Ima's stories of their adventures in Jericho, I'd been firmly convinced. His red hair and blue-green eyes fit the exact description my mother had given of the Canaanite woman who'd sacrificed herself to rescue my mother so many years ago.

Even though I loathed pulling myself from the paradise of fine linen and cushions that had embraced me all throughout the night, I slipped from the warm cocoon, hissing as my bare feet hit the frigid stone floor.

I glanced over at the man who'd come to rescue me, feeling a slight pang of guilt that he'd been forced to lay on this cold floor with little more than a wool blanket, but it was obvious he was a well-honed warrior, and therefore used to sleeping on the ground. Besides, he owed me for the large black-and-purple bruise on my hip from when he'd tossed me off his lap, and for the hours I'd spent trembling in fear that he was planning to consume me, body and soul.

Liyam lay on his side, jaw slack and one hand tucked beneath his cheek, giving him the appearance of a wild-haired little boy instead of a feral mercenary. Something about that thought jarred me, and I skittered from the room, determined to put some distance between myself and the man who'd killed my friend, yet whose eyes held such shadows as he'd told me of how brave and honorable Sheth was and how he'd begged to be spared more torment by the Aramean brutes.

I padded down the hallway, thankful that no one else seemed to be stirring this early. I dreaded a run-in with the guards who'd escorted me to Liyam's room last night and whatever disgusting things they might have to say about what they assumed had happened within it.

As I stepped out into the kitchen courtyard, I shivered in the predawn chill. Already a few of the other cooks were going about their regular morning tasks, lighting cook-fires, scraping ashes from ovens, but all of them stopped what they were doing when they noticed me approaching.

My skin blazed as I took in the expressions on their faces, which ranged from curiosity to sympathy, and on some, disgust. Even though I'd expected a reaction from the women I worked alongside every day, the reality of facing them every morning after leaving Liyam's quarters for the foreseeable future made undeserved shame unfurl inside my gut.

Nothing happened! He did not touch me! I wanted to shout. But of course, I had to continue acting the abused slave or I'd place us both in danger. So I dropped my eyes and headed for the washing pot, prepared to spend my day looking as humiliated as possible.

I accomplished the ruse quite well throughout the morning, and thankfully none of my fellow cooks were bold enough to say anything, so I hoped the incident was more or less forgotten. But when Odeleya appeared at my side as I was pushing the heavy quern back and forth on its stone saddle, grinding a large measure of barley, her troubled expression stirred everything back to the surface. She crouched down beside me, setting the jug she'd been carrying on the ground.

"Are you all right?" she asked, her wispy brows pinched. "I was so worried when you did not come to the servants' quarters, and I cannot sleep when you are not next to me."

The poor girl must have been beside herself all night. Although she was occupied most hours of the day fetching water for the household, we always curled up on the same pallet, sharing body heat and whispering together. Since she'd been disappointed that she wasn't yet allowed to assist me more in the kitchen, I filled her head with as much of my mother's cooking knowledge as I could as she drifted off to sleep in my arms. For as short a time as we'd known each other, I felt a strong sense of responsibility for Odeleya, as if she were my own child.

"I am sorry," I said, working to sound unaffected, but likely failing. "I was obligated to be elsewhere for the night."

She gripped my arm, her fingers digging into my skin. "I heard what that man demanded—"

I winced at the devastation in her tone but was unsurprised that she'd already heard the rumors. I covered her hand with my own and smiled up at her. "I am fine, Odeleya. Do not worry for me."

"I cannot help but worry. I can only imagine what you've been through. . . ." She gulped in a large breath, tears gathering in her doe-brown eyes.

Guilt welled up at the sight. How could I possibly lie to this guileless child who was hurting for me, even though everything she thought I'd endured last night was a complete fabrication?

"Listen to me," I said, winding my fingers into hers and turning to face her. "I am well. Truly. Do you see any bruises on me?" I stretched out my arms for her to inspect and then gestured to my face and neck.

"He did not hurt me," I said, wishing I could wash her fears away completely with the truth. "And he vowed that if I came to his room every night without complaint, he would not do so."

Her lower lip quivered. "But you can't—"

"You must trust me," I interjected. "No harm will befall me, I assure you."

A tear slipped down her cheek. "Maybe you can escape?" she whispered. "I will help."

"Hush," I said, with a quick glance around the courtyard to ensure that everyone else was occupied. "I meant what I said. He did not hurt me. And this is where I need to be. The Moabite will likely be sent off with the army soon, and Barsoum made him vow that his meals would not be affected." I winked, hoping she would be swayed by my easy manner. "The commander's greedy stomach will keep me safe."

She did not laugh at my jest, only continued staring into my eyes with piercing intensity. Odeleya might be young, but she was not unintelligent. I had the distinctive sense that she'd somehow picked up a shade of inconsistency with my lukewarm reaction to my supposed violation. Perhaps I should have filled her ears with what she'd expected instead of attempting to assuage her fears.

"I have endured much in my life, Odeleya," I said, hoping she would equate my statement with the lies I'd told her of my past. "But I trust Yahweh with my every step. Will you do the same?"

She chewed on her lip, still gazing at me with mingled confusion and fear. But then her eyelids fluttered, and she heaved a sigh. "All right," she said. "I trust you without question. But if you need my help in any way, please tell me. You are the only friend I have in this world, and I cannot bear to see you in pain."

Liyam was not at the evening meal. For as much as I'd prepared myself to feign fear in his presence and play the part of a shamed and abused slave, I was almost disappointed I wouldn't have the opportunity to do so. Instead, only Barsoum's most trusted men joined him at the table.

Had the man Malakhi sent to rescue me already failed in his mission? By his performance here last night, he'd been plenty capable of passing himself off as a Moabite mercenary, and Barsoum had practically fawned over him. Surely he'd not already been discovered?

My fears were quelled when Khaled came into the room late, moving as if his entire body was stiff. With one eye blackened, his hand bandaged, and a bloody scuff on his well-shaven chin, it was clear he'd been recently thrashed.

"Still smarting over your loss to the Moabite?" mocked Barsoum as he took in the appearance of his once-favorite underling.

Liyam had done this?

Khaled's expression soured further, but he did not respond as he yanked out his chair and sat down. His raw and abraded knuckles curved around his wine cup before he lifted it to his mouth and drained it in one long draft.

Barsoum laughed as I padded forward to refill the cup. "Come now, Khaled. Every man has a bad match from time to time."

Liyam and Khaled must have been sparring this afternoon. I'd heard some shouting from outside the walls of the villa, and Barsoum was particularly fond of arranging matches within his company. He seemed to almost delight in pitting his men against each other, encouraging them to scrabble for his favor. If anything, it was a good sign that he'd set Liyam against Khaled; it meant Barsoum saw him as worthy of the pairing and therefore above suspicion for the time being.

I could not help but contrast the way my father and Malakhi respected the men beneath their command, how they strove to lift them up, encourage their strengths, and teach them how to rely upon one another, instead of gleefully provoking jealously and competition the way Barsoum did.

After leveling a few more emasculating jabs at Khaled, Barsoum indicated for me to begin serving. "Regardless of his triumph against you in the match, Khaled, our mercenary friend will not be joining us tonight," he said. "I have something to discuss with you and the rest of my war council. Information that will not leave this room for the time being."

The restrained anger melted from Khaled's face in a moment, replaced by his usual haughty demeanor. Whether or not Barsoum toyed with his pride, he did count Khaled among those he trusted most.

"I have received a missive." He lifted a small packet of folded papyrus. "From both the king of Edom and the king of Moab. They are sending a delegation here to discuss our mutual interests in the south. In the meantime, we will step up training and recruiting. We will show the Edomites and Moabites why our armies are superior to these disorganized Hebrew tribes and how easy it will be to crush this new upstart leader if we work together."

A thrill traveled all the way down to my toes as I slipped a fresh piece of flatbread onto the commander's overflowing plate. *Finally!* This was the reason I'd come to Shechem. The reason I'd risked my life in this household. All these weeks of silent subservience had been worth the effort to discover that the potential alliance was with Moab and Edom.

Although it would be a relief to Malakhi and Othniel that this coalition did not include Egypt, it was no less concerning. Since we'd come into the Land, we'd maintained a fairly peaceable existence alongside the tribes descended from Lot and from Esau, both of whom held territory just to the east of the Jordan River; although there had been tension between us before, especially when they refused to allow our ancestors to cross their lands after the exodus from Egypt. But even so, how could our distant cousins consider allying themselves with King Kushan, who'd ruthlessly invaded their territory just as he had ours?

"And what have we promised these people if they join us?" asked Ishmid, the most shrewd of Barsoum's men, in my opinion.

"We will withdraw our forces from their territories completely," said Barsoum, his mouth full of lamb.

"The king is willing to forgo tribute from both Edom and Moab?" asked Ishmid, his next bite of meat paused in midair.

"For now the Hebrew territories are the greater prize," said Barsoum.

"The fertility in those regions is nothing compared to this one. It is the price he is willing to pay to put down these bothersome rebellions once and for all."

The rest of Barsoum's men seemed to accept this answer easily enough, a few of them agreeing that both Edom and Moab contained more desert than farmland. The land that had been promised to Avraham so long ago had grown exceedingly abundant in the years since our people began tilling the soil and building upon the progress the Canaanites left behind when they fled Yehoshua's army.

Yet none of them seemed to notice the temporary nature of his offering, the fleeting words *for now* tucked smoothly among the rest.

Kushan may offer the Edomites and Moabites their freedom for a time—since they too had been subjugated when his forces swept down from Aram-Naharim—but it was clear to me that once all the Hebrew territories were back under his control, nothing would be left of such treaties but ash.

I wished I had a method of getting this information to Malakhi. Yet without Sheth and Hanael's help, I was at a loss of how to do so. It would have to wait until I could get out of Shechem and carry the information to my brother myself.

But regardless of the way Liyam had blustered last night over my refusal to leave with him right away, I refused to step foot outside this household until I was armed with the exact plan our three enemies had for halting Othniel's successes. And that meant staying at least until the delegation arrived. Besides, I didn't plan to walk out those gates unless Odeleya was with me. Liyam could either stay and help me in that course of action, or he could go back to Shiloh with the message, alone.

CHAPTER
SIXTEEN

Liyam

"Enter," I called out at the timid knock on the door, since I had no intention of rising from my place on this soft cushion.

Even though I'd emerged as the clear winner in my match against Khaled earlier, he'd managed a well-aimed kick to my upper thigh that seemed to have bruised down to the bone and left me with a wicked slash in my shin from his blade. I'd resisted the urge to limp the rest of the day, knowing that any display of weakness might sway Barsoum's fickle sentiments and strip me of the favored position I'd earned by what I had done to Sheth. The cost of such a gain was too great to waste.

Tirzah entered the room with hesitant steps, shoulders hunched and eyes downcast as the two guards behind her grinned at me in lascivious encouragement that turned my stomach. But as soon as the door closed behind her, all subservience melted from her countenance. Her spine straightened and her expression hardened as she approached me, transforming her from cowed victim to sleek challenger in only four strides.

"Put out the lamp and lay down on the bed," I ordered loudly. Our performance may have fooled the guards last night, but I did not want to take any chances that they'd decided to hang about again.

Tirzah's eyes practically sparked with fury at my demand, but her mouth did not argue as she complied with the first part of my request. The room now dark, I heard her shuffle a few paces closer, but no farther.

"I think you know I have no intention of crawling into that bed with you," she snapped, her voice barely above a whisper.

Something about the way she slid so easily between pretense and reality, as well as her refusal to back down, stirred my intrigue, along with a healthy measure of respect.

"I won't lay a hand on you," I said. "I have no desire to harm you."

"Tell that to the bruise on my hip from when you shoved me to the floor," she muttered.

"That was for Barsoum's benefit. The man glories in brutality. Believe me, I took no pleasure in hurting you." I paused, shifting my position on the bed with a stifled groan. "Sit, Tirzah. We need to talk, and at the moment I can't move."

A rustle of fabric followed, and her voice came from closer by. "Are you wounded from the match with Khaled?" she asked.

"How did you know we'd sparred?"

"Barsoum made sure everyone knew that Khaled had been bested by you," she said, with something akin to amusement in her tone.

I groaned. "Which will only further encourage his animosity, no doubt."

"Oh for certain. He looked on the edge of murder when he arrived bruised and battered at the table. So I would say you've solidified his hatred of you."

"All the more reason that we should leave."

"I told you—"

I cut her off. "I know you want to finish this mission. And I admire your tenacity. But this is too dangerous. Each hour we stay is another opportunity that you or I could be discovered."

"As I was saying," she ground out, "I told you that I need to stay until I have the information I came for. And tonight I came closer to that goal."

"What did you learn?"

A long beat of silence followed. "Tirzah?"

"Regardless of the things you've told me, I still do not know whether to trust you," she admitted. "Especially after what happened . . ." Her words dropped away.

"To Sheth," I supplied, closing my eyes against the images his name dredged up again. I blew out a long, slow breath. "He wanted me to give you a message."

Her sandals scuffed the stone floor as she moved a couple of steps closer in the dark. "He did?"

"Yes. He wanted you to know that the knife was not your fault. That he was careless when he retrieved it." The poor man had been adamant that I ease Tirzah's guilt on this matter, and from the little gasp she emitted as I said it, it was obvious he'd been right to do so. I didn't know what knife he was referring to, but I assumed it had something to do with how he and his friend had been discovered as spies.

She sniffed, and I wondered if she was crying. Which also made me wonder whether it was not just the loss of a friend she grieved, but perhaps something more. I pressed aside my curiosity on this point, since it made no difference to me whether the two of them had been entwined in some ill-fated love match.

"I know that I am a stranger to you," I said. "But my goal in this is to bring you out of Shechem, unharmed. I vowed to Malakhi that I would do everything in my power to do so. And in all honesty, I am fairly certain your father will have my head if I do not."

Something that sounded like a choked laugh came from her mouth before being quickly muffled.

"I thought he was going to strangle your brothers when those messengers arrived from Shechem," I continued. "And as a father, I wouldn't have blamed him at all. Your poor mother had to practically tie him down to keep him from rushing in here with his sword drawn. His friend Baz was all for it too." I shook my head, remembering how the two of them had roared at her brothers that night, and yet how, in the midst of such turmoil, Moriyah had been inexplicably calm and collected as she soothed her husband's wrath. "I still don't know what Malakhi was thinking sending you in here," I muttered.

All Tirzah's earlier humor had fled by the time she spoke again. "He was thinking that I would be able to get closer to Barsoum than any *man* could. That I was plenty capable of making myself invisible as a cook. And that in doing so I could get information here that will help win this war. And I have." Victory was evident in her tone.

"And? What is it?"

She paused again, perhaps weighing whether all the things I'd revealed were reason enough to trust me. I waited, giving her time to add my words together and come to the correct conclusion.

She huffed out a resigned sigh, and to my surprise I felt the cushion near my feet dip, as if she'd sat down on the bed.

"There is a joint Moabite and Edomite delegation arriving soon," she said. "They are planning some sort of three-way offensive to stop Othniel."

"Moab and Edom?"

"Yes," she said. "Barsoum plans to offer withdrawal from their territories in exchange for their help against us. That is why we cannot leave now. I have to stay long enough to know the exact details of when and where they will attack. If we can avert whatever they are planning, perhaps even prevent this alliance from being successful in the first place, then Othniel will only have one enemy to conquer, instead of three."

"Confirmation that they are working together should be plenty for Othniel to determine the next course of action."

"If you want to go, then you are welcome to do so. I'll find my way out in a few days."

This woman was beyond frustrating. "I am *not* leaving you behind, Tirzah."

"Then stay. Help me uncover what we need to know," she said, an edge of desperation in her tone. "I cannot fail in this. Not after what happened to Sheth and Hanael."

"You are not responsible for their capture, Tirzah. I've told you what he said about the knife."

"Perhaps not," she replied, although I could tell she was unconvinced. "But even more than that, we *have* to win this fight. Being here among the Arameans has made that even more clear to me. They will not be satisfied with just collecting tribute from us forever. The way Barsoum talks, Kushan means to pay us back for daring to rebel by displacing even more of us than they did eight years ago. If Othniel fails, they will round up thousands, maybe tens of thousands, and take them in chains to Aram-Naharim. If that happens, and if the rampant intermarriage between us and the remaining Canaanites continues, the people of Yahweh might be completely assimilated in a matter of decades. Don't you see? Our survival as a nation is at stake. And if I can do anything to help prevent that, then I will, even at the cost of my own life."

Even whispered in the dark, her vehement declaration caused my pulse to race unexpectedly. I'd heard Othniel speak of these things before we went into battle for Hebron, and I had been inspired by the reminders that our parents and grandparents had fought for this Land, and how Yahweh had preserved our people throughout the wilderness wanderings. But hearing a woman who would never raise a sword in battle so fervently declare her willingness to die for the sake of our people shocked me into silence.

"Think of your family. Your wife and children," she said. "Don't you want them to be free? To live under the Torah in peace and prosper in the Land Yahweh gave us?"

Pain speared the center of my chest. "I have no family."

"But . . . I thought you said that as a father you understood why mine was so angry."

I cleared my throat of the fiery lump lodged there. "They are gone."

"Oh, Liyam." She must have heard the bleakness in my flat tone because I felt the slightest pressure of her hand on my knee. "I am so sorry."

I did not respond to her useless apologies, and her touch retreated so quickly I questioned whether I'd actually imagined it in the first place.

Although her refusal to leave would further delay my search for my daughter's killer, I could not find fault in her passion to help our tribes regain what we'd lost. And perhaps the upheaval surrounding a foreign delegation's arrival would be the perfect cover for our escape anyhow.

"We will stay until the delegation arrives," I conceded. "But as soon as you gather the intelligence we need, we leave without delay. Do we have a bargain?"

"Thank you," she breathed. "We have a bargain. Although there is something else . . ."

I ground my teeth. *Infuriating, this woman.* "What now?"

"It is not just you and I who will need to escape when the time comes," she said. "I have a young friend. A girl named Odeleya. I won't leave without her either."

Exasperated, I scrubbed at my eyes with my fingers, seeing flashes of color from the pressure. "A child?"

"Yes, she latched on to me when I first arrived. She is alone here and vulnerable. I can't walk away knowing she'd be at the mercy of these depraved men."

"Where is her family?" I asked.

"They sent her away a few months ago, sold her here to cover their debts. She has no one who cares for her."

I heard the plea in Tirzah's voice when she spoke of this girl, so she must mean a great deal to her. Some neglected part of me squeezed at the way her concern for an orphan softened her sharper edges.

"I don't know how we will all get out unscathed, but I will do my best."

"Thank you, Liyam," she said, and the smile in her voice was unmistakable, even with nothing to illuminate it in the darkness. For some reason, I was irrationally frustrated that I could not see it for myself.

"If we work together," she continued, "I have every confidence we will succeed. But for now, I am beyond exhausted. Time to go to your pallet." She pushed against my leg, and I released a sharp hiss. The deep gouge Khaled had inflicted along the length of my shin had only just stopped bleeding but still stung, even though Barsoum's healer had cleaned and bandaged it with a honey-herb poultice. I tried to roll from the bed, but her hand curved around my ankle, halting my struggle.

"He really hurt you, didn't he?"

Defensive, and unsettled by the feel of her hand on me, I scoffed. "I've had worse from tussling with my nephews."

Still not releasing my ankle, she chuckled. "Just what my brothers would say. You could be missing a limb and insist you were fine."

She was right. I'd never admit to her that even the thought of laying on the frigid ground all night made my hip throb. I twisted to my side, dislodging her hand, determined to endure that vicious pallet without even a hint of complaint.

"Stay where you are," she demanded. "This bed is three times the width of the pallet Odeleya and I sleep on."

I froze, wishing I could see her expression in the dark. "You can't actually be suggesting we both—"

"There's no reason for you to be in pain all night," she bit out, and the cushion shifted as she slid farther away, making herself comfortable on the opposite end of the bed. "But just so you know, I never take my belt off."

Again, I was begrudgingly amused by her nerve. I sank down onto the cushion again, holding back a groan of relief. "Keep your knives sheathed, woman. I've bled enough today."

CHAPTER

SEVENTEEN

23 Nisan

I loomed over where Tirzah squatted in front of a bread oven, scraping cold ashes from its belly. I hated that I was here to humiliate her, but I had no time to wait. I'd left the training grounds and come straight to the kitchen courtyard, filthy and drenched in sweat from hours of exercises with the other foreign mercenaries Barsoum had hired over the past couple of weeks.

Tirzah twisted when she caught sight of my shadow, nearly falling onto her backside in her haste. She was normally so aware of her surroundings that I was surprised I'd caught her off guard.

"I want you in my quarters," I ordered. "Now."

Since the next meal was hours from now, I'd decided that my plan was worth barging into the courtyard to drag her away. I'd have her back to her duties before Barsoum noticed anything was amiss. What I hadn't considered was the hostility of the other women who were working beside Tirzah. Their eyes were trained on us, and if the murderous looks I was garnering were arrows, I'd be full of holes. Although I had to make a show of returning their stares with a menacing sneer, I was glad they were furious with me and proud of their audacity, because the things I was pretending to demand of Tirzah were abhorrent.

Prevented from responding to my command by her supposed inability to understand the language of the Arameans, Tirzah stood, brushed her sooty hands on her overgarment and dropped her chin, fully enrobed in her false persona.

I grabbed her arm and yanked, and although I only applied enough pressure to make it look real, she cried out as if I'd jerked her limb from its socket. Building on her inventive reaction, I snapped at her to close her mouth or suffer the consequences and strode toward the doorway, a seemingly chastised Tirzah tripping along behind me.

Near the door a young girl stood off to the side, two empty waterskins dangling from her shoulder and her face ashen. Perhaps this was the girl Tirzah had spoken of, since she seemed particularly stricken by what she feared I'd do to her friend. I scowled at her as we passed, and she cowered, but her eyes sought Tirzah, her lips moving, as if silently pleading with Yahweh for protection.

Once in the hallway, with the door slammed behind us for good measure, I let my grip slacken but continued tugging Tirzah behind me as I headed in the direction of the guest quarters.

When I was satisfied no one was around for the moment, I turned a corner and pressed her back against the wall, dropping my head to whisper in her ear. "There's a messenger being dispatched today with a number of missives from Barsoum. He will be coming this way any moment. If I create a diversion, can you retrieve a couple of them from his satchel?"

"Of course," she whispered back, her large brown eyes looking up at me without a shadow of apprehension. "How did you know about this?"

"I overheard Barsoum discussing it with Khaled this morning and watched the commander hand over the packet to the messenger. I suspect at least one of them is meant for Kushan. The man is heading out before the noon hour, on horseback. Whatever communication he carries must be urgent, perhaps demanding an answer before the delegation arrives." I gestured to a door two down from the chamber she and I had been sharing each night. "He came back here to his room to gather his belongings before heading out."

She hummed in acknowledgment, looking past my shoulder as if lost in her thoughts.

I'd watched her these last few days, fascinated by her unique ability to blend into her environment as if she were no more than a wisp of smoke. Barsoum and his men simply looked past her and spoke boldly in front of her, unaware she was keenly cataloging everything they said. For as much as I sympathized with Darek's fury that she'd been sent here alone, I was also beginning to understand Malakhi's sure confidence in her abilities.

She was nearly the complete opposite of how my wife had been. Where Havah had been timid and sensible, Tirzah was bold and spirited, walking the edge of recklessness at times. I'd found contentment with Havah in our arranged marriage; she had been good and kind and a comfort to me, especially after the losses we endured in the Aramean war. But Tirzah intrigued me in a way Havah never had, and watching her weave a cloak of invisibility during her interactions with the Arameans was beyond fascinating.

I flinched, realizing that I had no business allowing such thoughts to cross my mind. Not only was it traitorous to the memory of Havah, but I was here to fulfill my part of the bargain that would lead to justice for our dead child, not to get wrapped up in thoughts of another woman, no matter how captivating.

My sudden movement made her eyes snap back to mine with a quizzical lift of her brows. Then her gaze dropped to my chest, as if taking note of my appearance for the first time, and her nose wrinkled. "You smell awful."

I glanced down at the sweat and grime that covered my sleeveless tunic from a long morning of sparring. My arms were striped with dirty rivulets, and my torso spattered with blood from one of the Amorites whose nose had had an unfortunate collision with my fist. "I came directly from training. Barsoum has given me command over the most recent mercenary recruits."

"You are training men to fight us?"

"I have no choice—" The sound of a door opening nearby, and then sandals on stone, halted my words.

Reaching for the back of her neck, I yanked Tirzah close to my body, and without pause she feigned a whimper and shrank back. I dug my fingers into her silken black curls and tugged, forcing her chin upward.

"Do not pull away from me," I snarled, as the messenger I'd seen earlier came into the corner of my view. "You would not get far anyhow."

I aimed a menacing grin at her and pulled her head even farther back, exposing more of her slender neck. I briefly considered brushing my nose against the enticing length of smooth skin but immediately tossed the instinct aside, thankful she could not divine my thoughts.

With her eyes stretched wide in the appearance of fear, Tirzah darted a glance at the man who was approaching us in the hallway, and I slowly turned my head, annoyance in the curve of my mouth. The young Aramean's brows were drawn together as he warily approached. A leather satchel hung from his shoulder, undoubtedly containing the missives I'd seen Barsoum hand to him earlier.

"What are you looking at?" I challenged.

"Nothing," he replied, taking another few steps our way. He meant to slither by, caring nothing for the woman I was supposedly harassing, but I did not mean for him to do so.

"She's mine," I said, flaring my eyes, spittle flying from my lips. "Barsoum gave her to me."

He lifted his hands in concession, trying to placate the crazed man glaring at him.

With a sneer, I placed my palm on Tirzah's cheek and pushed her backward. She made a show of stumbling and knocking into the wall with a cry.

"If you think to put your eyes, or your hands, on *my* prize," I said, taking two menacing steps toward the messenger while stretching to my full height, "you will regret it."

"I have no desire to do so," the young man stuttered, taking in my wild appearance. "She's yours. I just need to get by—"

As soon as he attempted to pass, I reached out and grabbed his tunic, swinging both our bodies around so that Tirzah was in the perfect position to reach inside his pack. Without delay she moved into place.

I shook him and pressed my face close to his, dropping my voice into a dark whisper. "She. Is. Mine. If you see her in this hallway again, you will turn and walk away."

Tirzah already had her hand in the satchel, brows furrowed in concentration.

"I don't share my possessions," I said, narrowing my eyes to slits and moving so close that our noses nearly touched. "Do we understand each other?"

She lifted her hand from the bag, two wax-sealed missives in her palm. Within two breaths, they were down the front of her tunic. And within another two, she was back in place, cowering against the wall.

"I don't want your woman," the man said, his warbling voice emphasizing his youth. "I am leaving the city—now. She's all yours. I swear it to you, by all the gods."

This was who Barsoum entrusted with his important messages? The boy's beard hadn't even fully come in. The high commander was getting more and more careless with every passing day.

I barked out a laugh, as if the entire exchange had been nothing but a jest. The messenger gaped at my unexpected shift in demeanor. I grinned at him and released his tunic.

"Good. Then be on your way," I said, swiping a palm through the air as if ushering him onward.

Not waiting to see if he'd run off, I stalked over to Tirzah and dug my hand back into her hair, dragging her into a rough embrace.

"Now," I said, tugging her even closer, "where were we?"

"Get off me, you brute," she said, a deep pinch between her brows and her palms flat against my chest. "He's already—"

Before she could get out another word, two fists struck my lower back.

"Leave her alone!" called a small voice. "Stop hurting her!"

Stunned by the vehemence in the tone, along with the surprise that it was not the messenger behind me, I whirled around, inadvertently pulling Tirzah with me.

Before me stood the young girl from the courtyard. She'd seemed so stricken with fear then, so meek, but not anymore. Her mouth was pressed in a tight line, and her light brown eyes sparked fury, even though they were also filled with tears. Her small fists came down on the arm that was still clutching Tirzah.

"Let. Her. Go!" she commanded, each word punctuated by another futile blow on my forearm. This little thing actually thought to save her friend from me.

Tirzah struggled out of my hold and plowed toward the girl, her voice a low rasp as she grabbed my attacker's wrists. "Stop! Odeleya. No more!"

The girl looked back and forth between her friend and me, profound confusion on her face. "But he—"

"Hush," Tirzah demanded. Then, with a glance over her shoulder to ensure that the messenger hadn't returned, she turned and headed for the door of our room, dragging a bewildered Odeleya behind her.

I followed the two of them inside and closed the door behind me, then leaned back against it, curious to see how Tirzah would handle this latest obstacle.

She led Odeleya over to the bed, the one from which I'd been banished the night after my altercation with Khaled. She'd had mercy on my sore bones, but after one reprieve, I'd been forced to sleep on the ground again. However, I didn't mind, because enduring my hard pallet was much preferable to lying anywhere near the woman whom I found myself thinking about far too often.

"What were you thinking?" she demanded, even while keeping her voice low. "He's three times your size!"

Odeleya glanced over at me, her lashes fluttering as if she'd only just realized this truth. "I . . . he was hurting you. I couldn't just watch. I wanted to give you a chance to escape."

Tirzah stared back at her for a few moments and then gathered her close. "You stupid, brave girl," she muttered as she squeezed her tightly while Odeleya shuddered in her arms.

"You have lost enough" came Odeleya's muffled voice. "I could not bear to think he was taking more."

Tirzah sighed and looked past the girl at me, conflict in her eyes. I simply raised my palms in acquiescence; it seemed we had little choice now but to reveal the truth.

She pulled back and wiped the tears from Odeleya's face. "I am all right," she said. "Liyam did not hurt me. He has never hurt me, and he never will."

I was shocked at the certainty and trust such a statement inferred, but Odeleya's face crumpled at this declaration. "But I heard him in the courtyard and with that man, and you were crying out . . ."

"A pretense," Tirzah admitted. "It was only a performance to distract the messenger from our true purpose."

Odeleya's mouth opened, but no words came out.

"If I tell you the truth, will you keep it to yourself? What I have to say is of the utmost secrecy. Not just my life, but yours, his, and perhaps scores of others are at stake."

Odeleya's eyes were as wide as moons. "Of course. I would never do anything to betray you."

"I am a widow," Tirzah said. "But not because my village was raided. My husband died while forcibly conscripted by the Arameans, in retribution for a failed rebellion by others."

Although I'd assumed Tirzah was unmarried, I'd not considered how that had come about, nor had I bothered to ask Malakhi before I departed Shiloh. However, the revelation that she had lost her husband in such a way answered a few of my questions about her motives here.

"I was sent here by my brother," she continued, "to collect information that could potentially be useful in the fight against the Arameans."

"You are a *spy*?"

Tirzah's lips curved into a demure smile. "I am."

"And him?" Odeleya gestured to me.

"Liyam was sent to retrieve me when things did not go according to plan." The simple explanation was likely to prevent Odeleya from being frightened by the whole truth.

The girl went quiet for a few long moments. "Those men," she said. "The ones who were arrested. They were working with you, weren't they?"

Although plainly dismayed Odeleya had made the connection so swiftly, Tirzah nodded her head. "But Liyam is here to ensure that I am safe, and also that you are safe. We have a plan to escape in a few days."

"I want to help!" declared Odeleya, all apprehension set aside. "What can I do?"

Tirzah blinked at the girl's enthusiastic response. "No. You will continue on as you have. Gather water. Run errands for the household. Liyam and I will handle the rest."

Odeleya stood, fists on her narrow hips. "I am not a child," she said, defiance in the set of her small shoulders. "I have been on my own for many months. And of the three of us I am the only one who can move freely between this house and the Hebrew camp without suspicion."

Tirzah's brows shot upward. No doubt she was as shocked as I was by the girl's insistence. "That would only put you in danger. I'd never forgive myself if something happened to you." She winced, probably thinking of Sheth.

"Who would suspect *me* to be carrying messages? In their minds I am nothing but an ignorant child—a girl child, at that," she scoffed. "They don't even look at me when I leave the gates, and when I come back inside they barely notice. They've never even checked me for weapons like they do every other person who comes into Shechem. How would they know the words I carry in my head?"

"No," Tirzah said. "There is too much risk."

Odeleya straightened her shoulders, her chin lifting in an uncanny approximation of the brave woman she obviously revered. "I may not be counted as a woman yet, but I want to fight for our people too. I can do this, Tirzah, I know I can. Let me prove it."

Tirzah chewed on her lower lip in contemplation, and I wondered if she'd persuaded Malakhi and Eitan to send her here in a similar manner.

"It is only for a few days," I said, knowing that, like her brothers had, she would capitulate. Odeleya was right about her usefulness. Neither Tirzah nor I could get a message out of the city without suspicion, but if we could send the girl to someone in the camp, they might be able to get word to Malakhi about why we'd been delayed and that we were close to uncovering the details of the alliance. If anything, it would bring a measure of comfort to Tirzah's family that she was unharmed. "We can at least make an attempt, determine if she is capable."

Tirzah's lips pressed together in a firm line as she stared incredulously at me. I shrugged, indicating my willingness to try. This young girl had taken me on to protect her friend without any regard for her own safety, doing her best to fend off a man who'd faced thousands in battle and who could crush her delicate throat in one hand. In my opinion, she was nearly as brave as Tirzah.

Odeleya must have sensed a shift in Tirzah's resolve as a wide smile began to stretch across her face.

"All right," said Tirzah, and Odeleya squeaked in joyous response. "But you must do everything just as Liyam and I tell you, is that understood? There is too much danger for you to deviate even in the slightest."

The girl nodded her head and then flung herself into Tirzah's arms. "I won't let you down, you'll see."

Resigned, Tirzah kissed the crown of her head, but her expression remained troubled. "I need to get back to the kitchen. And you need to go fetch more water so no one notices you've been in here. But before we go, I have an idea for the first message you should carry to the camp."

While the two of them discussed her plan, I slumped back against the door and dragged my dirty hands down my face. Malakhi had better have good information for me about the location of Nadina's killer by the time I made it back to Shiloh, because this bargain was becoming more and more costly by the day.

EIGHTEEN

Tirzah

27 Nisan

My name echoed across the kitchen courtyard, drawing not only my attention but everyone else's as Odeleya bounded over to me, a smile on her face and a dripping waterskin over her shoulder.

I paused in my kneading, my hands sticky with dough, and wondered whether I'd made a grave misjudgment in telling the girl the truth. By the time she stopped in front of me, I'd already begun weaving together ideas for getting her out of Shechem before Liyam and me. Surely someone in the camp might have compassion for her, perhaps even be willing to take her to my mother in Shiloh?

"I visited my uncle!" she said, her grin wide and her affectation of carefree innocence convincing. "He's so grateful that you've been watching over me."

I stared up at her, thoughts circling around what she'd said but finding no place to land. An *uncle?* After what she'd told me about being sent to Shechem alone? Then sudden realization broke through the fog of confusion. She wasn't speaking of her own relation. She'd made contact with the man I'd sent her to find and was ensuring that the women around us thought we were only speaking of family members.

"Did you?" I replied, brows high. No one seemed to be paying us much attention, busy as they were with their duties, but I prayed none of the other women knew the true story of her past, aside from Roma, who never set foot inside Shechem.

Although I'd second-guessed my decision to involve her a hundred times over the last few days, I'd sent Odeleya to search for the Levites we'd encountered on Har Ebal, praying that somehow one of them might be willing to pass on a message to Malakhi. Since I'd armed her with only a general description of their leader, I'd truly not expected her to find him, and certainly not so soon.

"After the way he tossed you out," I said, building on her clever ruse, "I wasn't sure he'd have anything much to say to either of us."

"I did too," she replied with a careless shrug. "But he reconsidered after the things you told him."

The beat of my heart stuttered and then raced. Did this mean that the Levites had actually listened to me up on the mountain that night?

I scrambled for a reply that would continue the thread of our veiled references. "Perhaps he'll think twice before making such decisions so quickly."

"I think he may," she said, hefting the water onto her shoulder more securely. "In fact, he said that when you chastised him for hoarding all the wood and not sharing with other family members, you were right, and he repented of being so selfish. He said that whatever wood he and his friends gather is being divided among the rest of the family now, so they all can have more heat in this cold weather."

Joy began pulsing through my limbs. The message that Odeleya had so brilliantly hidden in plain hearing of the other women was as clear to me as sunlight through a cloud-break. The Levites had been affected by my rash reproof that night, and as a result, they'd been spreading word among the Hebrews that change was in the wind.

I reined in the shout of triumph that threatened to spill from my lips and kept my features bland. "I am glad to hear that. He was certainly stubborn before."

She nodded in agreement. "Oh, and he also said he'll make sure that your brother gets some fuel for his fire as well."

At that, I allowed a smile to meet my lips. "I'm glad to hear it," I said, wishing I had the freedom to ask more, but thrilled that the Levites had taken my admonition seriously. And Odeleya's success in retrieving such information, while playing up her youthful exuberance to avoid suspicion, smoothed the rougher edges from my worries over her safety.

"Perhaps next time you see him you'll let him know how much I appreciate his efforts to take better care of his family," I said. "In fact, they should probably distribute even more firewood over the next few weeks, in case another of those icy rainstorms comes up from the south. I have a feeling that this chilly weather is only the beginning and they must be prepared."

"All right," said Odeleya, looping a finger around and around a lock of her hair as if she were bored with the conversation. "I should go. I am supposed to bring water out to the plaza where some of the soldiers are putting on a display for the visitors. Zimora said to tell you that the commander requires refreshment."

My brows lifted. This was certainly new information to me. The representatives from Moab and Edom had arrived two nights ago, and rumor was that they'd been disguised as traders when they came through the gates of the city.

The visitors had spent their first day in Shechem being treated to the best of Barsoum's wine stores and feasting on the many decadent dishes my fellow cooks and I prepared, but so far had discussed nothing of importance at the table. The effusive welcome seemed excessive for the roughly garbed men from Moab and Edom who spoke for their leaders, but Barsoum never did anything without purpose.

"Good," I said, waving my doughy palm as if casually brushing her aside. "Do as you've been told."

Odeleya flounced out of the courtyard, calling out jubilant greetings to a few of the other cooks as she did so, as if she had not one care in the world. I suppressed a laugh that bubbled into my throat. I could not wait to introduce that girl to Malakhi; he'd be equal parts amused and impressed, I had no doubt. In fact, I was certain that my entire family would enfold her into their embrace so quickly that she'd have no more cause to mourn her own that so callously cast her aside.

After passing off my half-kneaded dough to one of the younger cooks to complete, I retrieved a large jug of wine from the storage room where Barsoum's hoard of fine drink was secured under constant guard, deep in the cool earth. I'd seen my grandfather's seal on this and many other such vessels among his collection and felt no small amount of satisfaction that the wine the Aramean commander would consume today was prepared by the same family that would soon bring about his downfall.

When I arrived in the plaza, I headed for the canopy under which Barsoum and his two guests were seated, where they were observing Liyam and his group of mercenaries going through a series of complicated exercises meant to impress. My path took me by the hulking white stone raised by Yehoshua to commemorate our conquest of the Land. Seeing it stained by urine and filth, thanks to the Arameans who took pleasure in desecrating such a sacred symbol, made my stomach churn with disgust. At the same time, the sight of the monument's degradation strengthened my resolve. When we won this city back, it would be cleansed, house by house, stone by stone. The many worthless idols that peered sightlessly at me from every niche in the commander's villa would be smashed and tossed on a burning refuse pile, where they belonged.

However, even as I approached the commander with renewed determination, it was impossible to take my eyes from Liyam as he bellowed out orders to the men in his command, while at the same time engaged in mock battle with an opponent. I'd become familiar with his strong form and stoic countenance over these past days of close proximity, but seeing him grappling with another soldier, his powerful bare torso on display and every muscle engaged in the struggle, unexpectedly caused my cheeks to flush with heat.

I stumbled, almost losing my grip on the jug, but thankfully kept myself and the wine upright. Chastising myself for such foolishness in the presence of Barsoum, I slipped around the backside of his table, praying the commander had not witnessed my blunder and relieved that Liyam was far too distracted to notice.

After filling Barsoum's cup, I moved to replenish those of the other two men, then shuffled backward to await orders.

"And this man is Moabite, you say?" said one of the visitors, his eyes trained on Liyam.

"Yes," replied Barsoum. "And one of the finest mercenaries I've ever hired, which is why I put him in command of this last batch of paid recruits. He's almost savage when he fights. It's a sight to behold, isn't it?"

"I've never seen him among my ranks," murmured the man, scrubbing his knuckles across his shaven head. A long rippled scar traveled from his eyebrow to his chin, lending him a fierce countenance. "But of course I'm not acquainted with them all. I leave that to my commanders."

His commanders? I'd assumed these delegates from Moab and Edom were little more than glorified messengers for their kings, men sent to deliver terms, not the kings themselves. Now the deferential treatment made sense.

"As you should," said Barsoum. "And from what I hear, the men beneath your leadership are plenty capable. After all, they held off our forces far longer than I expected."

The subtle reminder was not lost on me that, even if they had fought off the Arameans for many long months, eventually Moab and Edom had fallen. Nor was it lost on the king of Moab. His grip on his wine cup tightened ever so slightly, but he only dipped his chin in begrudging acknowledgment.

"We have been witness to the might of Kushan's armies, Barsoum," said the other man—the king of Edom, I now guessed, whose narrowed black eyes and lowered brows conveyed heavy suspicion. The man's long gray hair was secured at his temples by a wide headband of blue and green wool in a swirling pattern I'd never seen before. "It is the reason both our kingdoms surrendered back then. And, as agreed, we have paid tribute to Aram, and have been grateful that in turn you've left us alone. But what reason do we have for sticking our necks out in your struggle against the Hebrews? They are our distant cousins, after all."

Barsoum placed his folded arms on the table and looked the man directly in the eye, even as the wood groaned beneath his weight. "Because if you join with us against this upstart Yehudite who has dared rise against us in the south, we will pull out of your lands. Completely. You'll no longer owe us tribute."

The two foreign kings glanced at one another, silent conversation passing between them.

"What is it that you want from us?" asked the king of Moab. "Our armies are well trained, but nowhere near yours in number."

Barsoum grinned, confident in his victory as he gestured for his manservant to step forward with a papyrus scroll. Then the commander snapped his fingers with a silent demand for me to remove his empty cup. As I complied, he unrolled the scroll atop the table, and I caught sight of a roughly drawn map but was forced to retreat to my place in the corner of the canopy without noting any details.

Barsoum pointed to the papyrus. "The Hebrews have taken back Hebron, Be'er Sheva, and Arad, as well as their surrounding regions." His tone was grim and tight as he listed these cities, as if admitting the losses was painful. "They're now stationed at Ramah."

He moved his finger upward on the map, and my breath hitched. Othniel had gotten that far north already? That was less than a day or two from here and almost directly south of Shiloh. Although I knew that the Hebrews would likely take some time to restock supplies, regroup, and give their men a rest before they made another advance, the fight could very well be here in Shechem within weeks.

"What I ask is that we coordinate our efforts. Bring your men across near Jericho and loop around them from the south and east. I will have my army break into two and attack from the north and west. We will completely surround them. Against our three allied armies"—he gestured to Liyam and his men—"along with the large collection of mercenaries I've added to my numbers over the past months, they'll have no chance. It'll take a day or two to crush them. If that."

Any response from the kings was cut off by a shout from Liyam to halt exercises and an order for his men to take a rest. In the distance I saw Odeleya scurry forward to offer water to the men and prayed that none of them would take notice of her. However, I had no cause to worry. Liyam stood directly next to my young friend, arms crossed as each man received his portion of cool water from Odeleya's hands.

A swell of gratitude for his presence here rose in my chest. He may be gruff, even bordering on rude when we were alone at night, but his quick thinking with the messenger had yielded a missive to King Kushan, and one to Barsoum's wife in Harran, in which he revealed details about his personal life that Malakhi would certainly find of interest. And something about the way Liyam had spoken of his lost family, as if they'd been taken from him by tragic circumstances, reassured me that he would do anything to protect Odeleya.

Barsoum ordered his manservant to fetch the leader of the mercenary unit. So as soon as Liyam dismissed his men, he strode up to the canopy, sweat and dirt coating his skin even more thoroughly than it had when he'd had me pressed up against the wall to fool the messenger. He dipped his chin in a semblance of deference to Barsoum and his guests and then dragged his forearm over his face, clearing the droplets of sweat that kept trickling into his eyes.

"How are the men coming along?" asked Barsoum.

"Fairly well," replied Liyam. "Although I had to order fifty lashings for two of the Amorites who decided not to appear for the drill this morning. They won't make that mistake again." His unaffected tone made it clear he felt no sympathy for the men.

Barsoum chuckled, flicking a glance at his guests. "Ruthless. As I said."

He introduced Liyam to the visitors, calling them simply by the names Belham and Shembaal, and giving no allusion to their status as kings. Perhaps no one but he and his trusted manservant knew of their true identities. They'd arrived on mules, after all.

"Are your new quarters adequate, Liyam?" asked Barsoum. "I apologize for shifting you to the barracks to make room for our guests. But I told Khaled to find you a comfortable chamber."

Liyam nodded his head, saying nothing of the fact that Khaled had instead assigned him to the smallest room, outfitted with nothing more than a stack of dusty animal skins and two threadbare blankets. Between shivering from the cold and the knots of pain beneath my shoulder blades from sleeping on hard-packed dirt, I'd barely gotten any rest these past two nights. It was even worse than the servants' quarters, where at least I'd had Odeleya for warmth. Liyam had continued to respect my request that he sleep on the opposite side of the room, even now that the chamber we shared was a quarter of the size. If there was anything I'd learned about the tight-lipped redhead, it was that he stood by his word.

"And the company?" Barsoum asked, flicking his fingers in my general direction but not looking back at me. "Satisfied in that respect? She's been keeping up with her duties in the kitchen, so you are still welcome to her, but I have many others you might choose from, you know. A number who are specially trained to fulfill their duties." He chortled at his own crudeness.

Liyam scratched his thick beard, lips pursed, as if taking his time to contemplate Barsoum's offer. He took so long to respond that my pulse began to flutter. So far Liyam had only touched me when it was necessary to deceive others, and I'd come to believe he was an honorable man. Surely I was not wrong.

"I am grateful to you, my lord," he said. "But I'm still satisfied with my choice. She may not be well trained, but she is exceedingly compliant. Does anything I ask without argument."

I could not resist letting my training slip for the briefest of moments and darting a look at him. His gaze was on me, his features devoid of emotion, but there was an unmistakable spark of mischief in his blue-green eyes. The man was goading me, knowing I could do nothing but remain silent and still.

Barsoum guffawed at Liyam's response and waved him off, giving him leave to return to his men. Then the commander rapped his knuckles on the table. "Now that you've seen both my conscripted soldiers and my mercenaries in action, my friends, let us adjourn to more comfortable quarters to finish our conversation."

The three of them left the table to make their way into Barsoum's private chambers, a place I'd thankfully never been summoned to. But I felt certain that what I'd overheard today, along with the messages Liyam and I had stolen, was enough for Malakhi and Othniel to formulate a strategy against their coalition. However, they needed this information as soon as possible, before the kings of Moab and Edom left the city. We must depart for Shiloh.

Tonight.

NINETEEN

I'd never cleaned the dining chamber as quickly as I had that evening, an easier task knowing that it would be the last time I did so. Once all the bowls, plates, and pots were scrubbed and returned either to the treasury or kitchen courtyard, I'd headed for the women's quarters to search out Odeleya. I found her in the company of two younger cooks just outside the doorway, giggling over some secret.

"Odeleya," I called out, adding a scowl and a note of censure to my tone.

She jolted at my voice, brows furrowed, but then came forward with meek steps.

"I asked you to fetch an extra skin of fresh water," I said, praying she would understand. "The commander requested it specifically for his guests this evening."

"I apologize, Tirzah." She ducked her chin in seeming contrition. "I must have forgotten."

I flattened my lips in a display of annoyance and doled out my words with care. "I allowed you to come here with me in order to be a help in this household. If you do not want to stay by my side and learn from me as you requested, then you must tell me now." I leveled a gaze at her, willing her to grasp my true meaning. "But you must make that decision tonight and then stick by it. Do you understand?"

She looked up at me, her soft brown eyes full of sincerity. "I won't leave your side, no matter what."

"Then you'd better hurry before it is dark. And do not dally near the well."

"Of course not." Odeleya gave a little dip of her head to acknowledge my false admonishment, making me certain that she understood I was asking her to hurry out of Shechem and wait for me by the well. She slipped past me without another word, and I lifted a prayer to the One Who Sees to watch over her this night and until she and I were safely in Shiloh.

"You have an early morning," I said to the two young cooks who'd watched our exchange with bewildered expressions. "Unless you want to fetch more water tonight with Odeleya, I suggest you both find your pallets."

I did not wait for their response but whirled away, my sandals hastening toward Liyam's chamber. However, my supposed rescuer was not in his assigned cell, so I spent a long stretch of time pacing back and forth, chewing my fingernails and arguing with myself about whether I should try to find him or stay put until he returned. Worried for Odeleya and desperate to be on my way toward my family, my thoughts swirled as I made pass after pass across the ten paces that made up the length of the chamber.

When Liyam finally pushed through the door, my relief was so acute, I had to catch myself before I barreled toward him with an embrace, then was forced to question where such an impulse had come from. My silent quandary was brushed to the back of my mind as I caught sight of his stormy expression.

"What is it?"

He blinked at me. Then he shook his head, as if clearing his thoughts. "Nothing. Khaled and I had words." He drew his long red hair into a tail at the back of his neck with both hands and let out a groan, casting his eyes toward the ceiling. "I think Barsoum's games are pushing the man past his limit. He's becoming more and more provoking by the day. Trying to goad me."

"Is he suspicious of your heritage?"

"Perhaps. But he seems more focused on . . ." Liyam grimaced. "On you."

"Me?"

"Yes, he's made a number of comments about"—he cleared his throat—"your charms. And intimated that you'll be in his chambers instead of mine very soon."

Blood drained from my head at the memory of Khaled's finger sliding up my thigh, and the furtive looks he sometimes gave me at Barsoum's table. I would be anything but safe within that man's company. Just another reason why the time had come to leave Shechem.

"I overheard the details of the battle plan," I said. "We need to get back to Shiloh and give Malakhi the information. It's time to go."

Liyam's blue-green eyes went wide. "Now? Tonight?"

"Yes. I sent Odeleya to wait for me by the well."

"How will we get past the guards?"

"I'll tell them that I am worried for the kitchen girl who did not return after fetching water and that you were sent with me to find her."

He nodded, his gaze taking in the room. "Is there anything you need to take?"

"Only the missives." I patted my middle, where the two packets of papyrus were tucked safety within a folded strip of linen that I'd tied around my waist beneath my tunic.

We left the room and headed for the east end of the building, utilizing the glow from a few high windows to find our way around the side of the barracks. I kept close to Liyam's large form as we slipped from shadow to shadow, heading down one of the back alleyways that would lead us toward the gates of Shechem.

Suddenly, a hand curved around my wrist and twisted it behind my back with a painful jolt. Although my gasp was cut off by the sensation of a blade at my throat, Liyam swung around with a silent snarl on his lips, sword in hand.

"And where might we be going?" came Khaled's voice near my ear. "It's late, my friends. You should be abed."

"Let her loose, Khaled," said Liyam. "This is between the two of us."

The man jerked my arm harder, causing a spike of pain in my shoulder, but I refused to respond to the obvious attempt at provoking Liyam. Instead, my fingers went to my belt, slipping into the slit between sheets of leather and grasping the narrow hilt of my knife. With Khaled's attention trained on Liyam and darkness surrounding us, the weapon now at my side was completely hidden.

Khaled chuckled. "You played Barsoum's game well, I'll admit, but there's always been something off about you, something I just could not put my finger on. But it seems my surveillance of your chamber these last few nights was worth the effort. There is no other reason for you—or your little *prize* here—to be out now unless you were up to something."

"We are up to nothing—"

Khaled cut off whatever fabricated excuse Liyam had been about to make. "I care nothing for your lies, but I am certain Barsoum will be quite interested in your reasons for skulking about. There have been rumors of more spies in our midst, you know."

Liyam took two determined steps toward the man holding me captive, a mocking sneer on his face. "Such a coward. Not able to best me in the sparring ring, so you take to attacking women instead."

"Only because you were stupid enough to show your underbelly." Keeping his gaze trained on Liyam, he breathed into my ear and then dragged his lips down the side of my face, causing my skin to prickle with disgust. "I don't know what is so special about this Hebrew wench, but it seems I'm about to find out."

Liyam's expression did not change, but his stance shifted from relaxed to battle-ready within the space of two heartbeats. "You will regret ever laying a hand on her."

"Down," Liyam said, in our language. Without hesitation, I dropped my full weight to the right, away from Khaled's weapon, forcing him to scramble to catch me, which threw him off-balance, exactly the way my brothers had taught me.

Liyam charged, and I rolled away from the scuffle, locking my knuckles around my knife handle as I did. As soon as I made a full rotation on the ground, I sprang to my feet. The two men were grappling, their grunts echoing through the empty alley. They were of similar height, although Khaled carried more bulk around his middle, but it was clear that they were well matched and neither seemed to be giving any ground as they tussled. I remembered the wounds Liyam had returned with the first time he'd sparred with the Aramean and knew that Khaled would not be satisfied with inflicting a few scrapes and bruises this time. He meant to be rid of his competition for good.

"Go!" grunted Liyam in Hebrew, as he jabbed a fist into Khaled's throat. Somehow he'd lost his blade in the chaos and was fighting with only his enormous hands. Although I ached to follow the command, run for Odeleya, and hope that Liyam would somehow triumph, my feet refused to obey. I slipped my other blade from my belt just as Khaled managed to roll atop Liyam. Although the men were little more than shadows barely outlined by the waning moon, my brothers had forced me to memorize the lethal places on a body, practicing them over and over until I'd known how to reach each one without thought, and I had no time to hesitate.

"Don't worry," Khaled growled, his knife now at Liyam's throat. "Before I pass her on to the others I'll—"

I barreled forward, using all my strength to plunge one knife into the unprotected gap beneath his arm, and the other into the side of his throat.

Warmth spilled over my hands as Khaled bucked and heaved against my attack, making me realize that somehow my aim to his pulse-point had been slightly off center. His weight knocked me to the side, where I landed hard, pain shooting up my elbow as I skidded over stone. He gagged and shuddered, his own knife forgotten in the dirt as he attempted to grab for the one lodged in his neck. His enemy distracted, Liyam gripped Khaled's tunic and yanked hard, rolling the man off himself and pressing his knee into his opponent's chest. Khaled's eyes were huge, the whites wheeling about as he gasped for breath, fruitlessly pawing at the wound in his neck. Liyam shifted, blocking my view of Khaled's horrified face, and suddenly everything went still.

The silence buzzed, the only sound my thundering heartbeat as I kept my eyes pinned on the unmoving body. Then, before I'd registered that Liyam had even moved, he was standing over me, his face shadowed from the moonlight, saying something over and over that my mind could not grasp.

As the fog of confusion cleared, I realized it was my name on his lips. "Are you all right?" he urged. "Tirzah?"

Dazed, I tried to move, but before I could push myself upward, Liyam slipped his hands beneath my arms and lifted me to standing, like a child. My knees wobbled, but he held me upright.

"Can you walk?" he said, urgency in his deep voice. "We can't wait. You need to get to Odeleya."

"I . . . I, yes. I can walk." I looked down at my hands, the blood on them swiftly cooling in the night air. Even though the color of my palms was hidden in the dark, all I could see was red.

Suddenly, Liyam's warm hands were on either side of my face, pulling my attention to his stern expression. "Tirzah. Look at me. We have no time. You must go. Now."

"But what about you?"

He shook his head. "Where is the missive? The one for Barsoum's wife?"

"Hidden in my tunic."

"Listen to me," he said, still not taking his palms from my face. The sure brace of his strong hands and the reassuring tone of his voice infused me with a surprising sense of calm. "Go to Odeleya. Find the Levites and ask them to help you get to Shiloh. You must be away from this valley by dawn. Do you understand?"

"Yes . . . of course . . . but aren't you coming too?"

"I need to stay. You and the girl will be safer if I draw suspicion from your escape."

"But they will know . . . about Khaled," I stammered. "Barsoum—"

His thumbs brushed my cheekbones, a soothing motion that was likely unconscious on his part. "Don't worry about that. I have a plan."

"How will you get out of the city?"

"I got in fairly easily, didn't I? I'll meet you in Shiloh soon." A small grin tugged at his mouth that did nothing to reassure me. I'd only known this man for a few weeks, but the thought of running off while he answered for the blood I'd spilled tonight made my gut wrench. He dropped his hands, and I immediately missed the warmth and reassurance. "Hurry. Give me the message. Someone could come at any moment."

Heeding the urgency in his tone, I twisted around. After wiping my palms down the length of my thighs to clear Khaled's blood from my skin, I slid my arm down the wide neck of my tunic, wrestling with the folded linen around my waist until one of the papyrus notes was in my hand. The one destined for Barsoum's wife had lost its seal, so even in the dark it was easy to distinguish.

"Take the other to Malakhi," said Liyam as he accepted the note. Then he strode over to Khaled's body and tucked it securely beneath one of the leather bracers strapped to his wrist. His plan instantly solidified in my mind. He meant to charge Khaled with the theft of the missive. But how would he explain the two gaping wounds in the corpse, along with my absence? Would yet another man die because of my rash actions?

"Go," said Liyam in a rasping whisper, jolting me off that painful trail of thought. "Odeleya needs you."

I nodded, peeling my eyes off the dead man to take in the tall, moonlit form of the one who'd come to rescue a woman he'd never met and now was choosing to stay behind to protect her.

"Be safe," I said, shuffling back a few steps and taking one final glance at the man whose heartbeats I'd ended, before I turned away.

"Tirzah?" Liyam called out softly, making my sandals halt in place. Then he was next to me, handing over my two blades, now wiped clean.

"You served Israel well this night," he said, his tone firm but gentle.

Nodding once, I slid my weapons back into their secret places inside my belt, dragged in a deep breath, and forced myself to move forward. There was a young girl waiting in the darkness who was relying on me to bring her to safety and a missive beneath my belt that might mean life or death for my people. Pressing the bloody scene from my mind, I headed for the gates of the city while formulating a plan to get past the guards without suspicion and pleading for Yahweh to lend me courage. There was nothing to do for Liyam now but to pray that the One Who Sees would watch over him as well.

CHAPTER

TWENTY

"Odeleya," I whispered into the darkness, then twice more when there was no answer. Was I too late? Had she been frightened and somehow slipped back into the city? The guards had been only too easily fooled by my tearful plea to allow me out of the gates to find the girl who was lost in the dark, my overwrought tears annoying them so much that they'd acquiesced, but I was certain that even if I wanted back in, they would not reopen the gates until morning.

Besides, not only was it imperative that I reach Shiloh as soon as possible, but any lie Liyam had spun might be contradicted by my reappearance. I could not risk his life or Odeleya's by returning. Yet the thought of leaving my young friend behind, of never seeing her again, caused a swell of acute pain in the center of my chest.

A hand touched my arm, and I sucked in a quick gasp of surprise. "It's me," whispered Odeleya. "Where have you been? Where's Liyam?"

Taking a slow breath to calm the racing of my heartbeat, I pulled her into an embrace, needing to feel her in my arms as I silently rejoiced that she'd not slipped away from me after all. I kissed the top of her head.

"I'll tell you everything later," I lied, since there were few details of this night's events that I cared to ever let past my lips. "Right now, I need you to lead me to the Levite I sent you to find."

"Of course," she said, slipping her hand into mine.

"And Odeleya," I said. "We cannot be seen or heard."

Even in the sparse moonlight, I saw the gleam come into her eyes. She was thrilled by the idea of sneaking about, energized by the challenge. If I didn't know better, I'd wonder if this child came from my own womb.

Her small feet barely made a sound as we slipped into the labor camp and through the deep shadows between tents, avoiding the cookfires of Hebrews quietly gathered to celebrate Shabbat. Not since I'd left Shiloh had I been able to partake in the weekly tradition, and I longed to slip in among my brethren and indulge in the beautiful rest, especially after the soul-jarring events of tonight.

I was actually surprised that the Hebrews in this camp had taken to openly observing Shabbat again, especially with the Aramean stronghold in sight. But by the lilt of soft laugher on the breeze and the animated whispers of storytellers as we passed by fire after fire, it was clear that something here had shifted—a new boldness, perhaps, inspired by rumors of Othniel's victories.

Odeleya led me to a small clearing within the sea of nondescript tents, making me wonder how she'd found her way. Within the circle of woolen dwellings, another cook-fire flickered, surrounded by people whose attention was trained solely on a man at their center: the head Levite whom I'd met on the mountainside.

The words of Mosheh poured from his mouth, recalling the sight of the pillar of fire as it stood atop the Mountain of Adonai, how the people beheld the glorious sight of flame and smoke as they heard the thunder of the Voice from its core.

"The glory is still in our midst," the Levite said. "The Mishkan still sits at the heart of our land, and within it, the Ark that contains the Covenant between us and Yahweh. No enemy can take that honor away from us. We are the beneficiaries of an eternal vow spoken by the Righteous One who cannot lie. And as Yehoshua exhorted us from this very mountain"—he gestured up to the peak of Har Ebal at his back—"we must be strong and courageous, for Yahweh our God is with us."

The man's gaze traveled slowly over the people, as if catching their attention one by one. "We are his *am segula*, his treasured people, and although he has punished us for our disobedience for the last eight years, he will deliver us if we call upon his name." His eyes connected with mine, causing chilled flesh to arise on my arms at the realization that his words echoed the ones I'd spoken to him. He blinked twice at me, expression unchanged, before moving on to catch the next person's gaze. "He has not forgotten, and neither shall we."

Knowing he'd seen us, Odeleya and I slipped back into the shadows between tents as the people around the fire began to stand and make their way to their own dwellings. Once the group had withered to only a few, the Levite found us, silently gesturing for us to follow. He led us to his own tent a few paces away and held the flap aside for us to step into its warm embrace.

"Yitzak!" said a startled woman, dropping the juglet of water she'd been holding.

"Hush, Rehuva," ordered her husband, a finger to his lips. "Say nothing more."

Although wide-eyed, Rehuva obeyed, motioning for Odeleya and me to take a seat on the only two cushions inside the tent. We took them without argument, since it would have been rude to brush off such unquestioning hospitality.

"Now," said Yitzak, without preamble, "tell me how you came to be here and how I can be of help."

"You know what I am?" I asked.

"Between the few things your young friend has told me, the cryptic nature of your message to a vintner in Shiloh, and what I deduced from our brief acquaintance on the mountain, I believe I do."

"I must get back to Shiloh tonight," I said.

Yitzak's black brows rose. "Tonight?"

"There is no time to spare," I replied, unwilling to share any more. I refused to endanger his family. "If it were just me I would not hesitate to go without escort, but . . ."

"I can take care of myself," said Odeleya.

I squeezed her hand. "As you have proven, my friend. But we are not within the walls of Barsoum's villa anymore, where there are guards in place to ensure our safety. We must travel through rough land in the dead of the night, and there are dangerous animals that populate these hills."

Odeleya's eyes went wide. "Oh. I had not considered that."

"I'll send two of my men with you," said the Levite. "There are few weapons here among us, only what can be hidden well. But we will ensure you both get to Shiloh safely."

"Thank you," I said, pushing to my feet. "Then we will stay no longer."

Yitzak stood as well. "Rehuva, give these ladies a couple of woolen wraps for their travels."

"We could not take—"

He lifted a palm to halt my protest. "The gift you have given us is of far greater worth."

Confused, I looked back and forth between the Levite and his wife, who was now smiling at me.

"The things you said to us that night on the mountain have changed everything," he said. "We stayed there until dawn, on our faces around that abandoned altar, repenting of our foolishness, our pride, and our cowardice."

My insides churned with an emotion I could not name, but suddenly I felt exceedingly small and inadequate.

"What did you say?" Odeleya asked, her tone pitched high and her eyes wide with anticipation.

Embarrassment crept over me, making me itch to leave the tent. "I barely even recall my words."

"Because they were not *your* words," said Yitzak. "And as a result, we all agreed that the Torah commands and the stories of our forefathers are more precious than our own lives, and if the Arameans decide to slay us for speaking the truth, then so be it."

The air within the tent practically vibrated, and I could not take my eyes from the Levite. Next to me, Odeleya seemed to be holding her breath as she gazed up at me.

"You may have come to Shechem for another purpose, but you are leaving behind something far more precious—hope." He smiled widely, all vestiges of the cowering, uncertain man on the mountain washed away. "When Othniel arrives in this valley, he will not find a camp full of beaten-down slaves. He will discover a multitude of people who are prepared in both body and spirit to join the fight for the Land. Not because we are mighty, but because Yahweh is."

I was nearly too stunned to reply and had to clear my throat of emotion twice before I spoke. "Haven't the Arameans been suspicious of your stories around the campfire?"

His grin was mischievous. "Oh for certain. There were more than a few instances of guards scattering our gatherings in the first weeks. But we refused to let that stop us and just regathered again in different areas—in shadowed places, out in the woods, or within tents. But lately they've either tired of patrolling our long-winded storytelling, deeming it unworthy of their time, or they are too busy preparing for war to care anymore. So, other than the few guards watching us at the entrance to our camp, they've left us alone for the most part. What they cannot understand is that the words of Yahweh, along with the renewed spirits of our people, are more dangerous than any weapon they might have taken from our hands."

Odeleya had slipped both her arms about my waist, her soft brown eyes nearly as wide as her smile. The sight of her young face looking up at me with such adoration brought my attention back to the flight we must undertake this night. As much as I wished to stay and find out more about what had happened among my people in this camp, there was no more time to waste.

"I am honored to have been of service," I said, still feeling a tinge of embarrassment at his effusive praise. "But we should be on our way."

"Of course," he said, gesturing again to his wife, who stepped forward to wrap woolen mantles around the two of us and press a few rounds of bread into our hands.

After thanking Rehuva for the gifts, Odeleya and I followed Yitzak through the black night to another nearby tent and were soon joined by two young men, both whose imposing labor-hardened frames would no doubt cause any wild animals to think twice before attacking our small party.

Before we walked away from Yitzak, he stopped me and pointed to the southeast, where the black shadow of Har Ebal stood, and at its peak, the altar of Yehoshua. "A fire will burn there again soon. And when it does, be assured that it was your iron strike against our flinty hearts that created the first spark."

TWENTY-ONE

Liyam

I'd been lounging at Barsoum's cedar table since dawn. Waiting. Planning. When the commander finally lumbered into the room, with Ishmid and a younger man I'd never seen before close behind him, I kept my arms folded across my chest, legs stretched out in front of me, and an expression of disinterest on my face

"What is the meaning of this, Liyam? Zimora told me you are in here with a body . . ."

His voice trailed off as he caught sight of Khaled's corpse. The young cook who'd stumbled into the room a while ago and had left pale-faced to fetch her master for me must not have noticed the identity of the body in question when she relayed the message.

Barsoum's face went florid. "Who killed my second-in-command?"

Pressing away the image of Tirzah flying at Khaled with her knives flashing in the moonlight, I shrugged a shoulder. "I did."

"You—? What—?" Barsoum spluttered, fury making his skin deepen to a shade of crimson I'd never seen on a man's face before. His indigo-blue eyes were outlined in stark white.

Both Ishmid and the younger man had already drawn their swords at my admission, but I refused to allow a hint of vulnerability during this exchange, so I stayed seated and forced my muscles to remain relaxed. I'd had plenty of time during the dark hours of the night to come up with a plausible explanation for my actions and the right way to manipulate Barsoum's line of thought.

"He was stealing off with my prize."

Barsoum blinked at me, as if he'd somehow forgotten how to speak his own language. "Your . . . your prize?"

"Yes. The girl." I flitted a hand toward the corner where Tirzah usually stood like a beautiful, sharp-eyed kestrel, blending with the shadows to watch over her prey. "I had no intention of killing him, but when I confronted him while he was sneaking out of the city with the prize you so generously gave me, I was forced to defend myself against his attack." I gestured to the bruises and scrapes on my face and then the long slash directly below my jawline where Khaled's knife had pierced the skin just as Tirzah had jammed her own into his throat. "It was him or me. I chose to keep breathing."

The younger man who had come into the room behind Barsoum spoke up. "And where is this woman you were squabbling over?"

I lifted a brow as I took in the stranger's appearance. He was likely a few years younger than me, tall and broad-chested, and something about him seemed vaguely familiar.

However, I did not acknowledge him as I spoke directly to Barsoum. "No idea. She skittered off as soon as Khaled attacked. She probably thought I'd deal with her next. And she would be right. I don't tolerate betrayal."

"Ishmid," said Barsoum as he lowered his bulk into his sturdy chair with a groan and wiped the sweat from his brow. "Go find the girl. Let's hear her version of these events."

Although he cast a wary glance at me before he left the room, Ishmid complied. I'd held off summoning Barsoum until dawn to give Tirzah time to get away. I could only pray that she'd gotten help from the Levites and that she and Odeleya were well on their way to Shiloh.

The other man stepped closer, as if sizing me up, making me realize that his eyes were the exact same dark blue as the commander's.

"This isn't really about the girl," I said. "I was beginning to tire of the timid little mouse anyhow. What concerned me more was that Khaled was sneaking out of Shechem just before the gates closed for the night. And he kept looking over his shoulder while I was confronting him, as if he were watching for someone."

Barsoum's eyes narrowed. "Who?"

"I can't tell you. But whatever he was up to, he certainly was worried about being caught."

"Who do you think you are to cast suspicions on my father's second-in-command?" said the stranger. Ah. Now the resemblance made sense. This man was the commander's son. Indeed, he very much looked like what Barsoum might have at his age, and before eight years of regal excess and relative idleness.

"Alek," snapped Barsoum as he pounded a fist on the table. "This is my concern. Not yours."

The commander turned back to me, the look of shrewd consideration in his gaze reminding me that this was the same man who'd led the successful offensive on the Hebrew territories.

"Khaled has been my right hand for twelve years," he said. "I trusted him with my life."

"Then perhaps your trust was misplaced," I replied. "Something smells foul. A loyal man does not sneak off in the night. Nor undermine his commander, even if it's about a woman."

Barsoum continued watching me for a few long moments, as if scrutinizing my face for any hint of wavering. I kept my breaths steady and my face blank.

"Alek. Search the body," he said then, falling directly in step with where I'd been leading.

"For what?" Alek's reply was replete with disbelief.

"Whatever can be found," replied the commander. "There must be some clue as to what Khaled's motive was last night."

Alek searched Khaled's body, patting down his bloodied garments with a grimace. "There's nothing here."

"Check his belt," said Barsoum. "And beneath his bracers."

Alek obeyed with a scowl that melted away the moment he tugged the hidden note from beneath the leather wristband.

"Give that to me." Barsoum snapped his fingers at him as if he were a dog.

A flash of pure rage flickered in Alek's dark eyes, but he managed to tamp it down as he handed over the folded papyrus Tirzah had stolen so skillfully.

Barsoum unfolded it, his eyes going wide. "This is a letter to my wife. I handed it directly to the messenger a few days ago."

"Is there anything that might be used against you?" I asked, praying he did not feel the gentle nudge of my words. "Or something that would hint to your negotiations with Moab and Edom?"

"No. It is only a note to refuse her request to be moved closer. She's been fussing about being left alone in Harran for so long and wanted to be housed with the other commanders' wives in Kedesh. I told her it was not safe and to wait until we have the Hebrews in hand."

"Seems harmless enough. Was that the only missive you sent with the messenger?"

Barsoum's chin jerked up. "No. I sent one to Kushan, telling him of the deal with the foreigners. There was also one to the commander in Merom, asking that more infantry support be sent here, and one to Megiddo, telling them we need more chariots."

"If he stole this one, then he undoubtedly took the others."

"No," said Barsoum, shaking his head in disbelief. "Khaled could not have been working against me."

I shrugged again, as if it were none of my concern. "The only reason someone would have for intercepting messages like that is to give them to the enemy."

Barsoum cursed loudly, his face going red again, and he crumpled the papyrus in his meaty fist. He unleashed a foul tirade against Khaled and his treachery, vowing to string his corpse up in the plaza and then to mete out vengeance on the man's family. I hoped, for their sake, that Othniel would come to Shechem before such vile threats could be carried out.

"You had something to do with this," Alek said, his sharp gaze narrowed on me. "Father, surely you cannot trust—"

I interrupted him before he could speculate further, pushing belligerence into my tone. "What profit would any of this gain me? I am here for one thing: silver. And as long as I am being paid well, then my allegiance is secure. And I've been rewarded very well in Shechem. I did not set out to catch a traitor in the act, simply to retain what was mine. I earned that prize by dealing with the Hebrew spy. And whether I was finished with her or not, Khaled had no right to touch her."

"If he was up to something, he would have taken off after killing Khaled," Barsoum barked out in my defense. "There would be nothing to gain from him staying. And I saw with my own eyes the damage he inflicted on that spy. Not to mention I heard the man's screams all the way from my chambers. It is obvious who the traitor here is." He spat in the direction of the body. "We just need to figure out who he was working with and where those other messages went."

Ishmid came back into the room and relayed that "the cook" had disappeared last night and hadn't been seen since. Neither had the girl who fetched water for the kitchens. He'd said that the guards reported that Tirzah had used the excuse of chasing after the girl to slip out of the gates and had last been seen heading southwest, toward the well, weeping and carrying on. The news gave me even more hope that the two of them had indeed made it safely out of the valley.

Barsoum explained the situation to Ishmid, who went slack-jawed at the news of Khaled's supposedly traitorous actions.

"We should find the girl," said Alek. "She must be part of this conspiracy or she would not have run away."

I laughed. "The girl was shapely and compliant, and I admit she cooked well, but she was about as sharp as a mud-brick." I shook my head, as if all too amused by his idea of Tirzah being a spy. "Khaled only wanted her for one thing."

"He's right. Some fool woman is not worth our time. No matter how good her food was." Barsoum scratched at the wispy hairs atop his balding pate. "But there have obviously been spies in this household. There's no chance Khaled was working alone. Liyam, since you've proved yourself fit to the task, I want you and your men in charge of security here."

"But he is nothing more than a foreign mercenary—" Alek protested.

"Are you questioning my decisions?" boomed the commander, spittle flying from his mouth. "I say who I trust to carry out my orders. Not you."

"Of course, my lord," said Alek, bitterness dripping from his tongue.

The acrid tone was not lost on Barsoum. "You will go to Megiddo. Tell the commander there about my arrangement with Moab and Edom, since my messages obviously went astray."

Alek bristled. "But I just arrived—"

"And now I am telling you to go," said Barsoum, jutting a beefy finger at his son. "If I say you will take a message, you take it. If I say you scrub my floors, you get down on your knees. Understand, boy? Or are you as feeble-minded as your whore of a mother?"

Alek said nothing, but his jaw worked back and forth, as if he were holding back a vitriolic response.

"That's what I thought," said Barsoum. "Perhaps if you can handle this assignment without getting tied naked to a tree, I'll reinstate you to your original rank instead of continuing as my errand boy."

Alek's brows shot high. "Truly?"

Barsoum shrugged, his eyes going back to the letter still clutched in his hand. "You may only be the offspring of one of my more useless concubines, but you are still my blood. Go on. I'll prepare a missive for you to carry after I discuss things with Liyam and Ishmid."

Alek left the room, but not before glaring at me with all the animosity he'd been holding back from his father.

"Are you a traitor too?" Barsoum asked Ishmid.

"I am your brother," said Ishmid simply, surprising me with this new information. "You know I would never even whisper a word against you. The blood in my veins is the same as yours."

"Did you guess?" Barsoum jerked his chin toward Khaled's body.

Ishmid followed his gaze. "I had my suspicions that his allegiances lay with his own interests, especially with regard to the king's favor. . . . But did I guess he would collude with the Hebrews? No."

Barsoum let out a long sigh, leaning heavily on his elbows. "I don't have time to deal with this issue. That Yehudite is already on his way north with a much larger force than we'd expected, and I'm still negotiating with Moab and Edom, so they cannot know that our coalition might no longer be a secret."

Frowning, he looked back at the body of the man he now considered a traitor. "You are my second-in-command now, Ishmid. The place you always should have held, apparently. I will trust you to lead my army against the Hebrews. And Liyam, I trust you to root out any spies in this household . . . no, in this city. Start by searching Khaled's quarters."

Ishmid and I both nodded, accepting our commands without argument but only one of us planning to obey them. Thankfully, I knew of only one Hebrew spy in Shechem and she'd been gone long before sunrise.

CHAPTER

TWENTY-TWO

12 Iyyar

The villa was deserted. No bustle of servants shuffling up and down the hallways, no smell of fresh bread on the air or chatter from the kitchen courtyard. Even Barsoum's regular guard had been sent away. My mercenary unit alone remained to protect the commander from his own folly. Only the shuffle of my own sandals as I strode the corridor could be heard now in the silent building, since I'd ordered my men to remain at their posts outside and barred the door behind them.

Barsoum had been cowering here in his chambers since yesterday, when word of his army's crushing defeat had arrived.

Few survivors, had been the words of the messenger from the battle-field near Ramah. *Moab and Edom did not come.*

Even more satisfying than hearing that Othniel had defeated Aram's forces was that Barsoum's plot to encircle our army with help from the foreign kings had failed. Tirzah must have made it to Shiloh and delivered the message to Malakhi. Barsoum had been certain of the strength of his bargain with the kings of Moab and Edom when they departed, so the Hebrews had to have interfered in some way.

In my relief, I was forced to admit to myself that I'd slept fitfully during these past weeks she'd been gone, my empty chamber seeming far too quiet without her steady breaths across the room and too cold without the heat of indignation in her eyes when I challenged her. But Tirzah had done what she set out to do and was now safely in the arms of her family. Her mission was complete.

But every time I'd considered walking out the gates of Shechem to return to my hunt for the trader, I'd had the distinct soul-deep impression that my own job here was not done. And so, against every desire, I'd stayed.

However, when a fire atop Har Ebal had been spotted last night, a fervent blaze that could be seen from any point in the valley, I knew that my time in this place had come to an end. I had only one more task to finish before I renewed my search for my daughter's killer. A task that I did not relish, yet one that would ensure a swift victory for Othniel when he arrived.

I knocked on the door of Barsoum's chamber but did not wait for a response before I swept inside. The high commander of Aram's forces startled at my abrupt entry. He'd been leaning heavily on the windowsill, gazing out over the city he'd claimed as his prize eight years before—the city that would soon return to its rightful owners. The sweat trickling down his fleshy face and the fear flickering in his eyes told me that he knew this all too well.

"Any word from Megiddo?" he demanded. "Or from Alek?"

"Nothing," I replied.

Curses flew from Barsoum's lips against the commander at Megiddo, whom he accused of coveting his power and position, the inept commanders he'd sent to Ramah, including his own brother, and most of all the "wretched" Hebrews. As he raged, his face grew redder and redder, spittle flying from his lips, until all that was left of the once-revered high commander was a stomping, ranting child who'd drunk enough wine already this morning to bring down a team of oxen.

By the time Barsoum had run out of foul words to describe both his enemies and his allies, he was swaying, anger having given way to desperation. "I'll pay you three times what I offered before. No, ten!"

"For what, my lord?" My teeth gritted at the regard I'd had to show this bloated snake for all these past weeks.

"To get me out of this city, of course! Take whatever is in the treasury, divide it between your men, I do not care. I must escape this place."

"The gates are closed," I said. "There is no other way out. The Hebrews have us surrounded."

And indeed they did.

The fire on the mountain must have signaled the people in the camp to revolt. By dawn, hundreds of laborers using little more than their own hands, a few building tools, and a small number of weapons that had likely been buried beneath tents for months—if not years—had overtaken their guards. The few units of Barsoum's army that had been left behind to protect Shechem were now ensconced within the walls, praying to their worthless gods for a rescue that was now certain not to come.

And Othniel was on his way, if not already at the gates.

The messenger who delivered the news of the loss at Ramah had also reported as much, along with the news that a strange blue-white cloud that sparked lightning and roared like the sea had been spotted over Shiloh, so terrifying the Arameans in that city that every one of them had fled. Shiloh had been won without the Hebrews even lifting a sword.

Barsoum groaned and slumped into his chair, running his shaking fingers through what was left of his hair. "There has to be some way out of this cursed city. A tunnel. Something." He poured another cup of drink, his hands trembling so hard that wine splashed onto the table. "I won't be taken by that Yehudite and his rabid pack of dogs."

"Don't worry," I said, squelching a smirk both at his foolishly dismissive portrayal of Othniel and also the underlying terror beneath those words. "I have a plan."

Though not one you will approve of.

Relief bowed the meaty shoulders of the high commander as he leaned his elbows onto the table, dropping his head into his hands. "I knew I made the right choice in putting you over the mercenaries. I knew that after what happened with Khaled, that treacherous worm, you were the only one I could trust to protect me."

"Of course," I said. "I am nothing if not loyal to my commander."

Although my commander's name is Othniel, and he has been raised by Yahweh to reclaim our Land from your slimy hands.

I moved to the window, silently peering out over the city and marveling at the strange stillness that had overtaken it in anticipation of what was headed this way. Barsoum took the time to drink another cup or two of wine and mutter to himself about insubordination, betrayal, and how he planned to storm into Megiddo to repay the commander who'd refused his orders to send reinforcements to Shechem.

A shofar sounded in the distance.

"What was that?" barked Barsoum from behind me.

A slow smile spread over my lips. Barsoum's villa was situated at the highest point in Shechem, and this room, with its wide, regal windows facing eastward, gave me a perfect view of the narrow gap between Har Ebal and Har Gerizim. Through it poured Othniel's army, and the second shofar blast from its heart, the one that ordered my fellow tribal brethren to attack, was the signal I'd been waiting for.

"He has come," I said, turning around so Barsoum could finally see my large grin.

"Megiddo sent reinforcements after all?" he said, hopefulness in the slur of his words. I ignored his question, glad to see that his eyes were glazed from drink. It would make my task all that much easier.

"I heard of you eight years ago," I said, leaning back against the sill and folding my arms over my chest. "Heard of how you swept into this land in such triumph, mowing down Hebrews with your iron chariot and slaughtering the rest with an iron sword fashioned by Hittites. The first of its kind on the battlefield. You were a man who inspired his men to fight without hesitation for a land that was not theirs, for a king who lusted after its fertility. You were hailed as fearsome, ruthless, and a brilliant strategist."

Barsoum blinked at my unexpected speech, confusion sweeping over his wine-ruddied face.

"And yet . . ." I pushed away from the wall to stalk toward him. "When I came here, I found this." I swiped my hand toward his pathetic carcass. "A pampered, overindulged drunkard. A man who somehow managed to hold on to power even though the reasons for his reputation were overstated. A coward who didn't even lead his men into battle at Ramah."

More *shofarim* blasted their war cry near the entrance to the city. I'd been at Hebron when those enormous cedar gates had been breached with surprising ease and had little doubt that Shechem's would succumb just as quickly.

I slipped my sword from its sheath, and Barsoum's eyes went directly to its well-honed blade, the one I'd sharpened to a razor's edge on a whetstone just this morning, with him in mind.

"But you—I trusted you," he spluttered, the color draining from his face. He pushed off his chair and stumbled backward until his enormous calves were pressed against his bed.

I reveled in his bewilderment as I advanced slowly, stretching out his burgeoning terror. "Only one of your many fatal mistakes. The first being entering Israel's territories at all. The second was profiting off the backs of Hebrew tributes, getting fat off the sweat of their brows, and in becoming so self-indulgent that you could not see the danger right in front of your face."

"You are Moabite!" he screamed. "What do you care what happens in this land?"

"Am I?" I smirked.

His eyes went so wide that I could see the bloodshot whites all around. "You are *Hebrew*?"

"Not only that," I said, showing my teeth. "I am one of those Yehudite rabid dogs."

Barsoum lunged for the dagger that had been sitting on a stool near his bed, but I charged, knocking the weapon from his sweaty fist before he could get a good grip and using my full body weight to push him sideways. Slamming his temple against his iron bedstead as he went down, Barsoum landed with a thud.

He lay sprawled halfway on the floor, eyes wheeling and blood trickling down the side of his face, calling out for his guards.

Tossing the dagger across the room, I moved to stand over the once-revered commander of Kushan's forces, my sword pointed at the lumps of flab beneath his chin.

"Don't you remember?" I pressed the tip into his skin. "You sent your guards away. Left me in charge here. And even if anyone cared to come to your rescue—and they won't because they are too busy trying to defend Shechem against its rescuers—they would have to break through the door I barred when I sent my men outside."

"I should have known you were one of them." He spat and cursed me, but his torrent of filth was cut off by a deeper jab of my sword.

"As I said, you were too dull-minded to see the danger right in front of you. But the greatest threat wasn't even me. It was your timid-as-a-mouse serving girl."

"What are you talking about?"

"Tirzah. The spy sent here months ago to listen to your every word. To pass along every one of your secrets. The one who slipped out of Shechem with the missive that thwarted your plans with Moab and Edom. And the woman who felled Khaled when he caught the two of us attempting to escape."

He screamed a foul curse and tried to roll to his side, but I slammed my foot into his chest, pinning him down.

"And this," I said, leaning over him and bellowing into his face with all the force of the black rage I'd been harboring for the past few months, "is for the Hebrews you enslaved. The women you ordered violated. The children murdered or sold to satisfy tribute. My brethren whose blood was spilled on the battlefield at your orders. For Sheth and Hanael, the two brave spies you had mercilessly tortured and slaughtered. For Tirzah, whom you gleefully offered up to rape. And for Yahweh, whose Land you defiled."

Then I ended the eight-year tyranny of Shechem with one swift plunge of my sword.

I headed for the kitchen courtyard, thinking to avoid any of the mercenaries who might still be guarding the front door and instead heave myself over the wall to join the battle as soon as the gates were breached. It would not do to be caught inside the villa when Othniel's men arrived, since none would pause to confirm my heritage during the chaos of an invasion.

I crossed the silent kitchen courtyard, somehow conjuring a shadowy image of Tirzah standing near the bread oven the day I'd dragged her off to steal messages, her outward appearance of subservience such a contrast to the warrior she harbored inside. I still could not believe she'd plunged her knives into Khaled to save me that night, nor that she'd walked away afterward without falling into pieces.

I knew without a shred of doubt that she'd never shed a man's blood before and hoped that the memories of those moments would not haunt her the way the battles I'd been a part of haunted me. The way Sheth's pleading voice still manifested in my dreams. And yet dispatching Barsoum to his worthless gods was all too easy, so perhaps at my very core I was broken beyond repair. Something had certainly shattered deep inside the moment I'd heard of Nadina's death. Now I only needed to survive this day so I could finish my mission to destroy the man who'd crushed my soul along with my daughter.

Determining that climbing atop one of the still-burning bread ovens in one corner was my best chance to scale the tall mud-brick fence around the courtyard, I found an abandoned pot of flour and used it to snuff the flames. Then, placing my sandaled foot in a small niche on one side, I lifted my body from the ground. However, a sob from somewhere nearby halted my progress. I paused to listen. The sound repeated, and I realized it was coming from the women's quarters, where Tirzah and Odeleya had lived together until I'd arrived in the city.

I hissed at the scalding pain on my palms, my hesitation giving the heat from the mud-brick oven time to inflict its sharp bite, but I could not clear an unbidden vision of Tirzah and Odeleya huddled together on their mat in that same room, terrified and vulnerable. Othniel would win Shechem today, I had no doubt, but that would not stop Aramean soldiers from bursting back into the villa before the battle was won and slaughtering these women purely for the sake of vengeance.

Convicted, I groaned and leapt back to the ground.

By the sound of the many whispers and sniffles that seeped through the cracks and windows, it seemed that all the Hebrews who'd served in Barsoum's kitchen were hunkered down inside.

I pushed on the door handle, but it did not give. The women must have barred it from the inside. A few panicked cries erupted as I made a second attempt.

"They're coming!"

"Don't let them in here!"

"I do not want to die!"

"I won't hurt you," I called out in Hebrew, but the only responses I received were shouts to leave them alone and loud calls for Yahweh's protection. I sighed, shaking my head at both their audacity and their stubbornness. It was best they remained barricaded within anyhow, until the danger had passed.

The only thing I could do now was guard them and wait. With my back against the door, I slid to the ground, laid my sword across my knees and pinned my eyes on the back entrance to the villa. I'd do well to rest until it opened, and I was forced to defend myself from either vengeful Arameans or my own kin.

All too soon the distinctive noises of battle came close. The Hebrews had broken through the gates of Shechem with as much ease as they had Hebron, as if the hand of Yahweh had opened them himself to Othniel's advance. Blood rushed in my ears at the clang of metal-on-metal, the shrieks of agony, and the unintelligible clamor of hundreds shouting, grunting, and cursing each other's gods. Those all-too-familiar sounds made my body ache to stand beside my brethren.

Not long after the battle began, and sooner than I'd expected, a group of Hebrew soldiers plowed through the open door into the court-yard, weapons raised and eyes on me. I was torn between laying my weapon down in a show of submission and holding fast in case they refused to listen.

"I am one of you!" I called out as they warily approached, pushing to my feet. "I am of the tribe of Yehudah."

"He lies!" screamed a woman from inside the chamber. "He is a Moabite mercenary. A killer! A violator of women!" She must have been peering through a crack in the door and recognized me.

"I tell the truth," I said to the men, patching together the most believable explanation I could muster. "I fought with you at Hebron. I was sent here to gather information for Othniel." Knowing I must display my sincerity, I bent to lay my sword on the ground, then raised my palms.

The Hebrews swarmed me without hesitation, jerking my arms behind my back and forcing me to the ground, searching my body for the rest of my weapons, which were swiftly confiscated. I did not struggle and laid my cheek in the dirt with a resigned sigh. How would I prove my identity? I wore Moabite clothing and looked like a wild beast.

"What are you doing to these women?" snapped one of Hebrew soldiers.

"*Protecting* them," I said, then grunted when a Hebrew sandal landed in the center of my back. "Have we taken the city?"

"*We* have retaken *our* city," snarled one of them, his foot moving to the base of my skull to press my face harder into the dirt.

"I *am* one of you," I said, groaning with exasperation. "My father Tobiah stood at the battle of Jericho. My mother's sister is Rahab, the Canaanite woman who aided Yehoshua's spies to escape the king of Jericho. I, alongside my five brothers, fought together in the wars against the Arameans eight years ago. My sword cut down many enemies as we liberated Hebron, our city of refuge. And I worship the One True God, Yahweh."

By the time I finished my speech, more sandals had joined the group around me.

"Let him stand," said a voice of authority.

The pressure on my neck disappeared, and I lifted my head to survey the crowd. At least fifteen blood-spattered faces looked on, in addition to the four that had taken me captive, and more men continued to spill through the doorway.

But the one man who stood out from all the rest was the one whose gore-speckled black beard was shot through with silver, and whose knowing eyes were pinned on me with piercing intensity. Although I'd only seen him from afar, just before the battle for Hebron, and barely heard his words of encouragement before we attacked, I knew that the man standing before me was Othniel, nephew to the great warrior-spy Calev.

"You say you are Hebrew?" he said. "And kin to Rahab?"

I bowed my head, ceding honor to his high rank. "Yes. My name is—"

"Liyam!" called a voice from the back of the group of onlookers. Then a body pushed through the group, and with arms outstretched, my brother Shimon plowed toward me. "Brother!"

Behind Shimon came Lev, Yosef, Mikal, Oren, and finally my cousin Yavan, a wide smile across his face. Ignoring the high commander of the Hebrew forces before me, they greeted me each in turn, embracing me with ferocity as the rest of the soldiers looked on in surprise.

Yavan was last to kiss my cheek and slap my back with a strong embrace that spoke of his relief at the sight of me relatively unharmed. But mischief sparkled in familiar brown eyes that were not nearly as sunken as the last time I'd seen him in Shiloh.

He wrinkled his nose and pushed away from me with a feigned gag. "Still smelling like a cave full of boar droppings, eh, cousin?"

CHAPTER

TWENTY-THREE

Tirzah

15 Iyyar
Shiloh, Israel

Music filled every dip and hollow of the valley, as it had since word of Shechem's fall into Hebrew hands had made its way here two days ago.

From the animated chatter of women preparing yet another feast to the delightful melody of laughter of children who were finally able to jump and shout and play without fear of the Arameans, the joyful buzz of triumph had not ceased. But as excited as I was that this valley was free and that Shechem too had been liberated, I had been on edge for days, wondering why Liyam had not yet returned. He'd promised that he'd be able to escape Shechem as easily as he'd slipped into it. So where was he?

I stood now at the head of the trail that led up from the valley, watching, waiting, as I had nearly every day since we'd parted over two weeks ago, praying for the safety of a man who'd begun as a wild, terrifying stranger but whose absence was now ever on my mind. I could still feel the sensation of his palms cupping my cheeks as he steadied me that last night, calming me with gentle words in that deep voice that had become so familiar during our nightly talks in the dark of our room.

Since I'd come home, my worries for him had spiraled from concern into near-panic as the days went on and he had not appeared. What if Barsoum had not believed his story about Khaled? What if, instead of being hailed as a hero who'd uncovered a traitor, Liyam's true identity had been uncovered? What if he'd been charged with Khaled's death in my place? He'd done so much for me and for Odeleya, I could not bear to think that he'd suffered Hanael and Sheth's fate on my account.

My mother appeared at my side, yanking me from my increasingly desperate thoughts. "Daughter. Are you well?"

I swallowed the truth and forced a smile. "Of course. Just lost in thought."

She slipped her arm around me, gathering me close and pressing a kiss to my temple. "My precious girl. I am so glad you are home safe with us."

She'd been so kind when I'd returned to Shiloh, exhausted but triumphant as I handed Malakhi the missive I carried. Although I'd expected fury for my reckless behavior and deceit, my mother had crushed me to herself in an embrace that lasted for a quarter of an hour, whispering how sick with dread she'd been since my whereabouts had been disclosed, but how proud she was of me anyhow.

My father, however, had not been quite as forgiving.

Of course he too had held me close, kissing my forehead and thanking Yahweh for my safety. He'd listened patiently as I informed him, Malakhi, and Eitan of all that had transpired in Shechem, and explained about Barsoum's plot with the kings of Moab and Edom. But things between us had been strained, not the easy, playful camaraderie I'd always shared with my abba. His reticence toward me hurt, and I wondered how long he would punish me with silence.

"The men netted a large covey of quail this morning," said my mother. "I plan to roast them, but I need more fennel. Might you be willing to go down to Yuval and Tzipporah's home and fetch some? She has an abundance in her garden and is more than willing to share."

I knew what she was doing, giving me a task to keep my mind occupied and offering me a reprieve from the happy chaos around the tents. I'd not spoken a word about Liyam since I'd returned, other than to tell everyone how he'd protected us, but I had the sense my mother suspected why I'd been so anxious. She was nothing if not exceedingly perceptive.

"Of course, Ima," I said, avoiding her knowing eyes, then pressed a kiss to her cheek and turned to head for the little home on the far side of my grandfather's property.

Odeleya was nearby, laughing with two of Eitan and Sofea's daughters, who were both close to her age. She still clung to me like moss to a cedar, but she'd had no problem making friends among my nieces and nephews and had almost immediately settled in to her new life. Unfettered by the burden of daily survival in an enemy stronghold, she was finally allowed to be the young, innocent girl that she truly was. Whether or not my time in Shechem had been profitable to the cause of my people, I would never regret bringing her home with me.

She caught sight of me and took a few steps my way, as if to follow, but I shook my head and gestured for her to stay. Thankfully she took no offense and kissed her palm before waving it at me, and I returned the gesture with a grin. It was impossible to remain melancholy around Odeleya.

The day was bright and cloudless, and I hummed as I meandered along the rows between dense green vines, breathing in the smell of sun-soaked soil and leaves as I walked. Halfway down the path, I caught sight of two men off in the distance. Lifting my palm to shade my eyes, I saw that it was Malakhi and my father slowly making their way through the vineyard while deep in conversation.

Taking only a few moments to debate my decision, I slipped through a gap between vines, stepping over the low rock fences that held their tendrils aloft. Keeping my body low and my feet soft, I repeated the move again and again, fashioning a crossways path through the rows until I was close enough to listen in on their conversation. Crouching even lower, I kept pace, lengthened my breaths, and attuned my ears to their words.

"How long do we have?" asked my father.

"Two months? Perhaps three if we are fortunate," responded Malakhi. "Their movements will be fairly slow if my contacts in Harran are correct about their estimation of the army. They say Kushan has been preparing to come south since news of Othniel's victories reached him months ago, in the eventuality that Barsoum failed."

"He won't let Israel go without a fight," said my father. "Once he hears of the loss of Shechem and Shiloh he'll curse Barsoum's memory with every step toward us, but he *will* come."

My belly clenched tight as the images of waves after waves of iron chariots barreling toward us rose in my mind. We'd lost so many of our people the first time the full force of Kushan's army invaded, both to the sword and to slavery in Aram-Naharim. It could *not* happen again. Our nation would not survive.

"Do you agree with my course of action?" asked Malakhi, a hesitation in his voice that I'd never heard before.

"Why are you asking me, son? You've been the commander of this unit for over five years now and accomplished far more than I ever did in twenty-five."

"No. That is not the truth, Abba. Without you and your men, much ground would have been lost to the Amorites and other Canaanite tribes, even before Kushan set his sights on us."

My father sighed. "Perhaps, but the network you have created and the young men you've trained over these past years laid the groundwork for this fight. I'm convinced that without you and Eitan, Othniel's advances may have been far slower. We've reclaimed over half the territories now, and if we continue on this path, the rest will be back in the hands of our tribes soon."

Malakhi scoffed. "What Othniel has done over these past months has been nothing less than miraculous. If we've played any part, then I am glad for it, but it's Yahweh who has been winning this battle."

My father clapped Malakhi on the back. "I agree, but I believe he's been using my two sons along the way."

"And your daughter," said my brother, his affirmation making my stomach twist with nervous anticipation and my feet shuffle forward swiftly to catch the response. What did my father truly think of my time in Shechem?

Unfortunately his reply was only a murmur and I was left disappointed as the two parted ways, my father walking on toward the southeastern edge of the vineyard and Malakhi heading back the way they'd come. I dropped to the ground before he could see me, holding my breath until he'd gone far enough away before I peered through the thick vines.

"Tirzah," said my father, who was standing only five paces away, hands on his hips. I gasped at the surprise and then, face flushing, stood up to face him.

"Did you truly think that you could out-spy me?" he said, his mouth pressed in a line and his brows raised high.

"I—I wasn't—" I stammered.

"You weren't listening to your brother and me discuss the war?"

I shrugged, feeling like I was eleven again, getting caught in the act of snatching one of my favorite honey rolls behind my mother's back.

"Come here," he said, and I obeyed without question. To my surprise however, instead of chastising me further, he put his arm around my shoulders. The familiar gesture caused my heart to squeeze—both with gratitude and with guilt.

"Let's walk," he said, nudging me forward.

He led me to an imposing fig tree that stood on a bluff overlooking the Mishkan. Silently, we faced the valley, listening to the sounds of celebration floating on the breeze. Smoke rose from the courtyard of the Tent of Meeting, a renewed constant since the Arameans had left Shiloh. It seemed as if the priests were attempting to make up for the years they'd been restricted to only one daily sacrifice. But now a line of people, eager to give thanks to Yahweh, curled out the multicolored fabric gates and all the way down the side of the linen fences. After beholding the awe-inspiring beauty of the *shekinah* that had so terrified the Arameans when it had appeared over the Mishkan, the sky over Shiloh now seemed empty without it.

"This tree is your mother's favorite," said my father. "Has she told you that?"

I shook my head. My mother was so busy tending our family's needs that I'd rarely even seen her away from camp unless she was hefting water back and forth from the spring with the other women.

"She used to sit here to watch the sacrifices and listen to the services, before she threw off her veil."

I knew well the stories of my mother's self-imposed isolation, the pain and mockery she endured from others, and how the challenges she'd faced during the flight to Kedesh had unshackled her heart in many ways.

"I used to think that she was the most courageous woman I'd ever met, Tirzah. But I must say that you might have outdone your mother."

I gaped at him, astounded.

"She braved a long journey through dangerous enemy territory, lied to the king of Megiddo, and helped me drag a half-dead Yuval down the side of a mountain. And even more than that, she never shied away from accepting the responsibility for the mistake she'd made that landed her in the city of refuge." He turned to face me.

"But you, daughter. You went willingly into this fight. You could have stayed here with us, safe and secure. And yet you armed yourself with skills and knowledge for the purpose of battling against our oppressors. Malakhi has told me how little fear you showed. How determined you were. And how you made your case for service so compelling he could do nothing but agree. And the information you were able to collect and the way you used your skills to protect yourself, Odeleya, and Liyam—" He shook his head, as if unsure what to say. "I did not guess that you would have been capable of such things."

Blinking the moisture from my eyes, I cleared my throat of the tight emotion there. "I thought you were angry with me."

"Oh, I am angry," he said. "I am angry that you and Malakhi did it all behind my back and did not respect me enough to come to me."

I dropped my eyes, hating the disappointment in his direct gaze. "Forgive me, Abba."

"I would have never allowed you to go, out of fear for your safety. Even if you are a grown woman and were outside of my authority during your marriage, you are still my little girl."

"However . . ." He placed his fingers beneath my chin so I would face him. "I've had a few days since your return to consider the situation. To let my fury cool so I could think more clearly. Although I might not agree with how you went about it, and it makes me ill to think of you walking into such danger, it seems Yahweh used you for a greater purpose. Without you, the battle at Ramah might well have been lost."

"What do you mean?"

"Malakhi was able to waylay the kings of Moab and Edom based on your detailed description of their features and manner of travel, and he convinced them the vow from Kushan to return their lands was nothing but a lie. It was because of the missive you smuggled out of Shechem, complete with Barsoum's seal, that the kings returned to the east side of the Jordan and ordered their armies to return home, leaving the Aramean army to be crushed by ours."

I stared at him, stricken mute by the revelation that my time in Shechem, and my friends' deaths, had truly not been in vain, and that even my small efforts had made such an impact.

With a gentle smile, my father slipped his arm about my waist and dragged me close to him, pressing a kiss to my temple. "You did well, daughter."

Taking comfort in my abba's nearness and reveling in such affirmation after fearing that he would never forgive me for hiding the truth, I laid my head on his shoulder and looked out over the Mishkan again, conjuring up the swirling pillar of blue-and-white fire in my mind and marveling that Yahweh would deign to use me for anything, let alone to help win a battle.

We stood silently on the bluff until a commotion drew our attention to the path just below us that led from the valley floor up to my grandfather's house. A small group of men were climbing the hill, some outfitted in armor.

"Ah," said my father. "It seems as though Othniel has arrived to meet with Malakhi."

Slipping out of his hold, I stepped forward, stretching to watch the line of men ascending the path. When a head of familiar red hair came into sight around the last bend, my stomach flipped with recognition. Without another thought, I left my father to trail behind me, my sandals flying for camp. I'd not moved this fast since the day I'd chased Malakhi and his men through the woods, but Liyam was alive, and the relief flooding my bones gave me wings.

TWENTY-FOUR

There was such a crowd of curious people gathered around Liyam and the others that I decided my own welcome, and my many questions, would have to keep for later. I stood off to the side, content for now to take in the sight of him, unharmed.

However, Odeleya had no such restraint. Having just arrived with my two nieces, she called out his name and then plowed through the crowd and directly into him, her skinny arms wrapping about his waist.

"You are alive!" she said, pressing her face to his torso. "We were so worried!"

Liyam's eyes went wide, both palms splayed to the side in shock at the girl's exuberant greeting. They'd only interacted a few times in Shechem, so her reaction was a surprise to me as well, but as I'd discovered, it took little for Odeleya to latch herself to anyone who showed her even a sliver of kindness.

His body stiff, Liyam patted her shoulder while the men around him smirked at the sight of Odeleya's welcome. Then his gaze lifted, moving over the crowd until he caught sight of me. Our eyes locked, then held for at least four breaths. Thrown by the flicker of something warm under my ribs and the surprising brush of envy that I could not receive him with the same abandon as Odeleya, I composed a tight smile and nodded my head before willfully severing the eye contact and surveying the rest of their group.

Liyam was no longer the only red-haired warrior in our camp. Five others stood nearby, all looking so similar that they had to be related in some way. Once Odeleya released her grip on him and flounced back to her new friends, a few nudging elbows and covert comments from the men around him confirmed my suspicions. *Brothers*, I decided, since their familiar and teasing way with each other was identical to Malakhi and Eitan's. However, Liyam remained solemn as he endured the ribbing, as if he barely noticed their jests.

Malakhi was conversing with an older man whose bearing and composed expression immediately proved his authority. This must be the famed Othniel, the man undoubtedly chosen by Yahweh to lead this offensive against our oppressors. A sense of reverence came over me, for I had the distinct sense that the victories won by this seasoned warrior would be elaborated upon around fires for generations to come. And somehow Yahweh had allowed *me* to play a very small role in those stories.

Caught up in the sight of Othniel talking with my brothers and my father ten paces away, I nearly cried out when a large palm connected with my elbow. Heart racing, I looked up to find Liyam standing beside me, his eyes also on his leader.

"So," he said, without turning his head my way, "you and the girl arrived safely."

"We did. The Levites sent two of their men to escort us back. We came into Shiloh just after dawn."

He nodded. "I'm glad to hear it."

His manner was stilted and his tone brusque, as if we'd not spent nearly three weeks sharing the same room and working together. I felt my hackles rise at his detached manner, especially after what we'd been through that last night in Shechem.

"Barsoum is dead," he said. "I thought you'd like to know."

"Good," I replied, as the sharp memory of the worst of the man's crimes pricked at my heart. "Then justice has been served for my friends."

"Agreed."

"Is this she?" came a voice in front of us, before I could ask more of what had transpired since I'd fled Shechem.

I jerked my attention away from Liyam to find none other than Othniel standing before me.

"Yes. This is Tirzah," said Liyam.

Othniel studied my face. "I am told that your assistance has been invaluable."

Overwhelmed with equal measures pride and embarrassment at being praised in front of everyone, my cheeks went hot. "It was an honor to serve my people."

"Indeed," he said, his deep brown eyes betraying nothing of his thoughts, before looking at Liyam. "We have much to discuss. Malakhi has arranged a meal and a place for us to speak privately. We'll need a full accounting of everything that happened during your time in Shechem."

Liyam nodded wordlessly and then followed Othniel as he made his way back to my brother. I released the breath I'd been holding, but then was startled when Othniel called out my name.

"You too, young woman," he said, with a gesture of invitation. "We'll need your report as well."

Profoundly shocked by the summons, and with my heart thudding so hard I could feel the pulse of it down to my fingers and toes, I feigned calm and followed the men into my mother and father's tent to partake of a meal and a debriefing with the high commander of Israel's joint armies.

My mother entered the tent, carrying a juglet of wine and two baskets of steaming flatbread. Her eyes darted to where I sat beside Eitan, and the satisfied little smile on her lips made my chest squeeze. I'd been a bit intimidated to share a meal with Othniel, but her silent encouragement helped me sit taller on my cushion as she placed one overflowing basket at each end of the blanket before us.

Sofea and Rivkah entered as soon as my mother slipped out, bringing with them a wide variety of dishes for us to share. As the two of them laid out the colorful spread of stews, dips, and salads, Sofea glanced up at me and winked one of her brilliant blue eyes, making me press my lips tightly together with amusement. Rivkah did not even bother masking the delighted grin she tossed over her shoulder as the two women ducked out of the tent. She'd been the only other person, besides my brothers, to know of my mission from the start, since she'd been tasked with teaching me to speak the Arameans' odd tongue with proficiency and to read the strange slashing marks and shapes that made up their written language. Her affirmations throughout my training had bolstered me time and time again whenever I'd felt my courage flailing during the lead-up to my departure for Shechem.

The approval of these three women I so admired meant just as much as that of their husbands and brought a swell of emotion to my throat that I was forced to press down with a healthy scoop of herb-laden yogurt atop a portion of warm bread.

"Now," said Othniel, after a hearty swig of my grandfather's well-aged wine, "tell me of the Cloud. We were told that it arose over the Mishkan just as our battle at Ramah began, but I'd like to hear of it from eyewitnesses."

Eitan cleared his throat. "It happened just after the daily sacrifice," he said. "As you know, the Arameans only allowed the one in an attempt to placate the priests while tamping down the people's fervor.

"When the Cloud flared up, high over the Tent of Meeting," Eitan continued, "it was a shock, but knowing the stories from the wilderness, all the priests immediately fell on their faces before the column of blue-white light that was sparking bolts of fire. The Arameans, however, did not. Three of those who'd been overseeing the small crowd of Hebrews near the courtyard gates were struck dead by the fearsome sight, and the rest fled in terror. Within only two hours of the Cloud's appearance, every Aramean soldier had evacuated Shiloh, leaving behind the majority of their belongings, including a valuable cache of weapons."

I'd seen Eitan's thrilled expression when he returned from surveying the haul and surmised that it was no small amount of weapons they'd be doling out to our men.

"Somehow word of what transpired here must have made it to the Aramean ranks," said Othniel. "Because within hours of their initial assault, many of them began to retreat unexpectedly. Mass confusion broke out, and we were able to break through their infantry with surprising ease. Those taken captive confirmed our suspicions when they said rumors that the Hebrew god who destroyed Egypt had now set his sights on them. They feared the Cloud would leave its place in Shiloh and devour them."

"That must have been a sight to behold," said my father.

"That it was," replied Othniel. "But I still would rather have seen the Cloud with my own eyes. Who knows when, or if, it will again appear."

Then the high commander gestured to me with his wine cup. "I'd like to hear from you, Tirzah. You were in Shechem for how long?"

"A little over two months."

"Indeed. Start from the beginning, then. Tell me everything you gleaned from your time there."

I took a deep breath, willing my voice not to waver, and then told them of how I'd procured my position in the household, detailed each significant conversation I'd overheard during my time there, shared every bit of knowledge I had on the way their military was organized, and then explained how I'd ultimately escaped.

Othniel listened to my story without a word. At its conclusion, he took a few long, silent moments to ponder, his sagacious eyes still pinned to me.

"And the Levites?" he finally asked.

I blinked wordlessly at the odd question.

"I have spoken with one of them, a man named Yitzak. He lays the credit at your feet for a transformation within the Hebrew camp."

A flush rose on my cheeks. "What happened with the Levites was conviction by Yahweh, not because of me."

"That is not what I was told," said Othniel.

The eyes of all the men inside the tent were trained on me, curious looks on all their bearded faces.

"Daughter," said my father, "tell us what transpired with the Levites."

I dragged in a quick breath to brace myself. "I had a chance encounter with a group of Levites near the altar of Yehoshua on Har Ebal. I was frustrated that they'd been worshipping Yahweh only in secret together and failing to remind the people of the promises of the Covenant. Apparently, they took my unsolicited words to heart."

"That they did," said Othniel, now addressing the rest of the group. "Yitzak shared with me how Tirzah's courageous admonition inspired them to throw off the fear they'd been clinging to, and as a result, they revived worship in the camp, diligently spread word of our victories in the southern territories, and began regular retellings of the miraculous histories of our forefathers." He turned his knowing gaze back to me. "And I must say, young woman, after hearing all that transpired under Aramean rule in that city over the years, I expected a completely different reception than I encountered upon entering the Shechem valley."

"What happened?" I asked, my mouth going dry.

"The Levites had taken to keeping watch atop Ebal, praying, asking Yahweh for direction," said Othniel. "And when they beheld the otherworldly Cloud high in the air above Shiloh, they took it as a sign. Within an hour they'd lit a fire inside the altar. You see, they'd been whispering among the people that a signal would appear to alert them when it was time to throw off their chains and arise."

The night Odeleya and I had fled Shechem, Yitzak had spoken of a future fire to burn on the altar, but I'd not guessed his true meaning.

"Those who were able," Othniel continued, "overcame the guards around the camp, using the few weapons they'd had buried beneath tents, or tools from their labors, or even just sticks and stones. The rest bent their knees to pray, a loud chorus of supplications going up to the One Who Hears from the mouths of women and children. By the time we arrived in Shechem, the soldiers had all taken refuge within the walls, which were encircled by hundreds of the men they'd forced into labor for so many years. It was easy work to break through the gates and deal with those who hadn't already fled the area, in no small part because of you."

Was Othniel truly attributing Shechem's easy fall to my impetuous chastisement of the Levites? I looked to Liyam for clarity, but he merely lifted his shoulder to indicate that he agreed with the assessment.

I opened my mouth twice before closing it again, unsure how to respond.

"Well," said my father, his expression full of warmth and pride, "it seems that while you may have gleaned a few skills from your brothers and me, you also inherited your mother's boldness, daughter."

Overcome and blinking hard against the burn of tears, I could do nothing but place my palm on my heart and dip my chin in silent gratitude for such an honoring comparison. My mother was known far and wide for her declarations of wisdom and her bold proclamation of Torah promises to all who would listen.

Othniel then asked Liyam to inform Malakhi of how he'd managed to escape. Hearing how Barsoum had met his end was as satisfying as it was disturbing, but the man had been evil, with an ocean of Hebrew blood on his hands, and he deserved justice.

As I listened to him speak, I was struck by the deep vein of honor in Liyam. I'd sensed it from almost the beginning, but somehow I also perceived a certain brokenness in him. Late at night, during those weeks, we'd spoken of little more than the mission and whatever information we'd gathered during the day, since he avoided any personal questions by claiming exhaustion, but I would never forget the hollow way he'd spoken of his family being gone, as if snatched away by a shadowy hand.

Especially after seeing him with his brothers, who laughed and jested with such abandon, I could not help but wonder who Liyam truly was, what had happened to strip the joy from his eyes, and why he'd come to Shiloh in the first place. I did not know how long he would remain with us, but I determined to speak with him before he moved on with the army. If I could not shake loose some of that tightly held guardedness—and I would make my most valiant attempt—at least I could offer my sincere gratitude for his help in Shechem.

"Now, Malakhi," said Othniel, once Liyam had finished his report, "tell me what your men have seen in the north."

"Kushan will soon be on the move toward us," Malakhi responded. "If he is not already. My contacts in Harran gauge his army to be in the tens of thousands. Not nearly what it was before, when he was allied with the Hittites, but enough to overcome us if we are not wise in our strategy."

"He has no intention of giving in," said Othniel. "This fight is far from over, but Yahweh will be victorious, of that I have no doubt. We will incorporate some of the lessons we've learned and prepare the people." His eyes flickered to me for a moment. "When Kushan arrives, he won't find an assembly of cowering slaves eager to give him the fruits of our land in tribute, but a nation of warriors established beneath the banner of the Covenant."

Fervor built in my chest as he spoke, along with the conviction that his words were inspired by Yahweh himself.

"Do I have your support in this war? No matter the cost? No matter the length?" asked Othniel, his commanding gaze traveling over the group of us. For so long Malakhi and Eitan had been operating on their own, and the question of whether they would accept Othniel's authority was a valid one.

"Of course," replied Malakhi. "We stand alongside our brethren and will do anything we can to further your progress."

The men all nodded their heads, with the exception of Liyam, whose arms were crossed and whose eyes were trained on the empty cup in front of him. He shifted his weight, jaw working back and forth. I had no idea why he would not be the first to volunteer, especially after his victory over Barsoum. I'd not seen even the slightest whisper of fear in the man, so why did he now look as though he'd rather be anywhere else but here?

TWENTY-FIVE

Liyam

I could not answer Othniel's question with any degree of certainty. Playing a role in the reclamation of Shechem had been exhilarating, and the fact that I'd ended Barsoum's bloody reign over the city by my own hand was certainly satisfying, but Nadina's killer still walked free. And if I took my eyes from my goal, even to fight alongside my brothers, then I doubted the Moabite would ever be subject to justice. I loved my people and my God, but I had made a vow in my daughter's memory that I must fulfill.

I'd hoped no one had noticed my failure to answer, but Tirzah's gaze snagged on me, her lifted brows questioning my lack of response. Unsettled, I looked away, but I could not help remembering the way my chest had squeezed with anticipation as I'd searched the crowd for her upon our arrival, nor the delighted relief in her eyes when we'd locked gazes, as if she'd been counting the hours since we'd parted ways. I shook off that foolish thought and determinedly turned my attention back to the delicious food set before me.

When the meal was finished, Othniel asked Darek to take him to

Tirzah's grandfather and grandmother, eager to thank them for their hospitality and to pay his respects to a man who'd fought alongside his uncle Calev during the war for Canaan.

"Liyam," said Malakhi, as the rest of us stood to take our own leave. "If you have a moment to spare, I have something I must discuss with you."

"Of course," I said, my tone not betraying the rush of anticipation in my limbs. I could tell by his reluctant tone of voice that he had news of the one-eyed trader.

Tirzah slipped out of the tent behind Eitan, but not before she glanced back over her shoulder. During her speech to Othniel, I'd been absorbed in listening to her talk, watching the skillful hands that had stolen missives and plunged a knife into a man's throat for my sake flutter about as she described all that she'd seen and done. How Barsoum and the others had overlooked her time and again I would never understand. Her strength and vibrancy were unmistakable.

As if she could hear my thoughts about her, her brown eyes sparkled as she gave me an encouraging smile and followed her oldest brother out into the sun.

"I must begin," Malakhi said, "by offering my most heartfelt gratitude for keeping my sister safe in that city. I knew you were the right man to send, but I confess I laid awake many nights wondering if I should not have just gone myself. Yet not only did you protect Tirzah, you protected our intelligence and gave that Aramean commander a fitting end. And for that I am in your debt three times over."

"The only debt between us is the information I hope you already have in your possession. The rest I did for the good of my people and for the sake of justice."

"As it should be." He nodded, his silver eyes solemn. "You have served the tribes of Israel well, my friend."

Then he cleared his throat.

"And as I promised, I do have some news for you. I sent a number of messages throughout our network. But until last week nothing credible had been reported. Then one of the men I recently sent to Beit She'an sent word that he'd seen the man there."

My pulse sped, and I fought hard against the urge to plow out of the tent and head directly north to the enemy stronghold. "How long ago?"

"Six weeks or so. He set up a market stall, trading wares he'd brought down from Damascus."

So the trader had been far to the north all this time, and I'd wasted weeks wandering Moabite and Edomite territory, dragging my cousin along with me, for nothing.

"He is still there?" I pressed, hope flowing through my body in a mighty rush.

Malakhi's brows furrowed. "No, I'm sorry. He remained for around ten days and then left on the northbound road."

The rush of hope hardened into sharp disappointment. Beit She'an was within a day's walk of here. I should have refused Malakhi's offer and continued north as I'd planned. I could have had that monster in my grasp, had I not taken the time to traipse off to Shechem in pursuit of a reckless woman.

And yet even as that uncharitable thought passed through my mind, I cringed at my callousness. Tirzah might have been killed, or worse, had I not gone to find her, and that outcome was an unacceptable one. I did not regret my decision, only that I'd missed my chance to find my quarry in the meantime.

"There are many fishing villages alongside the Kinneret and all around the region," said Malakhi. "If he's going village to village in that area he could be there for months. With the upheaval of late, I doubt he would go farther north than Laish, but there are a multitude of small hamlets and farms he could stop at along the way."

"Then I'll leave in the morning," I said. "I'll scour every one between here and Laish if I have to."

"You won't be going on with Othniel, then?" he asked, and the disappointment in his tone caused a surprising pang of regret. But regardless of my respect for Tirzah's brother, I would not change my course.

"Thank you for your help," I said. "Now that I know he's moved north, I can narrow my search."

"You held to your part of the bargain; I only fulfilled mine."

I nodded acknowledgment that our exchange was complete.

"Now . . ." He suddenly clapped a hand to my shoulder, his demeanor softening. "Tell me, my friend. Exactly how much grief did my sister give you when you showed up in Shechem?"

Allowing a chuckle, I shook my head. "I'll say one thing. After watching her wield those knives on that Aramean, I am certainly glad that I finally convinced her who I was that first night, because I was likely only a few moments away from being unmanned."

Malakhi tipped his head back and laughed until his eyes glimmered with mirth. "Ah, Tirzah. There's no one quite like my youngest sister. We will likely rue the day we taught her how to bring down a man twice her size."

"Perhaps so, but there are not many men who would have walked into that household alone," I replied. "Nor insisted on staying until the task was complete after what happened to your men."

"Agreed."

"Truthfully, watching her spin a veil of silent lies to shield herself and hide in plain sight was one of the most fascinating things I've ever seen. She was a meek servant during the day, all subservience and silent feet, and a stern-faced warrior facing off with me and stealing my bed at night. She is like no other woman I've ever met."

Malakhi tilted his head to the side, searching my face with those cool gray eyes, his pointed scrutiny making me realize that I'd given away too much with such a statement.

I shifted my stance and cleared my throat. "I'd best return to my brothers. We have much to discuss." I had a difficult conversation ahead of me; my own brothers likely assumed I would be moving on with them, and I was certain they would have much to say about my decision.

"Of course," he said. "I won't keep you any longer. I need to talk over plans with Othniel anyhow. But thank you, again, for bringing her back to us. She is irreplaceable."

That she is.

I nodded, tight-lipped, and left the tent, then kept my head down as I moved past Ishai and Ora's house and headed for the woods. I needed a quiet place to collect my thoughts before informing my brothers that I would be parting ways with them, again.

However, I'd not gone far when a scream tore through the air, jolting me from my tumultuous thoughts. I tipped my ear to the side, searching for the origin of the sound through the dense tree line above the vineyard. Another loud cry, distinctly childlike, followed that one. My blood stilled as more youthful shouts and cries went up. Was it a wild animal? A stray Aramean? What horrors were these children facing?

I broke into a run, dashing through the woods, my skin whipped by needles, leaves, and twigs as I pressed toward the commotion with my dagger in hand.

Crashing into a clearing, I stumbled to a halt, half-blinded by the bright sunlight and stunned by the sight before me.

At least fifteen children were gathered at the edge of the clearing, jumping up and down in glee as Tirzah whipped a sling back and forth through the air, working up speed with every looping pass. Then she leaned forward and let the stone fly. Across the clearing a jar shattered, pieces of pottery flying in every direction, and Tirzah's audience burst into screams and whistles.

"I told you!" shouted one boy of about thirteen years—Malakhi's oldest son, if I was not mistaken. "Doda Tirzah is the best!"

"I could do that," said one of the younger boys, his face a mass of freckles just like Eitan's. "My abba is the one who taught her in the first place, and he taught me."

Tirzah turned toward her audience with a wide grin, her curls swirling about her shoulders as she clapped for herself, the sunlight illuminating her effortless beauty and setting hints of copper in her dark hair aflame.

A knot of something indefinable caught in my throat, and I stepped backward, hoping that my presence had gone unnoticed. But true to form, Tirzah's keen eyes missed nothing. Her smile grew impossibly wider, and she crossed the space between us like a bird of prey swooping in.

"Spying?" she said, her eyes shimmering with amusement.

I lifted a brow at her tease. "No. I heard shrieking and thought someone was being mauled by a lion."

"Ah," she said, her tone disbelieving as she held my gaze. I'd noticed her brown eyes before now, but in the direct sunlight they reminded me of pools of rich date honey, sweet and warm. And I knew if I sank into them I'd never be free of their pull.

I cleared my throat and looked toward the splintered pot, needing a distraction. "You're fairly skilled with a sling."

"Fairly skilled?" She narrowed those lovely eyes, plainly offended.

"I've only witnessed the one shot, but it was impressive."

"Hmm." Her lips pressed together. "For a woman, you mean."

She gave me no chance to respond, whipping out an immediate challenge. "You can do better, I suppose?"

I lifted my palms. "I did not say that."

"It was implied. But if you'd rather not embarrass yourself in front of the children . . ." She let the provocation hover, lifting her brows as she glanced over at the crowd of onlookers. Fifteen sets of young eyes were on me now, full of anticipation for a contest between their doda and me, but one enticing set of brown ones looked at me with wicked satisfaction, fully assured that her challenge would not go unanswered. She would only mock me if I walked away now.

"All right. I'll shoot."

A chorus of shouts went up from the children, and a couple of them raced to arrange two broken pots at the far end of the clearing, even farther than the remains of the one Tirzah had destroyed.

One of the freckled boys handed over his own sling. "My brother is right, you know. Our abba is the best slinger around, and he taught her everything he knows. You haven't a chance."

A dormant spark of competitiveness rose inside me at his dismissive tone. "Perhaps your abba has never gone up against me."

A few of the children had rushed to Tirzah's side, proudly lifting stones they'd searched out to load into her sling. Each child received a kiss of gratitude, even the youngest, whose rock was as big as her palm. Tirzah crouched before the little girl and pressed her lips to her forehead. With such shimmering golden-brown curls and big blue eyes, this child must belong to Eitan and his foreign bride.

"Thank you, my sweet Lunah," she said, the tone of her voice as soft and soothing as a lullaby. "I want to save this one for my special collection. It's too pretty to throw. Can I do that?"

The little one beamed under the attention and nodded her tiny chin. A sharp pain struck the center of my chest, stealing the breath from my lungs at a vision of Nadina gazing up at me with the same adoration. But somehow, in this sunlit meadow, with youthful chatter and hopeful smiles all around me, I was able to tamp down my instinct to flee from the image and instead let the memory of my daughter's precious face remain. I could no longer remember the exact melody of her laughter, but I vowed in that moment to dwell on the image of her smile daily, so it would never fade. I would not let the Moabite steal that from me too.

With a wink, Tirzah stood and drew her own sling from her belt. "Shall we?"

Taking our places behind a toe-drawn line in the dirt, we readied our weapons as Tirzah ordered the children back to the tree line. I'd been slinging since I was as small as Lunah and had lobbed many a stone at the Arameans in battle, both eight years ago and at Hebron, so I doubted this competition would last very long.

Tirzah gestured for me to go first, so I stepped forward, whipped the sling through the air a few times as I aimed carefully, and then let my missile fly. The jar popped into the air for a brief moment and then landed on its side. It was not the impressive display Tirzah's earlier shot had been, but satisfying nonetheless.

Although undoubtedly biased against the wild-haired stranger trying to best their aunt, the children cheered for me anyhow, and I found myself bowing slightly in acknowledgment of their exuberant accolades.

Tirzah reached up to pat me on the shoulder, sending a small jolt of awareness through me. "Well done, my friend. You're fairly skilled with a sling."

With that little dig, she spun away to line up her shot. The second was even more violent than the first, splinters of pottery exploding into a shower and one large piece slamming into a nearby tree with a thump.

My eyes went wide at the damage. There was no way Tirzah had the same amount of strength in her arm as me, but somehow she'd managed to get up enough speed that my brawn meant nothing.

"More! More!" shouted all the children, shrieking again as if a wildcat were on the loose.

Helpless against their enthusiasm and the goading gleam in Tirzah's eyes, I found myself once again at the line, my sling whizzing through the air, with a touch more heft this time. My target cooperated this round, the pot spinning into the sky with an explosion of shards. I barely squelched the grin that pressed to the surface as I turned to Tirzah. "Your turn. Unless, of course, you yield."

Narrowing her eyes, she turned her back on me as she moved into position. Her third pot shuddered and broke into two, but did not give quite the show the first ones had. The children still went wild at her successful shot, crowding us and demanding one more round.

"One more," she said, running her fingers absently through Lunah's golden curls. "Liyam likely has far more important things to do than play with us."

Nearly everything about Tirzah in Shiloh was the opposite of what I'd witnessed in Shechem. There she'd been in tight control at all times, focused on her mission, and always at the ready. She'd even slept perfectly still on the bed she'd stolen from me, hands by her sides, as if prepared to spring to life with those wicked knives even in sleep. Here she was no less a force of nature, full of brash confidence and mettle, but seeing her interact with these children who obviously adored her, her expression relaxed, her laughter bright and without restraint, she was beyond fascinating, and my eyes were increasingly reluctant to pull away.

She shooed the children back to their place, and we waited while the two oldest boys reset the pots, this time atop a fallen tree even farther away. I wasn't sure if I'd ever hit a target from such a distance before, since in the chaos of battle one rarely knew if shots successfully connected with their marks.

"You seem a little uncertain, my friend," said my smug opponent, dangling her sling back and forth by her side as her lips curled slightly. "Shall we forfeit this round? I'd say we are about even."

I stalked so close that I could see the narrow band of blue that encircled her brown irises, all restraint somehow turned to ash by that condescending little smile, and reached for her hand. Lifting it by the wrist, I slid my finger into the curve of her palm and plucked one of her remaining stones from the very center, letting my skin brush against hers in a slow retreat.

"You first this time," I rasped, continuing to hold her gaze captive as I dropped her hand. Then I turned my back and returned to my place, loudly repeating my insistence that she take her shot before me. The children heartily agreed, their excited shouts overriding her stuttering arguments.

Even as she whipped the sling through the air I knew my tactic had worked. Her missile hit the lip of the jar but only managed to tip it backward with a pathetic wobble before it keeled over. She scowled and refused to look my way.

With a quiet chuckle I took my place at the line, taking my time in surveying my target before I looped the sling around to the left, the right, and then back again. As the weapon whistled through the air I concentrated on its weight and balance and gave it at least four more complete passes before finally sending my pilfered stone toward its final, gloriously explosive destination.

Victory humming in my bones, I turned to face Tirzah, incapable of restraining the grin that spread across my face. Locking gazes with the woman who'd been a stranger a few weeks ago, but who now occupied more than her fair share of my thoughts, I found myself wavering on my decision to leave tomorrow. I now knew which direction the trader was headed. Surely an extra day or two here in Shiloh would not matter so much, would it?

TWENTY-SIX

Tirzah

As my traitorous nieces and nephews screamed appreciation for my opponent's winning shot, Liyam turned to me with a triumphant grin that reached into my chest and yanked the breath from my lungs.

The smiles he'd displayed in Shechem had been for Barsoum's benefit, tinged with sarcasm or hints of malice, but this one was unencumbered by forethought, wide, and generous. Tiny lines fanned from his jewel-like eyes, proving that, like his brothers, Liyam knew how to laugh, and often.

I resolved to hear that sound soon or die trying.

Surrounded by all the children now, Liyam accepted his accolades and even answered a few of their questions about his use of a sling during battle, but that spectacular smile had eroded, leaving only his usual solemn expression behind.

"All right," I said. "Liyam has endured enough interrogation for now. It's time for you all to return to camp. There are chores to be completed."

Protests and groans abounded, but they obeyed. My nephew Amit, who looked so much like my brother Gidal that it still brought tears to my eyes, carried little Lunah on his hip as they walked toward home. With her chin on Amit's shoulder and her golden curls shimmering in the sunlight, Lunah lifted a little palm to wave good-bye with a grin, a small gap showing where she'd just lost her first tooth.

I waited until the children were entirely out of sight before I turned to Liyam, a hundred questions about the last weeks he spent in Shechem on my lips and wondering how I might provoke another of those delicious smiles. But his eyes were on the place where the children had disappeared into the trees, an expression of unadulterated grief on his face.

I said his name in a gentle tone, but he did not respond, just kept his gaze pinned to the tree line as if his mind had moved far beyond it.

Stepping closer, I wrapped my hand around his forearm. "Liyam," I repeated.

He looked down but seemed to be seeing straight through me. So I waited until the shadows cleared from the blue-green depths, giving him time to find himself again.

He cleared his throat and stepped back, pulling his arm from my grasp with a frown, as if confused how I came to be standing so close to him. Although I ached to understand what had just gone on inside of his head, I offered an alternative for his sake.

"Tell me what happened after I left Shechem," I asked. "How did you convince Barsoum not to hang you from the ramparts?"

The stiff set of his shoulders softened. "I kept the body hidden in the alleyway until dawn, to give you time to get out of the valley, then dragged it back to the villa. When Barsoum saw the corpse, he flew into a rage, demanding to know how his second-in-command could have come to such an end."

I was grateful for the warm sunlight across my shoulders because the words chilled my bones. I felt no remorse for attacking the man, because he would have slaughtered Liyam had I hesitated, and then would have inflicted himself on me, but I would never forget the details of that night. The terror. The terrible silence. The blood.

"I told him that I'd returned to the barracks just to catch a glimpse of him sneaking off with *my* prize."

"You suggested that Khaled and I had been . . . ?"

"Indeed. It offered an excuse for your absence, since my story was that I'd intercepted the two of you fleeing the city together, and sometime during our bloody skirmish, you'd disappeared into the night."

"And Barsoum believed this?"

"Not at first, but when the body was searched for evidence and the missive discovered tucked into his leather wristband, the commander's quick defense of Khaled became furious curses against a man he'd trusted for years."

I could imagine the scene would have been quite a spectacle, as Barsoum was known for his bellowing rages. "So he did not think I was involved in the conspiracy?"

"It was suggested, but I mocked the idea, and Barsoum easily fell for the ruse."

I scoffed. "He'd never have considered that a woman could best him anyhow."

"Very true," he said, then finally met my gaze with piercing intensity. "But best him you did."

"What did he do after you convinced him of Khaled's duplicity?" I asked, ignoring the pang of warmth his affirmation sparked.

"He was so grateful for my *faithful* service that he offered me another reward."

Blood drained from my head into my feet. I swallowed against the tightness that had gripped my throat. "Another woman?"

Liyam peered at me, his lips quirking. "There were women offered, yes."

I glanced away, doing my best to not spit on his feet and dash from the clearing. "I suppose it would have been considered suspect if you hadn't accepted."

"I did not say I accepted."

I jerked my head back to look up at him in surprise. "Oh?"

Although his mouth remained still, Liyam's eyes were bright as he studied my face. "I told Barsoum I'd already chosen the only prize I wanted and that I had no desire for another after such betrayal."

Giddy relief filled the hollow of my chest, a ridiculous reaction since not only was this man brimming with secrets and safely ensconced behind layers and layers of walls, he would be leaving with the army soon. And once this war was over, he would undoubtedly return to his home far to the south. I'd never see him again.

"And he believed this excuse?" I asked, willing my voice to remain steady.

"Thinking that he'd also just been betrayed by a man he counted as friend, he was remarkably understanding, although he told me I was welcome to any of his collection of women if I changed my mind."

A flat noise of annoyance rose in the back of my throat, but Liyam either did not hear it or chose to ignore it.

"But that was not the reward I was referring to," he continued. "He placed me and my unit in charge of protecting his household, since he was worried that Khaled was not the only traitor in his ranks. He decided that my actions were assurance that I would protect him with my life."

"For a man touted as such a genius in the war eight years ago, that was a remarkably foolhardy decision."

"True. Even up until the moment I drew my sword to gut him he thought me thoroughly loyal. I think his time in Shechem caused him to become complacent. He reveled in the adulation and excess his favor with the king offered, and as a result his once-sharp wits degenerated over the years. The man you and I met was not the keen strategist and brilliant warrior we lost the Land to, that is for certain."

"And does Malakhi have a new assignment for you?"

Liyam furrowed his brow.

"Your talk in the tent?" I prompted. "I assumed you would go on with Othniel's army, but I wondered if Malakhi had given you a special task."

His jaw moved back and forth, as if he were grinding his teeth, a pensive expression on his face. The faint question of what Liyam might look like if he tamed the flaming beard that covered half of his face floated through my mind as he hesitated.

"No . . ." he said finally. "He was fulfilling his part of our bargain."

"Which was?"

"I retrieved you from Shechem, and he aided with my search."

"And what are you searching for?"

"A killer," he said, the word laden with bitterness.

A frisson of unease worked its way up my spine. "You were searching for a killer in Shiloh?"

"He is a Moabite trader who travels throughout the Hebrew territories. I followed his path here. Knowing your grandfather has many connections in this region, I sought his help."

"And did he know of him?"

He shook his head. "No one had seem him, at least not recently. But then word came that Sheth and Hanael had been captured."

"And Malakhi talked you into retrieving me."

"Yes. We made a bargain. I went to Shechem in exchange for his help finding the trader."

"And he has now fulfilled his end?"

"He has."

"But why are you looking for a killer, Liyam?" I asked, wishing I hadn't already guessed the answer. "What would cause you to pursue a man so far?"

"Because he murdered my little girl."

The bleak words slammed into me like a flash flood. My hand flew to my mouth, pressing back the urge to cry out. I'd known that he lost his family and sensed the current of grief beneath his gruff exterior. I'd thought that perhaps illness had swept them into the olam ha'ba, but to lose a daughter by someone's hand? No wonder he'd been so uncomfortable around the children, and why having Lunah wave her tiny fingers at him made it seem as though he'd been gutted by an iron spear. Something in her expression must have sparked a memory. It was *his* daughter he'd been seeing in his mind.

"Oh, Liyam—"

He ignored my pained response. "Your brother fulfilled his part of the bargain. I now have a clearer idea of where the man might be."

"And when you find him?"

He stared at me, his blank expression making the answer clear. I wished that I did not have to ask more, but knew I must.

"How did she die?"

"It does not matter."

"Of course it does."

Again his strong jaw worked back and forth, his sharply outlined cheekbones becoming even more angular as a dark shadow descended over his features.

"He drove his team and wagon over the top of her."

"No. . ." I expelled a huff of sorrow, my eyes stinging. "What a horrific accident."

"It was no accident," he sneered. "He did not even slow as she was trampled, just continued on the road, full speed."

"But you don't know—"

"What I know," he barked out, "is that my seven-year-old daughter, my only child, is dead. A man killed her, and he will be brought to justice by my hand, as is my right as her next of kin."

I spoke the truth of it, even as my knees wobbled. "You are a Blood Avenger."

"I am," he said, without hesitation, his crossed arms and resolute expression daring me to argue.

I accepted the challenge. "And you know about my mother? About the history of my family?"

"I do."

I took a step toward him, determined that he hear me. "Then you know what a blood feud did to our clan. How it destroyed the love between my father and uncle. How Eitan was nearly killed by Raviv because of the depth of his bitterness over a childhood mistake."

"The situations are not the same."

"Perhaps not, but if you pursue this man, if you murder him in retribution, it will destroy you, Liyam." I placed my hand on his forearm, where the muscle twitched beneath my palm. "The man deserves justice, I grant you that. But let the elders—"

His beautiful blue-green eyes were almost black with anger, and he looked every inch the warrior he was as he loomed over me.

"I will not wait for this war to be over and our laws back in place, Tirzah. I've heard this all before. From my brothers, my parents, your family; but I will not change my mind. My daughter's blood calls for justice, and that is what I will give her."

"Then you will lose your soul," I whispered, taking another step closer and placing my other hand on his arm. Compelled as I was to make him understand the gravity of my words, I also wished I could throw my arms around him and absorb some of the pain I now knew he carried. "Just like my uncle."

His eyes were on my face, then my lips, a flare of emotion glowing in them for a brief moment. But then, just as quickly, it was gone.

"I already did," he said, the words so quiet I barely heard them. "There's nothing left."

"Tirzah. Liyam."

Both of us startled at the sound of our names called from the tree line, our heads jerking toward the place where Malakhi had appeared. Flushing as I realized just how close Liyam and I had gotten as we'd argued, I dropped my hold on him and tripped back a couple of steps.

As my brother approached, his gaze moved back and forth between the two of us, and I wondered whether he would chastise us for being in this clearing alone.

But instead he merely met us in the center, a look of determination in his storm-gray eyes, and without preamble said, "I have a proposition for the two of you."

TWENTY-SEVEN

"Othniel has returned to Shechem, where he will be staging the remainder of this offensive," said Malakhi. "But before he left, he asked that I put together a team of spies with the goal of accomplishing what you did in Shechem."

"Uncovering military secrets?" I asked.

"If possible, then yes. We will need all the fresh knowledge we can gather before Kushan's army crosses the Jordan. But even more importantly, we need to encourage underground support and to revive the spirits of the people. Othniel firmly believes that what you did with the Levites must be repeated throughout the rest of the territories. There are Hebrews in and around all of the remaining strongholds on this side of the river: Megiddo, Beit She'an, Merom, Laish, and Kedesh."

My pulse skipped a beat. "You are sending spies into Kedesh?"

"I am." Malakhi's silver eyes glimmered. "I need a team to infiltrate the city that can not only quietly recruit and train Hebrews willing to rebel against our captors, but also would be willing to seek out remaining Levites, of whom we think there are still a good number in the area, and call them to their duty. If the people of Yahweh rise up and remember who they are—and who he is—nothing will stop our armies from being victorious over the Arameans this time. Nothing."

A strong sense of overwhelming fervor gripped me, just as it had on the mountain with the Levites and in the tent with Othniel. But this time I took it for what it was: clear and certain purpose.

"Send me," I said.

Malakhi ignored my demand and looked to Liyam. "And you? Will you go and recruit those able to fight? Train them? Help us smuggle weapons?"

Liyam's face had paled, and his lips were pressed into a flinty line. "You know I must leave," he said.

"Kedesh is in the very center of the region where your trader is rumored to have traveled," said Malakhi. "And in fact sits adjacent to the trade road that leads to Laish. Even eight years ago it was a well-known center of trading. You will have plenty of opportunity to further your search *while* fulfilling your duty to your people."

Liyam flinched at the gentle reprimand, but I was astonished that Malakhi was again offering to help him seek out the man he meant to kill.

"Tirzah knows Kedesh inside and out," Malakhi continued. "In fact, we've discovered that our family inn is now a well-fortified dwelling place for some of the wives of commanders stationed in our territories. Which means these commanders will have visited from time to time."

"Possibly leaving their secrets behind . . ." I murmured as I contemplated the possibilities.

"Indeed," said Malakhi. "And who better than my little sister to burrow in among the wives and ferret out those very secrets?" He smiled at me, a silent reminder of my original argument as to why a woman was suited to such tasks.

I glanced up at Liyam, but he still refused to meet my gaze. If he ground his teeth any harder, he would soon have none left.

"I still have my people looking for the trader," Malakhi said. "You cannot search the entire Land on your own, and we need you. We know the two of you work well together, and I have faith that you will keep her protected."

"*If* I did this," Liyam said, inciting a thrill to rush through my limbs, "would I go in as a mercenary again? A Moabite?"

"No," said Malakhi. "We still have family in the area. Our uncle's widow and her family maintain a farm in the valley. We will send you there. Since they have been forced to supply the Arameans with goods, it will give you both an excuse to enter the city. Tirzah can talk her way into work at the inn, I have little doubt."

"We can do this, Liyam," I pressed, excitement building. "Like he said, we do work well together."

Liyam looked down at me, and the lifting of his countenance gave me a small measure of hope. He was on the verge of agreeing, I could sense it.

"There is one requirement, however," my brother said to me. "A condition that Abba insists upon before he consents to another mission. He is adamant that you be protected."

My back stiffened as my palm went to my belt, since even within the safety of Shiloh I did not feel comfortable without it. "I have my knives, and I've proved I am able and willing to use them when necessary. Besides, Liyam won't let me come to harm. I trust him with my life."

"As do I," said Malakhi. "But Abba feels that it is only right that if you go in as a team together, you must be bound not only by trust but also by covenant. You must be married."

The entirety of my blood seemed to pool into my feet. "Married?" I echoed.

"Most men will protect a woman they are not bound to, if they are at all honorable," said Malakhi. "But a worthy husband will give up even his life for the other half of his own flesh."

"But we were not married before," I argued. "Liyam's behavior toward me was nothing but upright, even though we were forced to share quarters."

"That was a different situation," said Malakhi. "It could not be helped. We cannot in good conscience send the two of you off together without being wed."

"But—" I began.

"This is not a negotiation, Tirzah. You will be married, or you will stay here."

Helplessly I looked to Liyam, my jaw agape, but he was a pillar of stone. I'd had no intention of marrying again in the first place, and the thought of this mysterious man being my husband, especially when his stated goal was to slaughter another human being for an accident, was so overwhelming I could barely string two thoughts together.

And yet at the same time, the idea of going to Kedesh, of being part of the liberation of my home, the place of my birth, had completely captured my imagination. I would do anything to take part in such an endeavor.

But could I marry this stoic, deeply wounded man beside me? I'd only known him for a few weeks, yet he'd proven to be trustworthy and loyal, and although he'd had plenty of opportunity, he'd never laid a hand on me with ill intent. Although he'd struggled with my decision to stay in Shechem at first, he'd not forced me to go, but instead supported me, listened to my concerns, and complied when I'd insisted on protecting Odeleya. And truly, if any man was worthy of changing my mind, it was the one whose presence I'd missed so keenly in the weeks we'd been apart.

"No," he said, his firm and abrupt refusal overriding any wavering in my own resolve. "I made a vow. And I will not marry again." Then he brushed past Malakhi and headed back toward camp without another look behind him.

We both watched him retreat as the sun relentlessly beat down on my head. I scrambled to push aside the jolt of hurt the sight of his retreating form provoked.

"Why are you doing this?" I asked my brother. "Why force this issue? If we stay with Raviv's family, would it matter all that much?"

"Like I said," Malakhi replied. "Abba and I believe that he will be even more protective of you as his wife. He is a good man, I have no doubt of it, or I would not even suggest this in the first place. Abba feels the same. But Liyam is also torn between his duty to Yahweh and his role as go'el haadam." Malakhi peered at me. "You know about his child?"

"He told me just before you arrived." My heart curled in on itself again at the mention of his profound loss and the anguish and fury I'd seen in his eyes as he spoke of the trader. "Why are you so willing to help him find the Moabite anyhow? You know what he plans to do."

Malakhi grimaced. "I do. But Abba and I discussed this at length. Liyam is not Raviv, who was bent on murdering a child and a defenseless woman in his blind rage. We both think Liyam can be persuaded from this blood feud before the man is found, so that he can instead be brought to justice lawfully."

He gave me a piercing look, but one that was colored with affection. "We all agreed that if anyone can break through to him, it is you—even Ima, who said that she knows Alanah would agree. But first you'll have to convince him to go to Kedesh with you."

"And I have to marry him to do that," I stated.

"He needs you," said Malakhi, with a gentle tone.

I thought of that brilliant smile that had burst through Liyam's tight control after the slinging contest. I'd already felt compelled to slip past his walls and draw out the buried laughter I'd seen glimpses of. Could I also dissuade him from spilling blood unnecessarily?

If I was successful in talking him out of killing the trader, then he would not forever carry the weight of murder on his soul. After all he'd done for me, and for our people, I owed it to him to at least try to prevent him from making such an irrevocable mistake.

Perhaps he and I could come to an agreement that would not only enable us to serve our people, but that would also give me time to dissuade him from his blood feud. And what better place to do so than in a city of refuge?

TWENTY-EIGHT

Liyam

"I thought we'd have to leave without you, brother," said Lev, when I returned to their camp at the bottom of the vineyard. "Othniel expects us back in Shechem by nightfall."

Yavan and my brothers looked as if they'd been waiting for me for a while. Their camp was packed away, with only the small cook-fire remaining as they sat in a circle, sharing a wineskin of Ishai's delicious vintage. Moriyah had been here, without a doubt. The six of them looked satiated, and a small stack of wooden bowls sat beside the fire. From the way she'd greeted and pampered me once she'd figured out who I was, I was certain she'd been thrilled to meet the rest of Alanah's sons.

I dropped to my haunches near the fire, prodding at the dying flames with a branch I plucked from the ground. "I'm not going with you."

A chorus of exclamations and demands went up among the group, overlapping and growing in volume.

"Yes," said Lev. "You are."

"We need you," said Oren, whose fiery red hair matched his temper to perfection.

"It's time to join the fight, Liyam," said Mikal, the oldest of us, whose deep voice was so like our father's that a pang of longing hit me. Even though I knew he would be on the side of my brothers in this argument, I still craved his counsel and presence.

"We aren't leaving without you," said Shimon. "You've been away long enough."

Only Yavan did not join in the protest, but even though I did not look up, I felt his glare on the side of my face. He knew better than anyone that these demands would do nothing to dissuade me.

"I have new information about the whereabouts of the trader," I said.

Curses went up around the circle.

"That foolishness? Still?" said Oren.

"Yes, the foolishness of justice for Nadina," I gritted out. "You remember Nadina, don't you? The little girl with the big brown eyes who used to beg to ride on your shoulders and wove flower necklaces for all the goats and donkeys in the valley? My only daughter, who insisted on sending each of us off to war with a kiss and a *kalanit* bloom tucked into our armor?"

Silence dropped over the group like a shroud.

"You know what I vowed—"

"Yes," said Mikal, cutting me off with a gentle but firm tone. "We understand your drive for justice, Liyam. We do. There's not one among us who would not feel the same if it had been our own daughter. But you've spent months fruitlessly searching. And we are in the middle of a fight for our nation's very existence. Is your quest worth turning your back on your brethren?"

"I'm not turning my back on my brethren. You know what I did in Shechem."

"And we are nothing but proud of you, brother," said Mikal. "But the battle is not over. We need every hand lifted against the enemy."

"I can do both," I said, frustrated that their prodding was making me reconsider my vehement answer to Malakhi and Tirzah in the clearing. "Malakhi asked me to go to Kedesh. To help build an underground resistance. And the trader is rumored to be in that area as well."

"Well, why did you not say so?" Shimon slapped my back. "We thought you meant to just wander off alone again like a wounded cat."

"No, not alone," I said softly. "He wants me to go with Tirzah. Work together like we did in Shechem."

"Is that the woman you were speaking with earlier? When we first arrived?" asked Lev.

"Yes. Malakhi's youngest sister."

"And the hardship in going with that beautiful young woman to Kedesh would be what?" asked Shimon. "From the stories you told of your time in Shechem, she's nothing short of a brilliant spy."

"And none too difficult to look at either," said Oren with a chuckle. "No wonder the Aramean commander offered her up to you on a platter. She brings to mind some queen of Egypt with all that shiny hair, lovely eyes, and long limbs."

I scowled at him, but he only wiggled his brows at me, unapologetic.

"There is no hardship in working with Tirzah. The problem is that Malakhi insists we marry if we go together to Kedesh. He said that her father will not allow her to take part in any more missions unless she has a husband to protect her."

Six pairs of eyes stared at me.

"And the problem is. . . . ?" prompted Lev.

"I have no interest in marrying again."

"Havah was a good woman," said Shimon. "But you can't mourn her for the rest of your days. It's time for you to move on, take another wife, have more children."

"I don't want more children," I ground out. "Losing Nadina like that was . . ." I cleared the needling grief from my throat. "I don't ever want to go through this again."

"I never took you for a coward," said Yavan.

My head snapped toward him. "What did you call me?"

"You heard me full well," said my cousin. "We have been at each other's side since before we could walk, and I've never seen you give in to fear once until now."

My eyes narrowed but he stood unmoved.

"She's a good match for you," he said. "From all the things you told us about her, she sounds very much like Doda Alanah. Sharp. Stubborn. Brave. And if the two of you can accomplish something together in Kedesh that will help liberate our people, then you should do it. There's nothing to be afraid of."

"I am not afraid," I snapped.

"Aren't you?" he said. "What else do you call it when you turn your tail and run from a challenge?"

A growl built in my throat as I pinned him with a glare. If the man was not a brother of my soul he would be breathing his last at this moment.

"Although," he said with a shrug, unaffected by the fury vibrating through me, "if you don't marry her, I suppose Malakhi will find someone else. He has plenty of other men he's already trained for such missions, and I'm certain one of them will be all too happy to gain her as a wife."

At the image of some other man with Tirzah, a wave of unbidden jealousy crashed over me, nearly knocking the breath from my lungs. Malakhi had indeed said that Tirzah must be married to take part in the mission—not that she had to marry me specifically.

Thanks to my weeks of feigning calm in Shechem, however, I was able to rein in the vehement curse that threatened to break free from my lips and kept my eyes steady on my cousin. "I'm certain they shall."

"Liyam." I stiffened at the sound of Tirzah's voice from a few paces behind me, the stick I'd been jabbing into the flames going still. "May I speak with you?"

How much had she heard of this conversation? Knowing Tirzah, much more than I hoped. Perhaps she'd followed me from the clearing and had been privy to all my brothers' admonishments.

"We must be off," said Mikal, standing, which led the others to follow suit. "You know our thoughts on this matter. If you choose to join us in Shechem, so be it. If not, then we will see you when this is all over. Back in the valley."

The command was clear. *Do what you need to do, but come home alive.*

One by one my brothers left the campsite, each reaching to grip my shoulder with firm affection as he passed. When finally Yavan approached, he stood above me, forcing me to tip my head back to meet his gaze.

"Remember that time we nearly got swept away in that flash flood? In the wadi south of home?"

"Of course." We'd been only about eleven years old, hunting on our own for the first time and too busy tromping about scaring all the game away and calling ourselves men to pay attention to the quick change in the weather.

"I'll never forget what you said as we clung to that boulder with the water rushing all around us, threatening to swallow us whole, and I thought my fingers could not hold on for one more moment," he said. "You kept telling me that it was almost over, that I had a lot more strength than I thought I did, and that you looked forward to telling everyone how brave I'd been when it was all said and done."

I stared at him, uncomprehending.

"You may feel like you are still underwater, my brother, but don't let go. And if someone reaches into the flood, take the hand that is offered. Don't push it away." Then he leaned forward, his voice low and an expression of sincere concern on his face. "And for all that is good beneath the sun, no one wants to marry an acacia bush, no matter how brave she is. Trim that prickly red mess on your face."

I shoved him back with a snarl, and he walked away, laughing as he wished Tirzah well and followed my brothers down the hill. Then I stood with a heavy sigh, scuffed some fresh dirt over the last of the embers of their fire, and turned to face Tirzah.

She stood about ten paces away, her back against a cedar tree and one foot propped against the bark, with such a look of uncertainty in her expression that she barely even resembled herself.

"I know that you have already said no," she said. "But I'd like to make my case for why we should do what Malakhi asks."

"There is no need—"

"Please," she interrupted, pushing away from the tree. "Let me speak my piece and then I will accept whatever decision you make."

Knowing it would do me no good to argue, I nodded.

"I am barren," she stated, her tone as flat and unaffected as if the statement were no more weighty than the color of her hair. But I was more than acquainted with the sight of Tirzah plastering calm over her turmoil. Only a flicker of grief in her eyes slipped past the walls before her expression went blank. "Therefore, there would be no children from a union between us anyhow."

"So you *were* listening earlier," I said.

"If you didn't guess I was, then you don't know me at all." She shrugged. "But that is beside the point, so here is *my* proposal. I want to go to Kedesh. I want to fight for my home with whatever weapons I have. To placate my father and brother, we will marry in name only, and once this battle is over and our Land free you can return to your home and I will return to mine. As there will be no true joining between us, the elders will have no problem granting you a divorce on the grounds of non-consummation."

"You want us to pretend to be married?"

"It will be no different from our time in Shechem, and it will give my family peace while I am away."

"But if we divorce, you would be considered sullied," I said. "Another marriage would be unlikely."

"I don't want to be married. I am happy serving my family and serving my people. If anything, it would give me more freedom. My father would never cast me off, even as a divorced woman, and I wouldn't have to endure any more questions about who and when I will remarry."

I studied her face. Nothing in her expression gave the idea that she was taking this lightly.

"You, of course, would be free to choose a woman of your own tribe, one who could give you children if someday you change your mind," she said, then shook her head when I began to argue. "I understand that your loss is too fresh to even consider such a thing right now, Liyam.

But perhaps in time you'll feel differently. For now, this would simply be an agreement between us."

"I must search out the trader," I said. "I won't renege on my vow."

"You know my feelings on the matter," she said, a frown pinching her brows. "But I will not hinder your search. I simply ask that you lend me your protection until we part ways. If it was your home, would you not do anything to see it freed?"

My mind traveled to my valley, where the hills were lined with silver-leaved olive trees and my family thrived alongside fertile gardens and the stepped terraces that my Canaanite grandfather had built by hand. As isolated as our portion of the Land had been, the Arameans had left us alone for the most part over the years. I could not imagine being driven from our homes the way Tirzah and her family had been.

"I need to marry," she said. "I would prefer that it be you because I've come to trust you . . ." Her words withered away, but her meaning was clear. She would indeed find someone else if I refused her. The fact that it disturbed me even more to hear it from her lips than Yavan's was a path I chose not to explore.

"All right," I said, my every argument defeated. "Let's go speak to your father."

TWENTY-NINE

Tirzah

The low tones of my family and friends talking around the fire floated through the night on an unseasonably cool breeze, lending a note of familiarity to the strangeness inside our marriage tent.

Liyam and I had shared quarters for nearly three weeks in Shechem without issue, since I'd been so focused on my mission I'd barely thought of him being so near. But as I lay in the dark only a couple of paces from the man who was now considered my husband, the silence between us thrummed with tension.

I shut my eyes tight, trying to force sleep, but nothing could block out the voices and laughter of those still celebrating our unexpected union up the hillside. Knowing that the Aramean forces were possibly only weeks away, there was no choice but to marry in haste, but although Liyam and I had agreed to Malakhi's plan only two days before, my mother had still insisted on preparing a wedding feast. I could not help but compare tonight's relatively subdued meal with that of my first wedding, which after a year of betrothal had included seven days of festivities, food, and endless dancing.

This evening had consisted of a brief ceremony, wherein Liyam and I publicly voiced our agreement to the marriage covenant. Then, after the meal and with little fanfare, Liyam and I were escorted by a small group of family members to this tent, with none of the sly teasing and effusive well-wishes they'd offered last time.

My eyelids popped open again, refusing to obey my command to rest. No sound came from Liyam's side of the tent, not even the rhythm of his slow and steady breaths that had become so familiar to me during restless nights in Shechem. Had he already succumbed to sleep? Or was he just as aware of the noisy chasm between us as I was?

"Are you awake?" I whispered, staring at the blackness above me and wishing there were at least stars there to count.

"I am" came his rich voice out of the stillness.

Unbidden, the image of him arriving at our wedding ceremony arose in my mind. With his long red braid still damp from his ritual cleansing in the stream and his beard neatly trimmed to his jawline, he'd been so altered I'd barely recognized him. With the wildness stripped from his appearance and dressed in a fresh garment borrowed from Baz, I'd found my eyes drawn to him time and time again.

"Tell me about your home," I said, determined to press aside the unease that had settled in the space between his pallet and mine.

"What do you want to know?" he asked.

"Anything. Everything," I said, shifting until I was on my side. "I cannot rest."

A soft chuckle came from his lips, and I held my breath, wishing it would develop into something more, but instead he went silent. I opened my mouth to apologize for pressing him, but then he spoke.

"My grandfather settled in the valley when he was ten years younger than I am now. He was Canaanite, his ancestors from Moab, and he was given the land by a tribal chieftain for bravery in a series of skirmishes against Edomite raiders. He built terraces all around the hillsides, stone by stone, over many years, to preserve the sparse rainfall. As you are familiar with the story of my mother's journey to repay the Hebrews for killing my grandfather and uncles, you likely also know that when she and my father returned after the conquest of the Land, Yehoshua gave them back the valley of her birth. Since that time we have rebuilt the homes, extended the olive and fruit orchards, expanded the wheat and barley fields, and planted prolific gardens. It is like a secret oasis in the desert . . ." His words trailed off, as if lost in memories of his valley.

"Tell me about your favorite place there," I urged, finding the sound of his voice soothing and desperate to know more of him.

"There is a wadi," he replied. "Just to the south of our homes, where a deep pool gathers in the rainy months. Yavan and I spent countless hours there swimming, floating on our backs watching the clouds, and wrestling in the green water. It is near the same place where my mother taught me to hunt when I was very small."

"Your mother taught you?"

"Indeed. Have you not heard of her skill with a bow?"

I smiled at the pride in his tone. "Yes, of course. She saved my mother's life with that bow. I don't know why I questioned it."

"You remind me of her," he said abruptly.

Taken aback by the comparison, I peered into the darkness, wishing I could see his face.

"When I arrived in Shechem," he continued, "I expected . . . well, I am not sure what I expected, but it was not a woman able to shift from meekness to vehemence in the space of a breath, courageous enough to steal secrets from the very mouth of a dangerous enemy, nor someone who would throw herself at a vicious Aramean to save my life. My mother is a force of nature, like thunder or lightning, but she can also run as still and quiet as that pool in the wadi. I've never known another woman who compared to her . . . until I met you."

I'd never heard him speak so many words together at one time since I'd known him, and for his speech to compare me to his mother made my throat so tight I could barely speak. "You honor me, Liyam."

A sudden burst of laughter from some of the men back at the fire broke into the silence, more than likely a response to some ridiculous tale Baz was spinning. My father's oldest friend was always at the ready with a story, real or imagined, to entertain a crowd.

Warm affection for my family, and those we counted as family, swelled in my chest. Within the week, Liyam and I would already be well on our way toward Kedesh, and I would miss the camaraderie of those who lived here in the vineyard. Tonight felt as much like a good-bye as it did a celebration, especially since I'd only just settled back into life among my loved ones. War with the Arameans was inevitable, and we'd lost so many men before, I could not help but wonder whether tonight would be the last I would see of some of them in this world, and my heart bled at the thought.

"What was Odeleya so upset over earlier?" asked Liyam, startling me from my desolate thoughts.

"She is heartbroken that I am leaving," I said. The girl had come to me just before the ceremony, begging to come with Liyam and me to Kedesh.

"She is much safer here."

That Odeleya would stay in Shiloh with my family had not even been a question, and I'd thought she would be excited to remain with the other children, whose company she seemed to enjoy so much, but I'd assumed wrongly.

"She is," I said. "But she thought I meant to not return."

Odeleya had clung to me, her body shaking as she pleaded with me to take her along, vowing she would be as much help as she had been in Shechem. When I realized she feared I was washing my hands of her, just as her own family had done, I understood the desperate plea.

"How did you convince her of your intention to come back?"

"I swore a blood oath," I said, my finger tracing the cut in the center of one palm. A matching one now marred Odeleya's hand too. "She calmed once I pressed our palms together and told her that she and I were now bound by blood and that no matter what, I would never abandon her."

"That was kind," he said, his tone gentle.

"I am grateful Yahweh brought us together," I said. "She has become like a daughter to me." I immediately regretted the words, fearing I'd aggravated his wounds.

"She would do well to have you as a mother."

The response shocked me into silence. For as many hours as I'd spent in his presence in Shechem, I'd seen none of the tender side to this intense warrior. I imagined that his wife and child had known a far different man than the one who lay near me now in the dark. As tempted as I was to ask about them, to know him better through his description of those he cared for, tonight was not the time for such conversations. But if I was to succeed in my goal of changing his mind about the blood feud, I would soon need to press into those wounds in order to draw out the poison.

"The sword you gave me as a wedding gift is far beyond what I would have expected. I wish I'd had something of equal value to offer you as *mohar*," he said, regret heavy in his voice. "I will make it up to you as soon as I am able."

"Think no more on that, Liyam," I said. "It was my pleasure to give you a weapon made by Eitan. There are few as skilled in metalwork as my brother. And you are deserving of such a prize after all you have done for me. You have given me something of far greater worth."

"And what is that?"

"There are not many men who would support a woman on such a dangerous mission, but from the very start you had faith in me and have now gone so far as to marry me so I can do what I believe I was made to do. No matter how masterfully crafted, a sword is paltry recompense for such a gift." I paused, then added in a whisper. "Eliya would not have agreed to any of this."

Liyam did not respond, but the silence inside the tent was no longer fraught with tension. We lay still, listening to the murmurs of my family members growing quieter as the hour grew late, until only the breeze whistling through the poplar trees and the hoot of an owl broke the stillness.

A rush of cold night air slipped beneath the woolen wall of our tent, causing me to shiver. Liyam must have heard the sound of my teeth clacking together, for all of sudden I felt the warmth of another blanket spreading over me and large hands gently tucking the edges around my legs.

"Won't you be cold?" I whispered.

"I have my mantle," he replied, the sound of his voice soothing. "Sleep now."

Obediently, I settled myself deeper into the cocoon he'd provided, secure in the knowledge that I could trust this man I now called husband with my life. Just before exhaustion claimed me, I found myself wondering what it might be like if this were a real wedding night and wishing it was his warmth I was curling into instead.

Part II

CHAPTER

THIRTY

Tirzah

25 Iyyar
Kedesh, Israel

What had they done to my city?

"What is it?" asked Liyam, responding either to the look of horror on my face or the strangled noise of dismay I'd let slip as we came up over the final ridge. I shook my head, unable to speak for fear that I'd weep in front of him and the four men Malakhi had sent to accompany us north.

The Arameans had done far worse than drive us and our neighbors from Kedesh; they'd stripped the place of its soul. The many leafy orchards that had once encircled the city on the hill were only ghosts of their former selves. Of the hundreds of trees beneath whose shadows I'd played as a girl, whose trunks I'd climbed, branches I'd dangled from, and whose fruit I'd gathered, perhaps only three in ten were still standing. Some of the olive trees in this grove had been so old that two men could not span the circumference with their arms.

Now many rotting stumps were left behind, their ancient carcasses no doubt wasted by an enemy who cared nothing for the Land.

Although I pointedly ignored him, I could feel my new husband studying my face as I walked beside him, taking in the destruction and blinking hard against tears. I could almost hear my brother, Gidal, mourning the loss from beyond his grave. The bountiful fruit trees of Kedesh had been his passion, having spent the years before his tragic death ministering to each one like a father would his sons. Now those that remained stood disheveled and diseased, a testimony to what Kushan had done to the Land of Promise and an insult to Gidal's legacy.

Even the white limestone boulders that once marked the boundary of the city of refuge were no longer visible, overtaken as they were by weeds and thorny vines. No longer was this a sanctuary for desperate manslayers fleeing for their lives, nor the weary travelers my mother had welcomed to her inn with shelter and a warm meal. It was nothing more than another heartless stronghold for our enemies, bereft of all that had made it a home and refuge for so many.

I would stop at nothing to see it restored to its purpose once again.

The walls of the city rose up before us as we neared. Those had at least remained the same over the past eight years, as did the enormous cedar gates through which I'd passed thousands of times. If only I could break into a run as I had as a girl, waving at Eitan's friend Chaim and the other guards as I headed for the inn after spending the day besting the boys at slings or archery out in the fields.

But just as the lamplight my mother had always kept alive in her window to guide travelers was no longer flickering there, Chaim too was gone; just one of the thousands of Hebrew lives snuffed out when King Kushan's forces swept into the Land.

Although the olive grove that once stood to the southeast of Kedesh no longer fully lined the ridge in silver-fingered glory, I spotted a path that led down into the valley, glad for the distraction from my mournful thoughts.

"Here is where we part ways," I said to Malakhi's men as I gestured toward the half-obscured trail. Although I'd walked its length only a few times before we left Kedesh, I knew my uncle Raviv's lands lay at its end. "Laish is only a half a day's walk northeast on this trade road."

The four young men had been given the task of stirring up support among the tribe of Dan, just as Liyam and I had in Kedesh. For as difficult as my own mission was, I did not envy them the task of attempting to sway the Danites to stand with their Hebrew brethren, especially after the underhanded way they'd taken the city of Laish just before the Arameans arrived. From all accounts, worship of Yahweh was so intermixed with heathen gods there, and intermarriage with Amorites and Arameans so prevalent, that the Torah was all but forgotten in that place.

After offering well-wishes to the men who'd walked with us all the way from Shiloh, I turned my sandals to the east, leading Liyam onto the snaking trail through the brush. I prayed that Raviv's family still remained in the valley and that we would find welcome among them. His widow was my uncle's second wife, so we shared no blood between us, but my father insisted that the peace made between him and his brother at the end of Raviv's life had broken down the walls that had once separated the two halves of the family.

Another partially obscured boundary stone lay at the very top of the ridge. Needing a moment to collect my thoughts and to rest my weary feet, I sat down on the limestone rock, vividly recollecting the last time I'd sat in this spot when I was barely fifteen, the day before I'd been forced to leave the city I'd been born in and all I'd ever known.

Stoic as usual, Liyam stood beside me, looking out over the fertile vista below, where a blue lake glimmered beneath a cloudless sky and a brown-and-green patchwork decorated the valley floor with promise.

"We thought we'd be allowed to stay," I said, my attention drawn to Har Hermon in the distance, its three-headed peak a witness to the many changes this Land had endured since Avraham had walked in its shadow so long ago. "The Arameans seemed uninterested in Kedesh when they first arrived, since its strategic value was negligible. But once they realized how plentiful this area is, they changed their minds." I swept a hand toward the farms below us, which seemed to be thriving in spite of what had been done to my city.

"Without warning, a large contingent of soldiers arrived and drove us from our homes, giving us only one day to collect our belongings and flee. Although it galled my father and my brothers to retreat, they knew that to stand against the Arameans that day would have meant the end of us all. So we left."

"Why did you not join your family in the valley?" Liyam asked.

"Many years ago, while in pursuit of Sofea, who'd been taken captive before they married, my brother fell into Raviv's hands," I said. "My father rescinded his claim on his inherited portion of the land to keep my uncle from murdering Eitan out of vengeance for his sons' deaths—a tragic accident that had occurred when he was only nine, if you remember."

Liyam said nothing, but I hoped that my subtle censure of his own pursuit nicked at his resolve.

"Although my uncle's widow did not hold a grudge against us, as it had not been her sons who had been killed, my mother had not seen her family in over two-and-a-half decades. Since Eleazar the High Priest had died a few months before the Arameans swept into the Land, she'd finally been freed from her imprisonment. So we went to Shiloh."

I would never forget the sight of my mother running into the arms of her father and my grandmother Ora, all three of them with tears streaming down their faces, after thinking that she would not see them again in this life. I could not imagine being separated from my own parents for so long. Although my mother was not related to Ora by blood, her bond with the blind woman who loved her so dearly was equal to a maternal one by any measure, so being wrenched away from both her parents had been devastating to her. "So much pain and loss," I murmured. "All because of a mistake."

"You will not sway me, Tirzah," Liyam spat out. "I will have no regrets when that trader is dead by my hand."

The sudden vehemence that spewed from his mouth shocked me. Even when he'd been locked in a deadly struggle with Khaled he'd not raised his voice, but had instead baited the man with cool indifference. Then he'd remained stunningly placid as he finished the job I'd begun when I plunged my knife into Khaled's neck. Somehow my regrets over my mother's sad circumstances had caused his defenses to flare to life with shocking intensity.

"You did not know her," he said, the words flying at me like arrows. "You did not hold her tiny body as her mother breathed her last. You did not search for shadows of your wife in her face as she grew, nor live for the moments she ran to you when you returned home from the fields. You do not lie awake at night straining to remember the echo of her little voice. And until you know what it is to have your heart trampled into dust, you have no right to judge my decision to avenge her blood."

I gaped at my husband, stunned by the bitter curl of his lips that dared me to push him further. Although I learned more about Liyam in those few sentences than I had in all the days I'd known him and wished I could ease the burden he carried, I could not leave such a statement unchallenged.

"Perhaps not," I said, although I was more than tempted to explain how I'd lost pieces of my own heart over the years as well. "But the One who made her in the first place *is* the rightful judge, and it is his laws to which you are subject."

Although my words were true, I immediately regretted their harsh tone. I had resolved to gently lead Liyam into rational discussion of the matter, not vex him into arguing over our differing opinions. The poor man had plenty of walls constructed around his heart; it would not do to hand him more bricks. I rose from my seat on the boulder and approached him warily, as one would a wounded animal.

"Forgive me," I said, then gathered enough courage to reach out and place my palm in the center of his chest. The solid heat of him soaked into my skin as I met his gaze. "I do not mean to tread in places I am not welcome. I will not press you to speak of these things again until you choose to do so."

Liyam took another deep breath, one that shuddered in his chest. Although he said nothing, his shoulders began to relax and his fists unclenched. We stood silently for a few more moments, until the vivid blue-green of his eyes outweighed the shadows once again. When he looked down at me, a bit of that trembling tension from within our marriage tent began to hum again as we stood only a handsbreadth apart, breathing in tandem, and my reasons for refusing marriage began to fade around the edges.

"We should go," he said suddenly, the sound rumbling against my hand.

"Yes . . . of course." I stepped away, his brisk words a reminder that although I valued his partnership, this marriage was no more real than the pretense we'd lived in Shechem. Without looking back at him, I returned to the path, pushing away the unexpected sadness that thought had conjured. As I headed down into the valley, I willed myself to focus on the mission before me, instead of the inexplicable pull I'd begun to feel for the man at my back.

Identical twin boys stood in the doorway, their matching eyes wide with surprise. Malakhi and Abra had also been born together, but these children were the exact image of one another, down to the curve of their little mouths as they gaped up at Liyam in awe.

I recognized them as my cousin Nessa's boys, who must be around twelve years of age now; but they were so stricken by the appearance of the red-haired giant next to me that when I asked to see their mother, they ignored me.

A crowd of onlookers had gathered outside the house, their wary glances making it clear that this clan saw few visitors from outside the valley.

"Itai. Ariel. Who is at the door?"

Nessa appeared, wiping her hands on a towel tucked into her belt and with a young girl peering out from behind her hip. "Yes? Can I help you?"

"Shalom," I said. "Do you remember me? I am your cousin Tirzah. Daughter of Darek and Moriyah."

Nessa's dark eyes went wide. "Tirzah? I have not seen you since you were a girl!" Instead of regarding me suspiciously as I'd expected, she pushed her boys aside and threw her arms around me. The memories I had of Nessa were few, and only directly after she'd been rescued by my father and brothers from Edrei during the initial Aramean invasion—the same rescue in which my uncle Raviv, her father, had been killed. Back then she'd been a broken woman, hollow-eyed and stripped of dignity by a husband who'd beaten her, and shaken by watching the father she'd thought cared nothing for her lay down his life for the sake of her and her children. Apparently much had changed in the last eight years. She gifted me with a huge smile, revealing a gap between her two front teeth as she glanced up at Liyam. "And who might this be?"

"This is Liyam," I responded. "My . . . my husband."

She looked back and forth between us, likely wondering about my hesitation. "Ah. Well, you are both welcome. Come in! Come in!"

She ushered us into the house, which was large in comparison to the other dwellings that made up the tiny village Raviv had founded in this part of the valley. The stone and mud-brick homes were located at the center of a large apple orchard, where the trees were already laden with miniature globes that would eventually shine red and green and gold among the dark leaves.

"Sit," Nessa commanded, gesturing to a low table around which were laid an assortment of pillows. "I will bring you food. The both of you look exhausted."

We nodded our thanks and accepted the bread and wine she offered without argument. We'd used the last of my mother's provisions last night, and my stomach was snarling at the neglect.

Once she was satisfied that our immediate needs were tended to, Nessa folded herself down on the floor. The twins also sat across the table from us, their dark eyes still trained on Liyam, but neither of them made a sound. Whether it was the red hair or his impressive height that had them in awe, I could not discern, but they were certainly enthralled with my husband. Nessa's daughter settled beside her, her little fist gripping the fabric of her tunic tightly, as if she feared her mother might flit away at any moment.

"And what is your name?" I asked the girl, whom I remembered as just an infant when we left Kedesh.

Her large brown eyes looked up at her mother in question.

"It's all right, Ruvi," said Nessa. "This is my cousin Tirzah. She grew up not that far from here."

Ruvi pushed herself upward to whisper in her mother's ear.

"No, we did not play together as little girls like you and Tovah do, but I certainly wish that we had. My sisters and I did not have other girls to play with back then. We spent most of our time climbing apple trees with our boy cousins."

The words lashed at my heart. Nessa was a few years older than me, but her younger sister Sariah and I were similar in age. If only Raviv's bitterness had not spliced our family in two. We'd been separated by only a ridge of trees, less than a hour's walk, and yet we'd grown up completely separate from each other, unaware that our cousins even existed.

"I would have loved climbing trees with you and your sisters," I said with a regretful grin at Nessa, then winked at her daughter. "I could climb higher than all the boys in Kedesh. Could shoot better and run faster too."

Ruvi smiled at me, and I knew I'd won her over. Something about the dancing light in her eyes reminded me of Odeleya, and my chest squeezed with missing her. I was grateful that she was safe beneath my mother's capable wing, but it had been difficult to walk away from her the morning we left Shiloh. I'd kissed her hair and promised once again I would return for her as she wept into my ima's bosom. She would love Kedesh, I was certain, and once the Arameans were gone I could bring her here and show her what it was like to live in the city of my birth, free and cherished by not only me but also my entire family.

"Now," said Nessa, dragging Ruvi into her lap where the girl settled against her mother's chest, "I assume you have not come to the valley for a simple friendly visit since no one comes to this area without purpose."

"We have not," I said, wondering at her choice of words. "We've been sent to prepare the people for war."

Her eyes flickered to the window and back, then she leaned close. "I would keep this information to yourself, even here."

Surprised by the shift in her demeanor, I lowered my voice. "Are there some among your clan who might not keep our secrets from the Arameans?"

"It is possible," said Nessa. "But more out of fear than sympathy for the enemy. The Arameans keep a close eye on everything we do. And we have been at the center of their sights a few times before."

"Because of rebellion?" I asked.

"No, because my cousins Yoash and Kefa made a poor decision to hide some of the harvest three years ago. Somehow the Arameans found out and raided our farm. They took everything that year, not just the tribute portion they'd demanded in the past. Since that time they've been far too aware of us and even send in men to watch while we harvest. There is not one apple that goes into our mouths without their accounting of it."

Dismayed by the knowledge that the Arameans kept a close watch on this farm, I frowned at Liyam, then back at Nessa. "Perhaps our plan is not so wise then. Should we find somewhere else to go?"

"No," she said. "Of course not! These Arameans are frightened. I can tell something has been happening because all of a sudden they are scrutinizing us more than ever, stepping up patrols and harassing the townspeople even more than usual. There are whispers of battles in the south. Is it true?"

"Have you not heard of Othniel?"

"No, who is this?"

"The nephew of Calev, the famous spy and warrior. Othniel is the leader of the tribe of Yehudah. He has retaken a number of our cities, not just those of his tribe, and has gained back over half the territories we held eight years ago."

Nessa's eyes stretched wide. "Has he? I knew something was happening, but not as much as that. Will he come here?"

"Perhaps. King Kushan is returning to the Land to reclaim what he believes is his. Whether he means to come down through Laish or further south is just one of the things we've been sent to determine."

"You are spying for your father's unit?" she asked, incredulous.

"My brother Malakhi is in command of my father's men now," I replied.

"Rivkah's husband?" She smiled broadly, the gap between her teeth making an appearance. "The handsome one?"

I laughed. "Oh, he'd love to hear you call him that."

"Even when Rivkah was running from marriage to that boy, she could never deny that his face was a thing of beauty." She winked. "Just do not tell my husband I said so."

"You have remarried?"

"I have," said Nessa, her dark eyes sparkling. "Dotan is a good man from our own clan and treats my children as his own."

"I am glad to hear of it," I said, and knew Rivkah would be pleased to hear it too, as she'd worried for Nessa after they had returned from Edrei. "But yes, Malakhi has charged Liyam and me with building a resistance here so that when Othniel and the others arrive, Kedesh will be prepared to stand and fight."

Nessa's lips pressed into a dismal line. "That will be a difficult task, cousin. The Kedesh you knew is not the city that stands today. We are some of the only ones who stayed in this area after the Arameans pushed you out; and of the twenty or so family groups that did maintain their homes eight years ago, over half have fled since then. If the soldiers are not stealing our goods or forcing our men into work projects, they are harassing our women and children. Anyone who stands against them is imprisoned and sent north to Aram-Naharim, more than likely to be sold into slavery or forced into conscription."

"Why have you stayed?" I asked. "When the opposition here is so great?"

"After what my father did to save me in Edrei, I have fought hard to remain on this land he loved, even though many among our clan were more than ready to abandon the orchards and head south. Thankfully, I am not alone in the fight. Yoash and Kefa insist that they too owe him a great debt for letting Rivkah and me slip away all those years ago, so they have taken over running the orchards and refuse to retreat either."

"So it is out of loyalty to your father that you stay?"

She nodded. "I may not have been born the son he so desperately wanted to replace Zeev and Yared, and there may have been little affection between us during his lifetime, but at least during the battle of Edrei he proved that he did in fact love me, or he would not have come to my rescue. And for that reason alone, for those few moments when I was his beloved daughter, I fight for this land."

The bleakness of such a statement caused my breath to catch. Raviv's brokenness had caused so much unnecessary pain, for both my family and for his. I'd always been cherished by my abba, so I had no idea what it must have been like for Nessa and her sisters to live in the cold shadow of two boys who had died long before her birth. But for whatever reason that she and her clan had clung to this land, a portion of which should have been my father's inheritance, I was grateful.

"I need to get into the city, Nessa. Back to the inn where the wives of the Aramean officers now reside. Is that possible?"

She regarded me with narrowed eyes. "Why would you want to go inside such a place? Did you not hear me say that Kedesh has become a dangerous city for Hebrews?"

"It is the mission Malakhi gave me," I said. "I must procure a job there."

She sighed. "I have a friend named Barucha who does the laundry for the inn. I might be able to connect you to her."

"I am grateful for any help," I said. "And Liyam? Would Yoash and Kefa need help in the fields?"

Nessa regarded my husband with a furrowed brow. "We could always use more hands. I am certain they will find a place for him." Then she glared at me. "Do you mean to tell me that you will be going in to spy in Kedesh while your husband here tends our trees?"

"I may be at the inn collecting information from gossiping women, but Liyam has an important task as well. And it sounds as though his mission to gather and train Hebrew men to fight against the Arameans will be just as perilous as my own."

Nessa's brows lifted high. "Indeed. You'd best be careful or you too will be shipped off to the north. There is no second chance for those suspected of rebellion in this region."

"Noted," said Liyam.

"And," said Nessa, her jaw setting and her dark eyes flashing black, "you won't be conducting any training on our land, so you'll have to find somewhere else to build your rebellion. I won't chance losing one more tree to those dogs."

Liyam nodded, taking in her demand without argument.

"Good," said Nessa, with a clap of her palms as she rose. "Now let's find a place for the two of you to stay."

Trailed by the silent twins and little Ruvi, who had so far not relinquished her grip on the skirt of her mother's tunic, Nessa led us to a door.

She turned to us with a frown. "The five of us share a chamber, or I would gladly give up my own. And my mother and her two widowed sisters reside in the other. Dotan is working on building another two rooms, but they are unfinished as of now." She smiled up at Liyam. "Perhaps you might be of help in that regard."

"I would be happy to do so," he replied.

"Oh, I am so glad," she said. "My husband would love to do it all by himself, but he lost use of his arm during the battle for Golan. And the other men of the clan are far too occupied with the fields just now to spend time working on our home. He'd hoped to have them completed before the rains return, but not without more help." She sighed as she opened the door and waved a hand for us to enter. "But I do wish I had more to offer you than a storage room."

I swept my gaze around the small space. "We are grateful for any roof over our heads. Besides, Liyam and I shared a room nearly the same size in Shechem and survived. Didn't we?"

Liyam hummed his agreement.

"Shechem?" Nessa's brows flew upward. "I thought you all have been in Shiloh?"

"It is a long story," I replied. "I'll explain tomorrow."

"Yes, of course. Itai, go fetch a lamp for them," she said to one of the twins. He darted away, his small feet making no sound on the dirt floor. The boys were not much younger than Rivkah's Amit, if I remembered correctly, but their slight frames made them look little more than nine or ten. Yet the silent, haunted look in their eyes was so ancient that it made me wonder how much they remembered of their time with the father who'd beat their mother and nearly starved them, and the terrifying flight they'd endured when the Arameans crashed into Edrei.

With a flickering oil lamp in hand, along with a few blankets and cushions Nessa had pressed into my arms, Liyam and I offered thanks for her hospitality and shut ourselves into the storage room.

The room in the army barracks had been similar in size to this one, but since much of the floor was taken up with jars of beans, peas, and grain, there was only a narrow space for us to fashion a pallet. Silently, we did so, then laid down alongside one another without exchanging a word. Liyam extinguished the lamp by smashing the wick between two fingers.

Once again, echoes of our wedding night began to vibrate in the two handspans between us. Unnerved by his proximity and the nearly uncontrollable impulse to reach out and slip my hand into his, I opened my mouth.

However, his voice came out of the darkness before I could speak. "I thought you said things were tense between your family and your uncle's family."

A thrill jumped in my chest at the curiosity in his tone and the unwitting opening he was giving me to speak of things that might lead him down a path that did not end in vengeance.

"They certainly were in the past. It was not until just after I was born that my parents even knew Raviv had remarried and had other children. However, none of us willingly ventured into this valley since he'd threatened my mother and brother's lives. But his final actions changed everything."

"He gave up his life for Nessa's?" he asked.

"And Eitan, Malakhi, and my father's as well."

"I thought he'd vowed to kill Eitan."

"He did. Numerous times. But something changed in the years after Nessa and Rivkah ran away together. From what I've heard, the man who laid down his life in Edrei was not the same one who spewed hatred in front of the entire assembly of Israel, along with Eleazar the High Priest and Yehoshua himself, during my mother's murder trial. I only saw him once, when he burst into our home searching for Nessa right after the girls disappeared, and I was only around nine years old, but I'll never forget his eyes. It was as if there was nothing behind them but death."

I wondered whether Liyam might flare with temper the way he had before when I'd spoken of the impact of Raviv's thirst for vengeance, but he said nothing at all, so I took a chance and whispered truth into the stillness.

"I know that I am not truly your wife, and I do not know you well. But you are a good man, Liyam. A man of honor. I could not bear to watch you lose yourself to the same darkness."

Then, giving in to my impulse, I slowly slid my hand across the gap and hooked my smallest finger with his. To my surprise he did not pull away, but neither did he further the contact by matching my palm with his or weaving the rest of his fingers into mine the way I hoped he would. After a while, embarrassment caught up to me, and I pulled my hand away.

Instead of dwelling on the sting of rejection, I forced myself to bathe in the memories of Kedesh the way it was, when the olive trees bowed with the weight of their fruit, Gidal's bees flitted from blossom to blossom up in the quince orchard, the Levites' sheep and goats frolicked in the fields around the city, and my mother's lamp still flickered on the windowsill of the inn to beckon the wanderer to her doorstep.

No matter the state of my city after eight years of being exiled, tomorrow I would see my home.

THIRTY-ONE

I shifted the bundle of papyrus reeds higher on my hip. Although the hollow sticks were not as heavy as I'd first thought they might be, their length made them unwieldy. But Liyam carried two such bushels, and I was determined to keep stride with him as we entered the city the moment the gates were opened at dawn. Ahead of us, Kefa and Yoash approached the Aramean guards, who demanded to know our business, as if the burdens we bore did not make clear what our purpose might be.

Since the apple harvest was still months away, Nessa's husband and her cousins had recruited Liyam yesterday to help them harvest reeds on the lakeshore, affording us a plausible reason to enter Kedesh. The four men had returned to Nessa's home later that afternoon, chuckling at some jest that they refused to share with the rest of us. For as brooding and stitched up as Liyam was most days, humor still managed to slip through his tight seams from time to time, like it had the day we'd competed with our slings. I prayed that when the man finally unclenched his tightfisted control, I would be there to witness the transformation. The change from wild mercenary to intriguing warrior on our wedding day had been shocking enough; I could only guess that an unfettered, genuine smile on that well-chiseled face and mirrored in those blue-green eyes would be nothing less than glorious.

"I've not seen the two of you before," said one of the guards, his eyes moving between Liyam and me. I cast my gaze downward and scuffled closer to Liyam, making a show of meek dependence on my husband. Inside, I screamed at the men who dared bar me entrance to the city of my birth and presided with haughty suspicion at the gates that had once welcomed travelers, traders, and manslayers alike with open arms.

"This is my cousin and his wife," replied Kefa, gently bending the truth. "We lost a few workers to illness last month, so we begged them to leave their home across the valley to help with the upcoming harvest. My cousin's wife will be working at the inn, so you'll likely see the two of them often."

The man narrowed his eyes. "I'll search the reeds before you enter."

One by one, the bundles were pawed through as the Arameans searched for weapons. Thankfully they did not lay a hand on me, but the knives in my belt seemed to pulse, as if calling out to the guards that they'd already killed one of their number and would do so again if necessary. Once satisfied with their search, the guards sent us on our way with a warning to tend our business within the hour and then leave the city.

Yoash and Kefa led us past the stone seats that lined one wall of the holding area between the inner and outer gates. Upon those thrones the elders of the town had once sat to hear cases of new manslayers brought to the city for refuge and to apply Torah laws in all matters. I could almost see Amitai, Rivkah's father, seated there, wisdom heavy on his silvered brow, as he discussed the particulars of each case with the other Levites of the council. Now that he'd passed from this life into the olam ha'ba, his son Tal would take his place on that stone seat once we returned Kedesh to its rightful owners. And those seats would be occupied sooner rather than later. I refused to consider any other outcome.

"We do not have long," said Kefa. "Only enough time to sell the reeds to the papyrus maker and barter for a few supplies. I would suggest you ladies go to the inn while we do so."

Liyam scowled. "I'll go with the women."

Kefa shook his head. "They'll be watching you much closer than Tirzah. It's best if you stay away so Nessa can speak with her friend unhindered. You'll only shine a light on your wife if you accompany them."

I placed my hand on Liyam's arm. "I'll be fine. From what Nessa says, the inn is populated mostly by women. The guards won't bat an eye at the two of us alone."

He looked down at me with furrowed brows, then surveyed the marketplace behind me with a wary frown. "I don't have a good feeling about this."

"I was alone in Shechem more than I was with you, Liyam. I'll be fine." I patted my belt, reminding him that I did not enter unarmed.

This reluctance to leave me was new, and I wondered whether something had shifted last night when my smallest finger was wrapped around his. My pulse flickered at the thought, but he did not argue again, only took my bundle of reeds and added them to his own burden before turning away without a word of farewell and trudging along behind Nessa's cousins.

"It seems you have much to tell me about your time in Shechem," said Nessa as she flicked her long braid over her shoulder with a sly smile. "That man is a tangled mess."

I sighed as I watched him walk away with all three of our reed bundles over his strong shoulder. "No more than I am, cousin. No more than I."

She slipped her arm into mine and urged me on. "First let's get you a job at the inn, and then you will tell me all. Yes?"

My greedy eyes took in the sight of my home, passing over the two hefty Arameans who stood on either side of the front door to the plastered exterior. More than a few cracks splintered its surface, and the oak shutters that Eitan and Malakhi had devised to protect the inhabitants from storms and heat now hung apathetically from weathered hinges.

I did not expect that the enemies who'd stolen our inn would care for it the way we had, but the neglect was far beyond my imaginings. Not even the double-trunked date palm that had once cast luxurious shade over the entire front of the inn had managed to survive the subjugation of Kedesh. Only a jagged and diseased stump stood testament to its once-prolific existence.

Caught up in mourning and seeing the ghosts of my memories whisking up and down the busy street in front of the inn, I barely noticed Nessa's murmured explanations to the guards, nor the knock she placed on the door.

A stern-faced woman opened the door, her disapproving gaze moving over us with swift efficiency.

"Shalom. I am here to see Barucha, the laundress," said my cousin.

"She's busy doing the work of two today," replied the woman. "Find her when her job is complete." Then she moved to shut the door, but Nessa was faster and slammed a palm against the wood, preventing it from closing all the way. The guards shifted, hands on their swords.

"Please," said Nessa, somehow keeping her tone light in spite of the three wary pairs of eyes trained on her. My cousin might herself make a good spy with such a coolheaded reaction. "Might we speak to her for only a few moments? We'll even offer our own hands to make the job go faster, if that will help."

The woman glared at Nessa. "What do you want with Barucha?"

"My cousin is searching for work. I've heard that one of your girls gave birth this week and another was stricken with illness and wondered if you might need someone to fill in the gaps their absence has left behind."

The woman's sharp gaze moved to me. "What can you do?"

"I worked at an inn like this one for many years. I am experienced with cooking for large groups, cleaning, laundry, and tending to guests' particular needs."

"Show me your hands," demanded the woman.

I turned my palms upward for her perusal, the roughness of their appearance, along with the many burn scars from cook-fires, on full display.

"Your cousin is right that we have lost two girls this week," said the woman, whom I now noticed had sweat beading at her hairline and a smear of red sauce on her tunic. "You'll cook now and prove yourself or leave."

I dropped my hands and straightened my shoulders. "I am ready."

"We shall see." She pursed her lips, her eyes raking me from head to toe and back again. "There is no room for you to live on the premises, unless you care to sleep in the courtyard or on the roof. Between the Arameans' wives and their maids, there is no space but under the sky."

"She and her husband live with us, just down in the valley. It's only a short walk."

"You'll be here at dawn and leave just before the closing of the gates?"

"I will."

She sighed, and the sound was as relieved as it was resigned. She must be truly desperate for help if she was willing to take on a worker with little question. She jerked the door back open and gestured for me to come inside.

"I'll send your husband to meet you at the gate this evening, Tirzah," said Nessa, taking a few steps backward. As I passed over the threshold, the Aramean guards allowed their hands to drop away from their weapons, giving me leave to finally take a full breath.

"If she lasts that long," murmured the woman, then slammed the door closed with a thud.

The exterior neglect of the inn had not prepared me for what greeted me within. The front chamber, once the site of so many family meals and neighborhood gatherings during inclement weather, had been sparsely furnished when we lived here, affording more room for guests to gather on cushions and rugs within its welcoming space. Now an Egyptian-style table sat at its center, with ten high-backed chairs surrounding its regal length. In each corner stood four double-wicked oil lamps on tall pedestals, which though unlit at the moment, must flood the entire room with light during the darkest of nights.

A cluster of smaller tables lined the far wall, swathed in fine fabrics and each containing two or three gods, along with an assortment of incense burners, as well as the remains of fruit and flowers that had obviously been presented to the sightless lumps of clay and sculpted stone. My nose wrinkled, both at the sight and the overripe smell, but thankfully the woman who'd barely allowed me inside was striding ahead and did not notice my disgust.

Idols in my mother's front room—in the place where she'd welcomed hundreds, if not thousands, of guests with the name of Yahweh ever on her lips and hospitality born of love for him in her heart—she would be horrified beyond measure.

"I am Tohdah," said my surly guide over her shoulder as she led me through the back entrance out into the courtyard. "You report to me and me alone."

"Understood," I replied, but was so caught up in the sight of the courtyard itself that I only half-heard her ensuing speech about the women who lived here, along with their penchant for making demands that could not be accommodated, no matter what lengths she took to please them.

Unlike the sad exterior and the altered interior, the central courtyard of the inn had changed little. Cedar posts lined both sides of the enclosed space, supporting the upper level with their impressive bulk. At the far end a narrow stone staircase led to the rooftop, where a few additional rooms were perched, one of which my three brothers had shared for years when they were boys. I'd spent many an hour atop that flat roof, peering over the wall to the ground far below, watching the clouds skim overhead or tossing pebbles at the sheep and goats that strayed from their herds to search out morsels along the plastered slope that encircled Kedesh.

In the far corner stood my mother's oven, a monstrosity built of interlocking stones with such precision that even after decades of use by Canaanites, Hebrews, and Arameans, it still remained as the proud centerpiece of the inn. If Kedesh were to be leveled, I wondered whether that oven might still stand, a lonely testament to the countless mouths it had fed and the hands that had tended its daily fires for lifetime after lifetime, including my own.

It was here within this courtyard that a number of betrothal ceremonies and wedding celebrations had taken place, my mother and father's included, along with those of the rest of my siblings. Only Eliya and I had not been joined within this precious place, having been married in Shiloh, but the memories of those celebrations—the food, the wine, the flowers, the dancing and song, were so engrained in my mind that I could practically taste, hear, and smell them as Tohdah led me across the courtyard.

It was from that staircase that a nine-year-old Malakhi had once fallen and knocked himself senseless while chasing Gidal during a rowdy game of war. And from that rooftop where the two boys had practiced shooting with the slings Eitan wove for them and I'd stood on the tips of my toes to search out the farthest points on the horizon and long for adventures. And on that long, low table in the very center where thousands of my mother's perfectly seasoned dishes were placed to the sensory delight of family and guests alike. So many memories flooded me that my stomach ached from the weight of them.

Tohdah broke into my thoughts by introducing me to Ednah and Hada, the two other women who worked at the inn. On their well-callused knees grinding wheat with a saddle quern, the ladies barely skimmed their weary eyes upward to note my presence as they continued the rhythm of their movements back and forth, back and forth. By the time Tohdah had finished outlining the numerous chores I was expected to perform over the course of the next few hours, I'd successfully pushed aside all echoes of the past in favor of the tasks at hand.

But when I approached the oven, I could not help but reach out to stroke the smooth surface of the stones that my mother had touched myriad times, a wooden spoon in one hand, her tunic streaked with flour, and unbridled love for her family and her city in her heart.

A vow arose within my own heart as I did so. *I will return this inn to you, Ima. Kedesh needs you.*

CHAPTER

THIRTY-TWO

Liyam

Mud seeped between my toes as I pressed farther into the marshy lake. The muck swelled up over my feet until my ankles were encased and the water touched my knees. I reached for another feathery reed and bent to saw its stem with my knife, as close to the base of the plant as possible. After harvesting papyrus for the better part of the day and part of yesterday, I'd become accustomed to the laborious task but could not help but be glad that I would soon need to fetch Tirzah from the city gates.

Leaving her behind this morning had been an exercise in restraint. For as assured as she was that she would be safe at the inn among the women, and that her knives were sufficient protection, Kedesh was anything but a place of safety. Shechem had been dangerous for both of us to be certain, but there was something about the way the guards had watched us as we entered, wariness mixed with a healthy portion of fear, that might prove to be lethal for anyone who lifted their head above the crowd of bent-backed Hebrews. It would be even more important that Tirzah and I not bring attention to ourselves here, and imperative that we not take any unnecessary risks, for this time it was not just the two of us at stake, but Nessa's family and anyone who chose to associate with us who would suffer if we failed.

Even so, I'd forced my feet to follow Yoash and Kefa to the papyrus maker, through the marketplace to barter for supplies, and then back to the valley without my wife. When Nessa said that Tirzah had easily procured a spot at the inn, I'd been more disappointed than relieved, which was foolish, since our goal had been to have her infiltrate that household. At least I'd had the papyrus plants to work out my frustrations upon as I anxiously kept track of the movement of the sun.

Dotan took the stalk from my hand and tossed it atop the pile he'd made on the bank. Nessa's husband and I had settled into a companionable rhythm throughout the course of the day; I would cut the reeds, and he would stack them with his good arm, and quiet and reserved as he was, he'd mostly left me to stew over Tirzah in silence as we worked.

Is she safe? I wondered as I hacked at another plant beneath the surface of the water. *What if the suspicious guards at the gate alerted one of their superiors to strangers in the city?* I yanked at the mangled papyrus, twisting it with all the force of my worry, but it refused to budge, so I must not have cut all the way through the reed. *What if something happened and I was locked outside, unable to reach her in time?* I sliced at what remained of the plant with fury, my belly churning at the thought of someone even worse than Khaled going after her.

Yoash and Kefa had started their harvesting this morning at the opposite end of the western shore, their animated voices floating across the surface of the water, but now our two teams were nearly at a meeting point. I'd told them yesterday of my mission in Kedesh and my plans to gather as many men as possible, and they'd been much less receptive than I'd expected, agreeing with Nessa's worries about the Arameans watching the farm closely. Eventually, they'd listed a number of neighbors and friends who they felt might be amenable to meeting with me but told me not to expect too much. The lukewarm response was concerning, to say the least. Perhaps the people of this region were even more complacent than they were in the south.

"So, tell me, Liyam," said Kefa as he bent to slice another feather-tipped papyrus stalk from its mooring. "Where do you hail from?"

"Yehudite territory, near the Salt Sea," I replied, wondering whether he'd noticed how anxious I'd been since leaving Tirzah behind and had determined to distract me from it.

"Not Shiloh?"

I shook my head and slid my knife under the surface of the lake once more, knowing what was coming next.

"What brings you so far from home, then? Surely not Tirzah? She's a lovely girl, but I don't know many men who would travel the length of Israel to procure a bride." He grinned at his own jest, but it was not from malice. There was an easiness to Kefa's character that reminded me of Yavan and his constant flow of teasing at my expense.

"I've not known Tirzah long," I said. "Other concerns brought me northward."

"Gathering support for Othniel?" Yoash asked.

"No, I've been searching for someone," I responded, wincing at the realization that I'd not thought of my pursuit of the trader all day. Not since last night, when Tirzah had spoken of Raviv's sacrifice for his daughter, had the idea of blood vengeance even crossed my mind. I'd been too distracted by my concern for Tirzah and the goal of searching out supporters of Israel to let my mind drift back to my daughter's killer.

I relayed my story to Kefa, and by the time I'd finished my tale, including the way I'd met Tirzah in Shechem, the three men had halted their work to stare at me.

"And after all this time searching for this one-eyed Moabite you've not come across anyone who has seen him?" asked Kefa.

"The trader was seen heading out of Beit She'an a few weeks ago, perhaps moving this way. I made inquiries at a few villages as we passed through the Kinneret Valley, without success, so I suspect he may have veered northeast back toward Damascus." I did not relish heading into Aramean territory to pursue him if he had, but I would do so if necessary.

Yoash stood tall among the reeds, arms folded across his wide chest and new suspicion in his gaze. "You know of our Uncle Raviv."

"I do," I said, bristling. "But our circumstances are different."

I had no interest in defending my decisions to these men, who although welcoming until now, I'd only known for less than a full cycle of the sun.

"Perhaps," he replied. "But we all lived with a go'el haadam for many years, so you can imagine why we might be concerned."

My brow furrowed. "From what I understand, you are related to Raviv's second wife. You had no connection to Moriyah or Eitan, so how would his vengeance have any impact on you?"

Kefa huffed a sorrowful laugh. "We may not have been the ones he so desperately wanted to exact judgment upon, but we felt the impact all the same. There was a reason why Nessa ran from this valley. A reason why the rest of us stepped softly in his presence. And a reason why our aunt Neshama rued the day she married the man."

Kefa began to tell the story that Tirzah would not have known to tell, giving life to the experiences of a family whose foundation was built on such rocky ground that it was a wonder it ever took root.

He told me that Raviv's fury at what he deemed his brother's betrayal had refused to be quenched, no matter how many years passed, and how each of those passing years saw him grow more and more bitter until the only thing that seemed to come from his mouth were curt demands on the best of days, or black curses on the worst of them. Eventually Neshama had been so terrified to make a misstep for fear of his sharp tongue that she barely spoke above a whisper in his presence.

"It wasn't until Nessa ran from his wrath," said Kefa, "that he began to awaken to the damage his single-minded focus on vengeance had wrought. Many of our clan had already left the farm, searching out other opportunities where they'd not have to endure his fits of temper and unpredictable rages. And with Nessa gone—the only one of his daughters who had any backbone to speak of—the rest were so cowed in his presence that they skittered into the shadows whenever he was around."

Yoash nodded in agreement. "And he also felt certain that he'd been cursed by Yahweh since he ended up with only four daughters who survived. All three male infants Neshama bore died before they took a breath outside the womb."

"Which is, of course, why the two of us tend this land, and not a son of his own blood," said Kefa, his eyes trained on me with an expression I could not discern.

"What does any of this have to do with me?" I said. "The trader I seek is not my brother. Once my score with him is settled, it will be done."

"Perhaps nothing," said Kefa. "I only know that we watched the light go out in the eyes of our aunt and saw Raviv's girls grow into women who feared their father more than they loved him. Perhaps you should ask yourself whether this pursuit is truly worth the cost."

His words so nearly echoed my mother's that I flinched and almost dropped my knife into the water. As I glared down at the mirrored surface, the silence between the four of us was broken only by the call of a crane from across the lake.

"I must go retrieve my wife," I said with a tight smile, then strode from the water, leaving their well-meant concerns on the mucky lakeshore where they belonged.

◆ ◆ ◆

Following the now-familiar path through what remained of the olive orchard, I headed up toward the city. The expression on Tirzah's shock-pale face when she'd first seen the conditions in Kedesh had nearly gutted me. I could only imagine how destroyed I would be if invaders had taken over my valley, chopped down many of the trees our family so lovingly tended all these years, and moved into our homes. This land, given to us by Yahweh himself, was sacred. Every part of it. It was no wonder that the enemy would not care for it as we did, since in their minds it was a resource to be used at their whims, not a gift to be guarded and cherished.

Even with the many stumps interspersed between the remaining olive trees, I could well imagine a younger version of Tirzah here, darting about between trunks, whipping her sling around, and filling the air with the melody of her laugher as she chased her brothers through the fields.

This marriage was not a true one; I'd barely even touched her and had only kissed her that first day as an act for Barsoum, but the more time I spent with Tirzah, the more I craved her presence. Those first pangs of guilt over looking at her as I once had Havah had seemed to wither away over these last few weeks in her company. And as Yavan had pointed out, Tirzah and I were indeed well matched. Her bravery. Her sharp wits. Her laughing eyes. All of it pulled at me like a relentless tide, making me want something more, and melting away all the reasons I'd had for avoiding marriage since Havah's death.

Yet even as I wondered whether we might change things between us, Kefa's words came to mind.

"We watched the light go out in the eyes of our aunt . . ."

If I succumbed to my want for Tirzah, might this quest for justice do the same to her? I could not deny that a deep well of bitterness lived inside me—something that had taken root with the loss of Havah and then multiplied a hundredfold when my Nadina was killed.

If I never found the Moabite, would resentment consume me as it had Raviv? Would it tarnish Tirzah's vibrance and chip away at her regard for me?

I thought of the way I'd snarled and snapped at Yavan whenever he prodded at me. How I'd thought nothing of dragging him through enemy territory as I pursued the trader. At how easy it had been to jam my sword into Barsoum's chest . . .

Had I become just like Raviv? A man so full of venom that all around him felt his bite? I winced at the idea of my family coming to fear me, tiptoeing around my anger, or even going so far as to flee my presence.

But just as I considered whether the cost of this pursuit was indeed too great, Nadina's face filled my mind. *"Abba! Pick me up!"* she demanded in her tiny voice. *"I want to touch the clouds!"*

No, I was not like Nessa's father. Our circumstances were vastly different. A woman and a young boy had accidentally killed his two sons, not a Moabite who willfully drove his team of horses over a child. The man deserved to die, whereas Moriyah and Eitan did not.

And even if I did give in to my growing desire for the woman now considered my wife and convince her to stay with me when I returned to my home, I had no intention of allowing my anger at a killer to taint our life together. I would protect her and care for her just as much as I had my first wife. I would never give her cause to fear me or allow her lovely boldness to fade. Besides, with Malakhi's help, I would find the trader and finish this whole matter soon enough.

"Liyam!" called Tirzah as she darted from the gates to meet me. She strode toward me with a brilliant smile painted on her lips, and my chest contracted with the pleasure of that smile being created for me.

"I have so much to tell you!" she said, her animated expression recalling my earlier thoughts about her as a young girl gamboling about like a lamb. Her gaze traveled down to my feet, which I'd not realized were still encrusted with dried muck from the lakeshore. Her eyes danced with mirth. "No time to stop and wash?"

"I was distracted," I said, glowering down at the muddy sandals that told the story of my hurry to get to her.

"Oh?" she peered at me. "And why was that?"

"Because my wife was in danger," I replied, unwilling to share how unsettled I'd been by Kefa's stories about Raviv. "And no matter that she can defend herself from one man, as she proved." I gestured toward the city. "There is more than one Aramean in there. If something happened, I could do nothing to get to her."

She blinked up at me. "You were that worried for me?"

"Of course. At least when we were in Barsoum's house I knew that you were only a few rooms away in the kitchen and under guard. But inside those walls I cannot reach you. Cannot see with my own eyes that you are safe. There are so many ways all of this could go wrong, Tirzah. Don't you see?"

"I do," she said, pulling at her lower lip with her teeth. "But things could have gone wrong in Shechem too. Don't you remember Hanael and Sheth?"

Sheth's bloodied face and pleading eyes appeared in my vision, then were overlaid by a horrific image of Tirzah being tortured in his place.

"Of course I do," I gritted out. "And you must not take foolish risks here like you did then, or it won't just be a couple of spies dying because of your actions. It could be all of us."

She flinched at my hasty words, and I was immediately struck by guilt for allowing my mouth to move faster than my tact.

"Tirzah," I began. "That's not what—"

She lifted a palm, which I noted was trembling. "No. You are right. I must be more cautious. Being at the inn today gave me a false sense of security, and I must not forget that it is no longer my home but a place that houses the wives of my enemies. I cannot allow myself to be complacent." Then she turned to head for the valley, defeat in the slope of her shoulders.

I'd done just what I'd vowed not to do only a short time before—chipped away at her beautiful brashness by lashing out at the very audacity and determination I so admired in her.

Mourning the loss of the sweet smile she'd given me before I'd tripped over my own tongue, I followed after her with muddy feet and a thorny tangle coiled inside my gut. For no matter how much I'd come to care for her—and my distress all day proved that I did indeed care for her much more than I'd even realized—I still could not betray my daughter. Nadina deserved justice.

CHAPTER

THIRTY-THREE

Tirzah

10 Sivan

It could have been any normal evening meal in my mother's inn, with twelve guests gathered around the long, low table Eitan and Malakhi had built, partaking of a lavish array of food. But instead of satisfying fellowship between family and friends, an argument had broken out between two of the Aramean wives, one that had risen in volume as well as spitefulness the longer it continued.

"You have no right to say that to me," said Chea, her henna-lined eyes fixed on Vereda, who'd insinuated that Chea was little more than a pampered prostitute.

"Truth is truth," said Vereda with a sniff and took a long draft of her wine. Then she lifted her cup and shook it in the air—a silent demand. Sighing internally, I obeyed, thinking that even though Vereda was a tall, willowy woman with wide blue eyes and golden hair, her imperious and arrogant personality more closely resembled fat, balding Barsoum.

Chea's face went ruddy, and her usually delicate features contorted into ugly malice. "You are just jealous that he chooses me over you most nights."

Why the husband of these two squalling wildcats chose to house them in the same inn during his absence, I could not fathom. They spent most days brawling over which of them was more favored and the rest of the time ordering the servants about like queens.

"You will be used for a time, it is true. And then set aside, just like the last of his cows," said Vereda with a pointed sneer at Chea's shapely bosom.

"You are nothing more than a sack of bones that becomes more shriveled every day." Chea ran her hands down her torso and along her well-rounded hips. "These aren't going anywhere anytime soon. So let's guess which one of us will be tossed out on her bony backside first, shall we?"

After two weeks of listening to these women tear each other to pieces, I now understood why Tohdah had wondered whether I would last in this job. It was an exercise in patience from moment to moment, dawn till dusk. Thankfully I'd spent months being ordered around by Barsoum and his underlings, or I too would have questioned my ability to keep my mouth sealed around these spoiled and vindictive women.

But instead of letting my thoughts about their selfish behavior spill from my mouth, I retrieved a tray of seed cakes that were drenched in date wine and sprinkled with a mixture of spices and walnuts and carefully placed one in front of each woman at the table.

By the time I'd finished doling out the indulgent cakes, Chea and Vereda had left off their arguing in lieu of devouring my creation. I'd taken a recipe I learned from my mother and altered it, using the vast array of exotic spices the women had brought with them from Aram-Naharim and the other nations they originated from. There were two women from Egypt here, four from Harran, three from Ur, and one woman whose dark skin and deep black eyes reminded me so much of Zendaye, my mother's friend and the mother-in-law to my sister Chana.

It had been at least two years since I'd seen Chana, traveling as she was with her husband's trading caravan to places I could only imagine.

I hoped they would return once the Land was in our control again; it had been far too dangerous for them to attempt such a trip during these past months of upheaval and war.

Once the women had their fill of my cakes, I poured another round of wine and then began to remove the soiled bowls and plates from the table. Most of the women ignored me as I did so, just as Barsoum and his men had done, but the two youngest ones at the very end of the table kept whispering to each other and glancing my way as I worked. Annoyed by whatever secrets they were telling about me but obligated to serve them with bland benevolence, I kept my eyes on my task but my ears open wide.

These women were gossips. And unlike the men they'd married who'd been trained to keep secrets, their mouths ran like rivers.

So far I'd discovered that Kushan was indeed on his way to our Land, but that his army was nearly half of what it had been when he came in before, due to a falling-out with some of the nations that had allied with him eight years ago.

Vereda and Chea were married to the commander who lorded over Megiddo, and now with Barsoum defeated, it was upon him to retain what was left of the territory they'd snatched from us.

I'd learned that the women had all been moved here as a precaution in the recent months, since Othniel had begun to march north, because Kedesh was tucked away in the highlands and without major strategic position like Beit She'an and Megiddo. Although after serving these coddled women over the last few days, I wondered if they hadn't simply been stashed here to keep from being underfoot in the midst of a war they seemed indifferent to.

After the meal had ended and the women were scattered to their rooms, I helped Tohdah clean the rest of the vessels and utensils, scrubbed the table that my brothers had so lovingly built for my mother, and then went up to the roof to help Barucha with the linens and clothing she'd spent most of the day washing in the stream.

Once all the cloth was flapping joyfully in the breeze atop the roof, strung across thin ropes that hung between sturdy poles my own father had erected for that purpose nearly thirty years before, Barucha thanked me for my help and wearily clomped down the stairs to head home. The poor woman was so overworked that she barely spoke, and when she did, her words were laced with sighs. I'd done my best to assist her whenever I could, but until one of the missing girls returned to help with the eternal job of washing the clothes of the women who lived here, most of which necessitated careful handling due to their expensive and delicate nature, Barucha was expected to bear the load. Tohdah had determined my skills were of better use in the kitchen.

The sun was at my back as I leaned my elbows on the wall and peered over it to the ground far below. Even with the loss of so many trees around the city, the vista looked much the same: the triple peaks of Har Hermon, the glittering blue lake in the valley, the stretches of green-and-brown fields. But the flocks of sheep and goats that had once lazily grazed the surrounding fields were gone. The sheepfold now housed a herd of pigs, which tainted the air with their putrid smell.

"Are you waiting for your man?" came a voice from behind me. I swirled around to find the two youngest wives, the ones who'd been watching me during the meal, standing on the rooftop a few paces away.

I blinked at the odd question, wondering whether I should pretend to not understand their language like I had in Shechem. It was the first time any of the Arameans' wives had addressed me directly, so I was unprepared. However, since none of them seemed to care whether I listened in on what they considered inconsequential gossip, it would not be as much of an issue as it had near Barsoum.

"Your man? Doesn't he wait for you down by the gates?" asked Larisa, the shorter of the two, whose wild brown curls darted about in the breeze. Her nose wrinkled as she giggled, a few fingers over her hennaed mouth. "The red-haired one?"

"Oh—Yes—" I stuttered, at a loss for why they knew anything about me. "That is Liyam, my husband."

"We saw him come for you," said Merit, the one whose shiny black hair trailed past her waist. The Egyptian kept it unbound like a little girl, but her perpetually somber expression, the heavy gold bands on her wrists, and the abundant black kohl surrounding her onyx eyes gave the impression of a young woman who'd seen far too much in her short years.

"He is so handsome!" bubbled Larisa, her giddy enthusiasm betraying her youth. "I've never seen a man with red hair quite that color. And such shoulders, like he could sling a woman over them without taking a second breath." She sighed and fluttered a hand in front of her blushing cheeks. "You are fortunate indeed."

"How did you see Liyam?" I asked. "He never comes into the city."

"We followed you yesterday!" Larisa said with an unrepentant grin. "The guards would not let us go past the outer gates, but we saw him greet you there anyhow."

"Why would you follow me?" My question was terse, mostly out of annoyance at myself because I was usually so aware of my surroundings. Perhaps I'd been distracted by the very thing they'd noticed—my husband. Whenever he met me at the gates my heart jumped around like a newborn lamb and my skin flushed hot. It was as frustrating as it was confusing and becoming more unsettling by the day. And the closet Nessa had put us in seemed to be growing smaller and smaller each night.

"We were curious about you," said Merit, her low husky voice a stark contrast to Larisa's bright tones.

"And there's nothing much else to do in this prison," said Larisa with a dismayed frown as she tugged at her finely pleated crimson gown. "We could lay around like Chea and Vereda, eating and drinking like Egyptian queens, but neither of us can stand being penned up here like animals."

I well remembered being their age, itching to explore beyond my horizons, eager to know all there was to know about the world. Being married so young and kept like vibrant birds in a cage while their husbands ground our people to dust was no sort of life at all. Neither of these two must be more than three or four years older than Odeleya, but the differences between my innocent young friend and these two worldly, overpainted girls made the gap seem much wider.

"So?" Larisa pressed, coming closer, her brown eyes impossibly wide. "Tell us about him. Is he as handsome up close as he is from twenty paces away? What does it feel like to be wrapped up in those big arms?"

My face went hot at the intimacy of her questions. *Of course he is as handsome up close*—I longed to say—*even more so.* I'd taken to watching his face as he spoke with the other men in the evenings around the fire, allowing my eyes to trace over his strong, red-bearded jaw, the faintly freckled tan skin at the neck of his tunic, and the powerful forearms that had grappled with Khaled in my defense. But it was when those blue-green eyes connected with mine, giving me a glimpse into the tangled-up, elusive soul within that I felt most drawn to him.

As for being wrapped up in those arms, that was a question I could not answer. Not that I did not wonder. Far too often.

But I'd caught him watching me too. And the tension in our little closet was not only from my side of the room. I did not think I imagined the way his shoulders relaxed as soon as I walked out of the gates every day, and how those jewel-like eyes took me in, from the top of my head to my sandals, as I approached him. He might say it was simple concern for my welfare after leaving me at the mercy of the Arameans all day, but my instincts told me something different.

However, I could not forget the flat tone of his voice as he'd told Malakhi and I that he would not marry again, nor the way he'd insisted that there was nothing left of his soul after the horrific death of his child. No matter how he might be drawn to me, it was plain that Liyam had no intention of allowing me inside.

Realizing that I'd not answered Larisa's intrusive questions and that the two young women were staring at me with bemusement on their faces as I'd been lost in thoughts of my husband, I flinched and took a couple of steps backward.

"If you will excuse me," I said, gesturing at the waning sunlight, "my husband will be waiting for me. The gates will close soon."

Their soft laughter followed me down the staircase, and I could only imagine what they might have seen on my face as I'd thought of Liyam. With a farewell wave to Tohdah, who scowled at me in response and then continued scraping warm ashes from the oven, I strode across the courtyard, worried that Larisa and Merit may have kept me too long. But just as I reached for the handle of the back door, it swung open, and an Aramean soldier stepped through the doorway. Tripping backward out of his way, I instinctively dropped my eyes to the ground and shrank into the shadows.

Three more soldiers passed through the doorway, none of them seeming to notice me, since they were busy discussing where best to procure strong drink after a long day of travel.

If I'd been only a few moments slower, if I'd not stepped into the shadows of the eaves when the first man appeared in the doorway, everything would have been lost. Because although I'd never seen three of these Arameans, the fourth was well known to me. I'd heard his voice on the road between Shiloh and Ramah. I'd felt the slide of his knuckles down my cheek and smelled his hot breath as he threatened me and my nephew.

Alek was in Kedesh.

This Aramean had seen my face, studied it in fact, before he'd been taken down by the men of my family and dragged away for interrogation, then left stripped and tied up in the woods.

My gut wrenched into a knot, and bile coated my tongue. He would remember me, without a doubt.

Liyam would be beside himself with worry if I told him about Alek being in the city. There would be no way he would allow me to step foot in the inn if I said a word, especially after his speech about how helpless he felt whenever I was inside the city walls.

But I'd been fine on my own for months before he arrived in Shechem. I'd simply have to be careful to stay out of sight until Alek left the city, use all the skills I'd learned in Barsoum's house to blend into the shadows and keep myself out of his way. His commander had obviously come to visit Larisa, who let out a squeal of pleasure as she fluttered down the staircase and into her much-older husband's arms. Hopefully he was only here for a night.

I could not leave my post at the inn now. I'd already overheard so much helpful information from the women, and perhaps I'd be able to get even more from Larisa after her husband left. She was certainly enthralled with me and my *handsome* husband, after all, so I could use that to my advantage. We'd had very little success in finding Levites in the area; the only ones Yoash and Kefa knew of refused to even listen when Liyam asked them to meet with us. So if I could not spark a revival among the priests here as Othniel had charged me to do, I could at least keep gathering valuable intelligence.

Besides, I owed it to my people to remain. I owed it to Eliya for letting him down and leaving him to die without an heir when the Arameans worked him into the grave. I owed it to Sheth and Hanael and Chaim and all the others who had died in service to Israel. I owed it to the people of Kedesh, who'd suffered under Aramean tyranny and lost their homes like my family had.

Before anyone could take notice of me, I bolted through the still-open door, through the inn, and back out into the street. Noting that the sun was beginning to drop low in the sky, I sped down the road and around the corner, barely making it to the gates of the city as the guards were just preparing to close the giant cedar doors and secure them for the night.

There, ten paces from the entrance, stood Liyam, worry heavy on his brow and his arms folded across his expansive chest as he glared with menace at the ground in front of his feet, reminding me all too much of the mercenary I'd met at Barsoum's table. The same one who'd grabbed me and crashed his lips into mine before I'd even known his name. Pushing aside the turbulence such a memory provoked, I assembled my features into the same cool serenity that I'd utilized in Shechem as I approached him.

His head jerked up at the sound of my sandals on the sloping road, and his entire body relaxed at the sight of me. His head tilted back, eyes on the sky above, and his lips moved silently, as if he were thanking Yahweh for my return.

Tears suddenly burned at the back of my eyes. The thought of this strong—and yes, handsome—warrior caring enough for me that he'd looked close to breaching the city walls alone was overwhelming. I may have suggested this marriage in name only, but suddenly I wanted nothing more than to be his, for good. And once Alek was gone and I had no more cause to hide any of my truths, I would find a way to be just that.

His guard may be well established and his walls high from the grief he'd suffered. But I was a spy. I'd slipped into places far more dangerous than Liyam's broken heart.

THIRTY-FOUR

Liyam

When Tirzah asked me to accompany her on an excursion the morning after I'd nearly blazed into Kedesh without even a sword in hand to find her, I'd been all too glad to go. If anything, it would keep her within my sights for a few hours.

Every day when she walked away from me and past those cedar gates, I felt as if I were holding my breath until I saw her face again. The hours in-between I spent either helping Yoash, Kefa, and Dotan in the fields and orchards, or training the paltry group of fifteen men we'd rounded up in the center of a thick wood just south of Raviv's lands. But whenever I stopped to take a breath or down a skin of water, Tirzah's mischievous smile, Tirzah's shining black curls, and Tirzah's laughing eyes came immediately to mind, which led me to worry all over again.

I could not lose her. Not like I had Havah. Not like Nadina. It was becoming clearer by the day that I would not survive if I did.

"How did you manage to talk Tohdah into letting you have this morning free?" I asked as we hiked up the slope above Kedesh. She seemed to know exactly where she was going, so I had been following along without question.

"I told her I had something to fetch. Something that would please the wives." She grinned at me over her shoulder, then pushed forward into an overgrown quince orchard that looked to have been neglected for many years.

"These don't look ready to pick yet, if it's quince you are after," I said, pressing back the still-green pomes hanging heavy on the branches so we could go farther into the orchard.

"No. Although when they ripen I'll make sure to bring Ednah and Hada out here to gather a few basketfuls." She stopped for a moment to cup one of the quince fruits in her hand, bringing it close to breathe in its scent. To my surprise, her eyes were glistening when she released it.

"This was Gidal's orchard," she said, looking around with a sad smile. "My older brother, the one between Eitan and Malakhi. He loved these trees, as if they were formed from his own ribs. I used to enjoy coming here with him, listening to him tell me all about how to care for the fruit and when exactly to harvest it." She paused, swallowing hard. "And it was just over there"—she gestured to the foot of one tree—"where a viper's bite stole him from us."

I'd not known she'd had another brother at all, let alone one who died in such circumstances. Between the both of us we'd sustained the loss of far too many loved ones, a commonality that I wished we did not share.

"I am sorry to hear that," I said.

"I was only nine. But I worshipped him." She sighed and ran her fingers gently over the leaves of the closest tree. "I am glad this orchard remains. It makes me feel as though he still lives on, in a way."

She gave me another sad smile and walked through the quince grove, onto a narrow path that wound its way farther up the hill. With barely enough room to place one foot in front of the other and the incline sharp and rocky, my sandals skidded more than a few times, nearly causing me to tumble backward down the hill, which Tirzah found all too amusing. My fleet-footed wife pranced ahead of me like a nimble ibex, a small pack slung over her shoulder that she'd refused to let me carry and her brown eyes twinkling back at me every so often. The breeze tangled into her luxurious curls, making me jealous of its invisible fingers.

"Just a little farther. Unless, of course, you need a break," she said with a playful frown.

I narrowed my eyes at her. "What can we possibly be looking for? Are you just leading me up here to push me off a cliff?"

"Perhaps." She pressed her lush lips together, suppressing a smirk. Then without a word, she darted off the trail and out of sight.

When I caught up to the place she'd disappeared, I found the entrance to a cave, barely wide enough for my shoulders and a head shorter than me. Bending down to peer inside, I called her name.

Suddenly she appeared out of the blackness at the far end of the cave, the biggest smile I'd seen on her face since she'd made that first clay jar explode with her sling in Shiloh.

"They're still here!" she said, then reached to tug me inside. "I prayed no one discovered them in our absence, and Yahweh kept our secret!"

Once past the narrow entrance, I found that the roof was higher than I expected and enough light had spilled inside that only the far wall of the cave was painted in deep shadow. Tirzah began pulling items from her pack: an empty pot, some flint, and a pile of old linens cut into long strips.

I watched in confused fascination as she sparked a fire with the flint, then set alight some damp brush she'd pressed into the bottom of a pot. She blew on the flame, causing a thin stream of smoke to curl upward. Then she wrapped the linens around every part of her exposed skin. Her neck. Her arms and legs. Her head and ears. All I could see was her eyes glittering at me as she told me to stay put and remain quiet.

She darted into the blackness, carrying her smoking pot, and I wondered if somehow she'd lost her senses. What sort of treasure could be found deep in a cave, and what use could smoke and linen coverings have in its retrieval? She must have the eyes of an owl to see in such darkness anyhow.

She was gone far too long, and I began to shuffle from foot to foot. Again, that suffocating disquiet I felt whenever she was out of my sight gnawed at me. Just as I'd decided that it was past time to retrieve her, she returned with a large, dripping clump of honeycomb in her hand.

She tugged the linens away from her face. "Gidal's bees are still here!"

"Gidal's bees?"

"When we were told that we must leave Kedesh, Eitan and Malakhi went to the quince orchard in the guise of harvesting some fruit for our journey, and they hid the hives Gidal had built just before he died. The last thing any of us wanted was for our brother's hard work to be destroyed by the Arameans—or worse, for them to reap its rewards. There's a small air shaft in the ceiling of the other chamber, which allows the bees to come back and forth and gave me just enough light to steal a portion of their treasure."

She plucked the pack from the ground and lowered the comb inside. "I'll take this back to the inn and press the honey from it. I told Tohdah that I'd stumbled upon a wild hive, so she practically begged me to fetch some honey, since the wives have been fussing about having only dates to sweeten their food."

"What was the purpose of the smoke?" I asked.

"Malakhi taught me to do that. Somehow it makes the bees more compliant, so they don't sting as much when you harvest the hive. He used to tell me as a girl that it made the bees too sleepy to attack."

Noticing that she was scratching her hand, I shuffled forward to grab her wrist. Then I lifted her arm so I could get a better look at the red welt at the base of her thumb. I brushed a finger over the spot. "You've been stung."

"It's nothing," she said, but her voice was barely more than a breath. "Gidal taught me to dab some honey on a sting to cut the pain."

Without releasing my hold on her, I looked into her eyes and saw my reflection within their luminous depths. How was it I only felt I could breathe fully when in this woman's presence anymore? My mind went to that first kiss, when I'd grabbed her like an animal staking a claim.

She'd trembled with fear in my arms then, but I would never forget the feel of her mouth against mine, no matter how brief the contact.

"Will you . . ." she whispered. "Will you tell me of your wife?"

Her question crashed through my pleasant thoughts about her lips, and I dropped her hand.

"My wife?" I blinked at her, off balance and wondering if the smoke that still trickled from the depths of the cave was clouding my head more than the bees it was meant for.

"I want to know you better, Liyam. You and I have been living in such close quarters for months now, but I feel as though in many ways we are still strangers." She paused, taking a deep breath, and glancing down at her hands. "I want . . . I want more of you."

Elation surged through my blood at her admission, but close on its wake was a pang of trepidation. I'd not spoken of Havah in a long time, other than the few times Nadina had asked about her mother. But Tirzah's gaze held nothing but earnest compassion, so I acquiesced.

"Her name was Havah. She was the daughter of one of my father's friends. I met her only twice before we married, but she was beautiful and very kind, so I had no problem with the match."

"And you came to love her?" she asked, peering up at me with a tight smile that made me wonder whether there was a small measure of jealousy entangled with the question.

"She was a good woman," I said, determined to speak the full truth. "A gentle and faithful wife who I indeed came to treasure, but we were only married for a few months when the Arameans invaded our lands. By Torah law I should not have fought in that war so soon after our marriage, but I was young, full of fury at the enemy. I insisted on joining the men of my family, determining that the need for any hand with a sword or a sling was too great for me to stay behind. When I returned a few months later, after we'd lost to the Arameans, I discovered that she was with child."

I'd been defeated and grieving the loss of so many men, along with our tribal lands, and only the rounded swell of Havah's belly as she ran to me upon my return gave me any hope after such a devastating blow.

"Her body was far more fragile than anyone guessed. And only a few months later she was dead. She fought so hard for Nadina. . . ." I paused, taking a deep breath to steady my voice. "She refused to give up during the labor, even though she was far beyond exhausted and nearly out of her mind with pain. I'll never forget the look of peace when my mother placed the babe on her chest, as if she'd caught a glimpse of paradise in our daughter's little face . . . and then she was gone."

"Oh, Liyam," Tirzah whispered, moisture brimming on her lashes.

"I should have stayed behind," I said, feeling all over again the help-lessness and the crushing grief as Havah took her last breaths. "I should have spent those months with her instead."

"You could not have known," she said.

"Perhaps not. But I will regret it for the rest of my days."

She was silent for a few moments, scratching at her bee sting with a frustrated frown. "I have to tell you something. . . ." She paused, chewing her lip thoughtfully, a struggle clear in her eyes. "I saw—" She stopped and shook her head.

"I know much of regret as well," she finally said, the words coming out in a strangely determined rush. "Eliya and I were married four years ago. He was a good man from our tribe, tolerant of my odd ways. Within only a few months we were expecting a child."

She'd told me she was barren the day we'd agreed to marry, so I was taken aback. My mind went directly to the future and what such a revelation might mean for us.

Seemingly unaware of the loud conflict raging in my head, she con-tinued. "He was so thrilled. Going on and on about his son and heir to anyone who would listen." She swallowed hard, scratching again at that welt on her hand with a pained expression that I knew had noth-ing to do with the bee sting.

"I lost it," she stated. "And then I lost another. When I suspected that I was with child a third time, I told no one. Not even my mother. I could not bear to face Eliya again. By that time he was so disappointed that he barely even spoke to me. I think perhaps he was even consider-ing finding another . . ." Her voice faded into nothing.

My stomach wrenched into a knot. Had her husband wanted to throw her over for another wife? I could not imagine anyone tossing this vibrant woman to the side.

"Before I even lost that last babe, Eliya had been taken by the Arameans, in retribution for a failed rebellion that he was not even involved in. I never had to face him with the news that I'd failed him, yet again."

"You did not fail him, Tirzah."

She shrugged, her lips curling into a grim smile. "My body certainly did. Something inside of me is too weak to carry a child."

"Is that why you push yourself so hard?"

She blinked at me in confusion.

"You are the most audacious woman I've ever met—and my mother is no soft-spoken maiden by any means. You trained with Malakhi, who is reputed to be the best of the best. You dove into a perilous mission in Shechem without hesitation. You refused to abandon that mission even when it went wrong. You took on Khaled to save me, though he was nearly twice your size. You are *anything* but weak, Tirzah."

Her mouth opened and closed, as if she were considering whether to argue the point. But then, to my great surprise, she stepped closer to me, bringing her warm, potent gaze to mine.

"And you, Liyam, are not soulless like you think yourself to be. Grieving, yes. Hurting and angry, yes. But not empty. I see you there, deep inside, beneath all the pain and bitterness." She closed the gap between us and lifted her hands to my cheeks. Standing on the tips of her toes, she whispered, her breath teasing my lips. "And I want more."

All restraint melted away by her words, I wrapped my arms around her body and dropped my mouth to hers, reveling in the honeyed sweetness of her yielding lips.

Mine. My mind repeated over and over as I pulled her even closer, and she responded by twining her arms behind my neck. *This woman is mine.*

When I finally came to my senses and slightly loosened my hold, Tirzah giggled against my mouth and then peered up at me with mischief in her golden-brown eyes.

"Tohdah will be wondering what has happened to me," she said. "She'll think I ran off with you to escape my duties."

Helpless to resist anymore, I laid another lingering kiss on her lips. "That sounds like an excellent idea."

"If Larisa and Merit catch wind of it, there will be no end to the questions about my *handsome husband*." She rolled her eyes toward the roof of the cave.

I lifted a brow. "Who are they?"

"Two of the wives. They followed me to the gate one evening."

"Where they caught sight of just how handsome I am, of course," I said, offering her a slow, confident grin. "Perhaps I'll have to meet these very discerning ladies."

She narrowed her eyes at me. "They're half your age. If that."

I laughed and dipped my head to brush my lips at the hinge of her jaw. "Only you, my lovely Tirzah." I kissed a path down the side of her neck, causing her to shiver. "Only you."

"I have to go," she said, her tone husky as she halfheartedly pushed at my shoulder. "Or I'll never leave and then I'll lose my position at the inn for certain. Honey or not."

I groaned as she slipped from my hold. She snatched up the pack with the honeycomb inside and darted to the entrance of the cave. She paused to look over her shoulder. "I'll see you tonight. . . ." *Handsome husband*, she mouthed before spinning away with another beautiful laugh, the last of my defenses clenched tightly in her skillful little hand.

THIRTY-FIVE

Tirzah

Where was Liyam?

I'd arrived at the gates that evening well before dusk. Tohdah had been so thrilled by my honey that she'd almost smiled, and when I asked whether she had additional tasks for me to perform before I left for the day, she'd waved me off with a snarling demand to "go on home." It was the closest to thanks I would likely ever receive from the woman, but it was enough. And I'd been thrilled to set my feet toward my husband, my lips still buzzing with the memory of our kisses in the honey cave and eager to be wrapped up in the strong arms that were even more warm and wonderful than Larisa or Merit could ever guess.

But the ram's horn had already announced that the gates were closing, and still my husband had not arrived.

Could he have regretted the intimate words we shared this morning? Wished he'd not revealed so much about his first wife or decided that a woman who could not carry a child was not worth the effort?

No. I'd seen the compassion on his face as I'd spoken of my lost babes and his determined sincerity as he insisted that I was not weak, not useless, as I'd secretly feared for so long. Besides, he'd been late before, after being caught up in his tasks around the farm or with recruiting men. He would come for me, I had no doubt.

I'd almost told him about Alek; it had been on my lips all morning, the secret begging to be freed, but when I'd returned to the inn with my bag full of honeycomb, I'd discovered that Larisa's husband and his men had only stayed the night and then left Kedesh at first light. Larisa had been pouting ever since, frustrated that she'd been only a stopover during his journey, an afterthought. Her whining had been so overwrought since his abrupt departure that the other wives were avoiding her, even Merit. I, however, had been more than relieved that collecting honey had kept me far clear of Alek and hoped he would not return any time soon.

Of course I'd fed Larisa's mood by feigning shock that her husband would leave his beautiful wife after such a short visit, especially after being separated from her charms for so many months, and then insisting she rest in the shade with some refreshment. I'd offered her a honeyed roll and a large mug of strong wine to ease her suffering and played the empathetic ear while she told me how terrible he was for leaving her there in Kedesh just to run off to a war council.

"That new high commander is a beast," she'd said, her tone petulant and betraying her true age. "Demanding that my husband drop everything and rush to Megiddo. I don't want to wait another week or two to see him when he returns on his way back to Laish."

"Why would the high commander do such a thing?" I asked, refilling her mug to the top, my brow wrinkled in sympathy even as I made plans for avoiding the inn when he did come back. I could not chance coming across Alek again. "If he had something to tell your husband, wouldn't a message suffice?"

She snorted, the sound incongruent to her pretty face. "Oh, it wasn't just my husband he summoned. It was all the commanders in this awful land, the ones who head the garrisons in Beit She'an, Merom, Golan, and a few other cities whose names I don't remember. Or care about." She giggled, the wine already having done its job.

"At least *your* husband is still here. And you have many nights, not just one, like me. And I'll bet each one is better than the last." She leaned closer, giving me a sloppy grin, heedless of my flaming cheeks. "Am I correct?"

I'd mumbled a non-answer and invented a task to attend, leaving her to guzzle her third cup of wine, and wondered how soon a messenger could be sent to Malakhi with the valuable information I'd just wheedled out of her.

The thought of sharing such a gem with Liyam and watching as his blue-green eyes lit up with pride for me had kept me humming for the rest of the day.

But here I stood near the entrance to Kedesh, the last of the stragglers slipping out of the city as the guards swung the heavy gates shut, and my husband was nowhere to be found.

Three men passed by me, giving me only a cursory glance as they headed off on the southern route, presumably toward their homes. But in the moment when the three of them had their faces turned my way, I'd recognized one of them.

I did not know his name, but I knew what he was. He was a good friend of Rivkah's oldest brother Tal. And he was a Levite. Not only that, but one of the *kohanim*, a priestly descendant of Aharon, who'd trained in Shiloh alongside Tal many years ago. Here was one of the very men I'd been searching for since we'd arrived in Shechem and one who had the distinctive tzitzit fringes peeking secretively from beneath his overgarment—which meant that even though he might not be actively serving as a priest in Shiloh, he had remained faithful to the Torah in spite of the Arameans.

Triumph shot through my blood, even as the men moved farther and farther away from me. But as I darted my attention back toward the ridge, searching for Liyam's familiar form, victory dissolved into frustration. I could not wait any longer. If I did not follow the Levite now, I would lose him, and who knew how long it would take before he returned to the city? Most of the people in the region avoided Kedesh unless they were desperately in need of something from the market or forced to deliver tribute to our overlords.

With one last glance toward the head of the trail Liyam took between the valley and the city, I made my decision. Of course he would be upset with me for leaving, but I had no choice. I would make it up to him by bringing back not only the news about the war council in Megiddo, but also the discovery of a Levite. Perhaps by the time I returned to Nessa's home, I'd have even convinced the man to join our cause and help flush out the rest of his fellow priests.

As I pursued the three men, who were very nearly out of sight already, I prayed that, as he'd done on Har Ebal on that frigid night near the altar of Yehoshua, Yahweh would use me to inspire his people to remember who they were and what they were made to do.

Grateful for the cloudless sky and brilliant moon that illuminated my path, I made my way through the olive orchard and over the ridge toward Nessa's home.

I'd not realized how late it was until I'd left the home of Avner, the Levite, but I was grateful that I knew this area like I knew the lines on my palms. Even in the dark I was able to find my way with ease, catching sight of the dark shadow of Kedesh crouching high on the hill and finding myself peering at its black walls, searching for my mother's lamp, even knowing it was not there.

It will be soon, I thought. Especially after tonight. I could not wait to tell Liyam everything that had transpired. I just hoped he'd not be too furious to listen.

I had followed the three men to a small hamlet only a short distance from the outer boundaries of Kedesh, thrilled that although I'd pursued them fairly closely, they'd not caught sight of me slipping along in the shadows of the trees that lined the path on either side.

The Levite took his leave of his friends and ducked into a small mud-brick house. Once the others had made their way to their own homes, I offered up the last of many prayers I'd whispered to the One Who Hears during my pursuit, slipped from my hiding spot behind a sturdy oak, and knocked on his door.

The man had been more than wary of a lone woman appearing at his door at twilight, just as he and his wife and five children were sitting down to their Shabbat meal, and he initially refused my request to speak with him, even when I told him that I knew Tal and that I'd been searching for a Levite for weeks. It wasn't until I informed him that I was Moriyah's daughter, and gave him plenty of details about her time in Kedesh, that the skepticism melted from his face and he ushered me inside, insisting that I join his family for the meal.

Over paltry but lovingly prepared fare, I explained what had led me to his door. I told him of Othniel's victories. Of the glorious Cloud briefly appearing over the Mishkan. Of the Levites in Shechem and how they revived the spirits of the people with the stories of our forefathers, leading to the altar on Ebal being set to flame and the ensuing victory. The longer I spoke, the larger the eyes around the room grew, until it seemed as though the seven of them were each holding their breath, awaiting my next words. As I finished by explaining how Liyam and I had come to inspire not only a rebellion against our oppressors but also a revival in our hearts that would lead to repentance and to a cry for deliverance, tears were tracking down the faces of both Avner and his wife.

"We prayed you would come," Avner said. "We prayed that Yahweh would stir love for him in the hearts of his people. But as much as we have tried to keep worship of the One True God pure over the last eight years, there is as much doubt as there is apathy among us." Defeat weighed heavily in his tone.

"We've heard little of the victories you speak of here. Most of the people in this region are spread out on their farms, so word travels slowly. We know the name of Othniel, of course, and about how he took Hebron back, but any other information passed along is mixed and sometimes contradictory. Many say the Arameans took back the refuge city as soon as it was reclaimed, and some said Othniel had been killed during a failed offensive. One of the reasons my friends and I ventured into Kedesh today was to see if we could hear more about what might be happening in the south. But the only rumor we heard was that King Kushan is coming back to crush us again—this time with the intent of wiping out our way of life."

I'd had to deliver the news that that particular rumor had been true, and how we had only weeks to stir the people of Kedesh and the surrounding areas to action. But by the time I departed Avner's home, we'd made a plan of action: Avner would seek out his fellow Levites, of whom he had knowledge of more than a few who'd been forced to take up farm labor to feed their families, and I would return with Liyam in a few days so the other Levites could hear what I'd told Avner with their own ears. He was confident that once the Levites comprehended how greatly needed they were in the battle for the Land—a battle that, as men consecrated for service to Yahweh, they were forbidden from joining by sword—they would arise without hesitation.

Avner had spoken a blessing before I left his home, offering words of protection and promise over me and my mission. Then he gave me an even more precious gift to send me on my way by declaring "Your mother's boldness, faithfulness, and generosity was an inspiration to all of us in Kedesh, Tirzah. We all miss her light here. But you are a credit to her. The same light lives in you, as you have proven this night, and I only pray that it will continue to spread to everyone you encounter."

Now with my heart overflowing with gladness and a smile on my face as I thanked Yahweh for guiding me to Avner, and for once again using me for his purposes, I pushed through Nessa's door.

Before I could even comprehend the number of bodies standing inside my cousin's home, or discern who all was gathered there, the room exploded into commotion.

"Where have you been?" demanded Kefa.

"Finally!" said Yoash with a grin. "I told you she'd come back."

Nessa was suddenly in front of me, her palms on my face, her dark eyes flashing with concern and frustration. "We have been sick with worry, Tirzah. Where did you go? Your poor husband is out there now searching for you like a madman with Dotan."

"I am sorry," I said, pressing my hands to hers, hoping to reassure her. "But I found a Levite. One who is excited about our mission here. I had only one chance to follow after him. I apologize that you were all worried for me, but it was worth it, I promise. I have so much good news to share!"

A few other men of Raviv's clan stood in a semicircle around me, their disapproving stares reminding me of Tohdah, which in turn made the information I'd wrangled from Larisa push to the forefront of my mind.

"We need a messenger!" I said, yanking Nessa's hands from my face, urgency returning as I remembered how little time Malakhi would have to intercept the council in Megiddo. "I have vital information that must reach my brother as soon as possible—information that might change the course of this entire war. I need a message delivered to one of his men in a village on the Sea of Kinneret. We don't have much time."

Knowing how well-managed Malakhi's network of messengers was, the missive could be in his hands in only two or three days if it was sent off tonight.

"I'll go," said one of the young men Liyam had been training in secret, bold confidence in his stance. "There's none faster than me, and I'm familiar with the villages around the Kinneret. I'll have no problem running through the night if necessary."

Within only just a short time the young man had been sent out into the night with my missive and directions to the home of Malakhi's friend in a tiny fishing village named Tagbha. As the frenetic pace of my pulse began to slow, I realized that the rest of the men who'd been gathered in this small chamber had disappeared, leaving only Yoash, Kefa, Nessa, and me. The most important person was still missing.

"Where has Liyam gone?" I asked, surprised that he'd not come back during the frantic preparation for the messenger's departure.

"Kedesh," said Kefa. "After all the surrounding areas were searched without a trace of you, Liyam went to plead with the guards to allow him entry."

"The guards refused to say much when he arrived the first time," said Nessa. "Only that they'd seen you right before the gates closed but didn't know if you'd slipped back inside or had run off."

Just as I was about to ask why Liyam had been delayed meeting me in the first place, the door flew open, and my wild-haired mercenary burst into the room.

He stalked up to me, eyes blazing. "Where. Have. You. Been?"

Then, before I could even open my mouth to reply, he grabbed my arm, whirled me around, and half-dragged me through the house and into our storage closet. It was black inside, so my senses were limited to Liyam's firm grip on my arm, the sound of his heavy breaths, and his large, warm presence in front of me.

"Liyam, I am so—"

My words were cut off by his mouth on mine and the feel of his big arms yanking me to him.

"I thought you were dead," he said against my lips, then kissed me again. "I thought I'd lost you just like . . ." *Just like Havah and Nadina,* my mind finished for him as his words dissipated.

It was then that I realized Liyam was trembling—this tall, strong warrior had been so frightened by my disappearance that his hands were shaking.

I reached up and placed my palms on his bearded cheeks. His hold on my waist tightened.

"I'm here," I crooned, stroking his face as I spoke. "I am safe. Yahweh watched over me. I've come back to you."

"Yahweh took them," he said, the words choked and husky. "He could take you too."

I laid my head on his broad chest, settling into his tight embrace to listen to the wounded heart inside beat, beat, beat, until our breaths moved in tandem and his trembling ceased. One thing became very clear as I curled farther into the extraordinary warmth his powerful body exuded: this was where I was meant to be.

"It is true," I whispered. "Yahweh could take me. Especially when I've committed my life to serving him in this way. But not today, my love. And until I breathe my last, whether that is a month from now or fifty years from now, I will stand by your side, wherever that may be."

One of his large hands had been stroking my back as I spoke, but it paused at my declaration.

"What does that mean?" he said, the words rumbling deep in his chest.

"It means that I want to renegotiate our agreement."

His heart began to pound against my cheek, and I smiled at the way his body tensed and his breathing quickened.

"You said you had no interest in another marriage," he said. "That you wanted to part ways when this was over."

"I did. And you said you would never marry again either. Is that the way you still feel?"

I held still. Waiting. Hoping.

"No" came the husky whisper. "No, I do not."

"Neither do I," I said, relief warming me down to my toes. However, as much as I'd come to realize that this man had stealthily crept into my heart, the painful truth still needed to be restated. "I cannot give you a child, Liyam. And it pains me to think of you being disappointed like—"

"No," he interrupted. "That means nothing to me. I want you, not what your womb can provide."

Elation swirled high at his admission. "Then perhaps it's time to cut a new covenant between us? One without condition?"

His reply was surprisingly hesitant. "You are willing to leave your family? Come back to my valley when this is over?"

My chest ached at the thought of being separated from my mother and father, my brothers and their wives, and all my nieces and nephews, but if Chana could travel the world with her husband and Abra could settle up past Merom with hers, then I could certainly be brave enough to follow my own to wherever he needed me.

"I am. I told you I would stay by your side." I paused, chewing my lip for a moment. "But perhaps Odeleya can come too? I promised I would never leave her behind."

He chuckled. "Yes. She can come. I would not even consider separating you from your shadow."

"Thank you. You are a good man, my husband. I cannot wait to see your lovely valley." I slid my hand up his solid chest and to the side of his neck. My fingers gently traced the curve of his ear, and I felt him shiver at the touch. "Besides . . ." I grinned into the dark. "I cannot wait to meet the fierce and famous Alanah."

He laughed, a full rich laugh that filled me up to overflowing and was every bit as marvelous as I'd imagined. "Oh, she'll adore you. I've known it from the beginning."

He kissed me then, soft and sweet, and I wished I could see his beautiful eyes and the emotion illuminated within their depths.

"My Tirzah," he said, his fingers tunneling into my hair as he drew back my head to press his lips to the hollow of my throat. "*Ishti.*" My wife.

THIRTY-SIX

Avner's face was barely visible, lit only by the small oil lamp he'd set on a stump at the center of the clearing. We'd selected this place for our meeting with the Levites because it was far from Nessa's home, isolated and surrounded by a wall of trees on every side, but I worried that it had been too hard to find, because it was well past midnight and no one had arrived.

Knees pulled to his chest, Avner stared into the flame, his mouth a tight line of discouragement. "I don't know where they are. I spoke to at least fifteen Levites. And all but two said they would be here tonight." He sighed, tilting his head back to gauge the slow glide of the full moon across the sky.

Liyam's long legs were sprawled out in front of him, but his hip was pressed to mine, lending me some of that unusual warmth that I'd come to realize was a constant for him. Being wrapped up in Liyam's arms for the past four nights, with no more gap between us in our little closet, had been nothing less than paradise. From the night we'd made our marriage a true one, it had become almost painful to be parted from him during the day. I'd always been one to kiss, hug, and offer caresses to my loved ones, but now whenever Liyam was near, my hands refused to keep to themselves. Nessa had twice caught us embracing on the side of the house and teased me relentlessly for it, but I suspected that she was glad that we'd found our way to each other.

"Perhaps Liyam and I should go to them one by one?" I asked, with a quick glance toward my husband. "If they are not comfortable meeting this way."

Avner shook his head. "No. We must come together. Look into each other's eyes, remember that we are not alone in our responsibility."

A shuffle of sandals and the skittering of pebbles directly to my right startled me, but Liyam was on his feet, dagger in hand, before I could even think to react.

Another small flame floated out of the shadowy tree line, and behind it, the two men who I recognized as Avner's friends. They nodded and murmured greetings before placing their light next to Avner's on the stump and then taking a seat on the ground.

"Anyone else?" asked Avner.

One of his friends bobbed his head. "We saw Lomal and Teyman on the path behind us. They'll be here soon."

One by one the Levites joined our circle, adding their own lamps and torches to the gathering. By the time all thirteen were seated, and my husband's steadying presence was once again at my side, Avner's dismal expression had transformed into joyful brilliance.

He stood and offered a blessing over the meeting, asking for Yahweh's protection, for the enemy to be blinded to our presence here, and for divine wisdom to be at the center of this circle. Then he gestured to Liyam and me.

"This is Tirzah, and her husband, Liyam. She appeared at my door a few days ago with a tale that I at first found difficult to believe, but it did not take long for me to realize that her words are indeed truth. Truth that I believe you all need to hear with your own ears."

Then he sat abruptly, his eyes on me and his smile encouraging. I'd expected him to be the one to speak to the Levites and explain our purpose here, but apparently that was not to be the case.

Somehow all the courage I'd had in Barsoum's home, and the strange unbidden brashness that had flowed from my mouth on Har Ebal fled at the sight of so many intent eyes on me. I hesitated, my body going rigid, but then Liyam squeezed my hand in his big, warm palm and leaned to whisper in my ear.

"Go on, my brave wife," he said, his breath tickling my skin. "Time to step out of the shadows."

How he knew me so well in such a short period of time, I could not guess, but he was right. If I was to do the work Othniel, and Yahweh, had sent me to do, I could not longer cling to the wall, content to blend into the background in attentive silence. I must step into the center and open my mouth.

And so I stood, asked Yahweh to use my lips for his purposes, and told them of Othniel and all that had been gained in the past months. Then I told the story of Shechem and how the Levites had been convicted to speak truth to the people, how they'd reminded them of our heritage and our identity as the am segula, which resulted in both repentance and revival. I told them of the miraculous victories in Shechem and in Shiloh. And then I told them how the man Yahweh had lifted up now asked for their help in reclaiming the rest of our lands. Then, my words spent, I sat down next to my husband and exhaled, trying to calm the swirling in my belly as I waited for their response.

They were quiet. Too quiet, for many long and painful moments.

But then one of Avner's friends pushed to his feet. "If Othniel is coming here, and he's been so successful, what is the point of stirring up the people now? Can we not just wait until Kedesh is retaken and then worry about rebuilding our priesthood? We've seen rebellions end badly many times over the past eight years. Land forfeited. People carted off to slavery. Executions. I'm not sure that I want to put my family in such danger."

"True," said Avner. "This is dangerous. And over the years some have lifted swords against the Arameans and lost their freedom or their lives because of it. But it was not yet time, and Yahweh was not in those failed attempts. Now that he has raised up Othniel, we can truly have hope for the first time since Kushan marched on Edrei."

"What good will any of this do?" asked another of the Levites, one of the last to arrive. "The king of Aram is not afraid of the prayers of a few priests. He respects only the sword. We are nowhere near the Mishkan, so there will be no glorious appearing of the Cloud to chase the Arameans away like in Shiloh."

"Liyam is already training men to fight, with slings, with spears, with swords and any other weapon we can muster," said Avner. "With your help in spreading the word, many more will join the cause."

I could only pray it would be so. Liyam and I both had been dismayed at the lack of enthusiasm about his call to action. Perhaps only about twenty-five men had volunteered, although the numbers had grown slowly day by day. Tonight's challenge to the Levites would be imperative. My husband and I could not do this work alone, and Kushan would not tarry while we waited around for the men of Israel to awaken.

"But it is *our* duty"—Avner slapped a palm to his chest—"as men consecrated by Adonai Most High to speak truth. We have hidden too long in our homes, cowering, keeping his words locked in our hearts instead of on our tongues." His voice grew stronger. "We must not only spread the word that Othniel is coming and that we must prepare for the fight, but also that we must turn back to Yahweh. The Arameans have held our Land for the past eight years because of our disobedience. Even before Eleazar died, so many of us had slipped into idolatry that it was almost like we were back in Egypt, laying at the feet of Isis and Osiris again. If we do not throw off our disgusting practices, burn the idols, wear the tzitzit, celebrate our feasts, and keep the Shabbat holy, then not only will we lose this battle, but we will also lose our Land. Perhaps forever."

The circle went quiet for a long while, expressions on faces ranging anywhere from wary to hopeful to pensive.

"I just don't think that the few of us can do much good," said the wariest of the group. "And more than likely the Arameans will catch wind of it and either send us off to slavery or hang us from the ramparts as an example to others with a mind to rebel. If Othniel is coming to deliver us, then let him come. But in the meantime I'll keep my head where it belongs."

Frustration boiled over, and I pushed to my feet. "Othniel is sent by Yahweh, of that I have no doubt. But he is only a man. Just as Mosheh was only a man. And even though we have won some battles, without the covering of the Almighty we will ultimately fail. Yes, the sword will be important in this fight, and we must raise up as many able-bodied men as we can to be ready, but without our hearts turned fully to Yahweh, without the am segula embracing their true identity as the beloved people of our Creator, then we will only slide directly back into apathy and idolatry like we did before. You are priests. Sanctified for the purpose of pointing the people to the Truth, of gathering us together without fear so we can be an example to the nations of who the Eternal One truly is."

"We can do that quietly. House to house if need be," offered one of the men whose features were in deep shadow. "I agree that it is our duty, but there is no use in drawing unwanted attention."

Sighing, I let my gaze fall on Avner's oil lamp atop the stump, its lone flame reminding me of my mother's beacon in the night.

"Look." I gestured toward the lamp. "Tonight when we arrived we had only one lone flame. It did little to push back the darkness. But as you all came out of the woods, your lamps and torches joined Avner's. Each one brightened this meadow a little more. Just imagine if we continued building this fire, spark by spark, flame by flame, and asking Yahweh to breathe on whatever fuel we had to offer. What would happen?" I gazed around the men. "There would be no containing the blaze. No chance of the darkness swallowing it. We could continue hiding those flames in our homes, worshiping in isolation, and waiting for rescue, or we could gather the faithful one by one, fan the embers of love for the God who rescued us from Egypt by his own hand, and watch to see what miraculous things he will do because of our collective plea for deliverance, just like when we were in bondage to Pharaoh. The Arameans can try to blow out a few flames—and they may succeed for a time—but there is no stamping out a raging wildfire."

There was no argument after that, only contemplative silence that emphasized the hum and whir of night insects and the far-off call of a mockingbird seeking his mate. Then, one by one, the Levites stood to their feet, took up their lamps and torches, and melted into the night with their flames. But even as they did, I had a clear vision of them spreading throughout the valley, lighting other little flickers in the night, one after the other. And when the time was right, that multitude of flames would come together into one beautiful and unstoppable blaze, and the darkness would be defeated once and for all.

CHAPTER
THIRTY-SEVEN

I followed Larisa and Merit through the marketplace, regretting my decision to attend them during their shopping excursion more with every step and with each new item they added to the market basket I carried.

I'd volunteered to accompany the two young women, playing the role of their maidservant and pack mule, only for the sake of Tohdah, who'd been pestered to the point of breaking by Larisa all morning.

When he'd come into town for that one night, Larisa's husband Teshun had forbade her from walking about Kedesh unattended, since he'd heard that there was escalating unrest among us Hebrews.

Therefore, the girl had been desperate to escape for nearly three weeks, and Tohdah was at the end of her wits with enforcing Teshun's directive. Larisa pleaded and pouted and raged, but through it all Tohdah stood firm, insisting that none of us had time to go with them in the midst of our many duties, and the guards had been ordered not to leave the entrance to the inn for any reason.

But this morning all of us had had enough of Larisa's tantrums, so for the sake of Tohdah's thinly worn sanity, I'd hurried through my tasks and told her I would go. Plainly defeated, she only waved me away with an order to return before the sun reached its peak.

The smug little smile on Larisa's mouth as we left the inn, with the largest market basket we could find under my arm, made it clear the crafty little fox's plan to wear us down had succeeded.

As soon as we'd set out toward the market, Larisa began teasing me about my "well-crafted" husband until I blushed. But then she exclaimed that the stew I'd made that morning was the most delicious thing she'd ever tasted, making me feel a twinge of guilt. She may be young and spoiled, but she was genuinely endearing, and I'd manipulated her just as much as she had me, sending messages to Shiloh that undoubtedly threatened her husband's life. I hoped that if Malakhi conducted a successful ambush of the war council, Larisa would never know my part in it.

The girls meandered through the marketplace, stopping at every single stall. They petted each piece of cloth, opened countless jars of unguent and perfume to compare the scents, harassed the spice merchant for tastes of all his offerings, and added item after item to the basket on my hip.

As we forged through the chaos of stalls, wagons, and tables that littered the center of the town, and the girls gossiped over Chea and Vereda's latest skirmish, I noticed an oddity. The papyrus maker dipped his chin in greeting as I passed, his eyes relaying secrets. Two familiar men carrying jugs of oil stepped out of the way of Larisa and Merit with muttered apologies but pointedly kept their eyes off me. Even one of the men who sat behind a table of ceramic and wooden idols briefly lifted a finger in a barely visible salute as I walked by. A while later, two women carrying laundry on their heads winked at me as they brushed past.

I did not acknowledge any of them, keeping my face blank as I pressed on through the crowd, but my excitement built with every new instance of silent recognition, because each one further confirmed what I already knew: Our efforts had not been in vain.

Since our fire-lit meeting in the woods that night little over two weeks before, a quiet but profound shift had begun taking place. Just as in Shechem, the Levites had taken up my challenge. Avner told me that house to house, tent to tent, farm to farm, the stories of old were again being spread. Reminders of our heritage were recounted over meals and around fires—from the courage of Avraham turning his back on idolatry to follow the voice of Yahweh to this land, to his astounding faith as he bound his precious son to an altar, to the sojourn in Egypt and the wave upon wave of miracles that freed us from Pharaoh's shackles. And along with these stories, the Levites spoke of Othniel and all that had come to pass in the south, making it clear that they believed Yahweh had raised him up, just as he had Mosheh, to deliver us from Kushan.

As a result of the Levites' efforts, the number of men coming to offer their hands and slings and even a few hidden swords to Liyam had grown steadily. In fact, they'd already been forced to split into smaller units in order to train under cover of darkness with whatever scavenged weapons or tools were available. Although I'd only been present at a few of these clandestine midnight training sessions, it was clear from the covert acknowledgments here in the market today that I was known among the Hebrews who were involved.

A brief flash of panic surged in my gut at the thought of such a vulnerability, for one ill-spoken word could mean my end at the hand of our enemies, but the fear was quickly replaced with pride over what we'd begun with only a small group of the faithful. The flames were beginning to spread.

Breathe life into our bones, O mighty Creator came the thought, the words spoken in my mother's voice—likely a long-forgotten moment of prayer I'd overheard as a child that had stayed with me.

"Just how much silver *did* your husband leave you with, Larisa?" asked Merit, who although she directed an exasperated frown toward me, seemed to be enjoying the outing just as much as her young friend, as evidenced by the alabaster jar of henna she'd just added to my groaning basket.

"Enough to ensure that we will have to go back to the inn and empty Tirzah's basket at least another time or two." Larisa grinned and winked at me before moving on to the next stall, which boasted a vast array of pottery from Aram.

"She'd best enjoy it while it lasts," muttered Merit.

"What do you mean?" I asked, wondering how I might possibly carry the fragile vase Larisa was bartering for atop all the other purchases she'd made.

"She is fourth in the line of wives Teshun has taken on, purchased from her parents when she was just twelve at the cost of several political favors," said Merit, her tone laden with pity. "None of the unions last long, and certainly not beyond each girl's sixteenth year. Larisa has a few more months, at most, before he tosses her aside for the next girl."

"Does she know this?" I asked, following Merit's gaze to her friend, who'd moved on to the next vendor and was squealing over a cage of baby monkeys carted all the way from Egypt.

"She does," said Merit, both resignation and concern for Larisa apparent in the sad smile that curved her painted lips.

I'd seen Teshun the day he and Alek had come to the inn. The commander from Laish had a pate that was as thinly covered as Barsoum's had been. His remaining hair was a mottled gray-brown, and a hawkish nose hooked over his barely visible top lip. Even as distracted as I'd been by Alek's dangerous presence in those moments, I'd noted the overly enthusiastic welcome Larisa had offered the man who was no doubt as old as her own grandfather. Now it made sense. It was desperation, not love.

"And you?" I asked, her honesty over Larisa encouraging my boldness. "What of your husband? Is he an old man like Teshun?"

"No," said Merit, and all the tenderness that had been in her expression as she'd regarded her friend melted away. "No. My husband stole me from my home. Took me far from the land of my birth three years ago when he was reassigned here and told me that if I ever dared to disobey him he would have my entire family slaughtered."

My chest ached from the weight of her words. No wonder Merit seemed to share none of Larisa's upset over being left here in Kedesh.

For all the fine linen dresses she wore and costly cosmetics that painted her eyes and lips, she was nothing more than a slave.

For that matter, even Larisa's situation was quite similar to what Odeleya's had been. The last of my guilt over sending off the message to Malakhi that could very well end the lives of both their husbands dissipated into nothing.

The two young women continued to visit every booth, wagon, and table in Kedesh, and I trailed behind them, increasingly grateful for the months when Malakhi had made me carry large rocks through the woods to build my strength. After the last couple of weeks working all day at the inn and then taking part in some of Liyam's training exercises at night, I was beyond exhausted.

Just as we approached the foundry, which had been built long before my birth, but was maintained and expanded by Eitan in his many years tending its forges and crafting weapons beneath its thatched roof, a commotion nearby pulled my attention away from the reminder that I missed my family to the center of my bones.

A group of Aramean soldiers was pushing through the market crowd, demanding that people make way. Behind them was a group of six bruised and battered Hebrew men, bound hand and foot, shuffling along as the soldiers prodded them with the butt ends of their spears.

Every bit of triumph I'd been reveling in as I'd counted all the strides we'd made since that night around the shared lamplight vanished as I recognized three of the men who were being herded along toward the plaza.

Avner the Levite and his two friends had been arrested, with another three men whom I guessed to be sons of Levi as well, and if the triumphant expressions of the soldiers who'd captured them were any indication, they did not have long to live.

CHAPTER
THIRTY-EIGHT

Liyam

With a knee planted in the cool dirt, I shook one of the lentil bushes, listening for the distinctive rattle that would indicate the pods were ready for harvest. Dotan had insisted they were nearing their time, so he'd be disappointed when I returned to tell him that they needed at least a week or two more to desiccate.

It had been nearly nine months since I'd left my valley, and the longer I aided Raviv's clan with their lands, the more I missed my home. I was happy to lend my hands to their work, but I would be more than glad to return when this was all over and slip back into the cycle of sowing and reaping in the valley of my birth.

The fact that I'd be bringing my wife—by whom I'd only become more and more ensnared as days went on—only heightened the desire to return. I looked forward to introducing her to my parents and the rest of my clan, to walking along the terraced hillsides with her, show-ing her every lovely and secret place in our valley, swimming with her in the wadi where I'd spent so many carefree hours.

I was ready to begin anew, and I looked forward to many years of admiring her bold spirit and being challenged by her wit and mischief. There was only one thing left to do before we could make that new beginning together, unencumbered and without the specter of Nadina's death hanging over me.

My name echoed across the valley, the anguished sound making me stand and whirl about, searching for its source. The last thing I expected to see was my wife, pale-faced and brown eyes as round as millstones, plowing toward me through the lentil field as if being chased by a pack of wild dogs. She landed in my arms with a strangled cry.

"What is it?" I demanded, pulling her closer. The sight of my courageous wife so distressed caused my heart to pound an uneven cadence.

"Avner," she said, the name muffled against my chest.

"What about him?" I asked. "Tell me."

She pulled back, tears edging her lashes. "Avner and his two friends have been arrested, along with a few others—all Levites. The Arameans dragged them through town, Liyam. And it looked as though they'd already been beaten. They must have been found meeting together." She shuddered. "I think the soldiers mean to have them executed, or at the least deported and sold into slavery."

My teeth ground together at the revelation. I'd known that the more our movement grew among the people, the more vulnerable we would be to discovery. But I'd expected that the Arameans would be much more apt to find some of the men training in the woods or fashioning weapons from whatever materials they had on hand, not to snatch priests from their prayers. But perhaps it mattered less who they were than that they were gathered together in the first place.

In the past few weeks, the guard at the gate had doubled, and the rumor was that soldiers had been told to keep a watch for any suspicious activity, no matter how innocuous it seemed. I doubted whether the soldiers had even paused to consider that Hebrew priests were not even allowed to lift a sword. They'd just followed orders. And after my time in Shechem I knew what would come next—the men would be used to set an example to the Hebrews about the cost for any measure of rebellion, let alone lifting up the name of Yahweh above their gods.

"We have to do something!" she said. "Now, before the Arameans make any further decisions as to their fate."

"What would you have us do? We are not yet prepared for any sort of offensive. And we've had no word from Malakhi that the time is right to move forward anyhow. I don't know that our numbers are sufficient even if it were time, and we are vastly under-armed."

"We cannot leave them to be tortured. They are not soldiers." Her face contorted into horror. "They will not last long, Liyam, not like Sheth, who was trained to endure such violence. Not only will they suffer, but they will possibly reveal all our efforts, and many more will be rounded up."

The guilt on her face was more than evident. She was reliving the day Hanael and Sheth had been arrested and feeling all over again the weight of her self-blame in the matter.

"Avner and the others knew the risk, Tirzah. It was what they agreed to when they heeded the call to service."

She flinched, and I laid my palms on her cheeks, brushing away the first real tears I'd ever seen her shed. I counted them a minor victory, an indication that she was learning to trust me enough to finally let them fall in my presence.

"Stop blaming yourself, ishti. That call to action was from your lips, but it was placed in your heart by Yahweh. Those men are obeying the command of the One who consecrated them for their duty and the words of Mosheh and Aharon at the foot of the Mountain of Adonai. You were only the vessel to remind them of that sacred duty."

She clutched my wrists, swaying closer with an expression of desperate entreaty. "There must be something we can do."

"I will think on it," I said. "Discuss it with the others. But you must trust me, wife. It is not time to barrel into Kedesh. We must be wise and cautious when we do so. Running in headlong without a well-laid plan will only end in more lives lost."

With a sigh, she rested her cheek against my chest, arms winding around my waist. "What if the people we've been trying to inspire and prepare see what has happened and decide that they want no more part in this fight? It was difficult enough to garner their support in the first place, and if we lose their faith now, then all will be lost."

Her worries were valid. Although more and more men had joined us since that meeting with the Levites, the swell of enthusiasm I'd seen when Othniel had called the men of Yehudah and Simeon to arms was lacking here. And compared to the constant stream of young men begging to take part in Malakhi and Eitan's efforts in Shiloh, we still were little more than seventy strong. There were some good fighters among that number to be sure, but even so, it was difficult to not be disheartened. And indeed, the arrest of these Levites might even unravel much of the progress we'd made.

I stroked her back, again and again, even in the midst of such turmoil reveling in the feel of my strong and independent wife taking solace in my presence, relying on me to calm her fears. "Whatever happens, we will trust that Yahweh's plan is the best one."

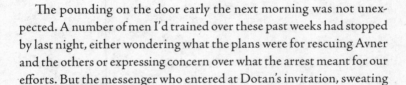

The pounding on the door early the next morning was not unexpected. A number of men I'd trained over these past weeks had stopped by last night, either wondering what the plans were for rescuing Avner and the others or expressing concern over what the arrest meant for our efforts. But the messenger who entered at Dotan's invitation, sweating and breathless, brought surprising news.

He'd run from Tagbha, the last in a line of messengers that had originated in Shiloh, and we stood in slack-jawed astonishment as he told us that not only had Beit She'an been overtaken by Othniel's army, but Megiddo too was now in Hebrew hands. When he described the way the ancient city at the heart of the Jezreel Valley had been stealthily infiltrated by Malakhi's men over a matter of ten days, and then taken from the inside instead of attacked outright, I'd been truly impressed with Tirzah's brother and his talent for inspiring men to feats of astonishing bravery, along with his willingness to apply creative strategies in impossible circumstances. Even in Yehoshua's time we'd not been able to take Megiddo, since the Canaanite kings employed a fleet of unstoppable iron chariots to defend it, and I assumed that was still the case with the Aramean who had controlled it.

Malakhi's words, from the day he proposed the union between Tirzah and me, came to mind: *"If the people of Yahweh rise up and remember who they are, nothing will stop our armies from being victorious over the Arameans this time. Nothing."*

Perhaps it was just for that reason that the impossible had been made possible in Megiddo, and from the sound of it, in Beit She'an.

"Can you believe it?" Tirzah whispered. "To think that my brothers had a hand in bringing down one of the last strongholds of Aram in the Land. I cannot even imagine how proud my abba must be right now. He must be bursting from his skin."

"I have little doubt of that," I said. "And not just because of Malakhi and Eitan's efforts. It was my brilliant wife's message that told them about the war council and when the best time to attack would be."

A flush came over her cheeks at my praise. I laughed at her uncharacteristic humility and pressed my lips to hers briefly, heedless of the audience.

"I do have some difficult news, however," said the messenger, distracting me from stealing another kiss from my tempting wife. "Since the bulk of Kushan's army is now near Golan, Othniel's forces have already crossed the Jordan near Beit She'an, determined to push them back in the direction they came."

"So we are on our own here," I said.

"I'm afraid so," said the man. "But Malakhi said to tell you that Othniel has faith that you will be victorious if you proceed beneath the banner of the Most High."

All jubilance over Othniel's victories withered into dismay. We'd spent the last few weeks whispering promises to the people of Kedesh that our army was coming, that Othniel was on his way. We'd been meant to join his efforts, not fight it alone. How could a group of seventy men, most with only the most basic of training and little more than farm tools and stones for weapons, take on a garrison of well-trained and well-armed Arameans?

Lost in thought, I did not notice the messenger had moved to stand in front of me, a hesitant look on his face.

"You are Liyam?" he asked.

I nodded, brow wrinkling.

"I was told to deliver a message to you directly, but I have little understanding as to what it means. Malakhi said to tell you that the one-eyed Moabite has been located in Megiddo."

My blood went still as my chest shuddered at the impact of his words and all its implications.

Voices all around me muffled as memories I'd stored up of my little girl arose in my mind. I closed my eyes, clinging to their echoing ghosts. Then my mother's voice broke into the elusive visions, delivering the final blow all over again: *Our precious little Nadina . . . Your daughter is gone.*

I'd spent nearly nine months waiting for this day, and I would not waste one more moment.

Shaking off the fingers that clung to my forearm and barely noticing that they belonged to Tirzah, I headed for the back of the house. I'd need my sword and a few other necessities, but it was best to pack light. Perhaps I could beg a bit of bread and dried meat from Nessa for the journey. I remembered well that as we'd passed near Beit She'an during our journey here, Tirzah had told me Megiddo was directly west of that city. If I kept my strength up, I estimated that I could make it there in four days, perhaps three if I pushed hard. I'd marched through the night before under Othniel's command.

"Liyam!" said Tirzah, shutting the door behind herself and trapping the both of us in our closet. "Liyam! Talk to me."

"I have no time. I won't lose him again," I said, not looking up as I pressed my mantle into a leather sack.

"Stop!" she demanded, snatching the bag from my hands. "You cannot fly off like this. We need you here."

Jaw grinding, I stood and placed my hands on my hips. "I have a vow to fulfill, Tirzah. You know this. You've always known this."

A flash of shock moved across her face. "But I thought you'd set that aside, after everything that's passed between us. . . . And what you learned about Raviv . . . I'd hoped you'd changed your mind."

"So you thought that because you and I made this marriage true I would simply forget my daughter? Forget how she died?"

Even as I lashed out, I knew that I was speaking my own indictment. Since we'd arrived in Kedesh, I'd put forth far too little effort to finding Nadina's killer. I'd been so focused on fulfilling my duty to Othniel and so wrapped up in Tirzah, allowing myself to fall into contented bliss with my new wife, that the Moabite trader had slipped to the recesses of my mind.

"No. Of course you would not forget Nadina." Tirzah's brows furrowed, a hint of betrayal in her expression before it was replaced with firm challenge. "But how is murdering a man honoring her memory?"

"I am lawfully exacting justice. Blood for blood. He either charged over her without remorse or he shrugged a shoulder as he watched her body fly beneath his horses' hooves. It is he who is the murderer."

"So you will charge in with the sword of justice and neglect the spirit of mercy?" she asked, her brown eyes flashing with conviction. "Yes, blood demands blood, but Yahweh gave us the refuge cities so that these cycles of blood feuds would not continue. His mercy should inspire ours."

"If justice for Nadina means the Moabite's family comes after me, then so be it. I'll deal with that when it comes."

"And what of me?" she cried. "You will walk away from me? Walk away from all we've accomplished in Kedesh when we are so close to taking it back? This city needs you, Liyam. I need you!"

"Do you?" I pressed. "Do you need me?"

She blinked at me, stunned.

"You're hiding something," I said. "You've been hiding something from me for a while now, haven't you?" I'd guessed as much in the honey cave that day, when she'd begun to speak and then had abruptly shifted into talk of Eliya instead. And over the past weeks whenever we'd lain together in this room, whispering on our pallet at night, she'd pointedly changed the subject whenever I asked her about whether she'd run into problems at the inn. And more than once I'd seen her studying the faces of Arameans she passed on her way out of the gates, a deep pinch of worry on her brow.

Her jaw gaped and her lashes fluttered, but then resignation came over her expression. "I have," she admitted. "A few weeks ago I was nearly recognized."

She briefly told me the story of her encounter with an Aramean soldier and his two companions on the road between Shiloh and Ramah and how the same man had shown up at the inn with Larisa's husband. I did not even want to consider what might have happened to her if he'd seen her in that courtyard and remembered her face.

Fury spiked through my limbs. "And you withheld this from me because . . . ?"

"I knew you would prevent me from going back to the inn," she said. "And he was gone by the next day, so there was no need to worry. He left while you and I were in the honey cave. . . ." Her voice melted away as she took in my glower.

"So you lured me to the cave that day to avoid telling me the truth."

"No—No, I took you there because I wanted to spend time with you, show you Gidal's bees. Because I wanted you to know how much I—"

"Don't trust me," I finished for her.

She flinched. "That's not true. . . ."

"It is. But I don't have time for this, Tirzah. I have a killer to find. We will discuss this when I return."

"What is the point?" she snapped. "If you go, everything will be destroyed anyhow. You are choosing vengeance over your duty to your people. Your God. Over me."

She closed her eyes and took a deep breath, as if to steady herself before she spoke again. "Leave the man in Yahweh's hands, my love," she said, her tone going soft. "Let *him* judge the heart of the Moabite. Cannot the God who shook the foundations of Jericho and struck down the firstborn of Egypt bring one man to justice if he deems him truly guilty of murdering your child?"

The earnestness of her entreaty caused me to pause. To consider her words for a brief moment. But just as quickly I pressed those faint doubts away. I would not take the chance the man would again escape his due.

I snatched my bag from her hands and slung it over my shoulder. "Stay here until I return. Do not set foot in that city. You are right that if I'd known you were playing with such fire I'd never have let you go in the first place. It is my duty to protect you, and you must rely on me to do so. There will be no more games of intrigue until I determine the safest course."

Rebellion pinched her mouth into a line. "I will not—"

Turning toward the door, I cut her off. "You are my wife, Tirzah, and you will do as I say."

The last thing I heard before I pushed out the door of the room that had become such an intimate refuge for the two of us in these past weeks was the pleading whisper of my name.

But no matter how much I loved the woman at my back, my daughter still deserved justice.

THIRTY-NINE

Tirzah

I smashed a round of dough between my palms, pressing my frustrations into its surface until it was nearly as thin as a sheet of papyrus. Muttering to myself about my high-handed husband and his edicts, I slapped the dough on the inside of the oven and glared at the flames.

I'd not even bothered pretending to obey his orders after he left. I might be the only person able to find out what had happened to Avner and the others, and I would not simply walk away because he'd chosen to run after ghosts instead of standing with Kedesh. With me.

If anything, it made me more determined to go. And no matter that Nessa and Dotan pleaded with me to change my mind, having been witness to our loud argument, I'd left for the inn shortly after Liyam stomped out of the house. Even after hours of scrubbing pots, grinding grain, shucking walnuts, and slicing quince fruit, none of my fury had abated.

And as angry I was with Liyam for tearing off to Megiddo, I was equally frustrated with myself for failing to change his mind about the blood feud. During these weeks of being together without barriers, I'd seen him come alive. The stoic, grim-faced warrior I'd met in Shechem had little by little transformed into the man I'd caught tantalizing glimpses of in Shiloh. He smiled. He laughed. He joked with Kefa and Yoash. He fashioned wooden swords for Itai and Ariel and taught them how to fend off each other's blows. He'd even, to my great astonishment, swung a giggling Ruvi atop his shoulders one day and let her use two hunks of his long hair as reins.

He'd not been the scowling, bitter mercenary of our first meeting. He'd just been my husband—the man who gathered me into his arms each night on our pallet and stroked my hair until I fell asleep listening to his river-smooth voice talk about the beauty of his home or adventures he'd had with his brothers and cousins over the years. Of course he'd not spoken any more about Havah and Nadina, and I'd not pressed him to do so, but I'd truly thought that his blood lust had cooled. I should not have assumed, however. I'd failed the man I loved.

"They're being held under the temple," said Vereda, her haughty tone pulling me from my rueful thoughts. She and another of the older wives had been lounging in the shade nearby, drinking pomegranate juice as their maids fashioned their hair into intricate designs that no one outside of the inn would ever see. "They'll be getting rid of one per day in the plaza."

Dread unfurled across my shoulders. I knew the place she spoke of. The old Canaanite temple had been stripped of its abhorrent items when the Levites first came to Kedesh, then ritually cleansed and used as a storage house for the tithes brought from all over the region. At one time, most of Kedesh was provided for from its vast stores, both Levites and manslayers alike. I'd been inside that building, had seen the door built into the floor that led to the black cellar below. In fact, Malakhi and Gidal had once gotten trapped inside accidentally, and the entire town had looked for them all night long. They'd been discovered down there just after dawn, clinging to one another, shivering and terrified.

"What is the purpose of that?" asked the other woman, as she plucked one of the spiced caramelized dates I'd made this morning from a dish at her side.

"To show these Hebrews that their god is worthless, of course," said Vereda, flitting a careless palm through the air. "They are priests of some sort. But they must be cowardly ones, since I heard they were found laying on the ground in the woods, crying out to their One God." She laughed, the brittle sound like a jangling sistrum.

"Shall we go watch this afternoon?" asked the other woman, with a note of morbid excitement. "It's sure to be a spectacle."

None of the women at the inn seemed to know what I did—that our armies had captured Beit She'an and Megiddo—or they'd not be lazing about like goddesses today.

"I don't see why not," said Vereda, patting the double plait her maid had just completed with a satisfied expression. "At least it'll be something to do other than waste away in this filthy pit of an inn."

Hearing the two of them so casually discussing the slaughter of the Levites caused every muscle in my body to turn to stone, but I forced myself to calmly continue shaping loaves of bread dough and pressing the rounds against the sides of the oven, pretending I could neither see nor hear their cold-blooded conversation.

Something had to be done. Today. Or one of Avner's friends, if not Avner himself, would pay the price for our hesitation. Liyam should be here, helping to make these decisions, but since he was not, I'd have to do it alone. Realizing that in my distraction I'd allowed the bread to burn, I snarled at myself and pushed the charred remains into the fire so I could begin again with another few rounds of dough.

Halfway through the second batch, this one much more carefully attended since Vereda and her friend had disappeared into their rooms, the sound of male voices in the courtyard broke my concentration.

Breath catching, I peered over my shoulder and caught sight of a group of Aramean soldiers, with Alek at its center. Of all days for the man to reappear in Kedesh, it was the very one in which my husband forbade me from entering the gates. And now I was trapped, out in the bright sunlight and no shadows to hide in. Turning back toward the oven, I kept my eyes on the bread inside, willing my body to remain as still as one of the cedar posts across the way.

Alek called out a demand for all the wives to assemble within the courtyard, his horribly familiar voice causing the hair on my neck to prickle.

A flurry of activity ensued in the corner of my vision as they complied, with Vereda and Chea demanding answers and Larisa's lilting voice unapologetically remarking how handsome a few of the soldiers were as the women gathered around my mother's table.

Still, I refused to turn around, forcing disinterest as I collected the perfectly brown-spotted loaves from the oven and placed them in a basket before beginning the process once again. I'd fooled Barsoum and his underlings for months; I could certainly make myself invisible for one afternoon. This wasn't the disaster Liyam had made it out to be. Perhaps after all this time my face was as anonymous to Alek as any other Hebrew woman.

I gave myself orders: Remain calm. Bake the bread. Don't draw attention. But I also allowed the slightest touch to my belt, reassuring myself that my knives were easily within reach.

"I do not enjoy bringing these tidings, ladies," said Alek, his tone void of any emotion. "But two of our strongholds have been overrun in the past week."

A few horrified gasps followed his revelation.

"Which ones?" pressed Vereda.

"A war council was assembled in Megiddo at the behest of the high commander, who hoped to reorganize our defenses and then strategize how to reclaim the ground that has been lost to these Hebrews," said Alek, ignoring her question. "And a number of your husbands were in attendance."

I knew what was coming, but I braced for the impact anyhow.

"The Hebrews somehow discovered this and ambushed many of the garrison commanders as they were leaving the city. Very few among their groups survived. At the same time, an uprising within the city threw Megiddo into chaos. We believe that a large group of Hebrews dressed as foreign traders and merchants slithered inside without notice. Megiddo is lost. And since their army struck Beit She'an two days later, it too has fallen."

Moans and muffled cries followed the announcement.

"Who?" demanded one of the women, her voice so strangled I could not discern her identity. "Who lived?"

"Only the commanders stationed at Merom and Golan," said Alek. "The rest were slaughtered. A few other soldiers and I managed to escape the assault. But even the high commander was struck down and his body hung from the ramparts of Megiddo."

Shrieks and wails filled the air. Ten of the twelve women here had lost their husbands in one day. Peering over my shoulder with a very slight turn of my head, I could see Larisa sitting straight in her seat, her pale features even more devoid of color. Beside her, Merit's face was turned downward as she stared at the surface of the table. What might be going through their minds? They were free of their tyrannical and lecherous husbands now, for good. But of course they were also adrift, having been stripped of their families.

Yet for as much as I wanted to run over, throw my arms around them, and calm their fears, the chaotic uproar of questions and demands and pleas to deaf gods had given me the perfect covering.

Dropping the last of my freshly baked bread in the basket, I left the oven burning and headed for the shadows beneath the eaves, my head down and my hands clasped at my waist. In the commotion no one would notice my departure for a good long while, and I was determined to make use of the time.

After informing them that he was now in charge of this city, since the man who'd administrated Kedesh was among the dead, Alek reassured the women that they would be safe here until arrangements could be made to move them back to Aram-Naharim. Vereda and Chea loudly argued against such a notion, insisting that they be evacuated immediately, unknowingly aiding my escape with their vehement protests.

The closer I came to the back door of the inn, the harder my heart pounded, but when I saw one of Barucha's abandoned laundry baskets at the foot of one of the cedar posts, one filled with dry and folded dresses, an idea blossomed in my mind.

Squatting, I rifled through the folded laundry, my pulse spiking as I felt the slide of sheer linen against my palms. After slipping an Egyptian-style pleated dress from the basket, along with a crimson headscarf, I smashed my pilfered items to my belly and dashed for the exit, with only one last glance over my shoulder toward the roiling crowd of women who were gathered around Alek and his men, chattering, crying, or firing questions at the men.

To my horror, I realized that Alek's dark blue eyes were on me, and any semblance of calm evaporated.

This was the end of it all. With his long-legged stride he would be across the courtyard before I even had time to close the door behind me.

But just as my knees began to go liquid, he looked away. No recognition in his expression. No shout to the others to apprehend me. Only a scowl of annoyance wrinkled his brow as he answered another question from Vereda about who was in charge of the Aramean forces now that her husband was dead and how soon a message could be sent to the man.

With rivers of relief crashing through my limbs, I dashed through the door, past a slack-jawed Ednah and Hada cleaning the front room, and out into the street. I should have listened to Liyam and not gone anywhere near the inn today, but now that I was in Kedesh and had a plausible disguise to implement my half-formed plan, I would not waste the chance to help Avner.

I ducked into a deeply shadowed alleyway, and with a haste fashioned from pure fear, I slid the expensively crafted Egyptian dress over my sleeveless tunic, retied my leather weapon belt around my waist, then arranged the crimson headscarf so that it veiled the bottom half of my face. Then, without hesitating for fear I'd second-guess my decision, I headed for the temple.

Keeping a vision of Vereda's gliding gait in my mind, as well as the haughty tilt of her chin, I approached the temple porch. Four guards stood at the entrance, a confirmation that Avner and his friends were indeed being held in the bowels of this foul place.

Summoning every bit of pretense I could muster, I approached the building as if I'd strode through its gaping entrance a hundred times—

and I had, of course, but never to prostrate my body before one of their many powerless gods. Before I'd even ascended the second stair toward the threshold, two guards stepped forward to block my progress.

"Let me through," I demanded, affecting Vereda's tone along with her pinch-mouthed sneer.

"None are to pass, my lady," said one of the men, without suspicion but with a tone that brooked no argument.

I narrowed my eyes. "I've come to worship, soldier. Now move out of my way."

Unaffected by my imperious display, he only repeated himself. "None are to pass."

Disappointed that my first attempt had failed, I scrambled for another idea. When it struck me like a clap of thunder, I had to press my lips together to restrain my gleeful smile.

I let my shoulders bow and pressed my fingers to my veiled mouth. Then, allowing the image of Avner and the others suffering unthinkable torment to fill my mind, along with my anger at Liyam for abandoning me when I needed him most, I summoned tears.

I gasped out a sob. "I—I need to go inside. Please. . . ." I shook my head, letting tears spill onto my cheeks. "You don't understand."

The guards exchanged wary looks.

"I cannot, my lady," said the first guard. "My orders are to keep everyone away while the prisoners are inside."

"I care nothing for prisoners," I cried out, then dragged in a long shuddering sniffle. "My husband is dead!"

The second guard shifted his feet, and I knew that he at least was beginning to soften.

"I just discovered he's been killed by these *Hebrews*," I sneered the word. "Slaughtered at Megiddo." I pressed my hand to my eyes, as if horrified by the vision. "I have to plead for his soul with the *baalim*. I must! I can only hope that it is not too late to intercede before his spirit enters the underworld. I must offer incense and blood, or he may be lost to me forever!"

I had no idea what strange beliefs these Arameans held to, only that their assortment of gods included those from all over the world, as if they'd simply adopted any new one they came across as they conquered nations and allied with others, but I did my best to cobble together a plausible-sounding mourning practice.

I sobbed, pleading with them to let me go inside, if only for a few moments, just to lay at the feet of the gods and plead mercy for my poor, dead husband. I dropped my face into my hands and feigned a wobble in my knees, as if I would collapse right here on the stone stairs outside the temple.

"Come now, men," said a voice as an arm slipped around my waist, steadying me against a firm body. "She's only a poor grieving widow. What harm could it be to let her inside?"

My flesh prickling with dread, I slowly slid my hands down my face and looked up through the tangle of curls that had slipped free of my crimson headscarf during my frantic pretense, through the blur of my false tears, and directly into midnight eyes that had scrutinized me on the road to Shiloh.

Alek lifted his hand, a smile spreading across the handsome face that belied whatever darkness lurked inside, and brushed his knuckles down my cheek, just as he'd done before. This time the wobble of my legs was no performance, nor was the choke of horror that burst from my lips.

"Hello again, little rabbit."

CHAPTER
FORTY

Liyam

The Kinneret Valley lay out before me, its heart a glittering blue jewel that reflected the heavens in glassy perfection. I stood overlooking the mouth of the Jordan as it emptied into the lake, high with late runoff from Har Hermon. It had taken me most of the day to walk here, for although I'd barreled out of the door of Nessa and Dotan's home fueled by anger and frustration, the furious pace I'd set had eroded hour by hour. With every step, more regrets settled into the places left hollow by the argument I'd had with my wife until I'd finally halted on the very edge of this bluff, my leaden sandals able to go no farther.

I scrubbed my hands over my face, watching the green river push its churning, frothing bulk into the sky-mirroring lake, which accepted the violence into its gentle embrace, drawing it deeper in until green and blue blended into calm stillness.

I remembered this place well from when Tirzah and I had passed through on our way to Kedesh with her brother's men not that many weeks ago. When we'd entered this valley I'd been fully convinced that our agreement was a wise one: she would be protected by my name, and I would be assured of Malakhi's help with my search. But even then I'd begun to wonder if my capitulation had less to do with my role as a go'el haadam and more to do with the woman who waded into the lake up to her thighs, giggling at the chill against her legs, then dove in without warning. She'd come up spluttering, a grin as wide as the horizon on her face, and then teasingly swiped a large arc of water toward where I sat on a boulder on the shore, watching her play. She was at once a child, full of joy and life, and a woman, whose spirit called to me, dragging me from the miry pit I'd been wallowing in and daring me to live again. And by the time we'd hiked up this very bluff I'd known that I could not resist her silent invitation much longer.

She was like wine to my blood and breath to my dead bones. And I'd walked away from her. I'd left her with devastation on her face and disappointment in her eyes as I threw her weaknesses at her feet in a bid to cover my own. Of course I'd been furious when I discovered she'd hidden the danger she'd stumbled across in Kedesh, but when she'd finally admitted the truth, I'd flogged her with it and belittled her, insinuating that her hard work and sacrifice was nothing more than a game. Then I'd watched as all the light drained from her eyes, just like Kefa warned me would happen. He'd been right. My mother had been right. The cost of letting bitterness fester in my soul was far too great.

I groaned at the weight of remorse on my shoulders.

I *was* no different from Raviv. I'd left my family behind in the valley, brushed off their concern and wise counsel in order to pursue what I considered the best course of action. I'd dragged along Yavan on my quest for blood, taking advantage of his loyalty. I'd barely even noticed when a defeated Shimon had parted from us, finally conceding that I would only continue to react with hostility to his gentle reminders that I'd left behind an entire clan of people, ones who still breathed, who needed me too.

And now I'd gutted my wife with the same bitter weapons. I'd been no more honorable than Eliya when he'd laid the blame for their lost infants at her feet and then had hinted at setting her aside for another.

She'd brought her vibrant colors into my bleak world, and I'd breathed death into hers.

These past weeks in Kedesh had been a challenge, to be sure. Drawing together a threadbare army of men who were much more comfortable with a pitchfork than a spear had tested my patience and my limits. But seeing their passion for Yahweh's land build by the day, seeing apathy replaced by fervor, and hearing the Levites remind us of our heritage and calling through the stories of the patriarchs had been invigorating and inspiring. Othniel had been right in commanding us to lift our faces to the Creator at the same time that we raised our swords against the enemy. This war would not be won with earthly weapons alone.

And yet even as I marveled at the changes in the people of Yahweh, I'd felt a certain distance from it all, a sense of being outside this fight. I could speak of trusting in whatever Yahweh had planned for our people, and even encouraged Tirzah to do so, but deep inside I wondered—*did* Yahweh care?

He'd certainly forsaken me.

He'd allowed our people to suffer beneath the tyranny of the Arameans. He taken Havah when I needed her, when our child needed her. And he'd not prevented the trader from trampling Nadina.

As I stood gazing out over the turbulent junction of river and lake, divided between the path before me and the path behind me, a vision arose in my mind, one conjured by the stories my father had told of the last moments before he stepped foot into Canaan.

I saw the Hebrews standing on the bank of the Jordan River, the same one I overlooked now, a vast army of Yahweh's beloved people. With forty years of wilderness at their backs, they could finally see the Promised Land with their own eyes. They'd endured the blaze of the desert. Plagues. Serpents. Rebellion. Doubt. Fear. War. But they were not the broken-backed slaves who had left Egypt. They'd been honed by struggle. Hardened by experience. Drawn together by purpose. Mercifully offered a Land flowing with milk and honey in spite of all their failures. And then, with their own eyes, they watched the waters of the Jordan cease and the walls of Jericho fall.

Perhaps I'd been looking at my own circumstances all wrong.

Yes, I'd lost my first wife, but Yahweh had allowed Nadina to live through her precarious birth. He'd given Havah the gift of seeing her daughter's face before she passed into the next life. He'd given me seven beautiful years with my child, of which every moment was precious. He'd guided me to Tirzah even while my heart was full of bitterness and rage. He'd given me the privilege of taking part in the reclamation of Shechem. He'd allowed me to bear witness to the transformation of the people of Kedesh and their new willingness to stand up to the Arameans.

Who was I to speak to the mind of the Eternal One? Or to turn my face away from the gifts he'd given me? Perhaps even the trials I had endured were gifts in a way, making me stronger, wiser, more prepared to accomplish his purposes. And if I trusted him like my mouth proclaimed, believed that he was the same God who shook the walls of Jericho into dust and crushed the might of Pharaoh, why had I not laid the burden of justice for Nadina in his capable hands as Tirzah had asked?

The truth of it was, I was no innocent either. I had lifeblood on my hands just as surely as the trader, even if it was in service and defense of my people. In all honesty, as I stood over Barsoum the day Shechem fell, my heart had been full of righteous anger as much as it had an unholy desire to see him suffer for all the pain he'd caused.

Perhaps I was the one in need of mercy.

A new revelation began to bloom in my mind: What if Yahweh had been hiding the trader from me, not only because I'd rejected his law with regard to manslayers, but also to protect me from becoming a murderer myself? And if that were true, wasn't that a mercy in and of itself?

Perhaps it was not the Almighty who'd forsaken me, but me who had forsaken him. I'd thought that all my anger and bitterness had been directed at the Moabite, but suddenly I realized that I'd blamed Yahweh even more and refused to trust or rely on him when he'd been nothing but merciful toward me.

My bones ached with the weight of sorrow I'd carried alone for all these months. Too weary to hold against the weakness in my legs, I fell to my knees, ignoring the sharp spike of pain from the jagged stones beneath me.

Then I lifted my face to the blue sky, confessing the murderous rage that had consumed me for so long. I confessed my refusal to give the Righteous One the reverence and obedience due his name. I confessed my bitterness toward him, my thirst for vengeance, my disrespect of his good and perfect laws. And then, my chest free of the burden of hatred and bloodlust, I dropped my head and allowed tears to flow for the first time since my mother had told me of Nadina's death. I wept for my beautiful girl. For the brevity of her vibrant little life. For the smiles I missed, for the laughter I craved, for the loss of her future days. I wept until the violent churning inside was swallowed up by an overwhelming calm, an inexplicable peace that soothed my soul and made it as placid as the blue waters laid out before me.

Emptied of the storm that had raged for so long in my soul, I raised my head and breathed deeply, taking in the fresh breeze that swirled around me and dried my tears, the graceful swoop of birds as they dipped low over the sparkling blue water, and the deep sense that this place, this verdant valley surrounded by hills, was in some way sacred.

Then, with fresh determination, I stood, turned my back on the wrongful vow I'd made, left my Nadina in the hands of her Creator, and headed toward my wife, with whom I had much to atone for.

The journey away from Kedesh had been arduous, like pressing through shin-high sand, but now I was a man newly freed from his shackles, my pace swift and unfettered. My mind was full of Tirzah and what I would say to her when I returned, of our little closet and the feel of her in my arms. She would forgive me; I knew my wife, and her heart was far too generous to ignore my sincere repentance. And now with all malice stripped away, I could cherish her freely the way I was meant to. Her light may have been dimmed by my careless words, but her flame burned too brightly for even me to snuff out, and I would shield it and nurture it for the rest of my days.

Before the sunlight even began to wane, I'd made it nearly halfway back to Raviv's valley. But just as the peaks of Hermon began to glow pink and orange and shadows stretched their long arms across my path, I caught sight of a figure in the distance. One moving at a surprising speed. Instinct urged my palm to grip my sword as I slowed my pace, a deep sense of unease coming over me as the figure drew nearer and nearer.

Then recognition struck. It was Eylam, one of the young men I'd been training in Kedesh—in fact, one of the first and most eager to be recruited. While not particularly proficient with a sword or sling just yet, he was well known for his speed and endurance and was regularly sent out as a messenger all over the region.

I halted as he approached, his chest heaving and tunic soaked through with sweat. It was clear the man had been running for hours at a full-out sprint.

He did not even bother with niceties as he skidded to a halt before me.

"Your wife," he said, gasping for breath. "Tirzah has been taken prisoner in Kedesh."

I did not pause. Did not ask how, or why, or when. I just ran.

CHAPTER
FORTY-ONE

"We cannot charge into Kedesh just to save your wife. We are not prepared," said Nahom, his arms folded tightly across his chest, the way they'd been since he'd arrived for this meeting. The older man, a friend of Raviv's and an elder of the tribe of Naftali, had been among the last to join with us, only days before.

I restrained an exasperated sigh. "As I've said before—a number of times—this is not only for Tirzah's sake. There are others being held prisoner too." *Although none whose loss would utterly unravel me.*

I scrubbed at my eyes with my fingers in a futile attempt at staving off fatigue, as I'd still not slept since my return to Nessa and Dotan's home well after dark last night. "The Arameans are so desperate to maintain control after the loss of Megiddo and Beit She'an that the situation within the city will only grow more dire. The time to strike is now, when they are least likely to expect it, when they think us weak and cowering beneath their threats."

I'd been making the case for uprising since well before dawn to this group of clan leaders I'd called to emergency assembly, hoping that the injustice of the situation and the news of Othniel's victories would be enough to stir their blood to action. But when I'd been forced to reveal that his army would not be coming north, perhaps for weeks, my call to battle for Kedesh had devolved into an argument. One I seemed no closer to winning than I had an hour ago.

"There's already one body strung up on the walls," said Nahom, defeat bracketing the pinched mouth of the old warrior. A scar ran from his temple to his chin, a product of the war at Edrei eight years ago. "And the rest of them are as good as dead."

Pressing aside the sorrow and guilt that had set up residence in my soul since I'd been told that it was Avner's body hanging from the ramparts, as well as the profound relief that it was not my wife, I leveled a glare at the man.

"And how many more?" I asked, frustration leaking into my tone. "How many more will we let the Arameans enslave? Rape? Slay? Have we not lost enough to this enemy?"

"I say we wait until Othniel comes," said Nahom. "We cannot possibly win this fight on our own."

"Othniel did not tell us to wait for him," I said, reminding them of the message from Malakhi. "He said that *we* would be victorious beneath the banner of Yahweh. There was less than one sword for every fifteen men at Shechem and yet the people in the camp overpowered their guards and had the rest of them hiding inside the gates—*before* Othniel even set foot in that valley."

Looking around Nessa and Dotan's small room, I met the eyes of each of the clan leaders. If I could convince them, then the rest would follow, I was certain of it.

The vision of my Tirzah, spine straight and voice unwavering as she challenged the Levites to fulfill their duty, rose in my mind, as did the realization of how to make these men see the truth.

"Do not forget," I said, my voice rising with new determination, "that I was there that day in Shechem. I saw how terrified the Arameans were. I looked into the high commander's eyes and saw fear before I drove my sword into his heart. He was not frightened of Othniel, who although raised up by Yahweh, is only a mortal. No, Barsoum was terrified of the God who'd delivered up his army to defeat, who ran the soldiers out of Shiloh with his Divine Presence, who filled the hearts of the people in the camp with impossible courage. The same God who shook the foundations of Jericho and buried Pharaoh's army in the depths of the sea."

Again I swept my gaze around the room, an infusion of conviction rushing through my blood.

"Kushan and his wicked commanders may have won eight years ago," I said. "They may have pressed our faces into the dirt for a while, but we have a weapon that they do not. One with infinitely more power than they could ever hope to wield. We have Yahweh. And just as Yehoshua told us before our fathers began that first loop around Jericho, he is with us. He will go behind us and before us. Without him it would be mere human effort, yes, and likely destined to fail, but with him as our shield and banner, no enemy will be able to stand against us. And I, for one, will not lay down and accept the loss of even one more Hebrew life.

"Not your son's." I pointed at Nahom.

"Not your brother's." I pointed at the man next to him.

"Not your cousin's." I pointed at Kefa.

"Not your daughter's." I pointed at Nessa.

"And not the Levites', who've been so brave to remind us of our heritage at such risk. And certainly not my wife's."

"And how do you mean for us to go about accomplishing this invasion?" asked Nahom. Even though his tone was still on the edge of wariness, his resistance was crumbling, I could tell. A burst of fresh energy battled my overwhelming exhaustion.

"Although we'd not planned to implement these measures until Othniel arrived," I said, "we've been setting things in place for weeks. At least half of the vendors and merchants in Kedesh are Hebrew, the majority of whom have already joined with us. Weapons have been smuggled inside the walls in skins of yogurt. In jugs of wine. Wrapped in spools of yarn. Tucked into secret compartments beneath wagons. Inside the carcasses of animals. Even the children have been gathering rocks and stashing piles of stones all over the city."

Nahom's surprise was evident. "And with these weapons a few merchants are going to overcome the garrison?"

"That is just the thing, you see." I grinned. "The Arameans have already done the hard work for us. It's the head of the month tomorrow—
the appointed day for us poor, downtrodden Hebrews to bring tribute
to our masters."

Ahead of me the guard prodded at the bundle of reeds Yoash carried
over his broad shoulder, searching for weapons. Keeping my expression
blank, I let my eyes travel over the rest of the Arameans who guarded
the outer gates behind us, counting six, and then shifted slightly so
I could take in the ones by the inner gates ahead of us. Four more.

Having already been searched, Kefa sighed wearily. "We've been
in and out of these gates a hundred times. Have you ever known us to
carry anything other than goods?"

The Aramean only scowled and gestured for me to come forward
with my own burden. I complied, watching from the corner of my
eye as three women entered through the outer gates, heavy baskets
of laundry balanced atop their heads. Two of the women seemed to
be having an argument over whose recipe for natron soap was more
effective on henna stains in linen. The third merely shook her head at
her younger companions, then brushed the back of her knuckles across
her brow, as if exhausted from a full morning of scrubbing bedding and
clothes. Sliding past the long line of Hebrews bringing their tribute to
the Arameans, the women came near, continuing their loud bickering.

Not even noting the approach of the women, who were well known
for coming in and out of Kedesh multiple times per day to do the inn
laundry at the spring, the guard poked his fingers into my bundle. At
the same moment, a wail began off in the distance, riding on the cool
breeze far from the walls of Kedesh, yet close enough to be recognized
for what it was. Mourning.

The guards went on alert, their swords coming out of sheaths as
another voice added to the doleful call, and then another. Yet, though

they searched the horizon for whatever danger was lurking outside the gates, nothing could be seen but the remaining trees that encircled the city.

"What is that?" hissed one guard to another.

"I don't know. Stay alert," said the other.

A few more voices joined the call and then more, until a circle of cries and laments enveloped Kedesh.

Then the distinct chant of the Shema lifted above the sounds of mourning.

"Hear, O Israel, Adonai your God is One . . ." began the ancient words, disembodied voices joining together as one haunting chant. The Levites and their families were carrying out their part to perfection, as were the many Hebrews who'd volunteered to join with them to lift high the name of Yahweh and plead our case before him.

"What should we do?" asked one of the soldiers. "Close the gates?"

The head guard frowned and shook his head. "It's only a few Hebrews mourning the two of them we executed. They'll quiet down soon enough. Or perhaps we will offer up two more to Ba'al today."

My gut roiled at the pronouncement. After they'd hung Avner from the walls as a warning, I'd hoped that they planned to send the rest off to slavery in the north, giving us more time to complete a rescue, but it seemed my hope had been in vain. Another Levite's body hung beside the first, the grisly sight a horrific welcome as we entered the gates.

Was my Tirzah next to be sacrificed? Or had the full day it had taken to implement my plan meant that she was already lost to me? I refused to let the thought of her precious body strung up in such disgrace to even remain in my head. For if I dwelt on it too fully, I'd never be able to push forward, and I needed all my wits about me now. I did not even know where she was being held and would have to fight my way through the city until I found her. I could only plead with the One Who Sees to guide me.

The sound of the Shema faded, and silence settled over the valley once again. The head guard laughed and announced that there was nothing to fear from a few pathetic Hebrews making noise to their weak god, and waved me on to join my friends so he could search the bundles of the next seven men in line behind me.

But before his arrogant smile had even left his lips, a shofar sounded from beyond the tree line, followed by wild shouts from every direction and more shrill and stuttering ram horn blasts.

Chaos erupted.

The laundresses plunked their baskets on the ground and ran for the inner gates, the oldest one outpacing the others in the flight. The head guard screamed for the outer gates to be closed, and the rest rushed to do his bidding, the ones near the inner gates abandoning their posts to do so.

But before the bars on the gates locked in place, Kefa, Yoash, and I—along with the rest of the men who'd abandoned their reeds and sheaves of barley and pots of grains and fruit—had already retrieved our weapons from the depths of the laundry baskets. Shouts and cries were ringing through the marketplace, the plaza, and near the army quarters. Because by slamming the gates of Kedesh closed, the Arameans were not shutting the enemy out, but instead locking themselves up tight with the army that had been here all along.

FORTY-TWO

Tirzah

I fumbled through the blackness on my knees, scraping my bound hands on the rough stone walls of this pit until I found the door above us in the low ceiling. They'd dragged away a second Levite a few hours ago, and I was determined to free us before another was murdered.

Carefully, I extracted one of my knives from the belt Alek had thankfully not stripped from me before shoving me into the storage hold beneath the temple. The four men imprisoned here still made no attempt to help, but they had not tried to stop me either. They seemed resigned to do nothing more than lay on the dirt floor of this pit, whispering prayers and mourning the loss of Avner and his friend, Yehud, who'd been taken to the plaza to die.

I jammed my knife in the crack I'd discovered with my raw fingertips, my shoulders aching from pushing on the trapdoor above my head. Whatever heavy object Alek had laid over the opening to this cellar refused to budge, but I had to find a way out of this hole. I would not give up until I did.

Thoughts of Avner's wife and children gutted me, provoking me to push my knife farther into the narrow gap between wood and stone with a strangled grunt. They'd so generously shared a meal with me that first night I'd barged into their home, listening to my stories with rapt attention. Because of my insistence that he join the fight, they'd lost him, and unless I found a way out of this cellar below the temple, four more families would be destroyed too.

I wiggled the blade, slipping it back and forth, hoping to catch a leather hinge or a latch of some sort, but there was no purchase. My knives were useless. My strength was useless. Every moment of Malakhi's training was useless now. If I'd told Liyam about Alek the first time I'd seen him, if I'd trusted him the way he'd trusted me, none of this would have happened. Now he'd run off to Megiddo and likely would not know what had happened to me for weeks. He would lose another wife, and I'd never be held in his arms again.

Losing all restraint at the thought of adding to Liyam's grief, breaking my vow to Odeleya and leaving her alone, and how utterly I'd failed everyone, I pounded on the trapdoor with my fists and let loose a cry of desperation. "Free us!" I screamed. "Let us out of here!"

Ignoring the painful scrape of wood on my knuckles as I banged on the wood again and again, I spewed a litany of curses against the Arameans and their gods, hoping they might be annoyed enough that they'd come after me and I could surprise them with my knives. It was only a half-formed plan and one that I knew was full of flaws, but I had to try.

Of course my demands went unheeded, only the blackness and the Levites hearing my unhinged tirade. When my throat began to burn, both from my screams and the sobs I'd been holding back, I dropped my arms, my knife falling into the dirt, and I covered my mouth with both hands to prevent myself from wailing in despair.

"It is time to rest, Tirzah" came an unfamiliar but kind voice out of the fraught silence that remained after my rant. "Sit down."

"I can't just give up," I choked out.

"You have fought well," said the Levite. "You have done what Yahweh asked of you."

"I failed," I said, wishing I could look the man in the eye. "All my efforts here were for nothing. Kedesh is not free. You all are suffering because of me. Avner and Yehud are dead because of me."

"No, they have passed into the world to come because they obeyed the call of our Creator to speak truth, and there can be no higher honor than to die in service to the King of the Universe. It was you, my dear, who reminded us of this and you who must now heed your own challenge."

"What do you mean?" my response came out in a strangled hush.

"You said that if we came together, each of us bringing whatever small sparks we had to offer, that the collective flames would be unstoppable. Your efforts alone are not sufficient to deliver this city into its rightful hands, and even if every man, woman, and child in Kedesh worked together, the battle might still be lost. But what did Mosheh tell our people when we stood with our backs to the sea?"

He let the question hover in the darkness, waiting for my response. The answer came to me immediately, in the voice of my mother, who'd been the first to tell me the stories of our deliverance while stroking my hair and whispering me to sleep as a child.

"'The Lord will fight for you. You need only be still,'" I said, tears burning behind my eyes as the words pressed past the knot in my throat.

"Yes," said the Levite. "And just as our ancestors learned as they followed the Cloud through the wilderness, there are times when Yahweh tells us to move. Times when he tells us to engage the enemy. And times when he tells us to stand firm and wait for him to fight the battle for us. You will only fail if you do not trust him for the victory."

"If I am supposed to be still and let him do it all, then why did he even bring me here? Couldn't he have raised up someone else to spur the people of Kedesh to action?"

"I do not know the mind of the Almighty, Tirzah. And you may not ever know what effect your words or actions have on the people around you, neither on the extent of their reach or their longevity. It is only your job to obey and to wait on the Deliverer." He paused. "But I will say this: I am grateful that you came here. My own flame had gone dormant, and Yahweh used you and Avner to bring it back to life. And even if my life ends here in this pit, I know that Adonai's words and promises will not."

Tears streamed down my cheeks as I remembered the look on Avner's face as he'd been hauled out of the cellar by two guards after volunteering to be first to die. There was no terror, no doubt, no regret. Only peace. He'd simply smiled at me, his face barely illuminated by a weak shaft of light, and said, "Fear not, our Deliverer will come" before being dragged away.

Somehow, at the center of my bones, I'd known that it was not Othniel he spoke of in his last moments. The look is his eyes had been too otherworldly, too knowing, much like my mother's whenever she spoke of her visions and dreams. And there was none more trusting of Yahweh's goodness than my mother, who'd reached out to him in her darkest moments and found overflowing mercy. I had little doubt that her quiet service to her friends, her family, and even to strangers would likely impact generations to come.

I longed for her presence now, for her steadying words of wisdom that were so woven into the fabric of my life, but it was her description of Liyam's mother that came back to me now: *"Although she is brave without question . . . I think it was her surrender to Yahweh that displayed the true depths of her courage."*

The Levite had been right to challenge my lack of faith. I was at the end of myself; there was no route of escape from this cellar other than death—there was no one and nothing left to turn to but the One who had promised to never leave or forsake me. And as my mother had so clearly shown by her words and her actions, there was no greater act of bravery than asking the King of the Universe to rescue me.

And so I did.

I dropped to my knees and laid my forehead on the cold ground. With my face in the dirt, I pleaded aloud with the God who spoke the heavens into being. I pleaded with the God who'd rescued my people from slavery. I pleaded with the God who lifted Yosef from a pit like this one to the right hand of Pharaoh.

By the time I was empty of prayers, I understood why Avner seemed so at peace as he was led away. It was as if there was nothing left of me, of my selfish need to push and run and fight and prove my worth to everyone around me. There was just me and the One who'd created me, and it was enough.

I had only to trust that Yahweh would take all my efforts, even those I'd made while wrapped up in my selfish desires and pride, and use them for his glory. If he could use the treacherous actions of Yosef's brothers to save our entire nation, then he could certainly use my well-intentioned but faulty ones for his purposes.

And so, with my heart free of the burdens I'd been carrying, I sat down as the Levite had told me to do, laid my head back against the cold wall of my prison, and was still. It did not take long for exhaustion to overcome me.

When some time later a loud rasp of stone over wood jerked me from the sleep my body had so desperately needed, the ominous scrape sent chills down my spine. Whatever had been laid atop the cellar door was being removed. Which of us would be next to be taken to the plaza? I prayed it would not be the Levite who'd spoken truth to me with such boldness.

If these were my last moments, I would make them count. I moved to my knees, ready to stand and volunteer myself if it would mean these men dedicated to Adonai's service might have even a small chance of rescue later. *I trust you, Yahweh.*

Lamplight flooded into the cellar, outlining the figure of a man, and I blinked against the brightness.

For one brief and painfully hopeful moment, I saw Liyam's face hovering over me, but when Alek's voice said "the girl" before one of the guards reached into the pit and hauled me off the floor by my elbow, the illusion was shattered.

"What of the rest?" asked the guard, when I lay scraped and bruised on the floor.

"Put back the stone," said Alek. "And then get back out there and join the fight."

The strange command made me realize that there was a wild commotion going on outside the temple. Shouts, cries, and guttural curses filled the air.

"What is happening?" I asked, a small glimmer of hope surging at the sound of a shofar being blown in the direction of the marketplace.

"Nothing that concerns you. It'll be over soon enough," he said, then reached down and grabbed my hair. Pain splintered through me as he yanked me upward by what remained of my braid and then dragged me down the hallway as I tripped over my own feet in an attempt to keep up with my captor.

Alek pulled me into a chamber, one whose walls were lined on both sides with idols. Their sightless eyes glared at me from their various pedestals or the tables they perched on, surrounded by wilting flowers and overripe food offerings. I had no names for most of them, but recognized the largest one that stood at the center of the room—a shoulder-high, gold-covered rendering of the goddess Ashtoreth, the same one whose blasphemous symbol had been burned into my mother's cheek.

Alek pressed my back against the idol and leaned down in my face. "I could not believe my eyes when I saw you across the courtyard, little rabbit," he said, a gleeful smile on his handsome face. "There you were, handed to me by the gods. But I thought I'd lost you, thought perhaps you'd slipped out the gates somehow, but then that loud and lovely display you put on brought me right to you."

He grabbed my face, gripping my mouth so hard that I tasted blood. "And now you'll pay for what you did to me. The perfect sacrifice to the baalim."

"Please," I cried out, my words muffled against his hand. For as much peace as had enveloped in the cellar after my outpouring to Yahweh, the madness in this man's eyes made it clear that I would not just die today, but also suffer. "I did nothing! My brothers—"

I halted, realizing my mistake as his dark eyes went wide and he sucked a breath through his nose.

"Your brothers?" he snarled. "It was your *brothers* who tortured me and left me tied naked to a tree?"

I tried to shake my head, but his hand clamped tighter around my jaw.

"I hated you Hebrews well enough when I learned that you ran my mother's clan out of Laish, leaving her at the mercy of the Arameans to be sold and used, again and again," he said. "But if I die today knowing I've repaid those dogs for my humiliation before my father, then I will go to the gods satisfied."

His disdain of my people was personal, as I'd suspected, but now I understood why. And whatever had happened with his father seemed to have brewed his contempt into outright hatred—hatred that was now concentrated solely upon me.

He sneered. "I'd planned to just slit your throat and offer your blood. But I think I have something better in mind."

The last thing I saw before agony split me wide open and blackness swallowed me was Alek's fist flying at my face.

CHAPTER

FORTY-THREE

Liyam

The temple was on fire. I'd seen the first wisps of smoke curling into the air as I fought my way through the plaza, determined to get to wherever Tirzah was being held and inexplicable urgency driving me toward the center of town. When one of the merchants I passed in my haste gestured toward the gaping entrance to the sanctuary, yelling that the prisoners were locked in the storage room beneath it, my bones turned to ice.

I plowed through the melee, vaguely noting that there were few Arameans left standing and those who remained were in a futile battle to fend off the Hebrews who surrounded them. The attack had been such a surprise to our enemies, and the eerie shouts and fervent trumpet calls of the Levites so unnerving, that most of them had little to no time to even arm themselves properly. We would be victorious today, but none of it would matter if Tirzah had been harmed, or worse.

Taking the porch stairs by twos, I barged into the temple, the smell of smoke acrid in my nostrils as I searched the dark antechamber for any sign of a cellar door.

A large stone idol lay on its back on the floor off to my right a few paces away, its strange placement drawing my attention. Darting over to it, I prayed that my Tirzah was beneath the wooden trapdoor it covered. Heaving my entire weight against the idol with a groan, I slid the blasphemous thing to the side and then snatched the handles of the door to lift it up and away.

Inside the shallow pit I could see four men covered in dirt and blocking their eyes from the feeble light I'd let into their prison. But my wife was not with them.

"Hurry," I said, laying my sword on the ground and stretching out my hand to the nearest man. "It's time to go. The temple is on fire."

They were weak, most likely from lack of food or water, and all four of them accepted my help in crawling out of the hole.

"Where is Tirzah?" I demanded as soon as they were all free.

"She was taken away a while ago. We could hear nothing down there."

Restraining my instinct to grab the man and shake him until he gave me a better answer, I cast my gaze around the temple, frantically searching for a clue as to where she'd been taken, and an orange glow from a doorway at the end of the long chamber snagged my attention.

"Go," I said to them, an urgent pounding beginning in my chest as I surged to my feet. "Get out of this place before it burns to the ground."

Leaving the Levites to scramble out of the temple by themselves, I darted across the antechamber, my burgeoning dread just as acrid as the smoke that was streaming from the doorway ahead of me.

While I was still ten paces from the room, I saw my wife at the center of the high-ceilinged chamber. Her back was against a golden idol and her arms bound behind her, head bowed and body horrifically still.

Two tall oil lamps had been tipped over at the far end of the room, a large assortment of papyrus scrolls spread out to fuel the fire. Already some of the idols at the far end of the chamber were engulfed; those with gold and silver overlay melted away as they were consumed, their faces dripping into ghastly screams of horror as they succumbed to the heat.

I bellowed out her name, terrified that I was too late. But her head jerked upward for a moment and then lolled forward again, as if she were fighting for consciousness, and relief pulsed through me. Her cheek and eye were swollen, beginning to darken with a bruise. Someone had struck her, and hard. Fury stoked higher in my veins as flames licked up the ornately painted columns toward the ceiling. I called her name once more as I stepped over the threshold.

Her chin tipped up again at the sound. She blinked blearily and shook her head a little, as if she did not truly believe that I was in the room with her. Then her eyes darted over my shoulder, going wide as she screamed, "Behind you!"

I whirled and jumped back just as a sword whooshed by my shoulder. Realizing I'd stupidly left my own sword on the ground back by the cellar in my haste to find my wife, I had only my hands to use against my attacker. I lunged, grabbing him by the tunic and yanking him toward me.

The man grunted, caught off guard by my swift response, but struggled against my hold with surprising strength. He brought his sword arm up, trying to slash my back, but I twisted away from the swing, receiving only a shallow gash on my shoulder as I retreated a few steps.

"You!" he screamed, at the same time I realized that it was Alek, the son of Barsoum, standing before me with my blood on the edge of his sword. "But you're Moabite! A mercenary!"

"I am Hebrew," I gritted out. "Just as I told your father before I ended his worthless existence."

Tirzah let out a rasping cry at the same moment that Alek bellowed a foul curse. "You *both* will burn," he snarled as he lunged forward, his dark eyes reflecting the flames behind me. I feinted right and then whirled to my left, avoiding the arc of his sword once again.

"Come now," I goaded with a taunting grin and a beckoning twitch of my fingers. "Your father hired me for a reason. Too bad he was too dull-witted to realize he'd invited an enemy to his table. And a spy to fill his bottomless gullet."

Just then a beam fell from the ceiling, crashing down only a few paces behind Tirzah, sizzling and sparking as it hit the floor, and drawing my attention toward the woman I loved for just enough time that I was unable to prepare for Alek's full-bodied attack. I hit the ground, my head slamming against the stone. Blinking hard against the lights flashing behind my eyes, I looked up to see the Aramean standing above me, his sword at my throat and his features twisted in hideous triumph.

"Two sacrifices in one," he sneered. "The baalim will be most pleased. As will the soul of my father."

Even though Barsoum had humiliated and mocked him in life, making it clear that his bastard son was of little consequence to him, Alek still hungered after his approval.

From the corner of my eye, I saw Tirzah outlined by the glow of the fire, frantically struggling against her bonds, which seemed to be loosening as she violently jerked her elbow back and forth.

I dragged in a smoke-laden breath and glared up at Alek, determined to keep his attention on me for as long as possible. "Your pathetic father died in his bed, sniveling like the coward he was. His depraved soul is where it belongs—with the demons."

Alek's midnight eyes went wide at my insult, but before he could push his sword into my throat, a knife lodged deep into the backside of his shoulder. He screamed, off-balance from the blow, and tripped sideways as he fruitlessly grabbed for the blade.

I surged to my feet, grabbed him by the back of the tunic, and threw him headfirst into the stone wall with all my strength. Then, before he could gather his senses, I snatched up his sword and plunged it into his chest, ending his life the same way I had his father's.

I ran to my wife, who'd fallen to her knees in front of the idol after she'd thrown the knife, coughing from the heavy smoke that filled the room, her wrists bleeding and abraded from the ropes she'd fought so hard to free herself from. Bracing against the heat that stung my skin, I reached for her, pulling her upright, and then slinging her into my arms. I dashed from the room, leaving Alek to burn alongside his gods.

"The others . . ." she said, struggling against my grip as I pushed through the smoky haze toward the entrance. "The Levites. The cellar."

"I got them all out," I reassured her, pressing a kiss to her forehead and breathing deeply of the scent of her skin, more precious than the fresh air around me. "They are safe."

"Oh, I am glad," she mumbled, her eyes dropping closed as though fighting against the darkness pulling her into its embrace. "He said to be still and Adonai would fight for us . . . and then I thought you were only a dream . . . but our Deliverer sent you, didn't he?"

Although I did not understand her ramblings, I tightened my hold on her, just grateful she was alive and in my arms. "I have you, my prize. Rest now. Kedesh is free."

FORTY-FOUR

Tirzah

15 Elul
Kedesh, Israel

Kushan, the King of Double Wickedness, was not only defeated by Othniel's army, he was driven from our land completely. And not until the last of his army had retreated across the Euphrates River to lick their wounds did the nephew of the great Calev lay down his sword, having accomplished the task Yahweh set before him. The Land was free again, the full inheritance of Avraham rightfully returned to his descendants.

And my mother was coming home.

A messenger had brought word that my family was returning to Kedesh well over a month ago, so from my post atop the roof of the inn I'd watched the road every day for the past two weeks, disappointed countless times when I saw only traders coming to hawk their wares in the market, or Levite families returning to their homes in the city.

Long arms slithered around my waist and a red-bearded chin landed on my shoulder. "Staring at the horizon won't make them appear any sooner, ishti."

"I know," I said with a sigh, leaning back into his embrace. "But I cannot help myself. This war has been over for nearly two-and-a-half months. I thought they'd be here long before now."

"Packing up an entire clan—not to mention the arduous walk here with animals, wagons, belongings, and lots of children—is no simple task."

"True," I said. "And we've accomplished much in the meantime. I am glad my mother will not see her inn the way the Arameans left it."

Liyam and some of the other men had worked tirelessly to repair the damage to the exterior. New plaster graced the front. The shutters were repaired. The long-neglected roof was given a fresh covering, and leaks were mended. And every last blasphemous idol that had sullied my mother's front room had been taken outside the city, smashed, and then burned alongside all the other lumps of clay and wooden carvings left behind by the foreigners who'd bowed their knees to such refuse. The cleansing of Kedesh had been the first order of business by the Levites, begun nearly the moment victory had been declared. I could only pray that our people would continue to reject the false gods they'd fallen into compromise with and stay true to Yahweh, so that we'd never again suffer chastisement like we had at the hands of the Arameans.

"Thank you," I said, turning around in the circle of Liyam's embrace so I could look up into his face.

"For what?" he said, before placing a tender kiss on my lips.

"For staying here. For helping me with the inn until they return."

For weeks he'd been restless, his gaze tracking off toward the southern sky whenever he thought I wasn't watching. I knew he was anxious for his home, his family.

His blue-green eyes held me in a potent gaze. "A few weeks of delay is no sacrifice when you have chosen me."

"My home is where you are now," I said, lifting my hands to stroke his cheeks, loving the feel of my husband's warm skin and the brush of his beard against my palms. "But I thank you for giving me this time with them before we go."

"I have you for the rest of my life, my prize. I can share you for just a little while longer." His hands told another story, gripping my waist possessively, pulling me closer.

"Ah, but you'll have me to yourself for only a few more months," I said with a grin. "And then you'll do nothing but share me with another."

The smile I'd been so hungry for all those months ago in Shechem now stretched wide across his face, just as brilliant and soul-stirring as I'd imagined it to be. One of his hands slid from my hip to caress my belly, where only the barest curve had just begun to show.

After having three pregnancies in the past, I'd been certain of the changes in my body not long after the victory of Kedesh, and since I'd determined to never again withhold truth from my husband, I had told him as soon as I'd realized that my cycle had not returned. All fear that the news might upset him or dredge up his grief over Nadina melted into nothing as tears of joy glittered in his jewel-bright eyes. Then he'd swung me into his arms with a gleeful shout, but nearly as soon as he'd done so, he'd placed me back on the ground, pulled me tight to his chest, and whispered with a tone full of compassion that no matter what happened, he would love me for the rest of his days.

Perhaps this babe would survive, or perhaps like the others it would be stripped away, but I could only lay my desires before the feet of the One Who Hears and trust his divine wisdom. My Deliverer had sent Liyam to rescue me, and the child within my body, so I would be still and let him fight for us, trusting in Yahweh to fill the hollow places, no matter the outcome.

Uncaring that we stood atop the roof of the inn in full sight of Kedesh, my husband kissed me, the depth of his adoration a heady elixir as he enveloped both me and our child in his secure embrace. Who would have guessed that being wrapped in the arms of the wild mercenary at Barsoum's table would become the safest place I could ever imagine?

"Truly?" asked Larisa. "Even up here on the rooftop?"

A low chuckle from Merit followed Larisa's grinning tease, their intrusion causing a groan of frustration to vibrate in Liyam's throat as he reluctantly removed his lips from mine.

"I thought I asked you girls to shell those pistachios," I chided, hoping they did not see the hot flush on my skin, and doing my best to appear unaffected by both their interruption and the unapologetic grip my husband's large hands maintained on my hips.

"Done," said Larisa with a shrug. "Barucha showed us a trick."

Tilting my chin, I surveyed their young faces, now clear of the heavy cosmetics they'd worn in their role as Aramean wives. "Or you talked Itai and Ariel into doing it for you."

Larisa just blinked at me, her eyes round as moons. "What would give you that idea?"

"Because only yesterday you swindled those two boys into carrying the linens to and from the stream."

Mischief tipped her smile upward. "Can we help it if they begged to be of service?"

Liyam's chest rumbled with barely suppressed laughter. He'd found no end of amusement at the frustrations these two young women had given me over the past weeks.

To my surprise, they'd pleaded to stay behind when the rest of the Aramean wives were placed on wagons headed for Damascus, Vereda and Chea howling at the indignity of being carted away like animals.

I'd assured Larisa and Merit that my mother would be happy to offer them refuge here, provided they carry their own weight around the inn. Teaching formerly pampered young women to grind grain, press olives, bake bread, and tend their own laundry had been a chore, but there were no more shadows in either of their bright eyes. I was certain that, as she'd done time and time again, my mother would nurture these girls, share her wisdom and love of Yahweh with them, and draw them into the fold of our ever-expanding family.

"Look! A caravan is approaching," said Merit, gesturing past Liyam and me. "Is that them?" Both girls had regularly joined me here on my watch over the past weeks, so they knew how anxiously I'd been awaiting my family's arrival.

Spinning out of Liyam's grip, I shaded my eyes against the glare of the afternoon sun. Just as Merit said, a long caravan of wagons and bodies was making its way toward the city gates.

From this far I could only make out the figures of a few children perched atop well-laden wagons and the lengthy strides of the men who headed the procession. But when a little brown-and-white dog with a hooked tail darted ahead of the crowd, my heart cheered. Baz's Toki was unmistakable.

I flew down the stone stairs, across the courtyard, out of the inn, and toward the gates, my husband's long legs barely keeping up with my frantic pace.

I saw my brothers first, their grins wide as I approached, and the sight of them unscathed from the battles they'd taken part in—both in Megiddo and later with Othniel up near Golan—caused a flood of gratitude to well up inside me. Little Imri was high up on his abba's shoulders, waving and shouting my name, and a number of my other nieces and nephews had also joined in the enthusiastic greetings.

But when I was within twenty paces of the caravan, I heard my name being shouted above all the other voices, and Odeleya came barreling toward me, arms outstretched. She plowed into me, a sob rising up from her small body that was echoed in my own.

"I missed you," she said, gripping the back of my tunic tightly. "So much. I am so glad you are safe."

I pulled back to press kisses to her cheeks and nose. "And I missed you."

"Please don't leave me again," she said, her narrow shoulders shaking.

I lifted my palm in the air and waited for her to mirror the gesture. Then I pressed our hands together, our small matching scars meeting in silent reminder. She clung to me as the rest of my family gathered around, the children offering a myriad of hugs and kisses.

Malakhi pressed through the crowd of chattering nieces and nephews, pulling me close, but Odeleya continued holding my hand as he did so.

"I am so proud of you, sister. You served our people well," he said with a kiss to my cheek, his affirmation filling me to overflowing. He pulled back, giving me one of his mischievous grins. "And I was right about him, wasn't I?"

"What do you mean?"

His silver eyes darted toward where Liyam stood talking with Eitan, and then back again. "I knew once he married you he'd give up anything for you, even that blood feud."

"You did?"

He nodded. "That day in the clearing . . . He looked at you just like how I looked at Rivkah. I had no doubts."

Eitan pulled me away from Malakhi, wrapping me up in his long arms. "I heard," he said, his hazel eyes shimmering with delight, "that those knife-throwing skills I taught you were quite useful."

I laughed, looking up at my oldest brother and remembering the days when I'd delighted in riding on his shoulders to pluck fruit from the higher branches. "That they were, but I'll still never forgive you for making me practice until I could not lift my arms."

He chuckled and pressed a kiss to the top of my head before passing me into Sofea's enthusiastic embrace. Rivkah followed suit, her new babe strapped to her chest, the tiny girl's golden-brown eyes nearly the same shade as her mother's. With an offer to hold the baby, Rivkah convinced Odeleya to release me for a few moments as my mother and father approached, their faces alight with pleasure and relief.

My abba reached for me first, holding me to his chest in a tight embrace that spoke far more than words could ever say. Why had I ever felt the need to strive for worthiness when my abba's love was so plainly unconditional and boundless?

"My precious girl, I am so glad you are safe," he murmured as he kissed my forehead, rocking me back and forth. Then, with the sheen of tears still in his eyes, he reluctantly gave me over to my mother's arms.

She held me tight, her familiar scent invoking a bone-deep serenity that I had not enjoyed since I'd last been in her presence. She placed her hands on either side of my face and looked into my eyes, wordlessly searching them for a long few moments before she smiled, the radiant joy in her silver eyes vastly overshadowing the puckered scar on her face.

"Your city is free, Ima," I said, fresh tears arising from a well I'd thought dry. "Welcome home."

FORTY-FIVE

Liyam

17 Cheshvan
Near Ein Gedi, Israel

"How many more days do we have to walk?" asked Odeleya, grimacing as she plucked a stone from her sandal. "I don't think my feet can endure much more."

"You said the same thing as we passed through Beit She'an," I said. "And then again after we left Shiloh. And once more when we passed by the ruins of Jericho on our way to the Salt Sea. And yet somehow, every day, your feet continue to do their duty."

She groaned. "I'd just never imagined we'd have to walk *this* far to get to your home."

"Just think. Our ancestors walked for forty years in the wilderness," I said. "They'd have been all too glad for a simple month-long journey through friendly territory."

She screwed up her small face with a disdainful expression that reminded me of Tirzah when she'd had enough of my teasing. "I don't have magical sandals like they did. Mine are almost worn through. And there's no manna or fresh quail to be had here," she grumbled, gesturing at the barren landscape around us and the salty sparkle of the lifeless sea below the ridge. "I certainly hope there's more to eat in your valley than dried goat meat and barley cakes. We can't even drink that water, and I'm perishing of thirst."

"If you can manage to survive for a while longer," I said, "I have a surprise for you."

Her light brown eyes flared. "What sort of surprise?"

"The kind that your aching feet and parched throat will thank me for." I grinned, and then scrubbed at the crown of her head with my knuckles. "But no more complaining."

She giggled and dodged from my teasing gesture, slapping at me with a playful growl.

Seeing this girl laughing and jesting with me after all the heartache and uncertainty she'd suffered filled me with a sense of awe. It was no wonder that she and Tirzah had bonded so quickly in Shechem; they were fashioned from the same resilient material. Yet for as much as Odeleya adored my wife, she'd also taken to shadowing me as well— something I'd at first been unsettled by, but now had come to welcome.

She was unfailingly curious, asking about every bush, every tree, every bird we encountered on the trail, and I found myself thoroughly enjoying filling her head with the knowledge my parents had given me about the Land and all its wonders. A pang of latent grief hit me as I found myself thinking how much Nadina would have looked up to Odeleya. Memories of my girl were bittersweet now instead of shattering, but I could not help wishing she were here, walking with us toward home.

"What are the two of you cackling about up there?" called Tirzah from where she lagged about ten paces behind us. Although she feigned annoyance, I'd seen her secret smiles; she was grateful that her little charge had taken to me. When I'd personally invited Odeleya to come south with us and join our family, Tirzah had been so overcome with emotion she'd been unable to speak for a long while, a rarity for the woman I loved. But somehow, the girl had burrowed under my skin, and I felt nearly as ferociously protective of her as I did my wife. A strange little family we were, but joined nonetheless.

Giving direction to the five men Malakhi had sent along to escort us on this journey, I urged Odeleya to follow them, and the short caravan of donkeys they led, up the jagged trail that broke off the main path and then jogged back to walk beside my wife.

"Perhaps we should put you on one of the donkeys, ishti. You're holding up the caravan."

She stopped to glare at me. "I am doing nothing of the sort. I could outrun all of you, even now." Her palm smoothed over the precious burden she carried, which had been growing more pronounced every day. Even as she did, her sharp-edged gaze softened and then become affectionate as I reached over to place my hand atop hers. It was past the time now when she'd lost the three babes before, and my hopes grew with each day that passed. Even so, I kept her within my sights at all times, my stomach curling every time she groaned or shifted uncomfortably. I would not rest easy until our child was in my arms.

"I have no doubt you could, my prize. But I learned my lesson about challenging you to contests the day we shot slings."

"You won that contest." She narrowed her eyes. "But only because you cheated."

"That was not cheating." I stepped close and pulled her palm to my lips, sliding my mouth from the base of her third finger down to the delicate skin at her wrist where her pulse fluttered, keeping my gaze locked with hers. "That was a well-planned battle tactic that yielded me the exact results I desired."

She sighed at my silent persuasion and came willingly when I hauled her into my arms for a long, slow kiss. Not since we'd left Kedesh behind had we had any time alone, and I meant to take advantage of these precious private moments with my wife. I trusted Malakhi's men implicitly with Odeleya's safety and knew she was likely already knee-deep in the pool beneath the waterfall my mother had shown me on a long-ago hunting expedition. I'd been thrilled when familiarity struck as we'd come upon the trail that led to the spring-fed falls. I planned to camp beside them for this final night before we came into the valley, and drink our fill of the cool, fresh stream that emerged from it and emptied into the Salt Sea below.

"They'll wonder where we are," she murmured against my lips.

"Let them," I said, sliding my hands into her curls and tilting her chin back so I could nip at her throat with a growl. "I need you to myself for awhile."

She laughed and pulled back to peer at me, her golden-brown eyes shining up at me with delight.

"You are so different now," she said, a note of awe in her tone.

"Am I?"

She hummed. "The heaviness is gone. Those weighted shadows I saw in you from the start have disappeared."

From the moment I'd left the burden of Nadina's justice on that bluff above the Kinneret, I'd been free. There would always be a hollow place in my soul when I thought of my daughter, but since I'd allowed myself to mourn, there was no longer that burning, tearing rage that had blinded me to everything but vengeance. I'd finally been able to relax, to delight in my wife, and to get to know her family without the burden of my blood feud between us.

Once they'd all returned to Kedesh, a spirit of gladness had seemed to descend over the city. Moriyah had been delighted to go back to her inn and within a week had organized a celebration that lasted for three days. Many of the original Levite families that had once been settled in the refuge city had returned, although there were more than a few who'd perished at the hands of the Arameans, and there were as many tears of sorrow during those gatherings at the inn as there were tears of joy. Even Chana, one of Tirzah's older sisters, had come to visit, traveling through with her husband's trading caravan, an event that inspired yet another feast.

I'd hesitated in pushing Tirzah to leave, delighted as she was at being among her loved ones. And truthfully, with as much as I enjoyed the company of her father and brothers, not to mention Baz—who was never empty of far-fetched tales of his and Darek's long service as spies for Yehoshua—I'd been nearly as content as she was to tarry.

But then, a month after they'd all settled back into the inn, my wife told me it was time to leave. Time to establish our life together in the place where my own had begun. There was no fear, no doubt, no hesitation in her assertion, only calm acceptance that her time in Kedesh was at an end.

I'd always known she was extraordinary, from the first moment I saw her in Barsoum's villa, her brilliant light skillfully tucked away in the shadows, but it seemed that every layer I discovered within my wife was more fascinating than the one before. She may have been offered to me as a prize by the Aramean commander, but in my mind she was a treasure given to me by Yahweh himself.

"Come," I said, slipping my arm about her waist and pulling her toward the trail to the waterfall. "Let's catch up to the others and rest for the night. Odeleya is no doubt pushing your brother's men into madness with all her chatter." I pressed a kiss to her temple. "Tomorrow you meet my family."

My greedy eyes traveled over the familiar dips and rises that encircled our lands. It had been over a year since I'd set sight on these rocky, terraced hills, and I'd not realized just how powerfully I'd missed my home. I'd seen majestic mountains, vast lakes, rushing rivers, lush rolling fields, and dense forests since I'd departed, but nothing was as beautiful to my eyes as the cluster of homes at the center of the valley, some of which my own hands had helped build, and the distant figures of my loved ones as they spilled from doorways or meandered in from the garden and fields, curious about who had arrived.

Then, just as when Tirzah's family had joyously greeted her upon their arrival at Kedesh, we were bombarded. A wall of red-haired brothers arrived first, slapping my back and kissing my cheeks, digging their knuckles into my sides with half-jesting admonitions for taking so long to come home and unabashed congratulations for bringing along such a beautiful new wife. My eldest sister, Natanyah, greeted me next with tear-filled eyes, her newest granddaughter braced on her hip, followed by my other sisters and their husbands.

Then came a flood of cousins, nieces and nephews, aunts and uncles, and an assortment of spouses. With each blessing for my return, exclamation over my new marriage, and word of welcome to Tirzah and Odeleya, the well of gratitude in my chest grew larger and larger until I was barely able to control the burn of tears in my eyes.

When finally my mother and father stood before me, I was taken aback by the way both of them had aged in my absence. Though they both looked just as healthy and formidable as they'd always been, there were more creases around their eyes and more silver strands on their heads, and I wondered if worry for me over these months had contributed to the subtle changes. Knowing the depths of my love for my own children, both the one I'd lost and the one yet to be born, I was certain it had, and I looked forward to repenting for the burden I'd left them with.

"Ima. Abba," I said, pride humming in my bones as I tugged Tirzah forward to present her to my parents. "This is Tirzah. My wife . . . And Moriyah's daughter."

A gasping sob came from my mother's mouth, and she looked back and forth from my face to Tirzah's. She stepped forward and lifted her hands to cup Tirzah's cheeks in her palms, staring into her eyes with an expression of wonder. "Truly? You are Moriyah's girl?"

"I am," said my wife, through her own joyful tears. "I have much to tell you of her, and many messages to relay."

My mother smashed her lips together as if to contain another outburst, her blue-green eyes alight. "I very much look forward to hearing it all. And getting to know the daughter of my heart-sister."

As the two women I loved best in all the earth embraced, I tugged Odeleya forward, making a sudden decision that I hoped she and Tirzah would approve of.

"And this, Ima, is Odeleya." I smiled down at the girl who'd unexpectedly taken up residence in some of those hollow places in my heart. "Our daughter."

A cry burst free of Odeleya's lips, and she slung her arms about my waist, weeping into my torso. The river of tears tracking down Tirzah's cheeks told me that she heartily agreed with my surprise declaration, and the joyful smile on my mother's face made it clear that she was more than delighted to add another grandchild to her lot. By Yahweh's grace, there would soon be another.

My father stepped forward, clapping his large palm on my shoulder and nodding his chin at me. Tobiah had never been a man of many words, but the tremble of his tight-pressed lips and the sheen in his brown eyes conveyed all he needed to say. *Welcome home. I am proud of you, my son.*

The last person to greet me was Yavan, who'd hung back throughout the flurry, but as my mother walked off with Tirzah under one arm and an overwhelmed Odeleya beneath her other, my cousin appeared at my side.

"So," he said, his gaze lifting to the western horizon where the sky had just begun to blush red. "Took my advice, did you?"

"She talked me into it," I said, with the same tone of feigned disinterest.

"Ah," he replied. "So it's like that. Fitting."

"Like what?"

"A mule being led around by the nose." His cheek twitched with barely contained mirth. "Or perhaps it's more like a buck panting after a doe—"

He had no chance to finish his thought because he was already locked beneath my arm, laughing and doing his best to escape my hold. His two youngest sons bounced up and down in front of us, cheering on our childish behavior.

Once both of us were sweaty and disheveled, and after my mother had halfheartedly ordered us to stop acting like her three-year-old great-grandsons, I released Yavan with a laugh and a feeble shove.

"It's good to have you home, cousin," he said with a wistful smile, one that reminded me of our lifelong history and how I'd abused his loyalty.

"I must ask you to forgive me, Yavan—" I began, but he stopped me with a vigorous shake of his head.

"No. There's no need for that between you and me."

I nodded, understanding exactly what he meant. We were brothers at heart. Forgiveness had already been given.

But something about the way his brow furrowed as he gazed off to the west made me think more needed to be said.

"What is it?" I pressed.

He paused, his jaw working back and forth as if he were grinding his teeth.

"Tell me," I said, knowing him well enough that I could see something was begging to burst from his lips.

"Your brothers and I had planned to wait for a couple of days after you returned, but I do not want you to hear it from anyone else but me."

A familiar sense of dread began to build at the base of my spine. I braced myself for whatever was to come, even knowing that it could be nowhere near as devastating as the last news I'd gotten upon my arrival.

"The one-eyed Moabite. You know he was seen in Megiddo? Malakhi sent word?" he asked.

It was all I could do to nod.

He cleared his throat. "Shimon, Lev, and I were part of the group that was sent into the city, disguised as traders."

Shock lifted my brows high. I'd thought he and the rest of my brothers had been with Othniel's army all this time, but it seemed I had much to learn about what happened while I was in Kedesh.

"We found him, cousin." His voice went low, his expression determined but making it clear that it pained him to reveal the truth. "We found him, and then we brought him back with us when we returned."

I flinched, my gaze instantly scanning the valley as my thoughts went hazy.

"He is in the city of refuge, Liyam. The man who killed your daughter is waiting for you in Hebron."

FORTY-SIX

The last time I'd beheld the city of Hebron was in the aftermath of the battle that had liberated it. No longer was it a wasteland of burning enemy corpses and wounded tribal brothers, but a city on a hill surrounded by green pastures and once again offering sanctuary to convicted manslayers. Including the one I'd come to speak with. The one I'd been pursuing for the last year.

Accompanied by Shimon, Lev, and Yavan, along with my wife, who predictably refused to stay behind, I'd made the two-day journey to the city of refuge with my heart lodged firmly in my throat and curiosity burning a hole in my chest.

I thought that I had set aside my urge for vengeance, left behind the terrible urgency to repay the Moabite for what he'd done to Nadina. But as soon as Yavan revealed the trader had been taken to Hebron, a painful wave of confusion had crashed over me again, tarnishing my joyful return home. Not only had the trader submitted himself to my brothers without hesitation, but he'd already been tried by a council of elders and sentenced to Hebron. He was safe there. Protected from my retribution for the rest of his life by a two-thousand cubit boundary around the city. And yet for some reason the man wished to speak with me, had asked that my family bring me to Hebron when I returned, but refused to tell them why.

I'd waited two weeks before heading north, knowing I needed the time to let the news settle into my bones so I could think clearly instead of blazing off with a sword in hand like I had before.

Besides, there truly was nothing I could do now, even if I'd not set aside my blood feud with the man. If I touched him inside that boundary line, I would be tried as a murderer and lose everything Yahweh had mercifully given me, including Tirzah and our baby.

There was much about Hebron that reminded me of Kedesh—its perch on a hill, the high stone walls, the thick gates—but this city was far more ancient. The bones of not only Avraham, but Yitzak, Yaakov, Sarah, Rivkah, and Leah lay within a cave nearby, bearing witness to not only the city's longevity but also its profound importance in the history of our people.

When the boundary stones that marked the farthest edge of the city were within sight, a group of three men approached us. Thinking that they might be Levites who kept watch over the road, greeting new manslayers fleeing their own blood avengers or turning away those who sought retribution, I did not hesitate to meet them at the invisible border between captivity and freedom. What I did not expect was to see an older man standing between two Levites, with one missing eye covered by a thin strip of linen.

I halted, stunned and horrified at the first sight of the man who'd crushed my little girl. Across the ten paces that separated us, the Moabite stared at me, his one eye betraying nothing of what he might be thinking as he surveyed the man who'd vowed to kill him.

My throat was on fire, swollen shut by screams of rage and a thousand questions. Thankfully Shimon spoke for me before it all came tumbling out in a blistering rush.

"How did you know we were coming?" my brother asked.

"A messenger passed you on the road," one of the Levites responded. "Brought word of three flame-haired men approaching the city. It was not hard to guess who you might be."

Of course, my brothers had been here before; they'd attended the trial, accompanied my nieces and nephews who'd testified to the Moabite's recklessness that day. I'd heard the entire story, along with the council's reasoning for their decision, but I wanted to look into that one eye and gauge his guilt for myself.

Suddenly, the man stepped forward, his singular gaze pinned on me so completely that it was as if the rest of my family was not even there.

"I didn't see her," he said, his voice firm even as his chin wobbled. "I promise you. If I would have known that anyone, let alone a child was on the road that day, I would have slowed my pace. I would have been more cautious."

Although I'd already heard this all from Yavan, I needed more. I needed to hear the testimony from his own mouth.

"How could you have not seen her?" I asked, surprised at the evenness of my tone, especially while nausea was tearing up my throat.

He gestured to his eye. "This was perhaps only half the problem. It was late in the afternoon, the sun was blazing on the horizon, and what was left of my vision compromised." A sound of distress burst from his throat. "I thought it was an animal. I vow to all the gods that my mind saw only a small animal darting in front of me. A coney or dog, perhaps. The very last thing I would have ever guessed was that a child had ended up beneath my horses' hooves."

He broke, his shoulders jerking as he sobbed. "I cannot imagine how much you despise me. I despise myself for not being aware. For taking your daughter from you. If I could go back, change my course, I would."

Regardless that I'd known his explanation of the event, my mind continued spooling through the details, trying to reconcile what I'd thought had happened and what he had experienced. One thing was very clear, however: this Moabite was not the slavering, bloodthirsty monster I'd conjured in my head. He was sincere in his remorse, brokenhearted, and contrite.

Without warning, he barreled forward, surprising not only me but also the Levites who followed him with arms outstretched and wide eyes as he crossed the boundary line and threw himself at my feet.

"Please," he said, the supplication wrenching at my gut. "I deserve to die. Your child's death is my fault. It does not matter that it was done in ignorance. It was reckless. I am guilty of bloodshed. I am in your hands. Kill me."

Far beyond stunned by his actions and the earnestness with which he pleaded for his own end, I could do little more than blink at him, paralyzed by confusion.

"What makes you so willing to give up your life this way?" came Tirzah's voice, her tone surprisingly gentle in the midst of such a fraught conversation.

"Because I know what it is to lose a child to a violent end," he said, pressing a fist to his chest. "Fifteen years ago, Amalekites raided my village in retaliation for the theft of a few cattle by a group of young men. They burned everything. Murdered my wife and my three precious girls, along with the rest of my clan. I did not even know the young men who'd stolen the cattle; they were from a neighboring village, not my own. But of course the Amalekites cared nothing for my explanations. They refused to kill me, telling me that suffering the rest of my life with one eye and nothing else was a fitting punishment."

"And why," asked Tirzah, "would you submit yourself to Torah laws that are not your own?"

"Because I have heard the stories of your Yahweh and how he brought Egypt low. I have seen the ruins of Jericho. My own father witnessed the ceasing of the Jordan River flow as your people crossed into Canaan. And after traveling from Egypt to Aram to Tyre and Sidon and all throughout Moab and Edom, I have come to believe that there is no God like yours, one whose power and might cannot be measured. I know that your law demands blood for blood. And so I will submit to his justice." He looked up at me, his one eye glistening. "And yours."

He bent his head, hands at his sides and neck exposed, awaiting my fatal blow.

I could feel the weight of my sword at my side. Could hear the blood rushing in my ears as the word *justice* reverberated in my head. He was past the boundary line, so by law and tradition I had every right to end him. To exact payment for Nadina's precious life.

And yet instead of the urge to unsheathe that sword, the image of my moments on that bluff rose above it all—the crashing, torrid swirl of the river as it came up against the powerful tranquility of the sparkling blue lake. Two perfectly balanced forces blending together in beautiful harmony.

Justice without mercy was tyranny, and mercy without justice was lawlessness. Yahweh had created both to work together, for his glory and for our good.

I reached out my hand to the man who'd killed my daughter and took a deep breath, remembering my Nadina's brilliant smile before I placed it on his head.

"You are forgiven."

His chin jerked up, profound confusion on his grizzled face. "But I deserve—"

"As do I," I said, remembering the hatred in my heart toward Barsoum as I ended his life and the dark rage I'd nurtured in the many months I searched for this man. "But even so, I choose mercy."

Then, leaving the last of my burdens in ashes on the road to Hebron, I entwined my hand with Tirzah's, left the trader to live out his life in peace in the city of refuge, and headed for my valley.

Epilogue

Moriyah

The first brush of sunset had just begun to paint the horizon as I poured fresh oil in the wide-mouthed lamp, the action as familiar as it was cherished even after eight years of disruption in my nightly ritual. After sprinkling a pinch of salt atop the glistening olive oil to ensure that it would not fill our chamber with acrid smoke when it was set alight, I leaned my elbows on the windowsill, drinking in the beauty that surrounded my beloved home.

There had been no question of whether we would return to Kedesh, reopen the inn, and minister to the people of the refuge city and the manslayers who would eventually find safe haven here. Darek had begun making plans for the journey north the moment we'd heard that the Arameans had fled back to the land between the Tigris and Euphrates.

The rumor was that when Kushan heard of the miraculous downfall of Kedesh so soon upon the heels of the earlier defeats at Beit She'an and Megiddo, he'd been so humiliated that he'd left his army behind at Golan, returning in disgrace to Aram-Naharim. Darek assured me that his reign would come to a swift end. Convinced of his weaknesses, neighboring kings would swoop in, bringing his arrogant quest to revive the empire of the ancient Akkadians to an end. He'd served his purpose as the means of our divine chastisement, and now he would melt into the inevitable anonymity of the defeated.

Countless had been the hours I'd spent gazing out of this window in years past, praying against the black visions I'd seen hovering on the northern horizon—even long before we'd been driven from Kedesh—but no more were my dreams tainted with such warnings. Now when I looked out my window I saw only the clear blue sky, the green of the pastures that were once again dotted with the Levites' sheep and goats, and the Land of Promise that had already begun healing from the wounds the Arameans left behind. The fruit trees my sweet Gidal had tended with such loving care would once again flourish, as would the shared gardens outside the city walls, along with the Levite families that once again called this place home.

After a nearly unanimous consensus among tribal leaders, Othniel had been asked to judge over the tribes, to oversee the rebuilding of our coalition, and to ensure that intertribal disputes would be handled according to the Torah. Although some called for a king, one who could stand up against future threats from other nations, Othniel refused to accept the office, reminding us that Yahweh was the true king and it was to him alone we should bow our knees.

I could only pray that his admonition would be heeded in generations to come. Hopefully the lesson we'd learned under Kushan had burned out the last of our rebellion, and idols and amulets like those consumed in the flames of refuse piles outside every city at Othniel's command would never be brought back inside our gates.

Releasing a long sigh, I lit a fresh wick before laying it carefully in the oil lamp. I knew from long experience that it would burn throughout the night, a beacon in the darkness that I'd first placed on my windowsill not long after I'd come to this city, weary and desperate after the perilous flight for my life.

"That was quite a sigh" came the voice of my husband from the doorway. "Missing our youngest?"

As was inevitable when my thoughts were deep in the past, my mind conjured the sight of Darek as he was all those years ago, when I was caught staring at the captivating broad-shouldered soldier across the dancing grounds. His hair was no longer a dark reddish-brown and his beard had been overtaken by gray, but he was no less handsome to me now, and my love for him had aged like fine wine, having become only richer and deeper as time passed.

"Always," I said, allowing a wistful smile to curve my lips. "But Tirzah is where she needs to be, at her husband's side."

"We will see her again," he said, approaching with a compassionate expression. "Now that you are free to attend ingathering festivals, we will meet in Shiloh from time to time, even if it is a year or two before they come back north."

As always when I thought of Shiloh, a pang of sadness hit my heart. My father had passed into the world to come just before we'd left the vineyard, which was why it had taken longer than we planned to return, but I would ever be grateful to Yahweh that he'd allowed me these years with him and Ora again, and I trusted that my adopted brother Yuval would care for my blind stepmother as if she were his own blood.

"True," I replied. "But it was hard to watch our youngest child walk away, knowing I will not be there when our next grandchild enters the world."

I had been in constant prayer over these past weeks, hoping that the babe growing inside Tirzah would live. Yahweh had impressed a deep sense of peace upon my heart before my daughter had even revealed she was expecting; indeed from almost the first moment I'd seen her precious face greeting us outside the gates. And I trusted that no matter the outcome, the One Who Hears would be near to her.

Darek brushed his knuckles down my cheek in a sweet gesture of understanding. "Alanah will be there in your stead, my love. And that should bring you great peace."

The thought did indeed settle my spirit. The sister-of-my-heart would care for my girl well, I had no doubt.

Snatching his hand, I pressed a kiss of gratitude to his palm. "Thank you for the reminder. But I do hope that Chana and Hakim will be able to come through Kedesh more often now that the Arameans are gone. I did not have enough time with our youngest granddaughter while they were here."

Darek strode across the room, heading for the washpot I'd just refilled with fresh water. "I am certain they will. And Abra and Liron will soon have another little one for you to cradle."

I'd been so thrilled when my oldest daughter and her family had returned to Naftali territory, along with the rest of Liron's family. The long years they'd been up near Merom had worn on me, and having them, and their five children, nearby again was a gift from Yahweh. I could only pray that one day all of my children would gather together again under my roof. What a celebration that day would be!

"How goes the harvest?" I asked, sitting on the edge of our bed as my husband dipped his hands in the water and began to scrub the day's dust from his face and arms.

"As well as can be expected with a group of men who don't know what they are doing."

I laughed at his disgruntled expression. "Malakhi and Eitan are struggling?"

"Well, they are young men, vigorous and strong, but other than helping out with the grape harvest on your father's land, they are not accustomed to the tedious rigors of using a sickle to cut down wheat for hours upon hours." He grinned. "Baz is also less than thrilled about spending his days tending the earth. I heard more than my fair share of complaints about aching backs this afternoon."

Since the war had ended and the threats to the Hebrew territories were negligible for now, our sons and their families, along with a few others associated with our clan, had settled on Darek's portion of land in the valley. Raviv's widow, along with his nephews who'd inherited the land after his death in Edrei, had insisted on returning my husband's inheritance. The agreement made between Raviv and Darek in payment for Eitan's life was declared to be canceled. Now the two halves of our clan were rejoined in the purpose of tending the orchards and fields together, the long-held rift between brothers erased by forgiveness and sacrifice.

"It will take some time for all of us to settle into new roles, I think," I said. "Without war looming over us, the boys will learn to think like farmers instead of soldiers."

Although I knew they were both a bit unsettled by the notion that their days of strategizing battles and smuggling weapons were over, and even though Malakhi had no plans to give up the unit of men who would monitor any threats, I prayed they would never be forced to lift a sword against foreign invaders again.

"Indeed they will," he said, coming to sit beside me with a groan that reminded me that my husband was no longer a soldier either, but a grandfather with bones that creaked and moaned just as much as my own. "And Eitan has plans for a new foundry in the valley, so he'll continue to utilize his metalsmithing skills."

"Zekai and Yoni seem eager to learn their father's trade, don't they?"

He nodded. "I have little doubt Eitan's skills will be handed down to many generations."

What a strange notion to dwell upon, that six lines had emerged from the union between Darek and me, and multiplied by our grandchildren and their children, a vast network of descendant branches would continue expanding throughout the future.

No matter where our branches spread, I hoped that they would flourish, remain faithful to Yahweh, and carry the light of his Torah wherever they went.

Darek slipped his arm around me, pulling me close and pressing a lingering kiss to my lips. "I, for one, have been more than happy to lay aside my sword and come home to you every day. To see you back in this place you love so much, tending to those in need."

"It is not so easy as it was before," I said, with a sigh. "I am no longer the young woman who dashed about this inn, doing the work of three while adjudicating arguments between Malakhi and Abra, ensuring Gidal had not forgotten to come back from the orchard before dark, and teaching Chana to weave and sew—all with Tirzah strapped to my back."

His fingers traced the faded scar on my cheek that had never prevented him from seeing my heart. "You become more beautiful to me every day, my love." His brown eyes captured me in his warm gaze that told me he too saw past the silver hair and wrinkles to the girl he'd watched dance with abandon under the moon, arms uplifted and a crown of flowers on her head.

The shrill blast of a shofar intruded on the sweet moment between us, ripping through the air with a familiar clarion call.

Setting aside the excuse of old age, I bounded to my feet, pulse stuttering in response to the summons and already heading for the door with my husband at my heels. The first of the manslayers who would seek refuge in my city since our return had arrived.

And just as I had been given comfort and compassion when I came through those gates, I would be the first to stretch out my arms to anyone who lifted their desperate eyes to my window and found hope in the light.

The Lord gave Cushan-Rishathaim king of Aram into the hands of Othniel, who overpowered him. So the land had peace for forty years, until Othniel son of Kenaz died.

Judges 3:10b–11

A Note from the Author

What a journey this series has been, one that expanded in ways I did not expect and held many surprises for me along its twisting path. When the idea of a book set within the cities of refuge sparked in my mind, it was one that I attempted to dismiss. I wondered whether I'd even have enough information to write about such places, especially when there is so little in the historical record about the sanctuaries Moses instructed the Hebrews to organize in Joshua 20. Indeed, there is much speculation that many of the Levitical cities designated by Moses were never even occupied. But the deeper I dug into these places of safety for manslayers, the clearer the picture of Yeshua within their just and merciful structure became. And what a joy it has been to imagine what might have happened in one of these cities that foreshadowed our Messiah so well.

When I was nearing the end of writing *Until the Mountains Fall*, I realized that I was dissatisfied. I wanted more. More of Moriyah and Darek. More of their family. More of Kedesh. And more exploration of the uneasy transitional period Israel underwent between the Conquest and the era of the Judges. So, inspired by stories of jaw-dropping bravery by both men and women throughout the long and turbulent history of the Jewish people, both within the Land of Promise and outside of it, I decided to write *Like Flames in the Night*.

While I was developing Tirzah's character and considering which of Moriyah's and Darek's traits she might possess, I came across an interesting article in *Forbes* about how the Israeli Mossad and the CIA actively recruit women because of their unique set of skills, including the ability to multitask; knack for deciphering underlying motives and vulnerabilities; ease in playing roles or shifting personalities; heightened spatial awareness; and swift discernment of dangerous situations. This, of course, made my little author mind spin, and tomboyish Tirzah blossomed into a talented spy to make her father and brothers proud and a daughter influenced by a woman of great boldness, love for her people, and an unshakable commitment to Yahweh.

Like Tirzah and Liyam, thousands of men and women put aside their own safety and comfort for the sake of reclaiming the Land given to Yahweh's people, and because of their sacrifice, the once-desert is blooming again in direct fulfillment of Isaiah's prophecies. I was particularly inspired by my brief visit to Israel a couple of years ago when our group toured the Ayalon Institute at a kibbutz in Rehovot, where an entire ammunitions factory secretly operated underground (quite literally) from 1945–1948, directly beneath the noses of the British Army and under the feet of unsuspecting residents of the kibbutz itself. From lying about the reasons they needed so much brass (telling the British they were making kosher lipsticks that their wives would adore) to smuggling bullets in milk trucks, to devising a system of ladders beneath industrial washing machines that hid the chug and clank of the noisy bullet-making machines, this effort was truly extraordinary and, in many instances, miraculous. Eitan and Malakhi's secret forges and clandestine training programs came directly out of my day at Ayalon, and I highly recommend a few hours there for every visitor to the Promised Land.

There is only a tantalizing glimpse of the eight-year period in which the tribes of Israel were subjected to Aramean rule, and as usual most of it is either glossed over, hotly contested, or discounted fully. But no matter when the king of Aram-Naharim (or Aram between the two rivers) swept into Canaan or how much territory he claimed for himself, the Bible is clear that this event came about directly because of the breathtakingly swift apostasy by the people who'd only years before stood in the valley between Mount Ebal and Mount Gerizim and reaffirmed the Covenant with all sincerity.

No one is certain exactly how Othniel achieved such a stunning success against the fearsome army of Aram, especially when the tribes of Israel were so disorganized and oftentimes at each other's throats. But regardless of the way it happened (and my imagined battle scenarios, including the appearance of the fiery Cloud above the Mishkan, are mere speculation), the Bible says that what precipitated Israel's rescue was their impassioned plea for deliverance. Tirzah's admonition for the Levites to speak truth boldly and lay aside comfort and safety in service to Yahweh is an important one for all of those who are called priests of the Most High (1 Peter 2:5). Imagine what could be accomplished by the Church if we actually lived like the free and redeemed people we are, without fear of any enemy, human or spirit, and let our collective lights shine bright against the darkness that surrounds us!

I'd like to thank my precious family for their unceasing support and encouragement to me during the past couple of years I spent writing this series. Chad, your continual self-sacrifice is the foundation of everything. Collin, your enthusiasm for life and words and story is a steady light on even my tough days. Corrianna, your servant heart and willingness to help lighten my load is invaluable. Thank you for patiently listening to me read this entire book out loud while I edited. I love you three to the moon and back.

Another round of thanks goes to my amazingly wonderful writing/plotting partners: Nicole Deese, Tammy L. Gray, Christy Barritt, and Amy Matayo. This book would not even exist without your enthusiasm for the premise and your creativity weaving together with mine to grow it from a tiny idea-seed into a fully blossomed story. Retreat time with you, my writing-sisters, is my favorite week of the year. Is it May yet?

Many thanks to the team at Bethany House, including Raela Schoenherr and Jen Veilleux, for honing the rough edges off my words and for their eternal patience with the rawness of my manuscripts, for Jennifer Parker's always flawless cover designs, and for every hand

and eye that contributes to the making of my books. It is a blessing to work with all of you.

Tina Chen, Joanie Schultz, and Ashley Espinoza, I can never thank you enough for your willingness to beta-read Tirzah and Liyam's story and for delivering honest and encouraging feedback. And Elisabeth Espinoza, thank you for answering my random grammar questions with such patience and skill.

Special thanks goes to our church family at Good Shepherd Anglican. Although our time in North Carolina was far too short, we found such a swift depth of community. Thank you for warmly welcoming us, for being the hands and feet of Jesus to our family, for your dedicated prayer support, and for blessing us abundantly as we took our bittersweet leave.

And finally, to every person who chooses to spend a portion of their precious time reading my stories, reviewing, blogging, and sharing with others, I offer my deepest gratitude. May the Lord bless you and keep you; the Lord make his face shine on you and be gracious to you; the Lord turn his face toward you and give you peace (cf. Numbers 6:24–26).

Questions for Conversation

1. Tirzah is the youngest of Darek and Moriyah's children. What part do you think her birth order might have played in her trajectory? Does she act like the typical "youngest child"? How does your own birth order affect your personality and relationships?

2. Do you feel that Malakhi's decision to allow Tirzah to go to Shechem was a responsible one? Was the risk to her safety worth the outcome? What risky decisions have you made in your own life? Were they worth the cost?

3. History is full of instances when people have had to lie, steal, cheat, or kill in order to save lives. Do you think that all of Tirzah and Liyam's actions were justifiable? If not, how do you think they could have acted differently in those situations?

4. Was the connection between Tirzah and Liyam's family a surprise to you? How did you feel about revisiting Alanah and Tobiah's valley?

5. Throughout the CITIES OF REFUGE series, themes of mercy and justice were interwoven with all of the main character arcs. How

do you think this theme was displayed within both Tirzah and Liyam's journeys?

6. Which of the hero/heroine couples from this series is your favorite? What made you connect with their love story best? Were there any characters you struggled to identify with?

7. Within only a short period of time after Joshua's death, the Hebrew people were fully engaged in idol worship, which resulted in their subjugation under a foreign king. Although this may seem shocking after all the miracles that happened during the Exodus and the Conquest, how is their swift apostasy mirrored in our own culture? Do you see any of these same issues within our own faith communities?

8. Tirzah's admonition to the Levites to put aside their fear and speak truth is a call that we, as Christ-followers, should all heed. In what ways can you more intentionally answer this call with those around you? What fears do you need to lay down in order to obey Yeshua's command to be a light in this dark world?

8. In many ways, Liyam's struggle is an echo of Raviv's quest for vengeance in *A Light on the Hill*. Did your perception of Darek's brother shift at all as we examined a different perspective of the *go'el haadam* in this story?

9. Did you find the conclusion to the CITIES OF THE REFUGE satisfying? What questions do you still have about the characters in this series? Are there any secondary characters you feel deserve their own stories?

10. Which part of the Bible do you think the author might explore next? Have her stories given you any new perspectives on the time period or about Yahweh's relationship with his people?

Connilyn Cossette is a Christy Award and Carol Award winner whose books have been found on ECPA and CBA bestseller lists. When she is not engulfed in the happy chaos of homeschooling two teenagers, devouring books whole, or avoiding housework, she can be found digging into the rich ancient world of the Bible to discover gems of grace that point to Jesus and weaving them into an immersive fiction experience. Although she and her husband have lived all over the country in their twenty-plus years of marriage, they currently call a little town south of Dallas, Texas, their home. Connect with her at ConnilynCossette.com.

Sign Up for Connilyn's Newsletter!

Keep up to date with Connilyn's news on book releases and events by signing up for her email list at connilyncossette.com.

More from Connilyn Cossette

Biblical settings come to life in this dramatic and evocative series about four young women who come face-to-face with tragedy and discover grace, hope, and redemption within the walls of a Levitical city of refuge.

CITIES OF REFUGE: *A Light on the Hill, Shelter of the Most High, Until the Mountains Fall, Like Flames in the Night*
